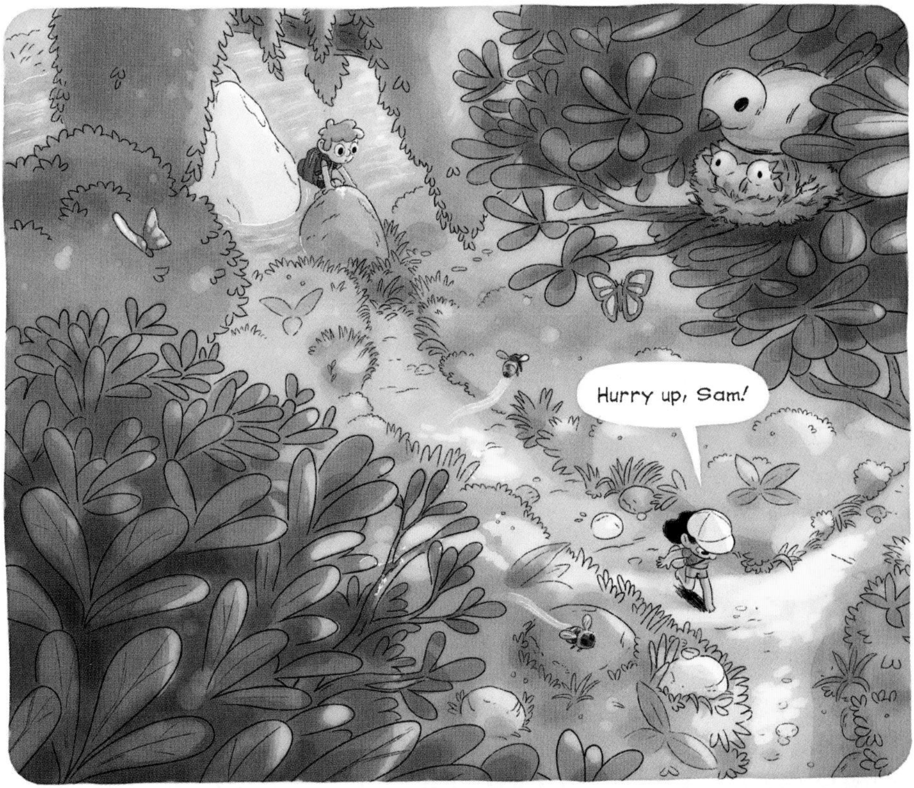
Hurry up, Sam!

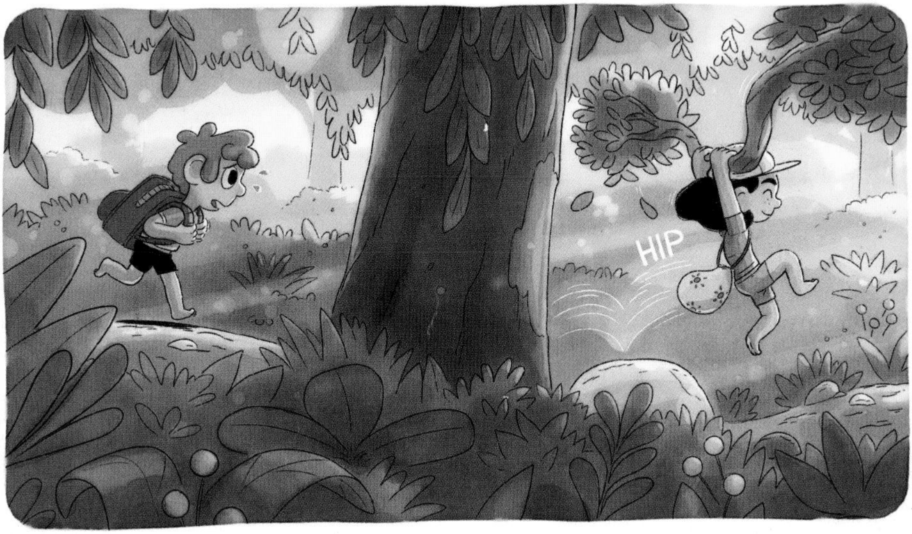
HIP

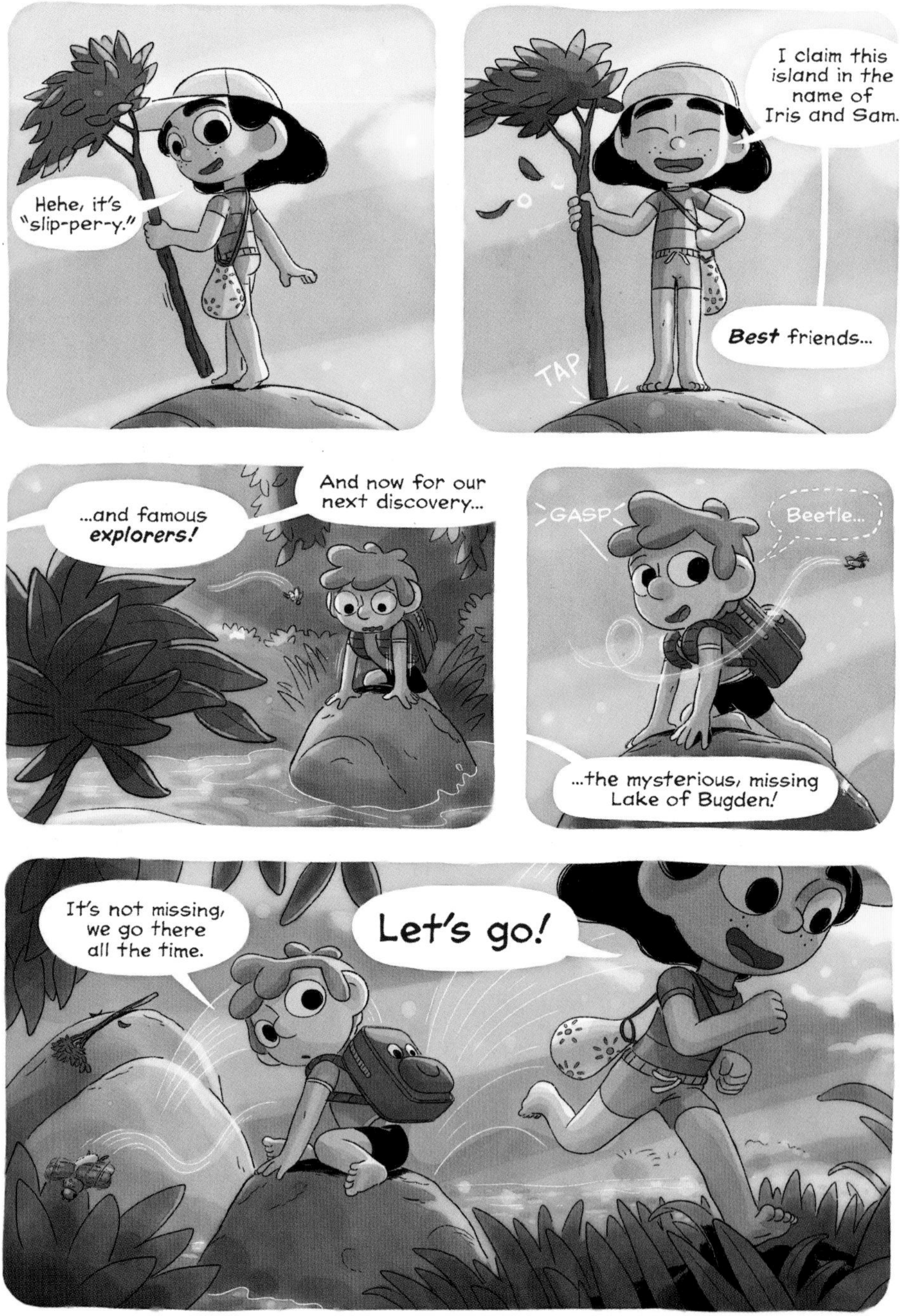
Hehe, it's "slip-per-y."
I claim this island in the name of Iris and Sam.
Best friends...
TAP
...and famous **explorers!**
And now for our next discovery...
GASP
Beetle...
...the mysterious, missing Lake of Bugden!
It's not missing, we go there all the time.
Let's go!

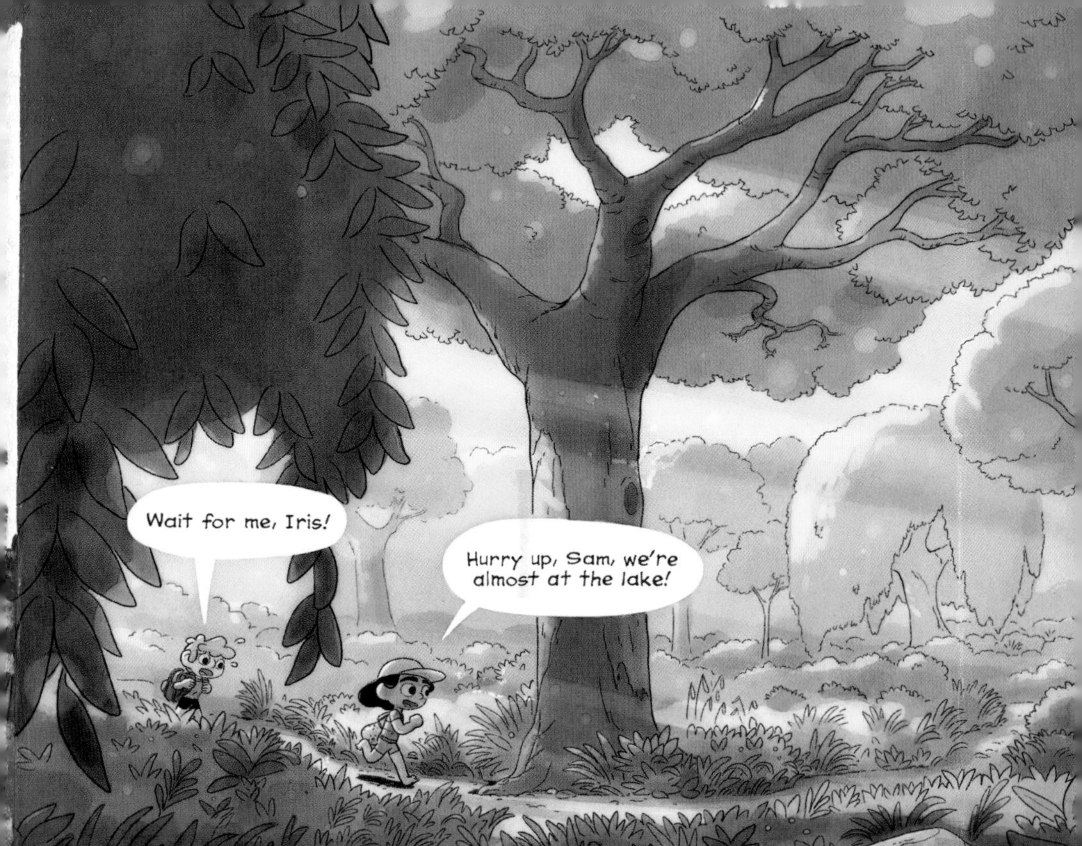

Wait for me, Iris!
Hurry up, Sam, we're almost at the lake!

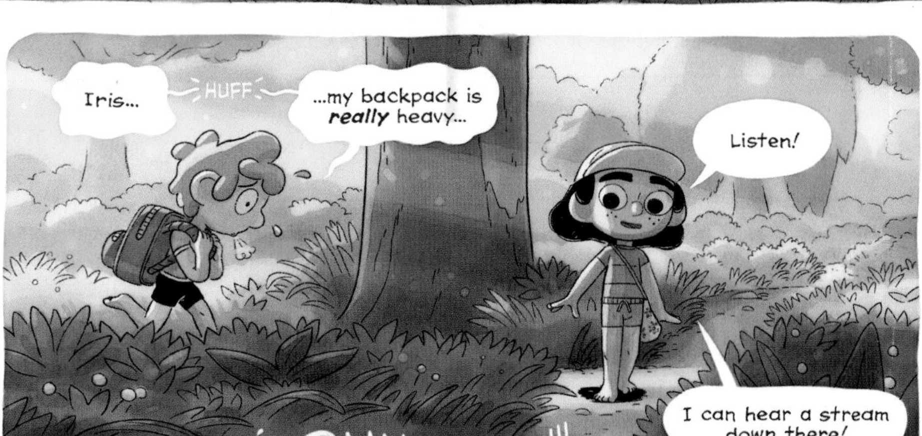

Iris...
HUFF
...my backpack is *really* heavy...
Listen!
I can hear a stream down there!
SSHHHHHHHHHH

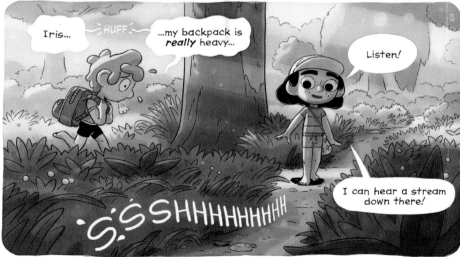

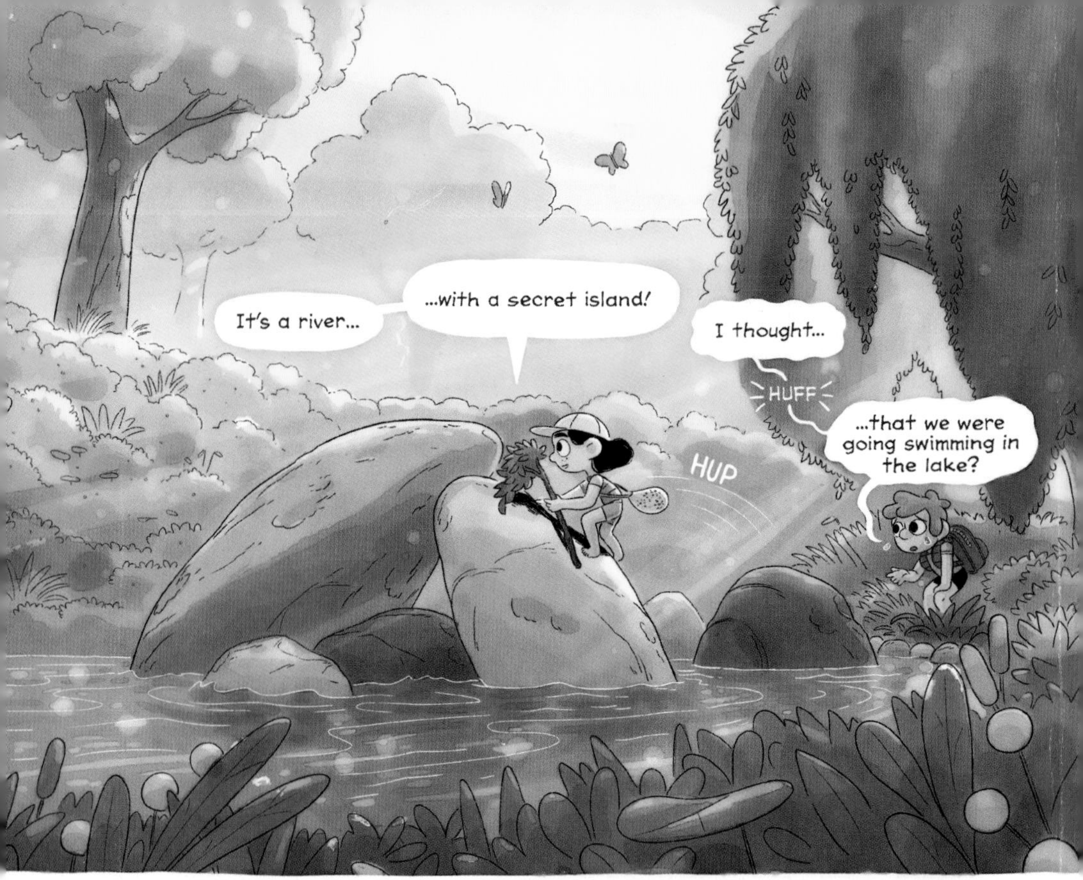
It's a river...
...with a secret island!
HUP
I thought...
HUFF
...that we were going swimming in the lake?

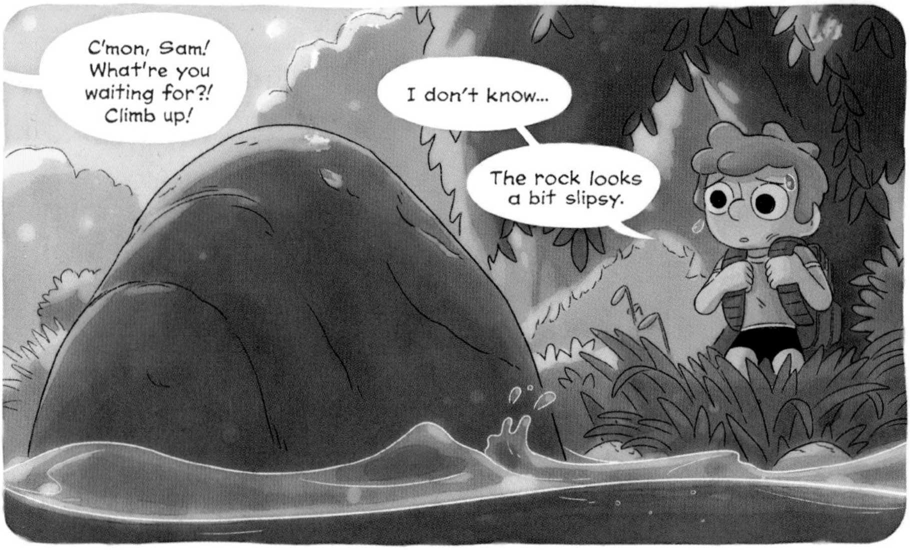
C'mon, Sam! What're you waiting for?! Climb up!
I don't know...
The rock looks a bit slipsy.

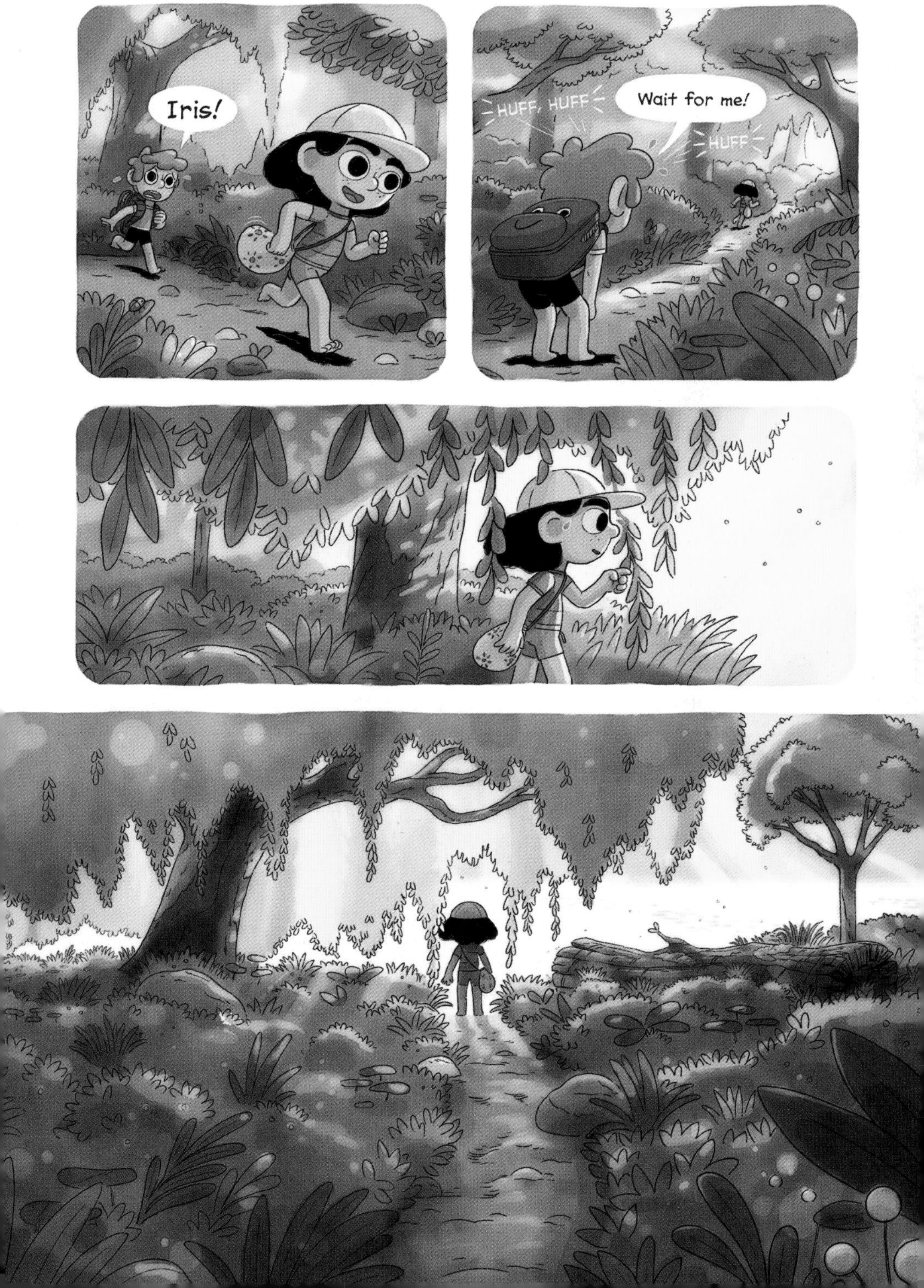
Iris!
HUFF, HUFF
Wait for me!
HUFF

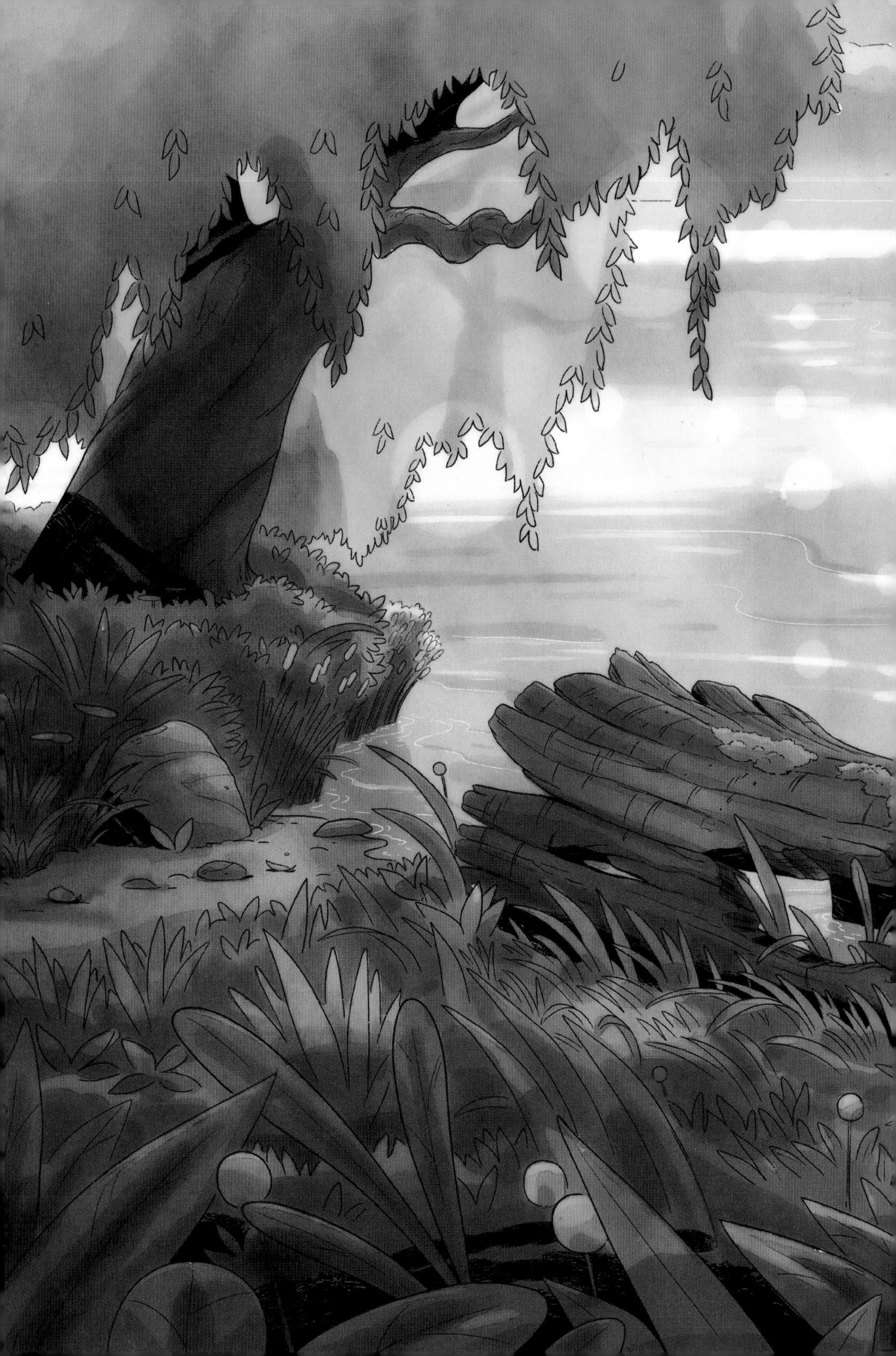

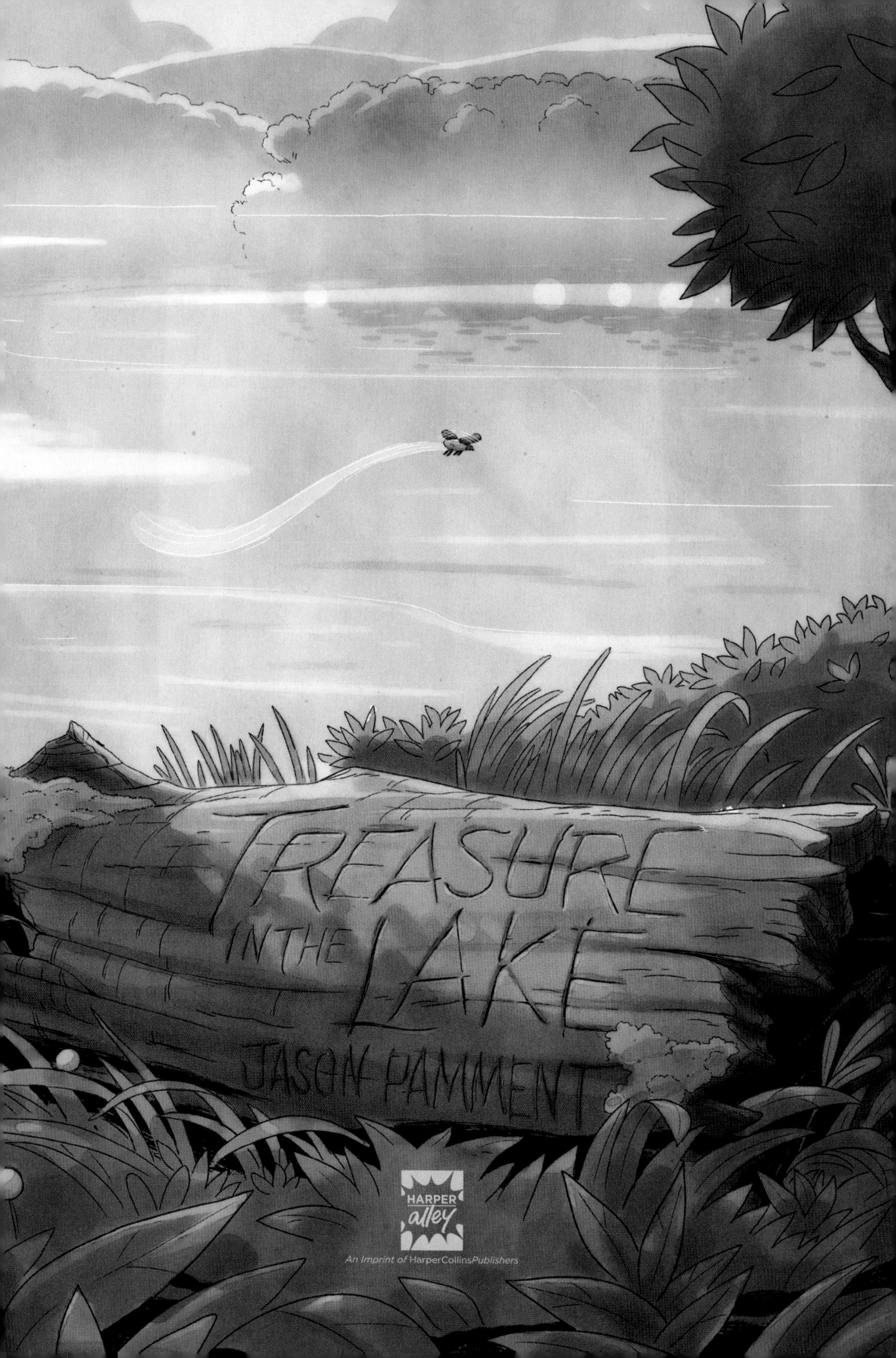
TREASURE
IN THE LAKE
JASON PAMMENT
HARPER
alley
An Imprint of HarperCollinsPublishers

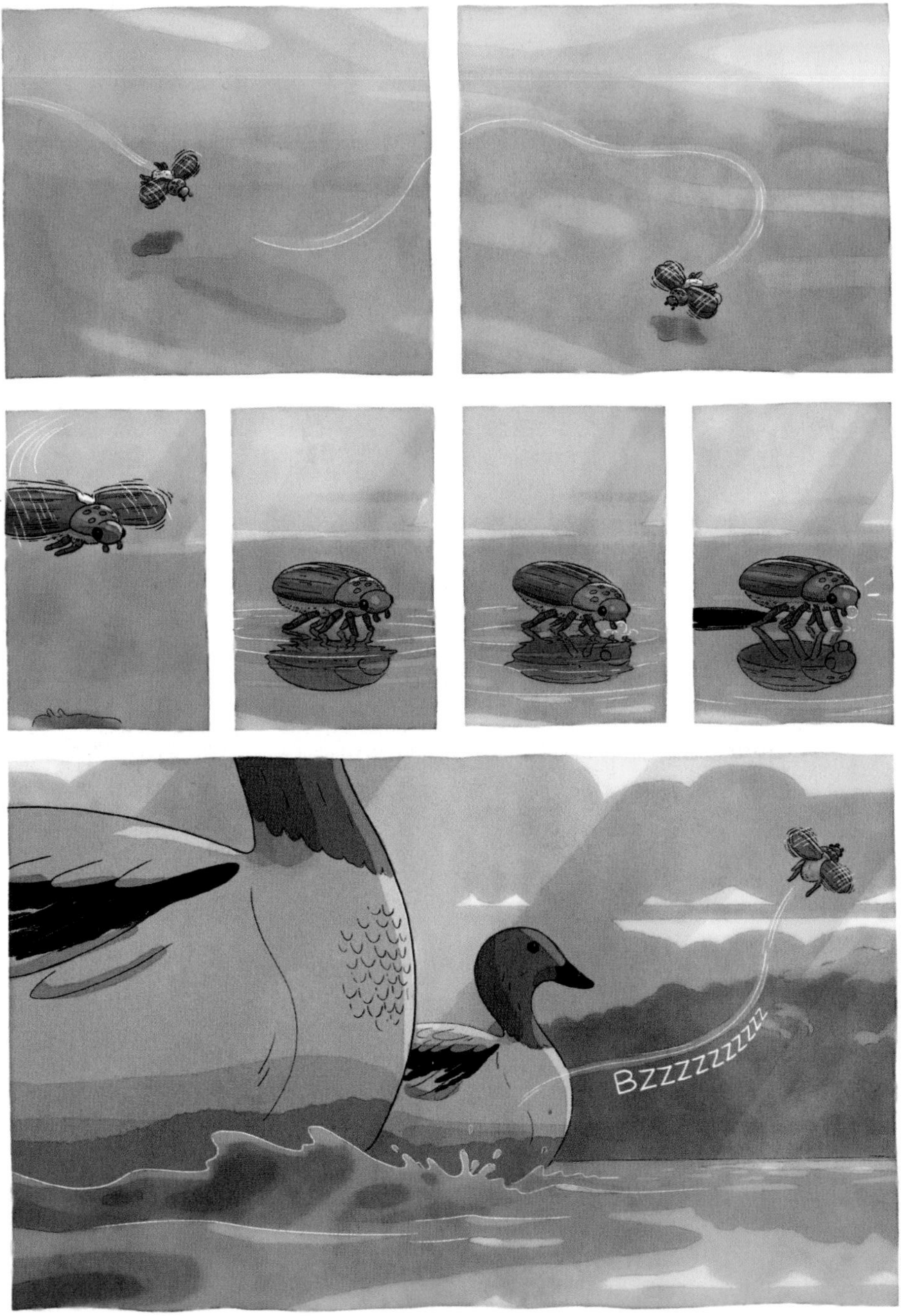
BZZZZZZZZZ

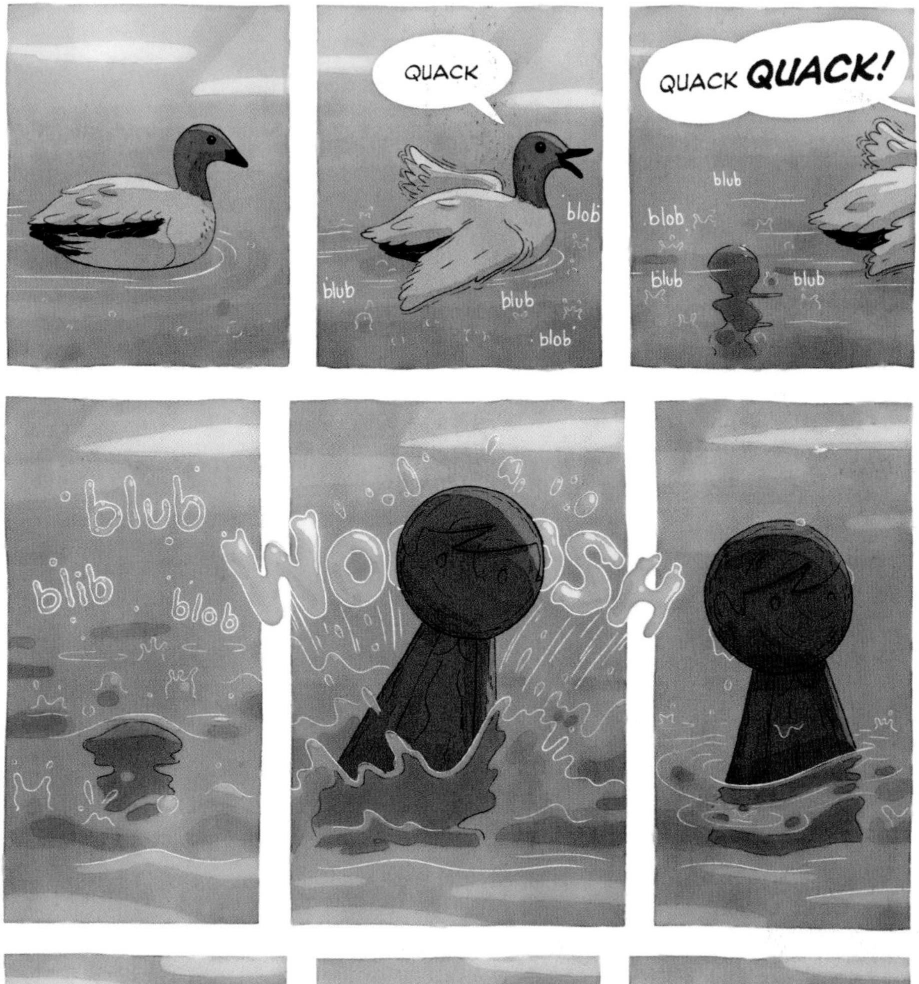
QUACK
blob
blub
blub
blob
QUACK QUACK!
blub
blob
blub
blub
blub
blib
blob

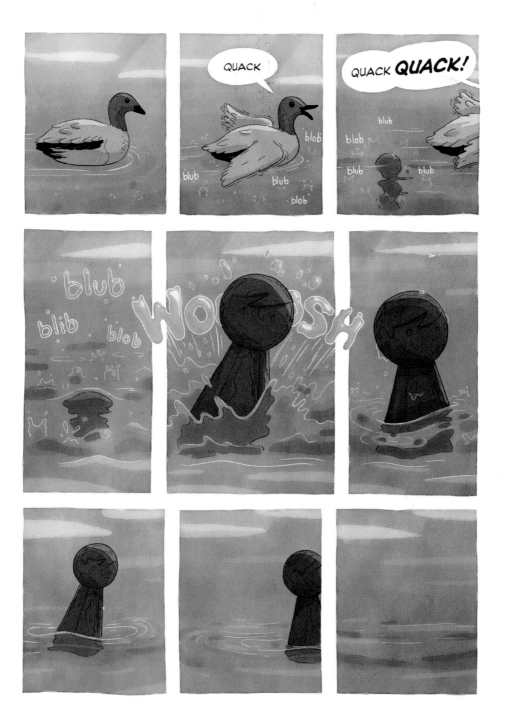

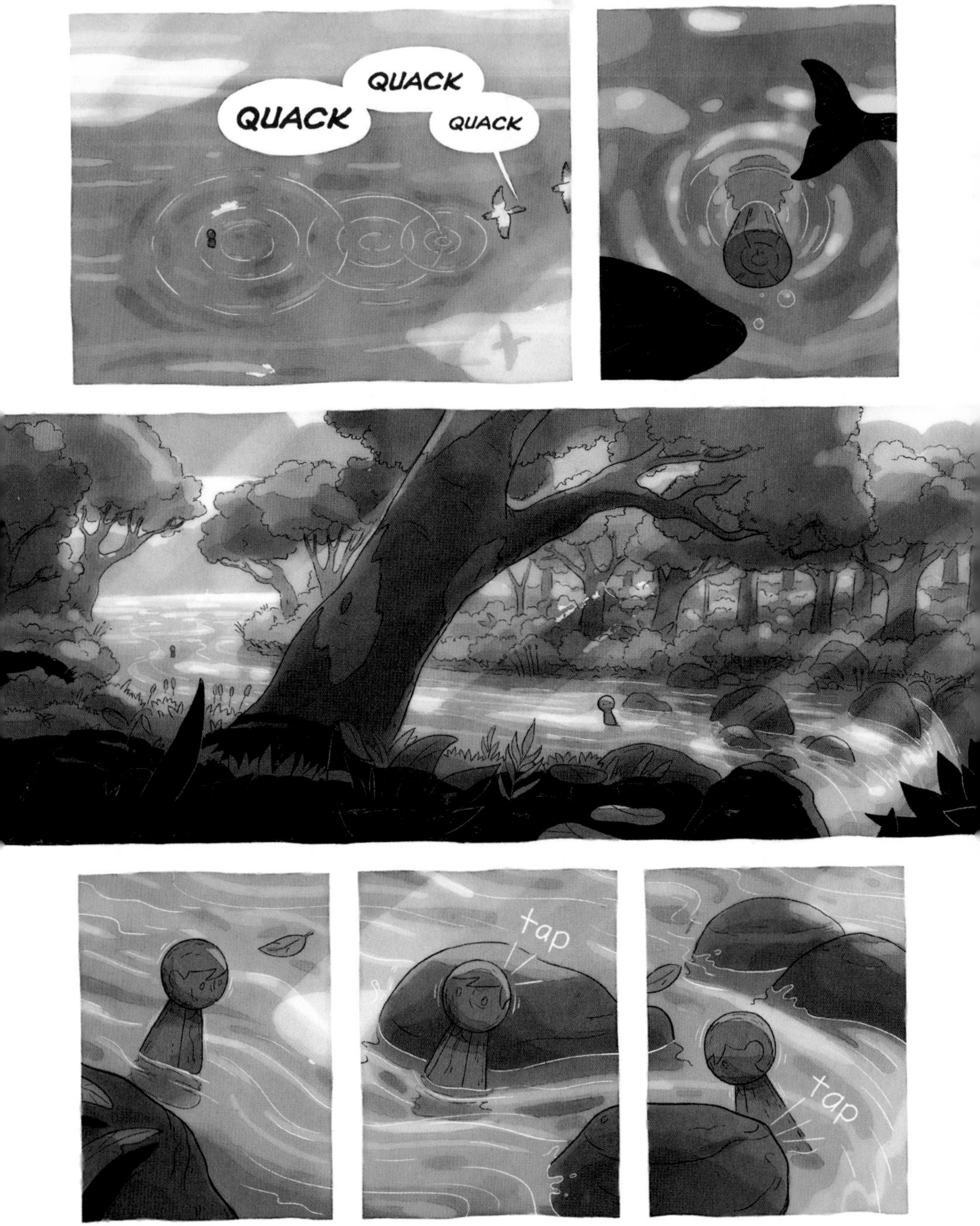
QUACK
QUACK
QUACK
tap
tap

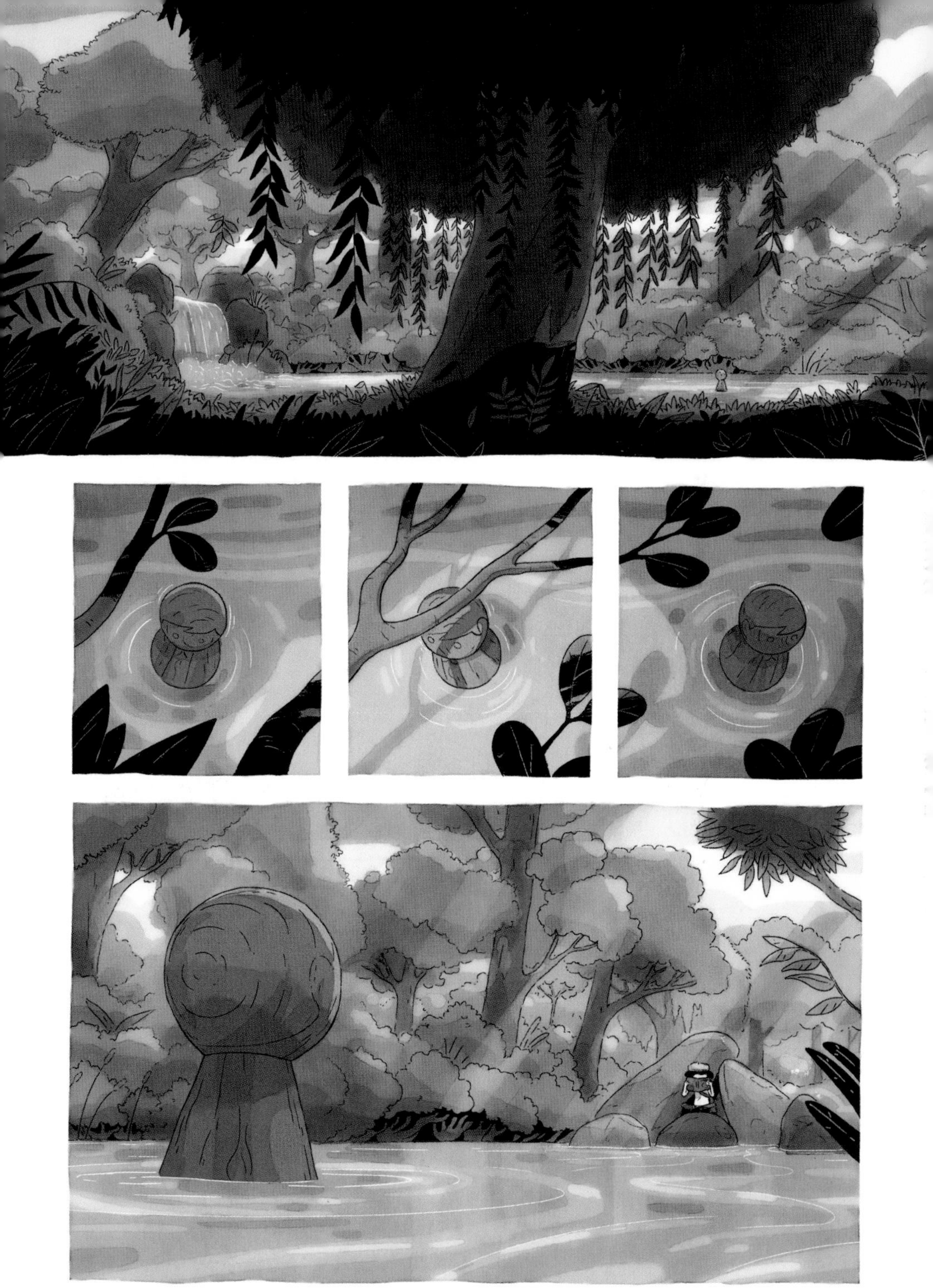

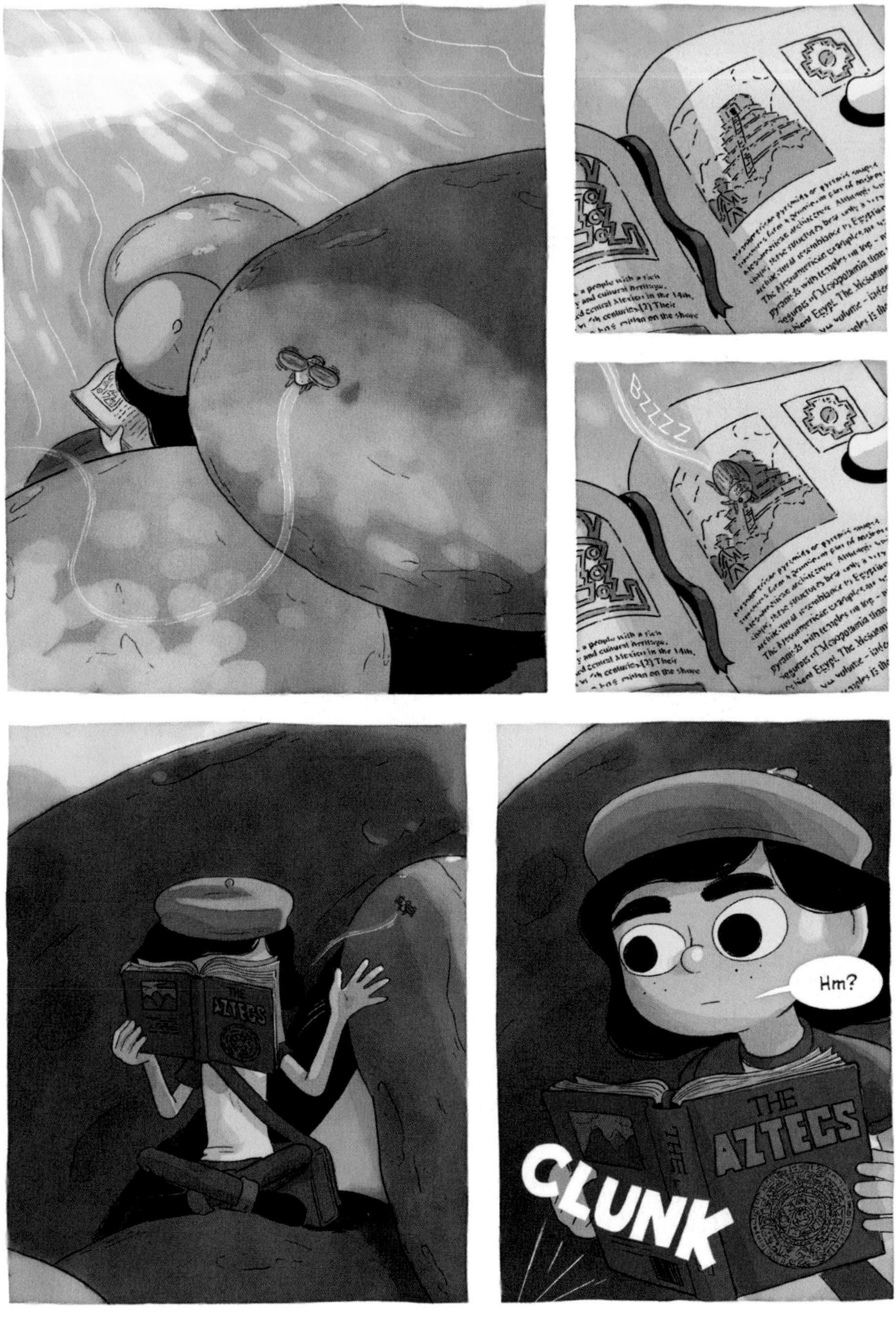
Bzzzz
THE AZTECS
Hm?
CLUNK

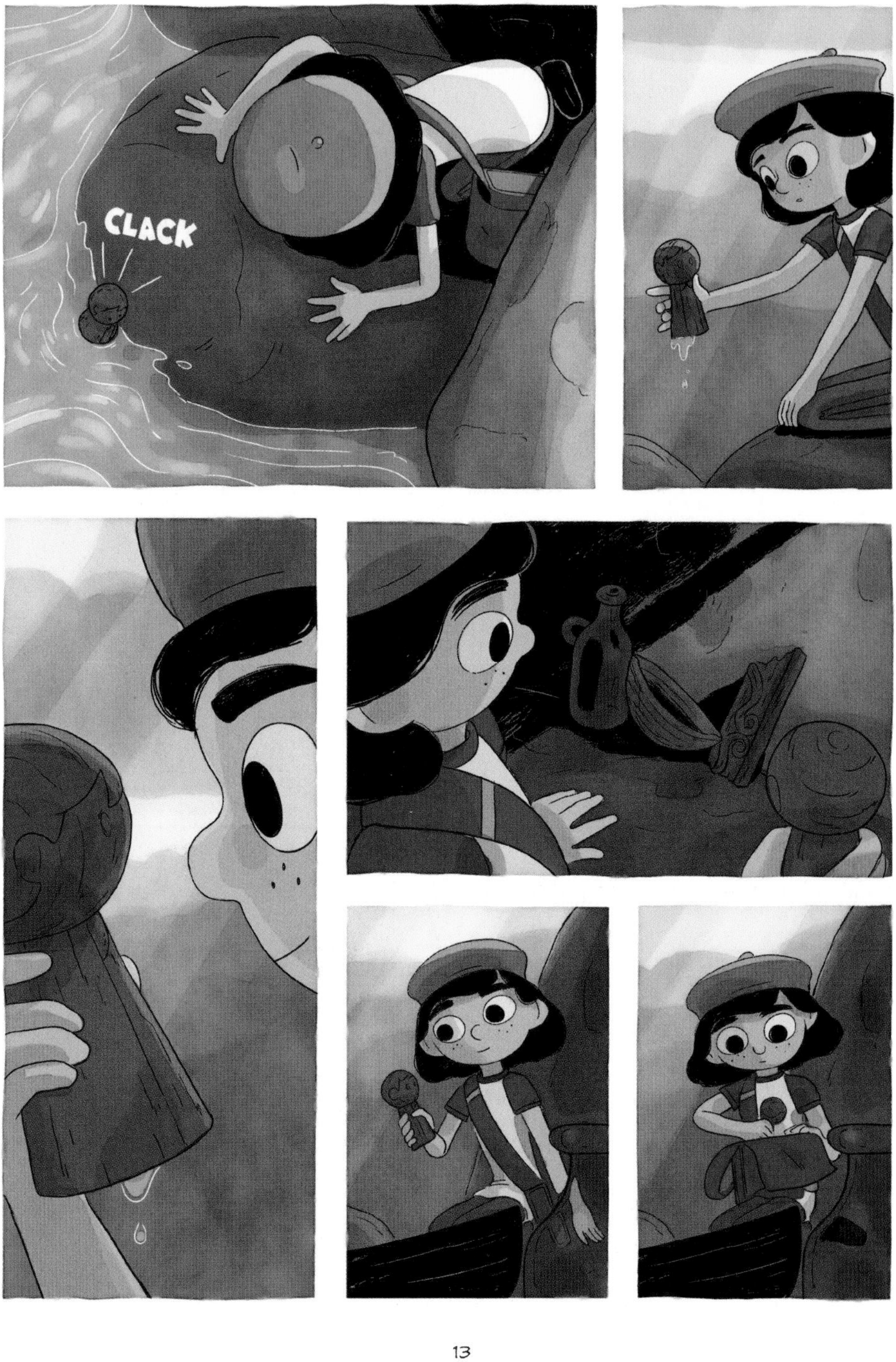
CLACK

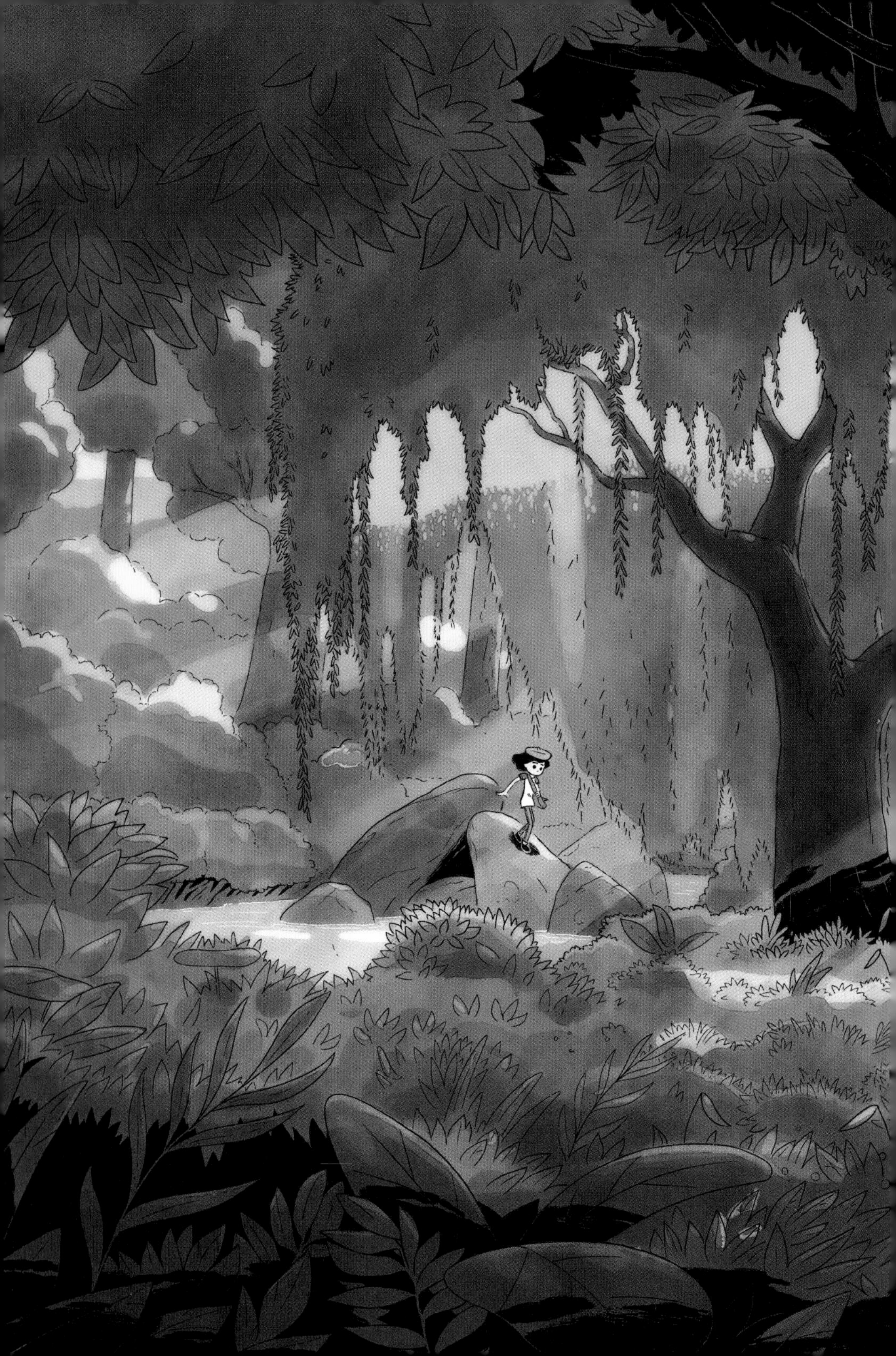

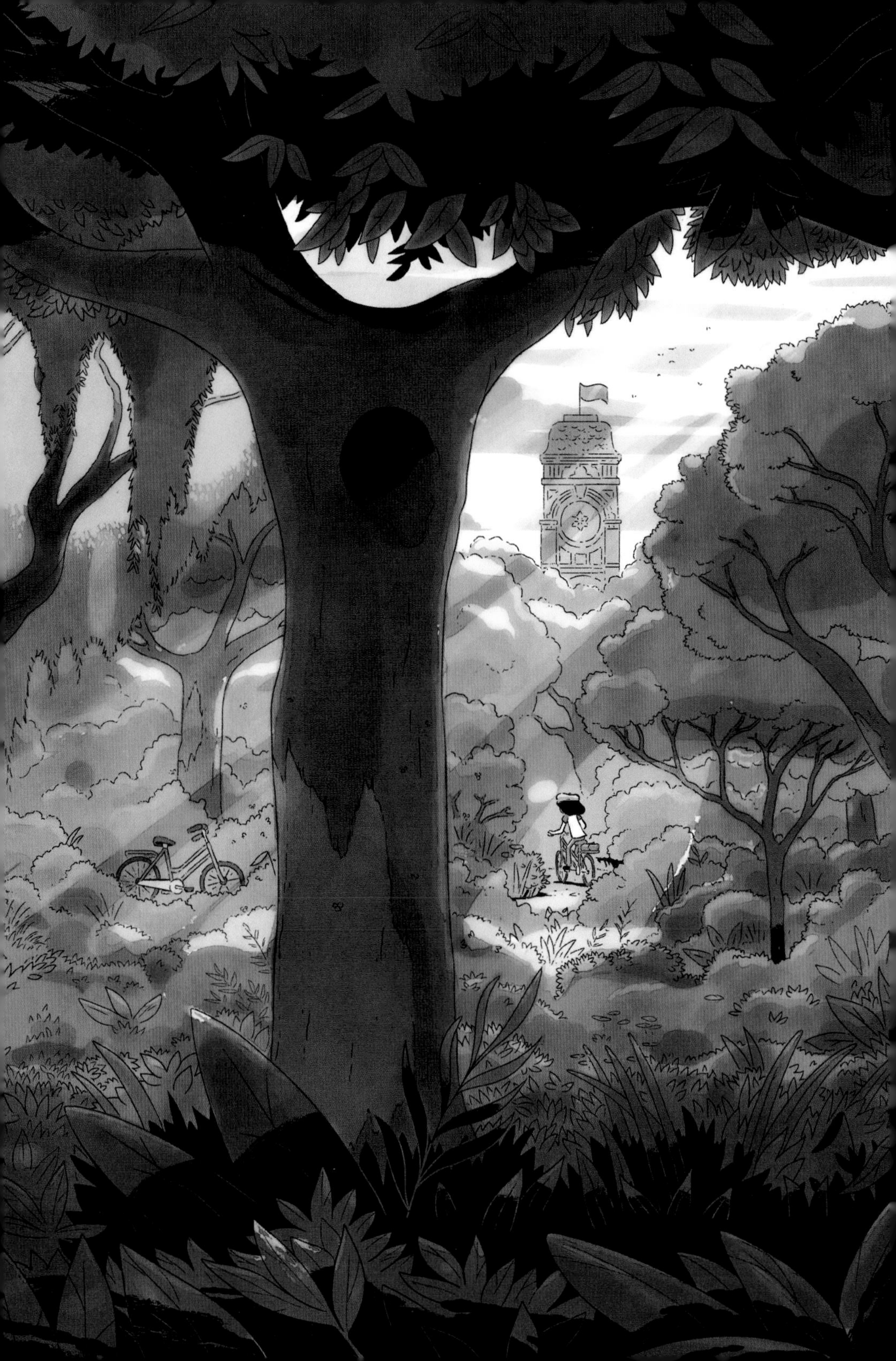

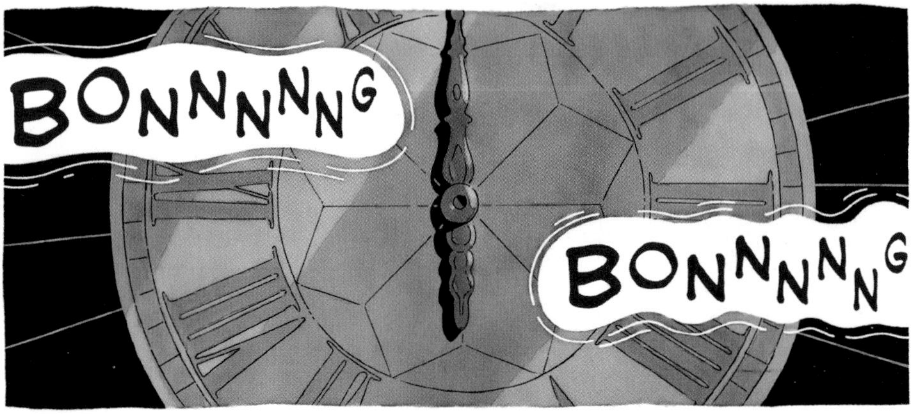
BONNNNNG
BONNNNNG

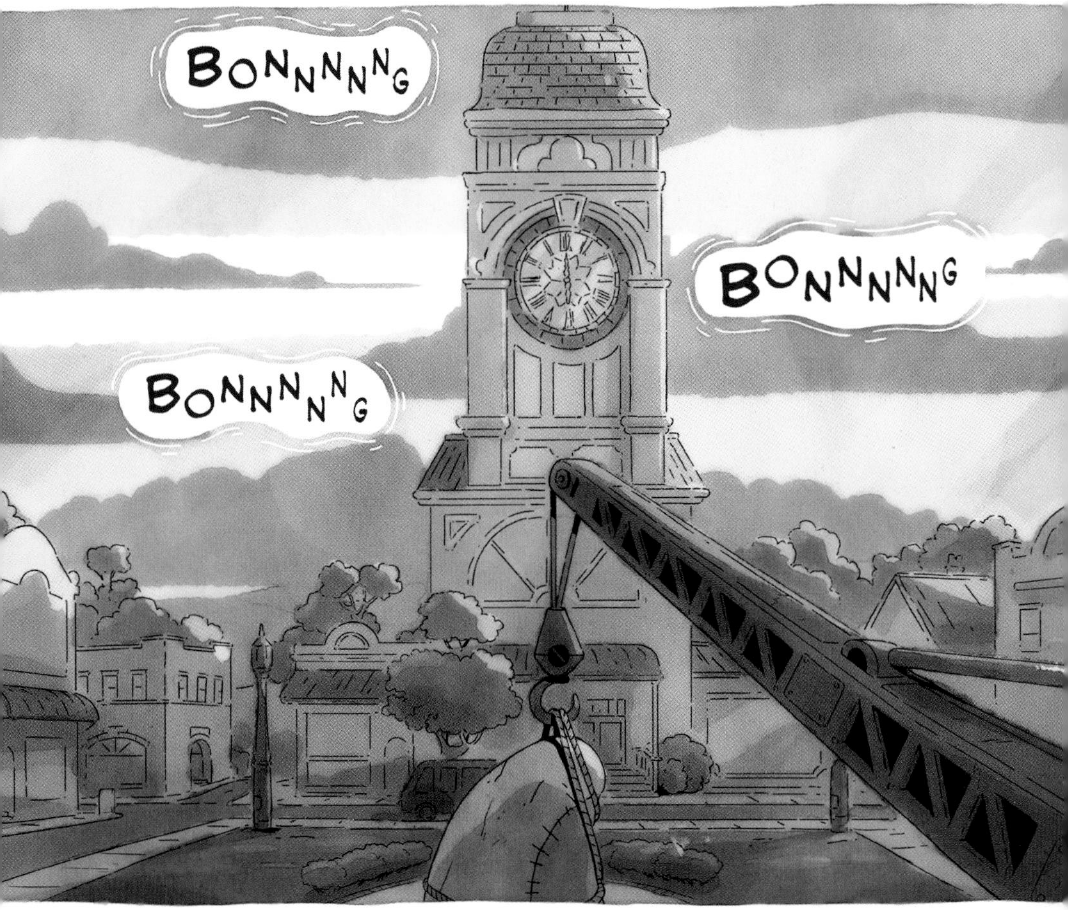
BONNNNNG
BONNNNNG
BONNNNNG

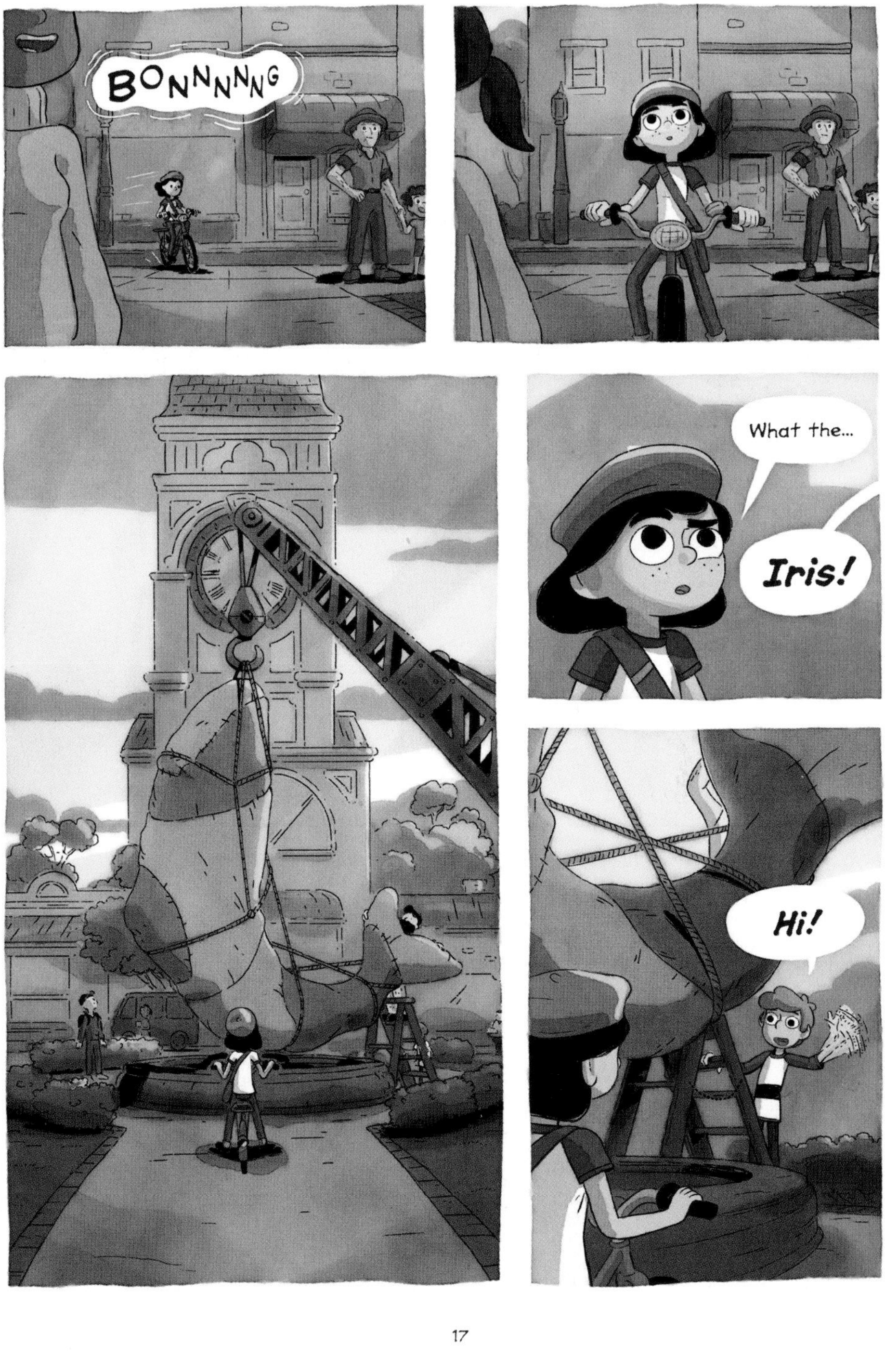
BONNNNNG
What the...
Iris!
Hi!

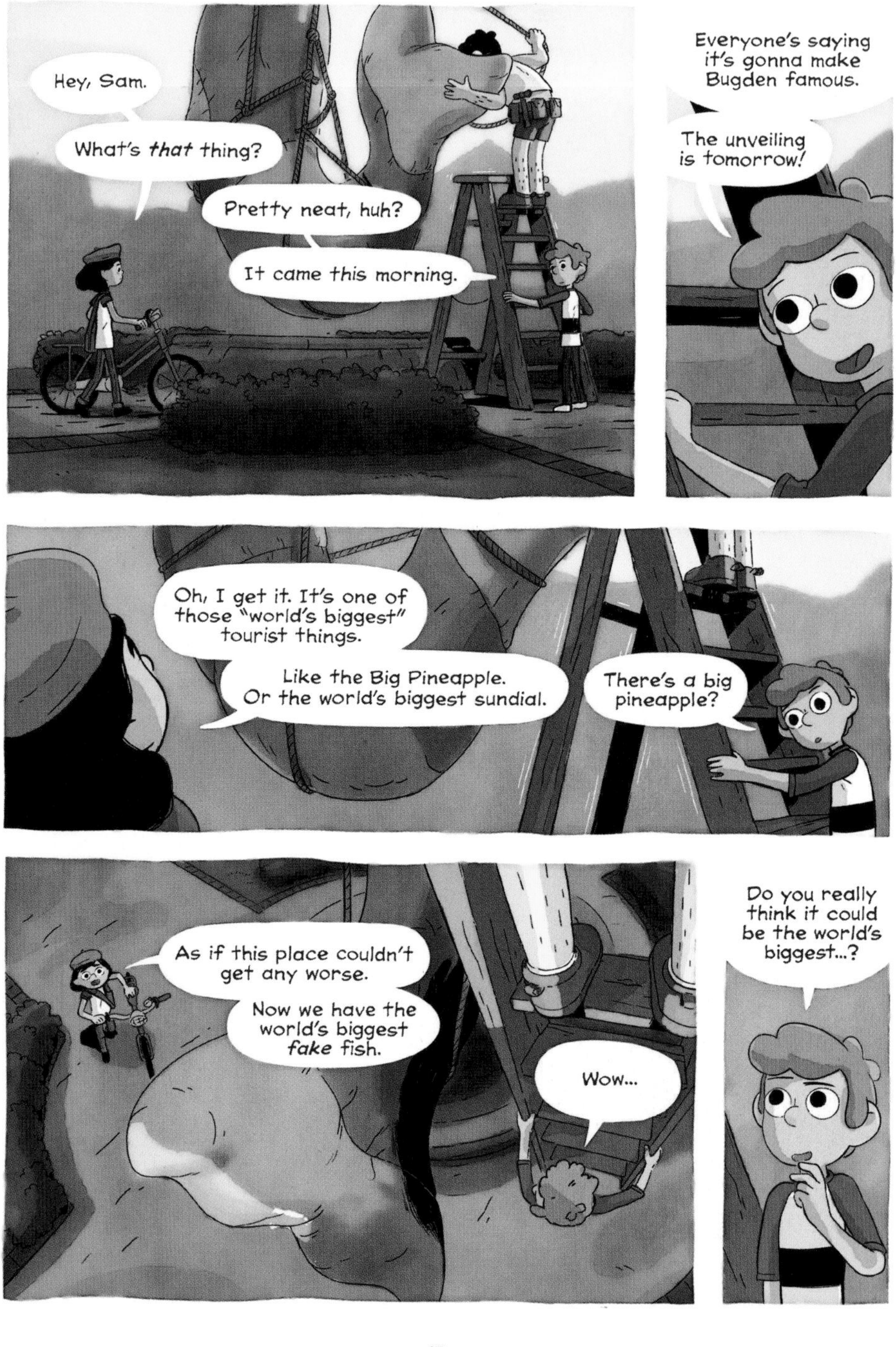
Hey, Sam.
What's *that* thing?
Pretty neat, huh?
It came this morning.
Everyone's saying it's gonna make Bugden famous.
The unveiling is tomorrow!
Oh, I get it. It's one of those "world's biggest" tourist things.
Like the Big Pineapple. Or the world's biggest sundial.
There's a big pineapple?
As if this place couldn't get any worse.
Now we have the world's biggest *fake* fish.
Wow...
Do you really think it could be the world's biggest...?

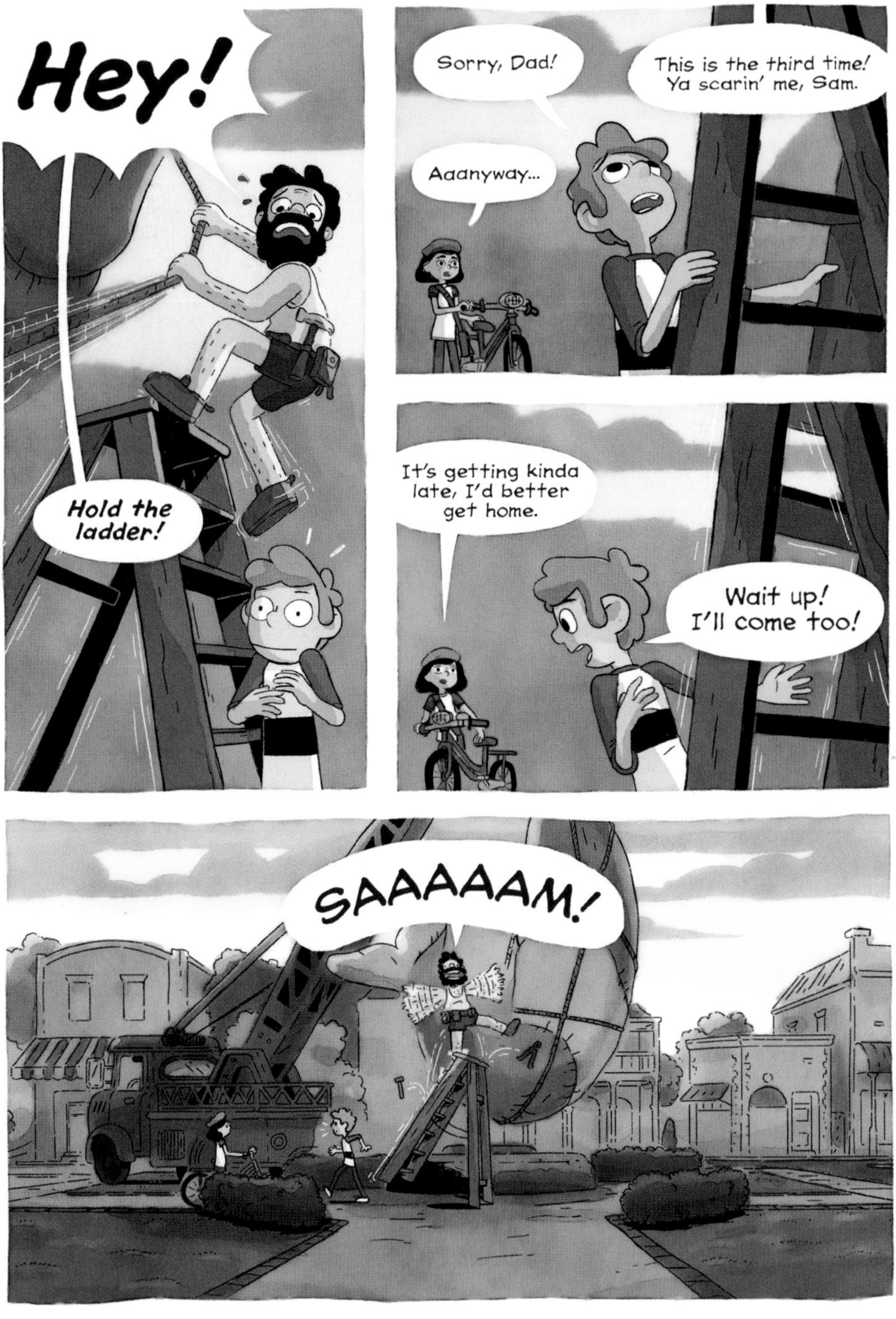
Hey!
Hold the ladder!
Sorry, Dad!
This is the third time! Ya scarin' me, Sam.
Aaanyway...
It's getting kinda late, I'd better get home.
Wait up! I'll come too!
SAAAAAM!

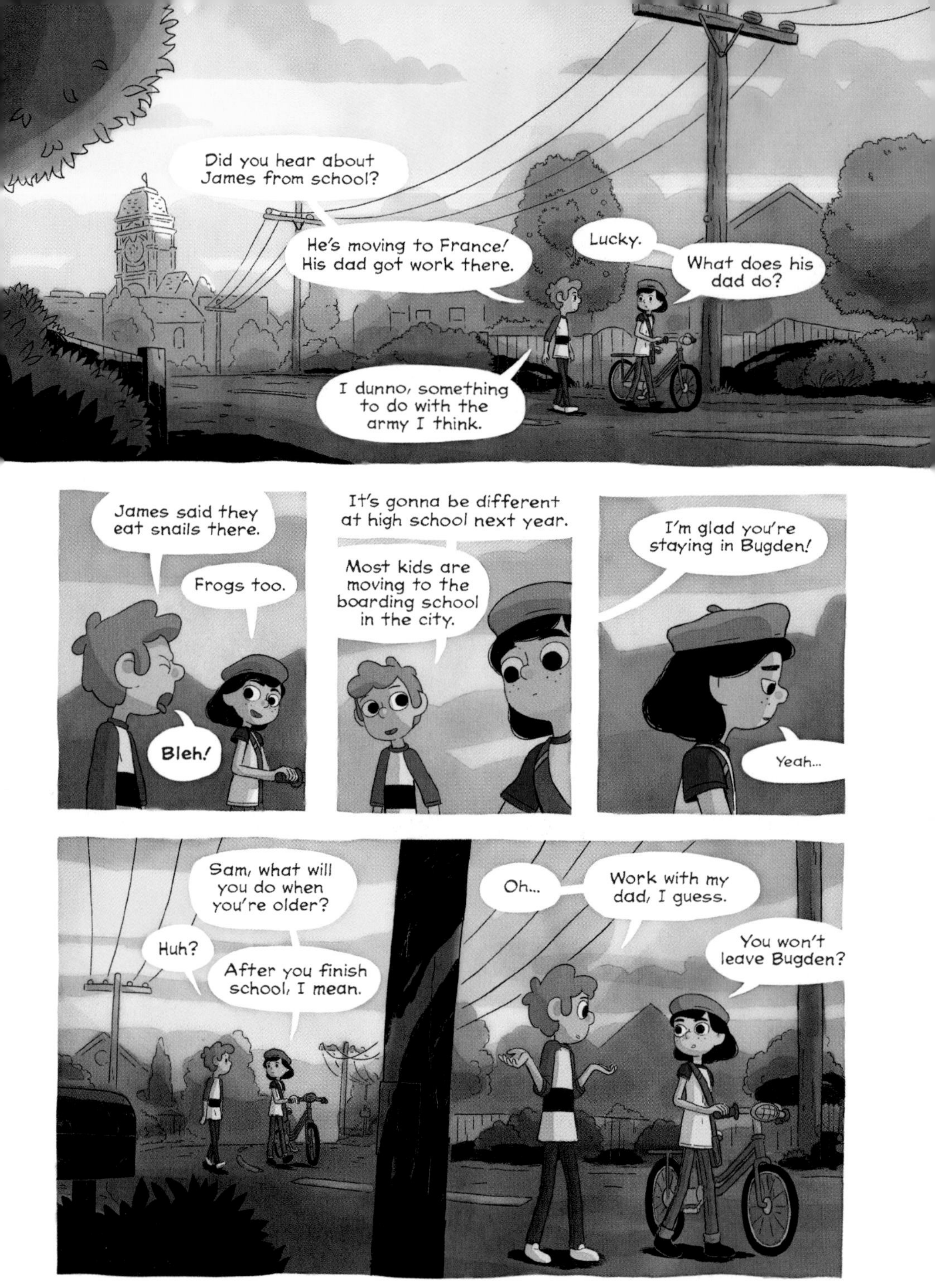
Did you hear about James from school?
He's moving to France! His dad got work there.
Lucky.
What does his dad do?
I dunno, something to do with the army I think.
James said they eat snails there.
Frogs too.
Bleh!
It's gonna be different at high school next year.
Most kids are moving to the boarding school in the city.
I'm glad you're staying in Bugden!
Yeah...
Sam, what will you do when you're older?
Huh?
After you finish school, I mean.
Oh...
Work with my dad, I guess.
You won't leave Bugden?

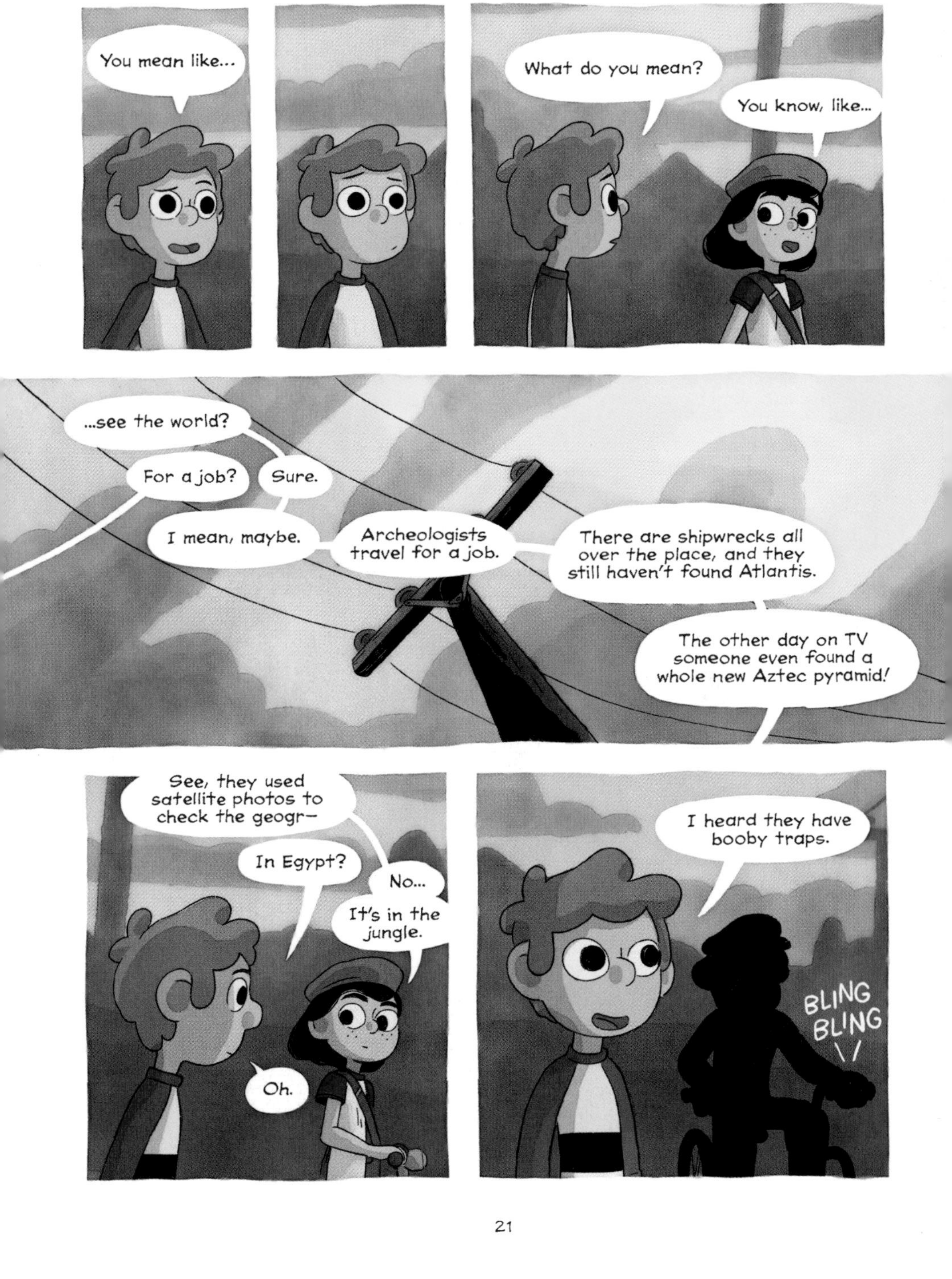
You mean like...
What do you mean?
You know, like...
...see the world?
For a job?
Sure.
I mean, maybe.
Archeologists travel for a job.
There are shipwrecks all over the place, and they still haven't found Atlantis.
The other day on TV someone even found a whole new Aztec pyramid!
See, they used satellite photos to check the geogr—
In Egypt?
No...
It's in the jungle.
Oh.
I heard they have booby traps.
BLING BLING

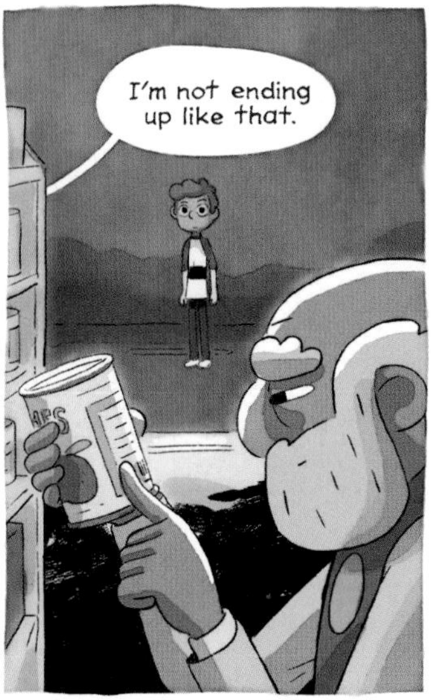
I'm not ending up like that.

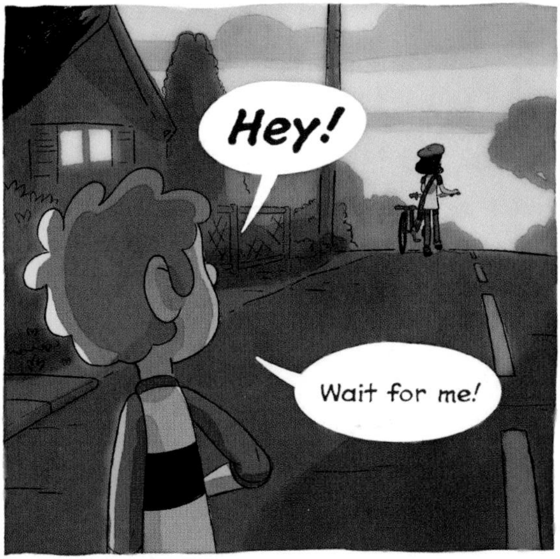
Hey!
Wait for me!

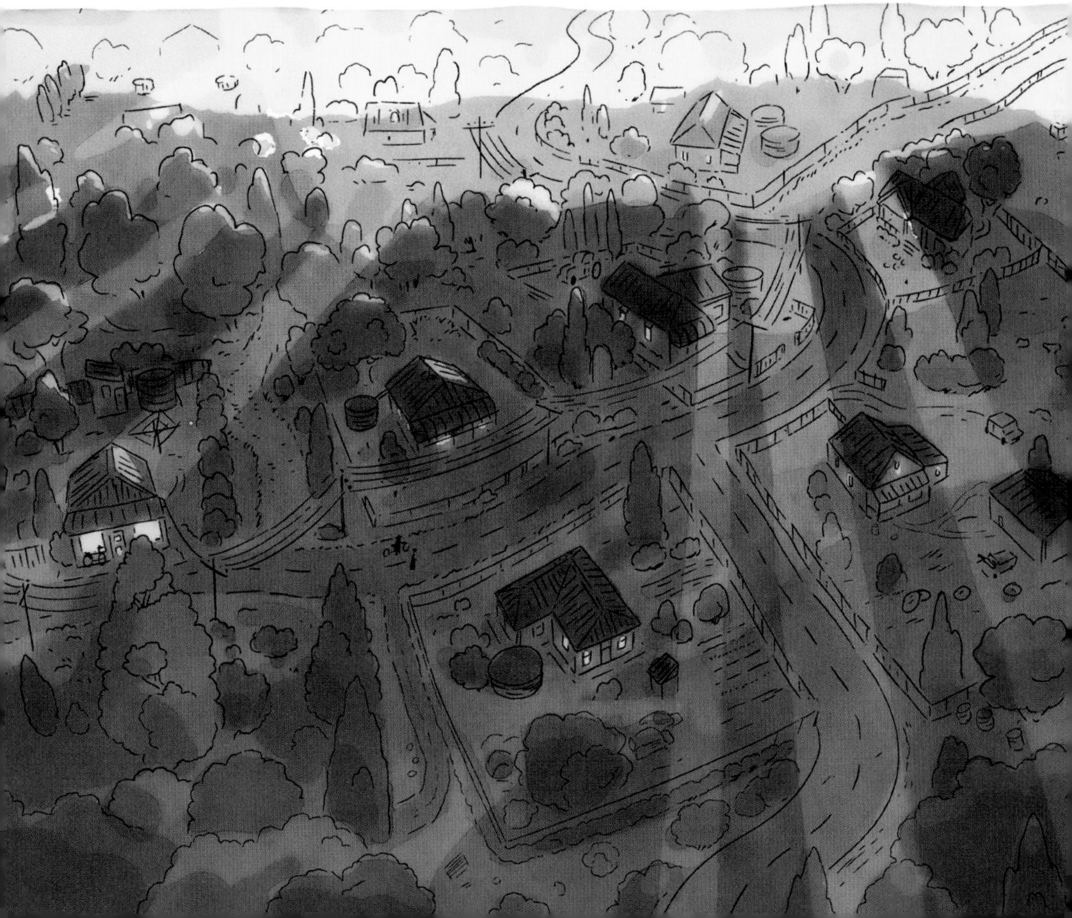

24

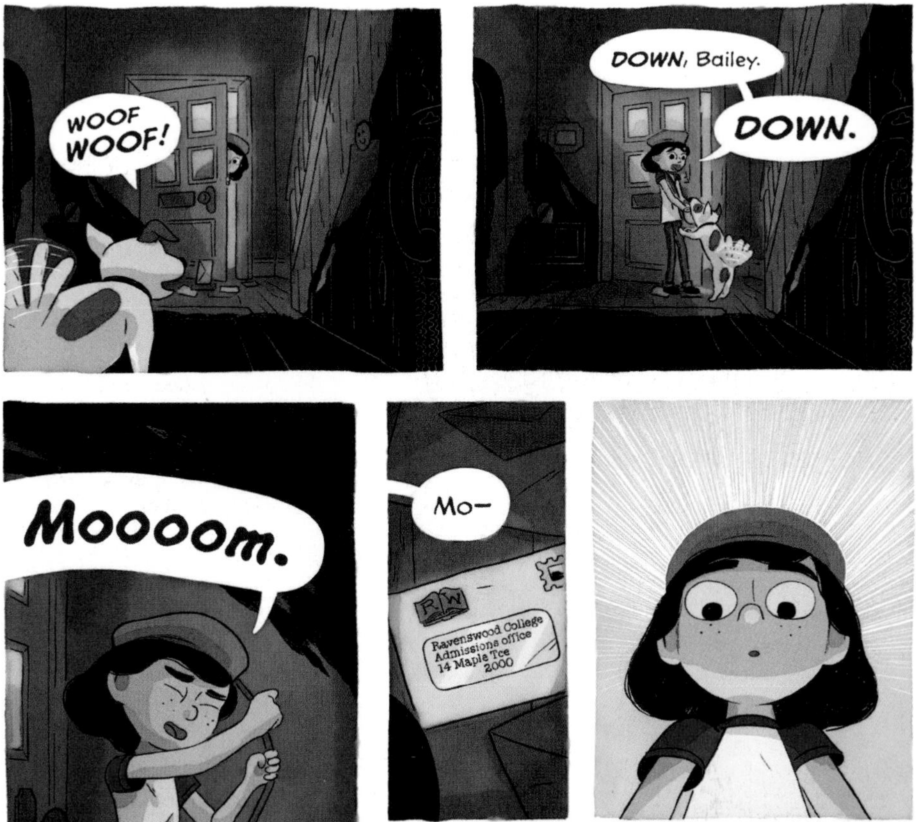
WOOF WOOF!
DOWN, Bailey.
DOWN.
Moooom.
Mo–
R.W
Ravenswood College
Admissions office
14 Maple Tce
2000
TEAR

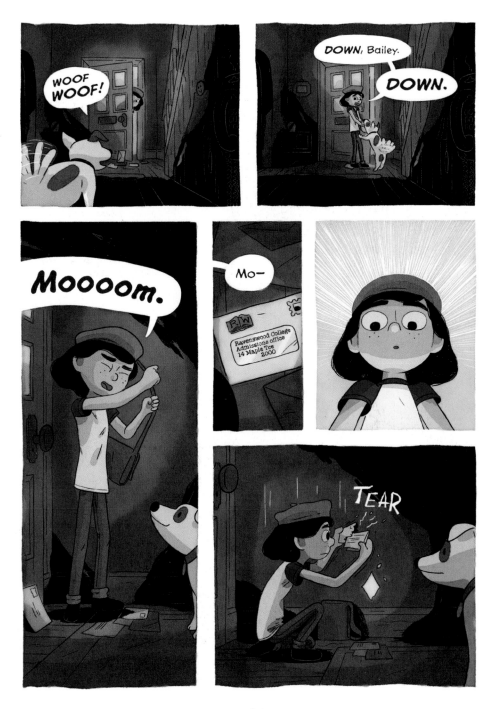

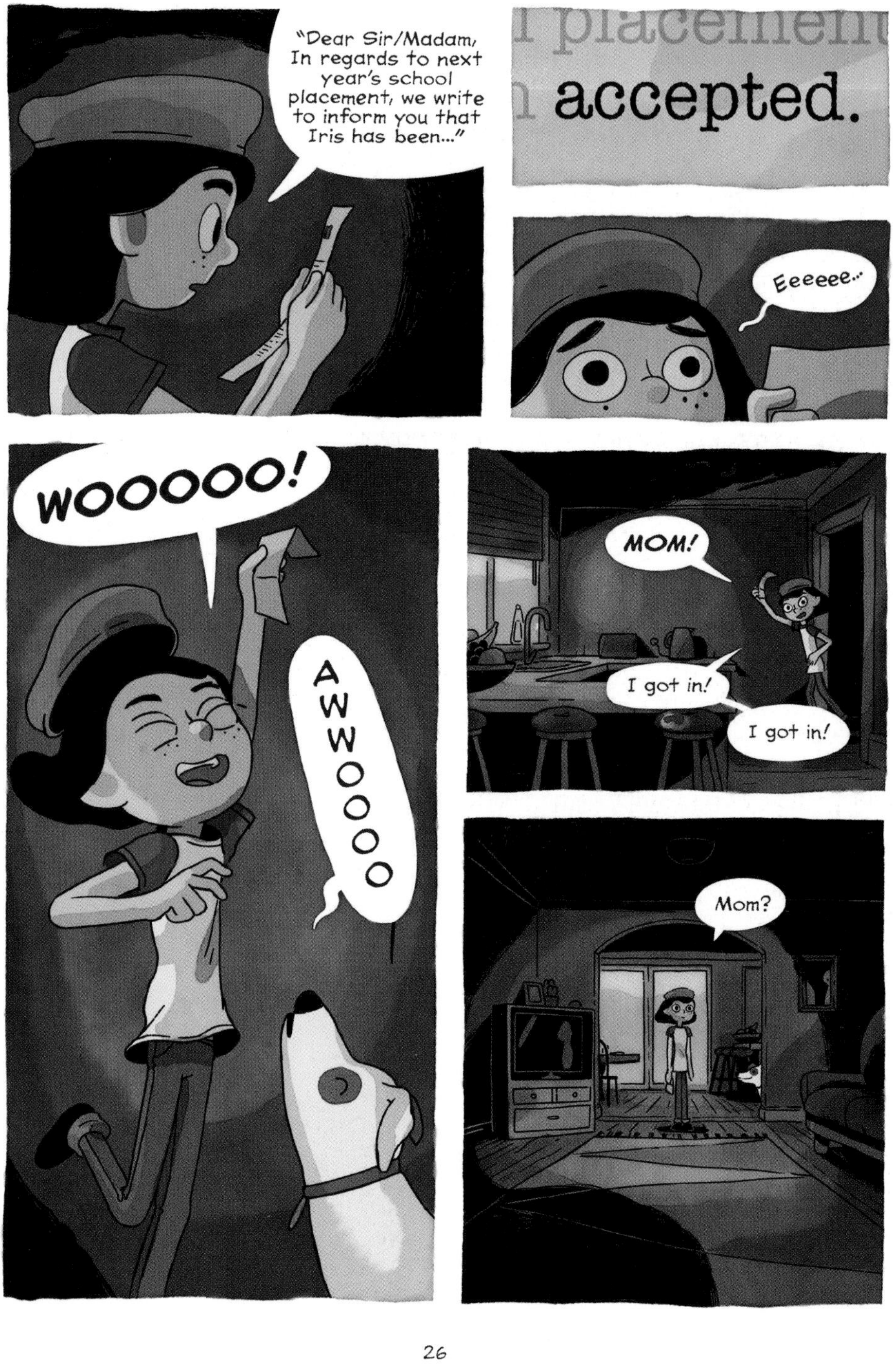
"Dear Sir/Madam,
In regards to next year's school placement, we write to inform you that Iris has been..."
accepted.
Eeeeee...
WOOOOO!
AWWOOOOO
MOM!
I got in!
I got in!
Mom?

Iris,
Taking your brother to the
city hospital. Don't worry,
everything's fine. Eat the
leftover spaghetti. I'll call
you later.

Love, Mom XOXO

Remember to feed Bailey!

THERE ARE LIMITS BEYOND WHICH MAN AND HIS PUNY EFFORTS CANNOT SURVIVE.

WE EXCEEDED THEM BY FIVE THOUSAND FEET.

WE'RE DEEPER NOW THAN MAN HAS EVER BEEN BEFORE.

GIANT SQUID ASTERN, *SIR!*

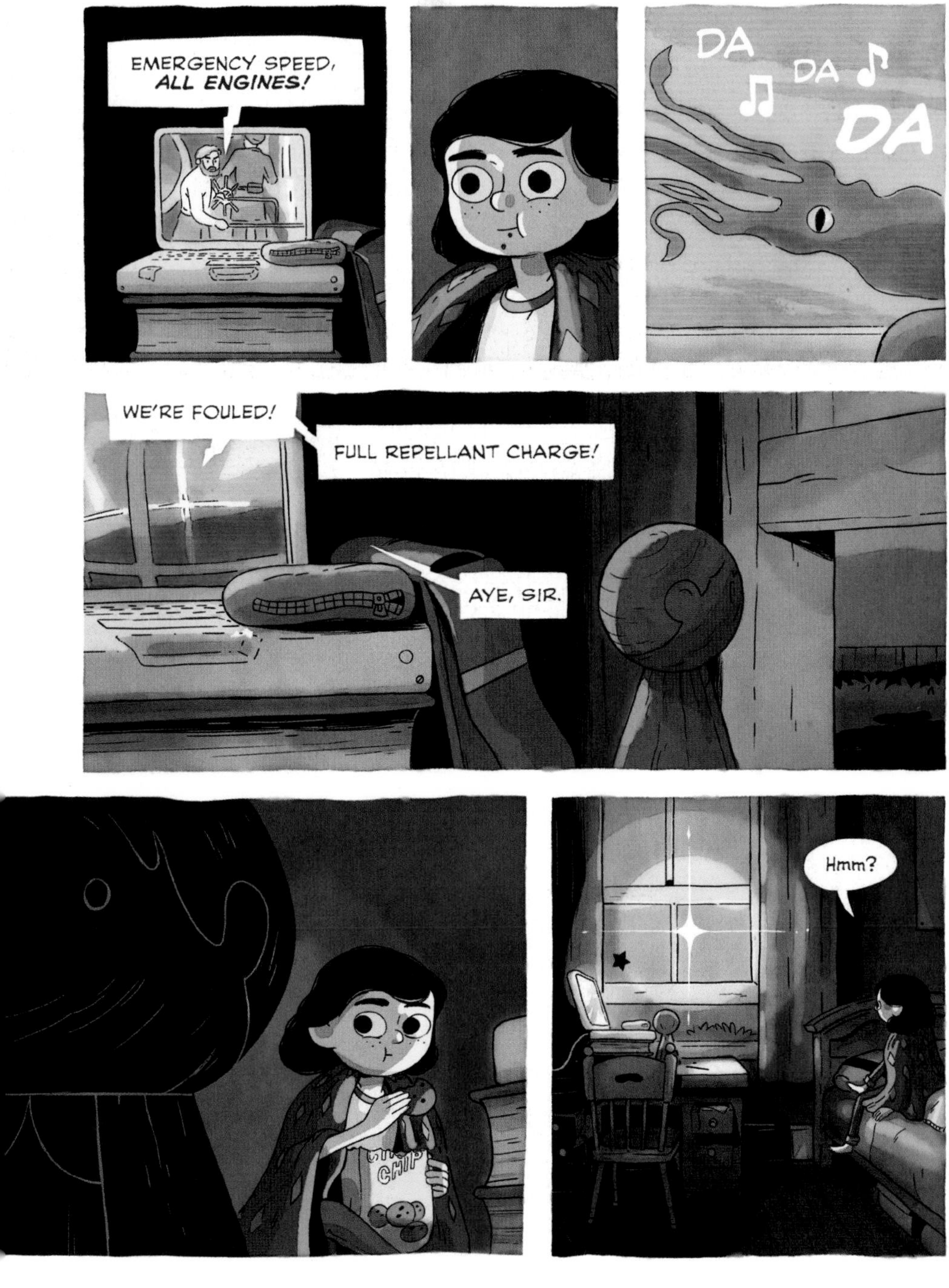
EMERGENCY SPEED, ALL ENGINES!
DA
DA
DA
WE'RE FOULED!
FULL REPELLANT CHARGE!
AYE, SIR.
CHIP
Hmm?

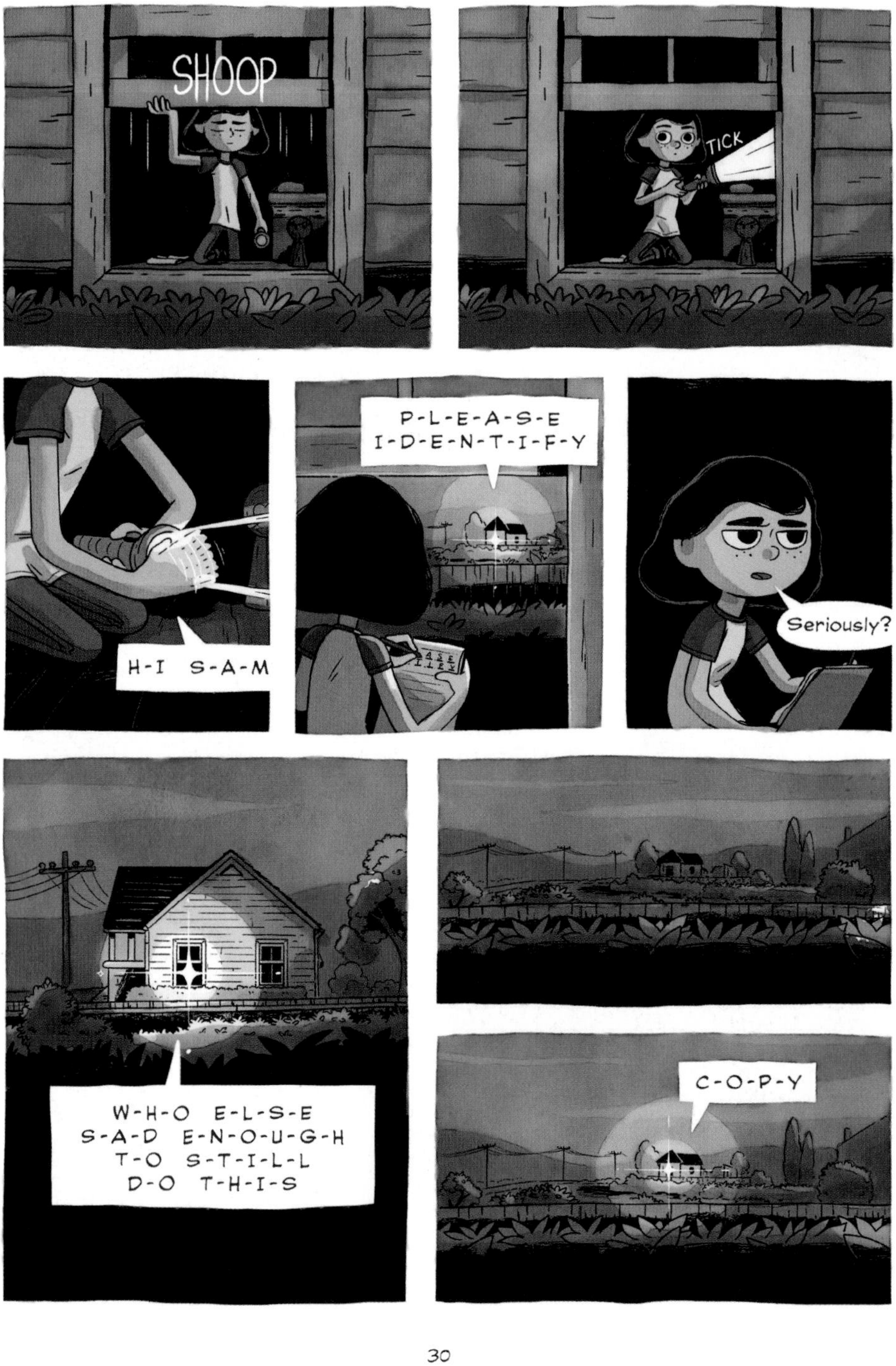
SHOOP
TICK
H-I S-A-M
P-L-E-A-S-E I-D-E-N-T-I-F-Y
Seriously?
W-H-O E-L-S-E S-A-D E-N-O-U-G-H T-O S-T-I-L-L D-O T-H-I-S
C-O-P-Y

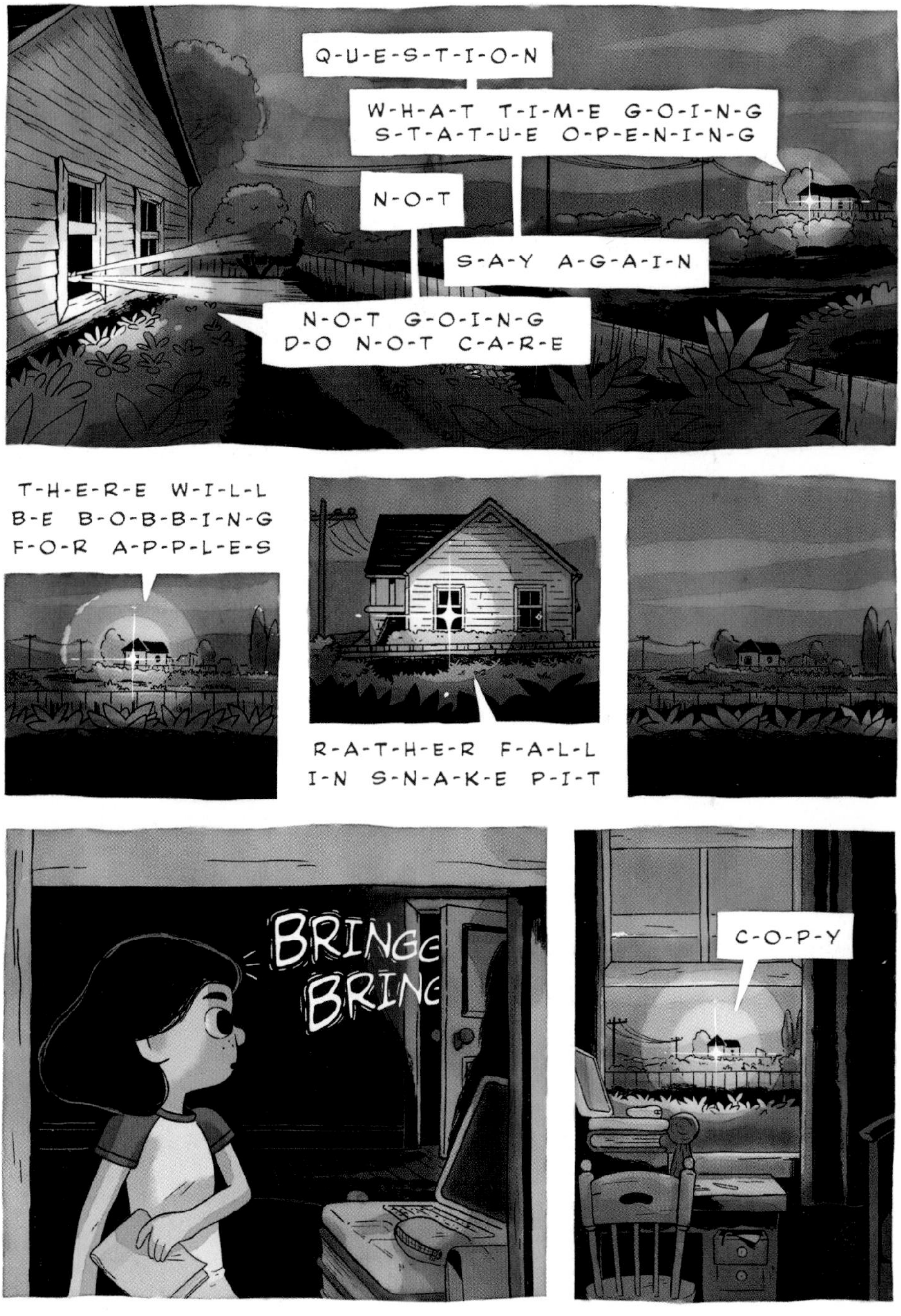
Q-U-E-S-T-I-O-N
W-H-A-T T-I-M-E G-O-I-N-G S-T-A-T-U-E O-P-E-N-I-N-G
N-O-T
S-A-Y A-G-A-I-N
N-O-T G-O-I-N-G D-O N-O-T C-A-R-E
T-H-E-R-E W-I-L-L B-E B-O-B-B-I-N-G F-O-R A-P-P-L-E-S
R-A-T-H-E-R F-A-L-L I-N S-N-A-K-E P-I-T
BRING
BRING
C-O-P-Y

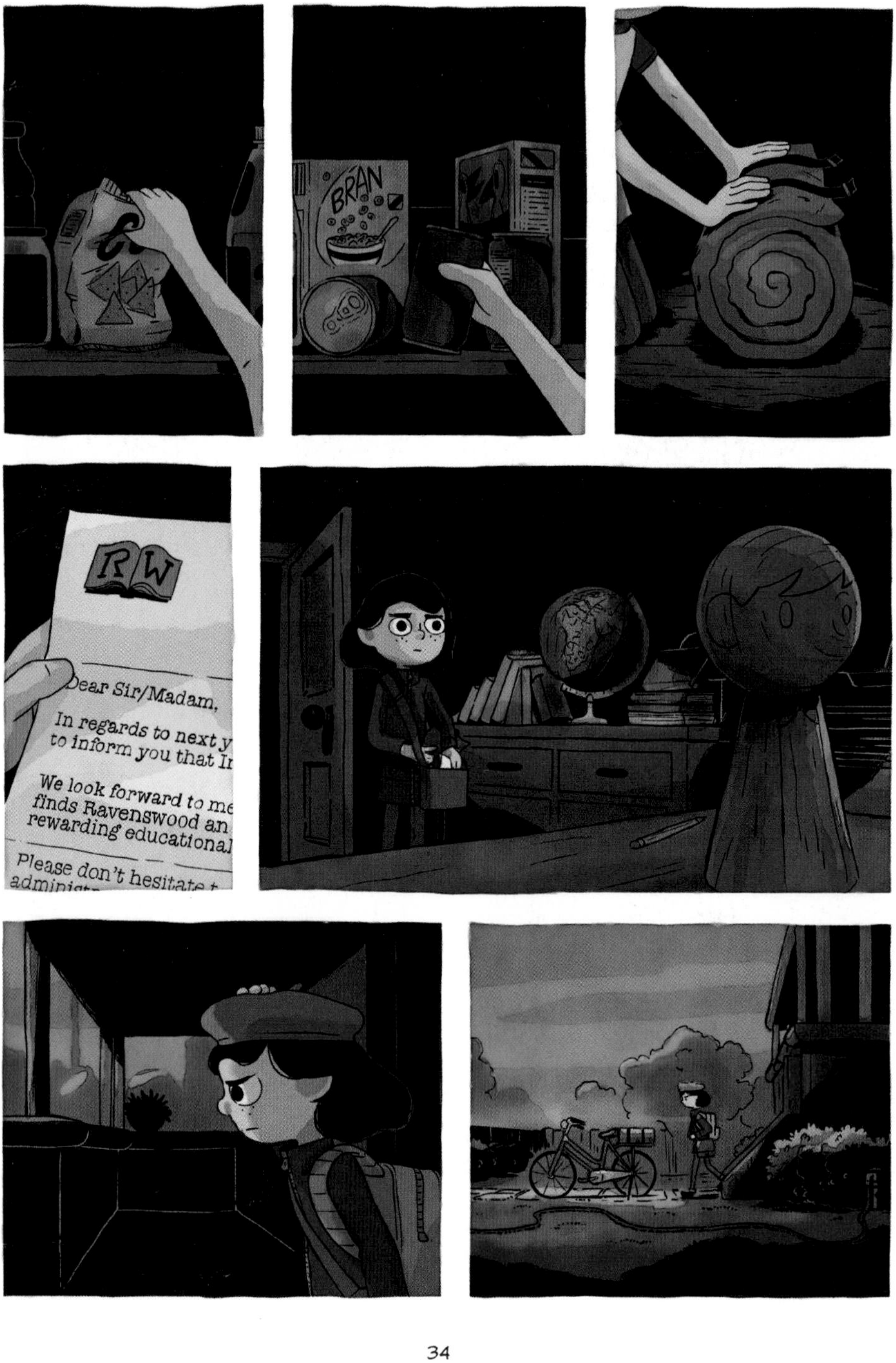
BRAN
RW
Dear Sir/Madam,
In regards to next y
to inform you that I
We look forward to me
finds Ravenswood an
rewarding educational
Please don't hesitate

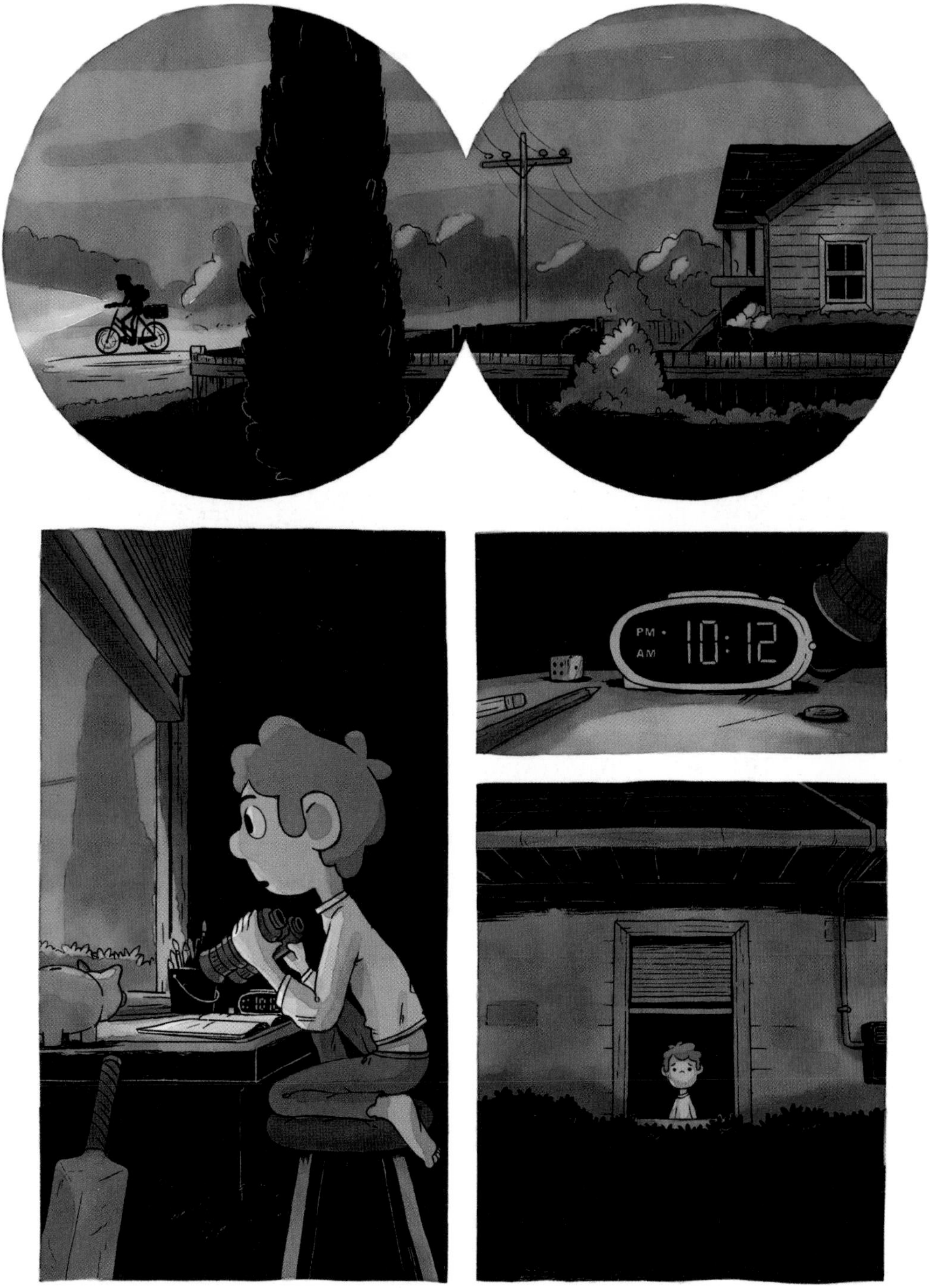
PM
AM
10:12

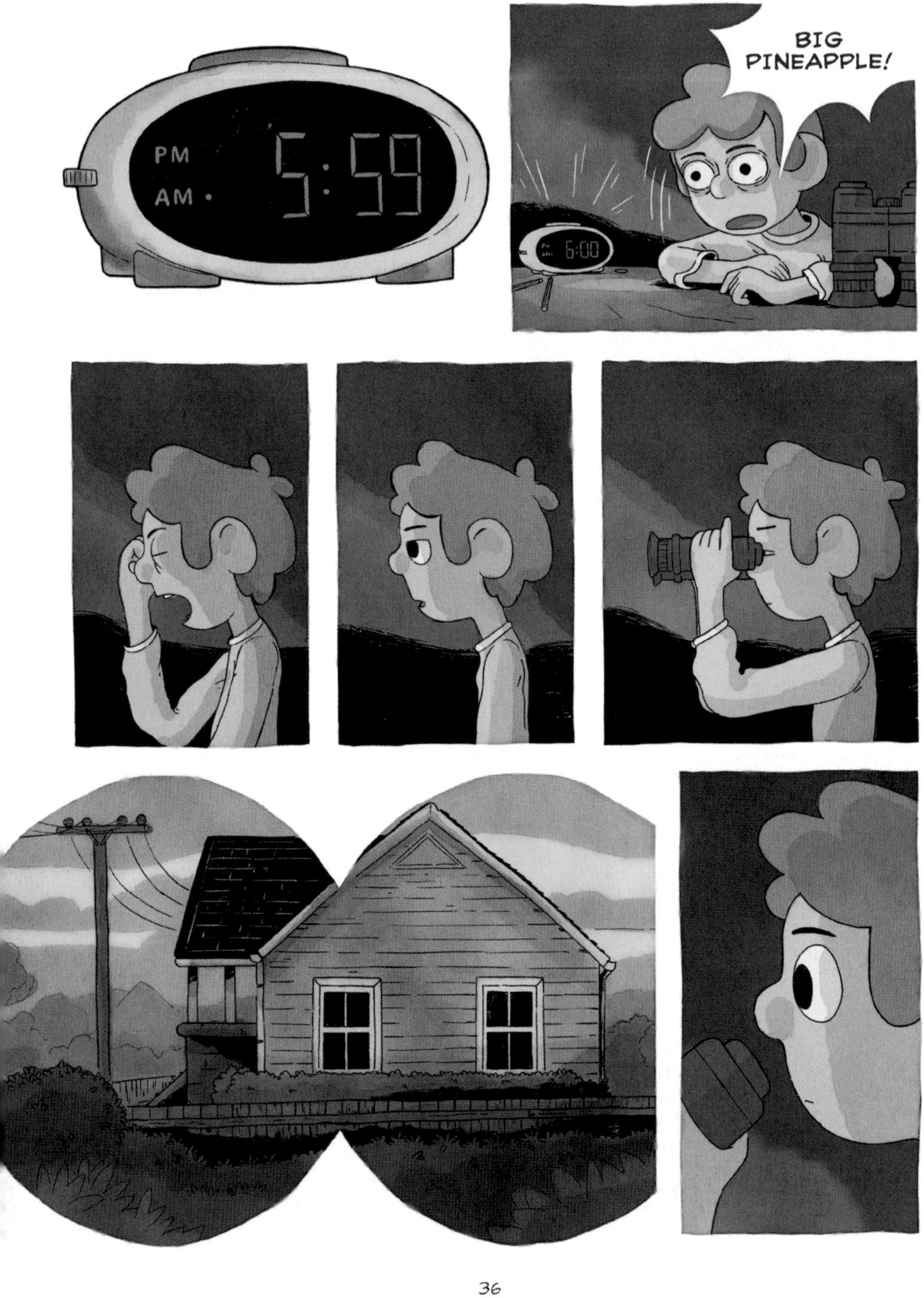
PM
AM
5:59
BIG PINEAPPLE!

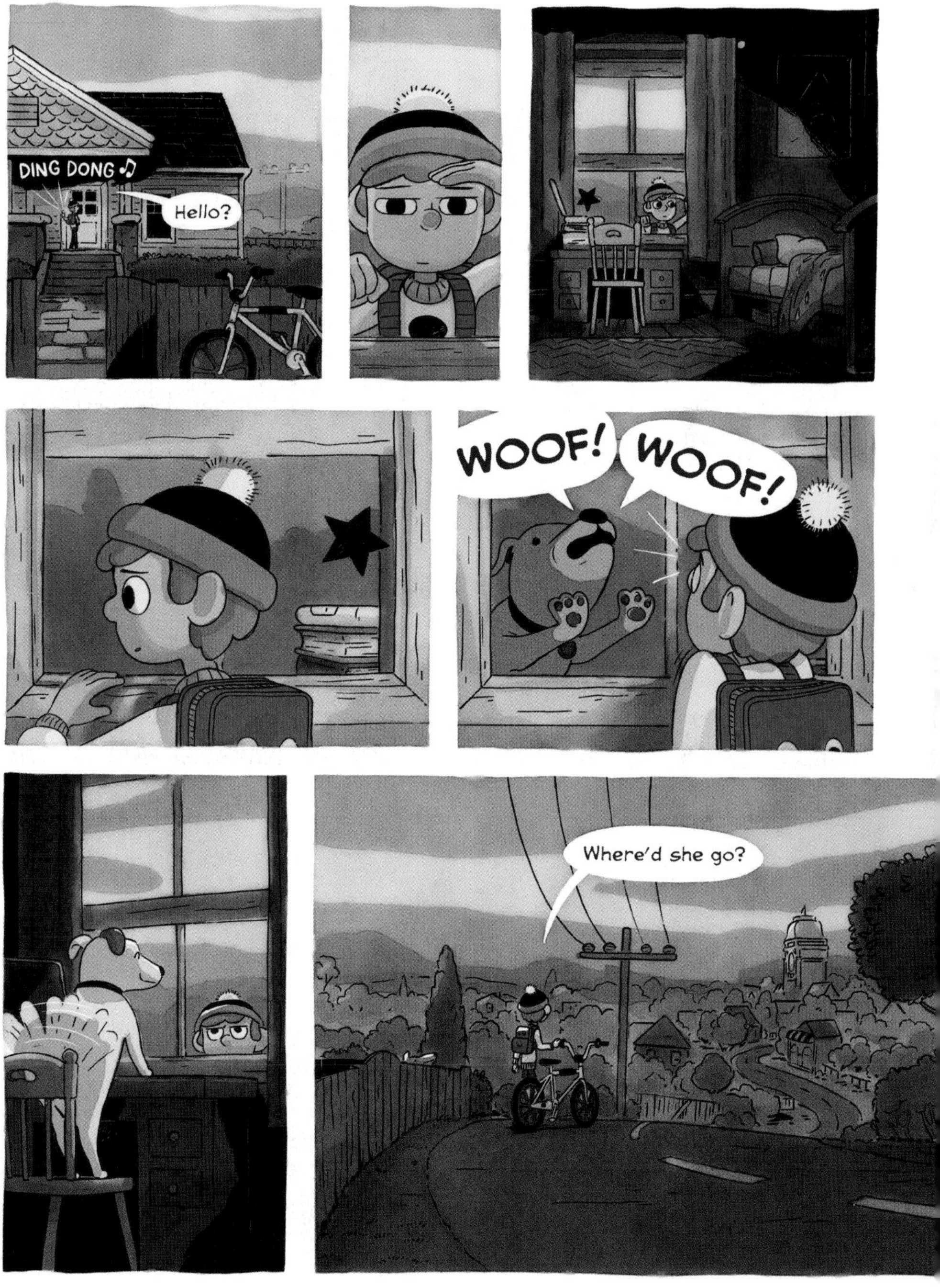
DING DONG ♫
Hello?
WOOF!
WOOF!
Where'd she go?

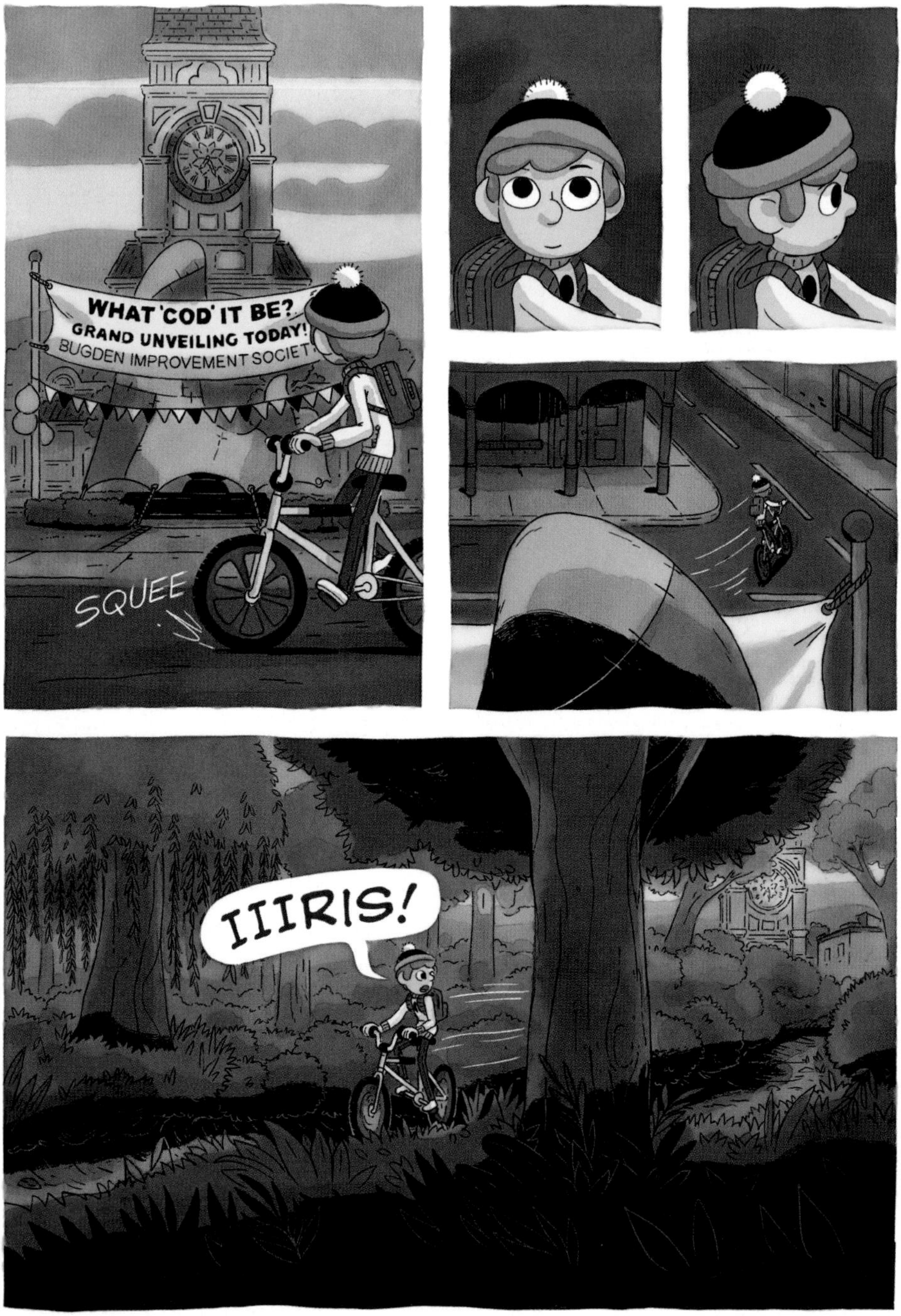
WHAT 'COD' IT BE?
GRAND UNVEILING TODAY!
BUGDEN IMPROVEMENT SOCIET
SQUEE
IIIRIS!

39

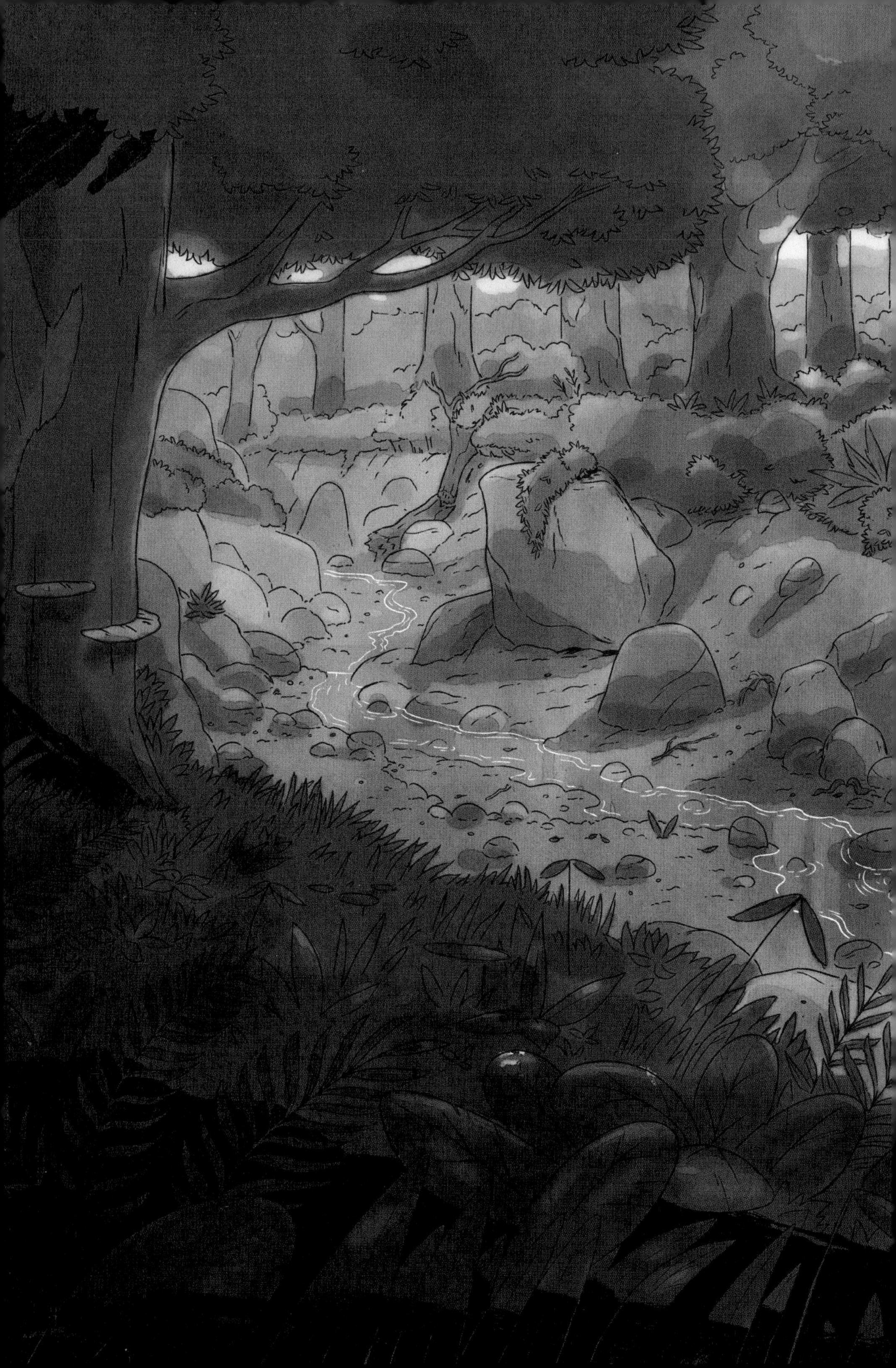

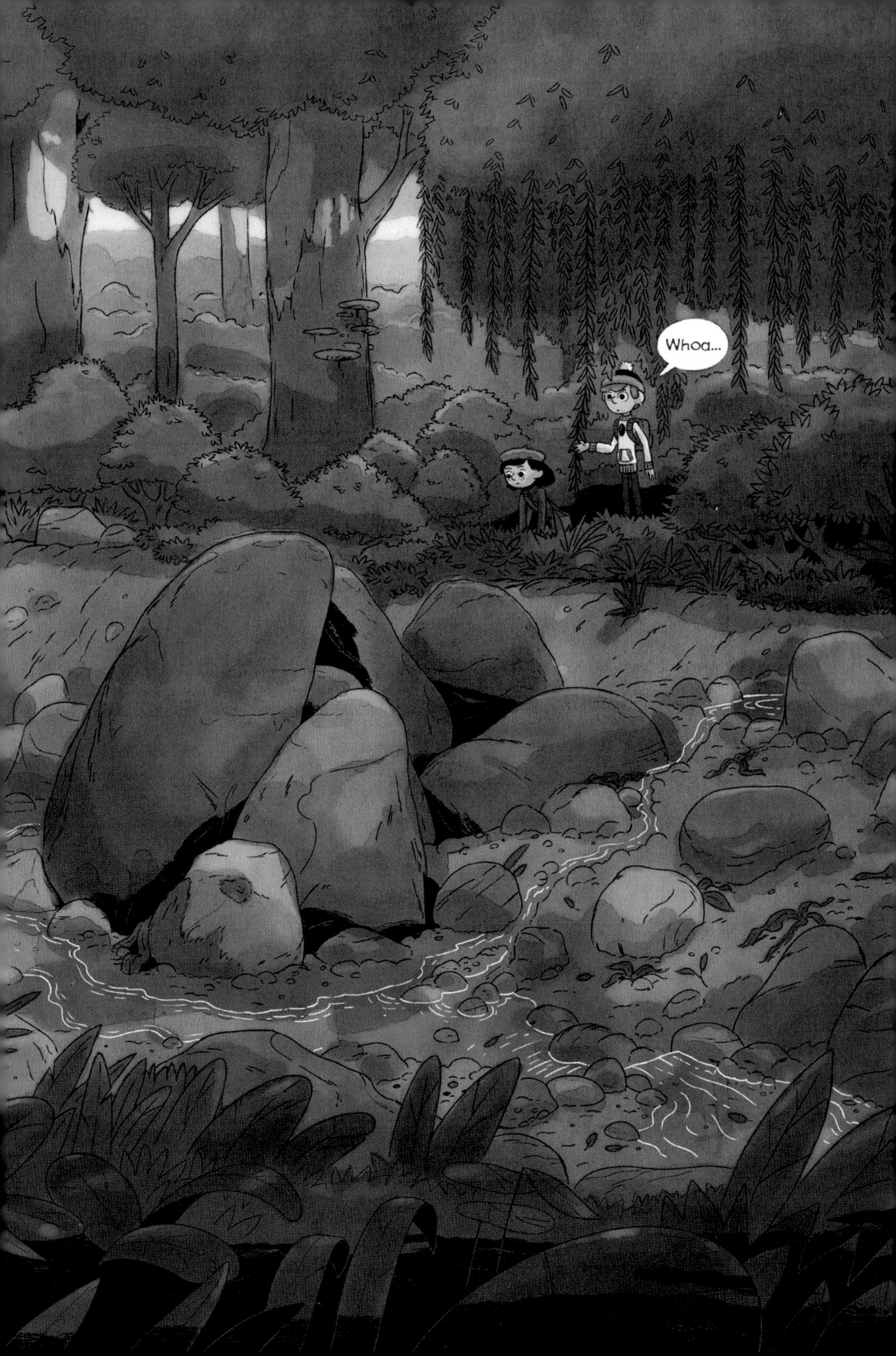
Whoa...

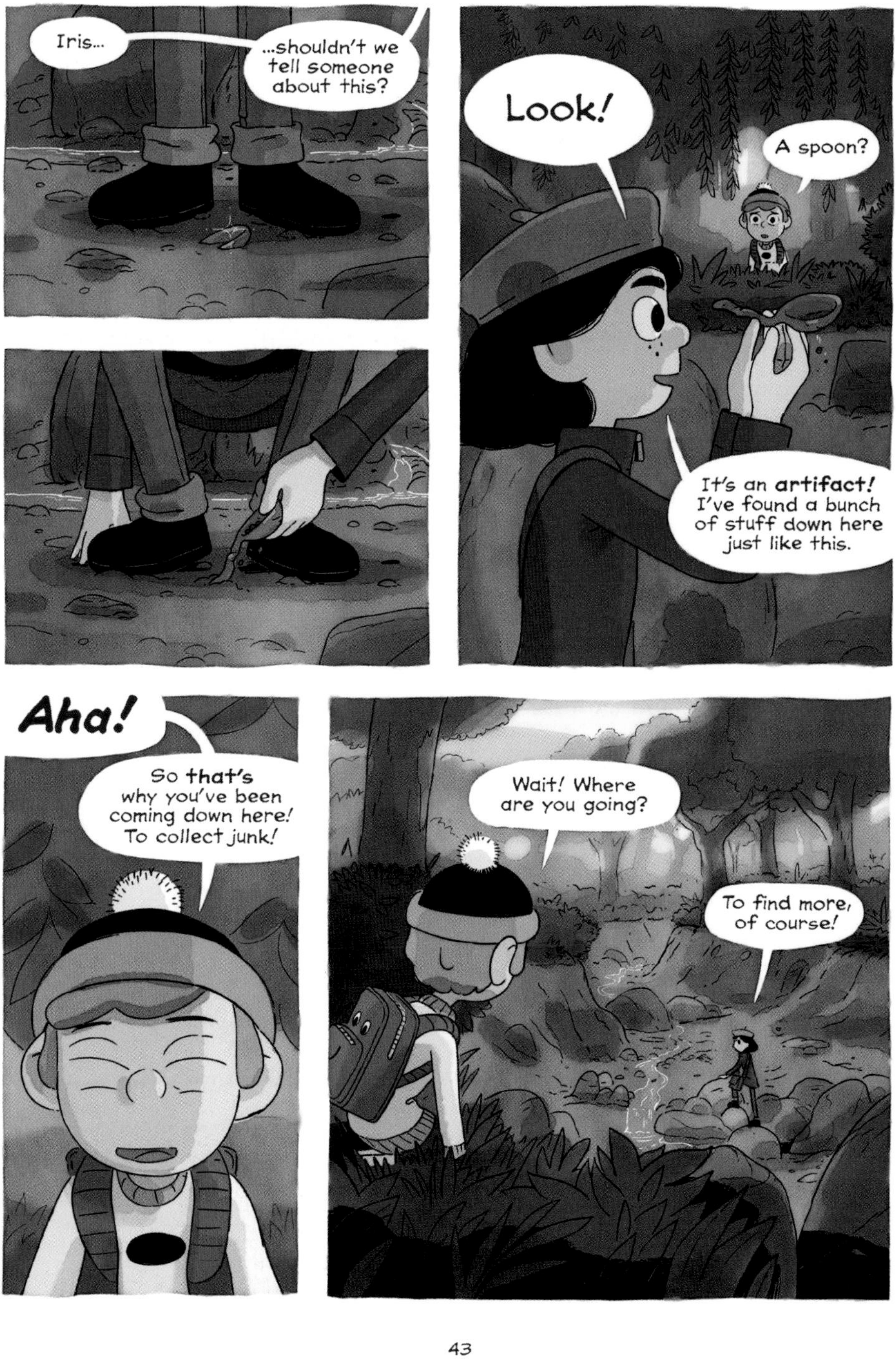

Iris...
...shouldn't we tell someone about this?
Look!
A spoon?
It's an **artifact!** I've found a bunch of stuff down here just like this.
Aha!
So **that's** why you've been coming down here! To collect junk!
Wait! Where are you going?
To find more, of course!

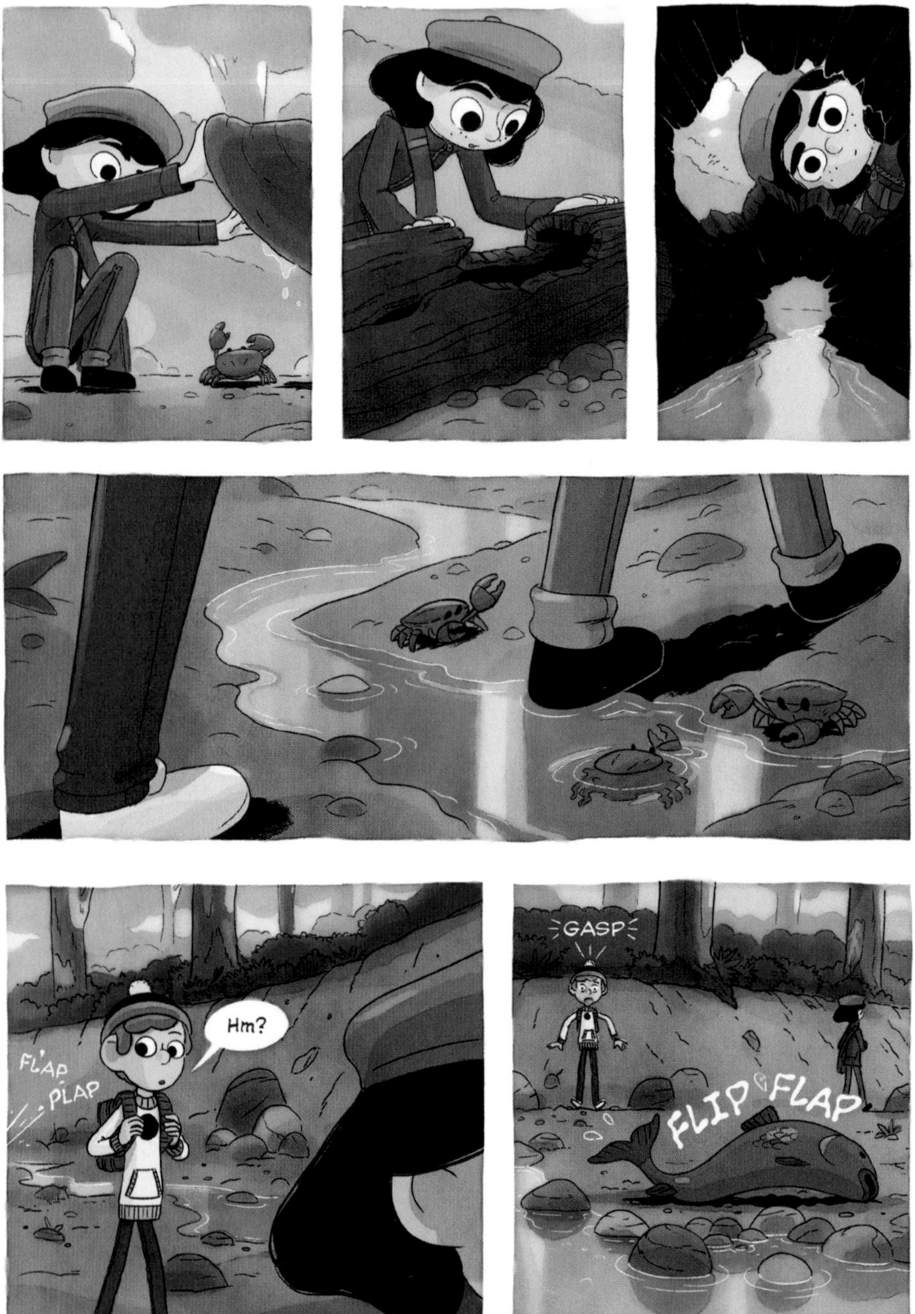
Hm?
FLAP
PLAP
GASP
FLIP FLAP

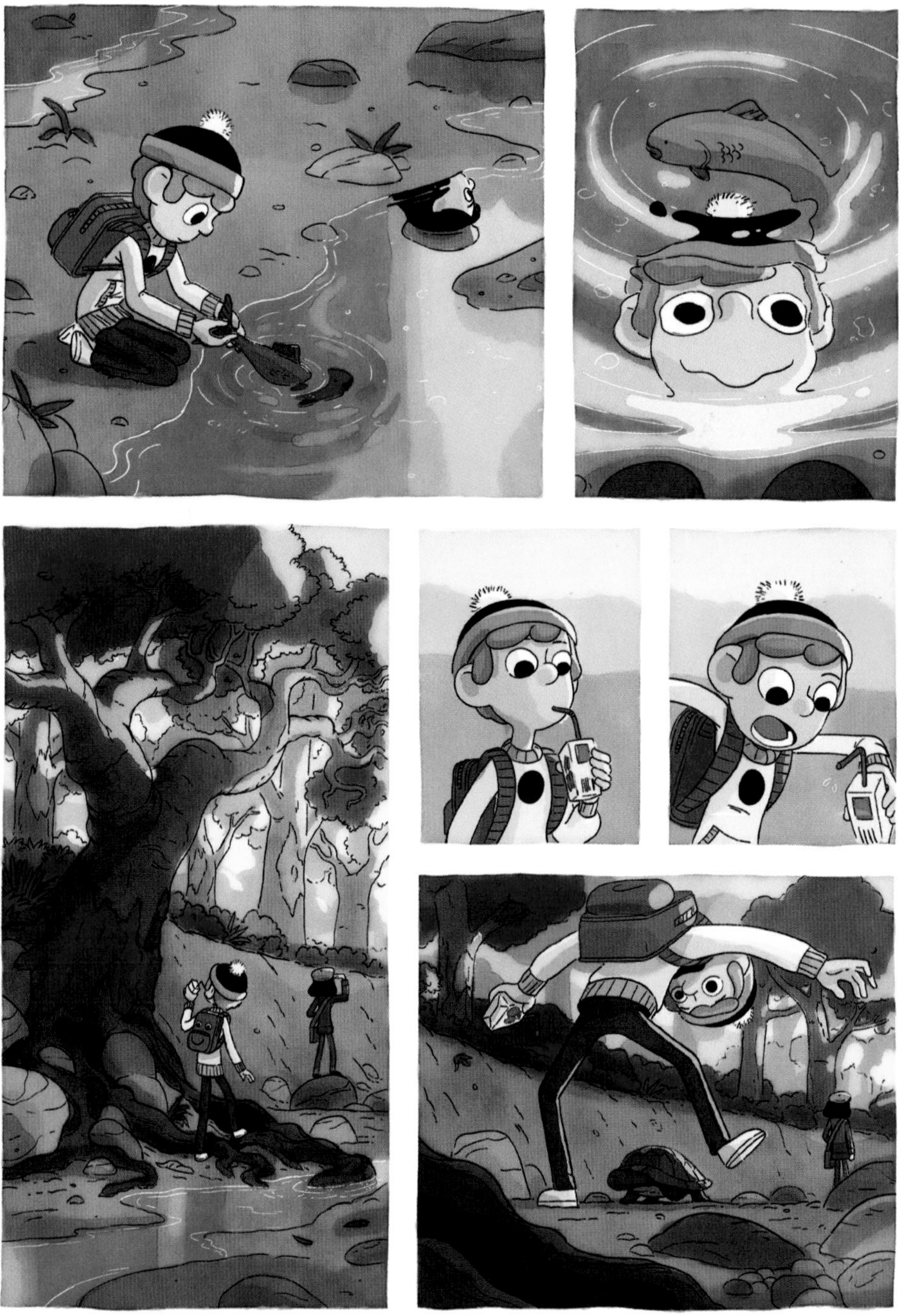

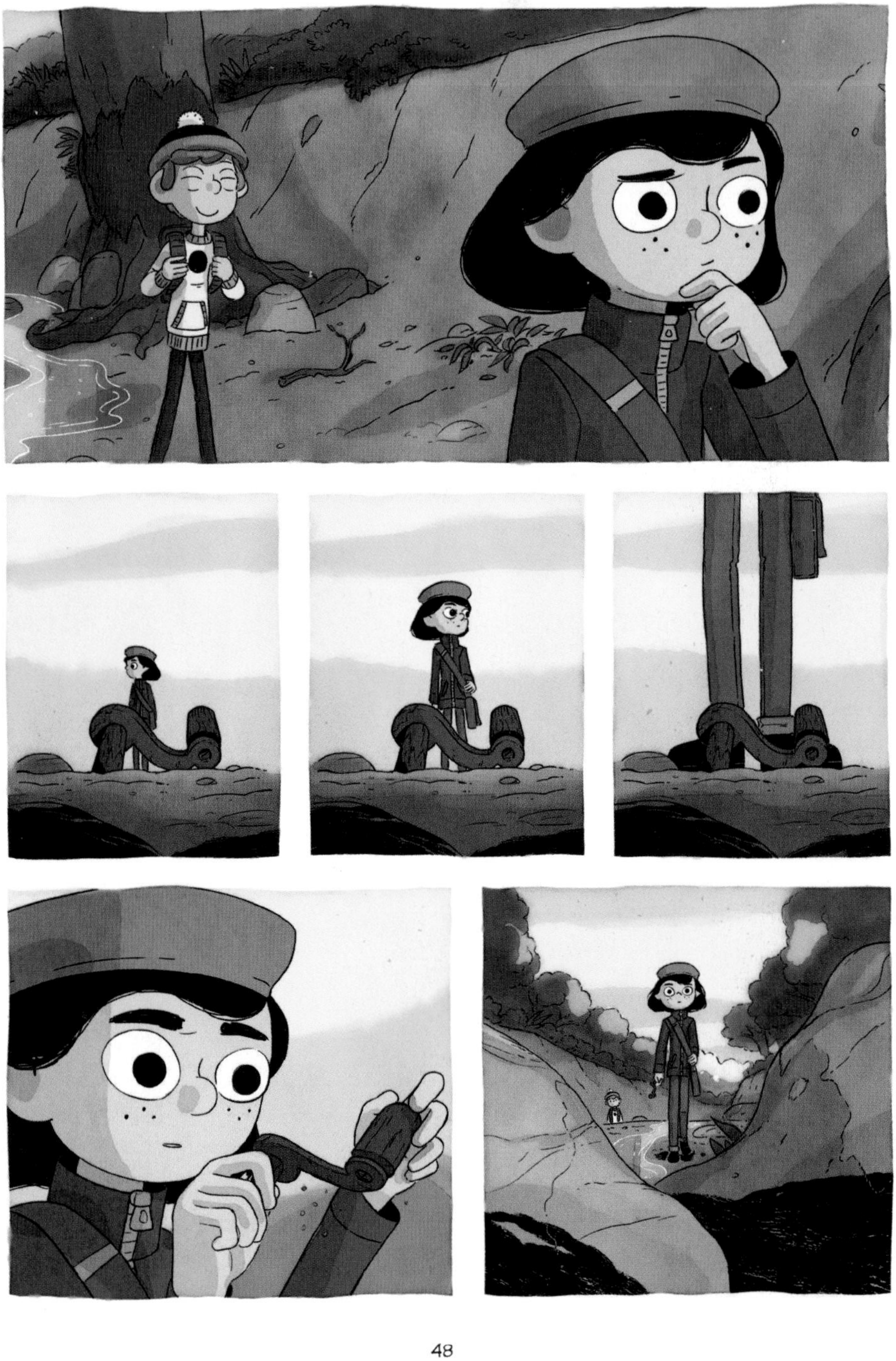

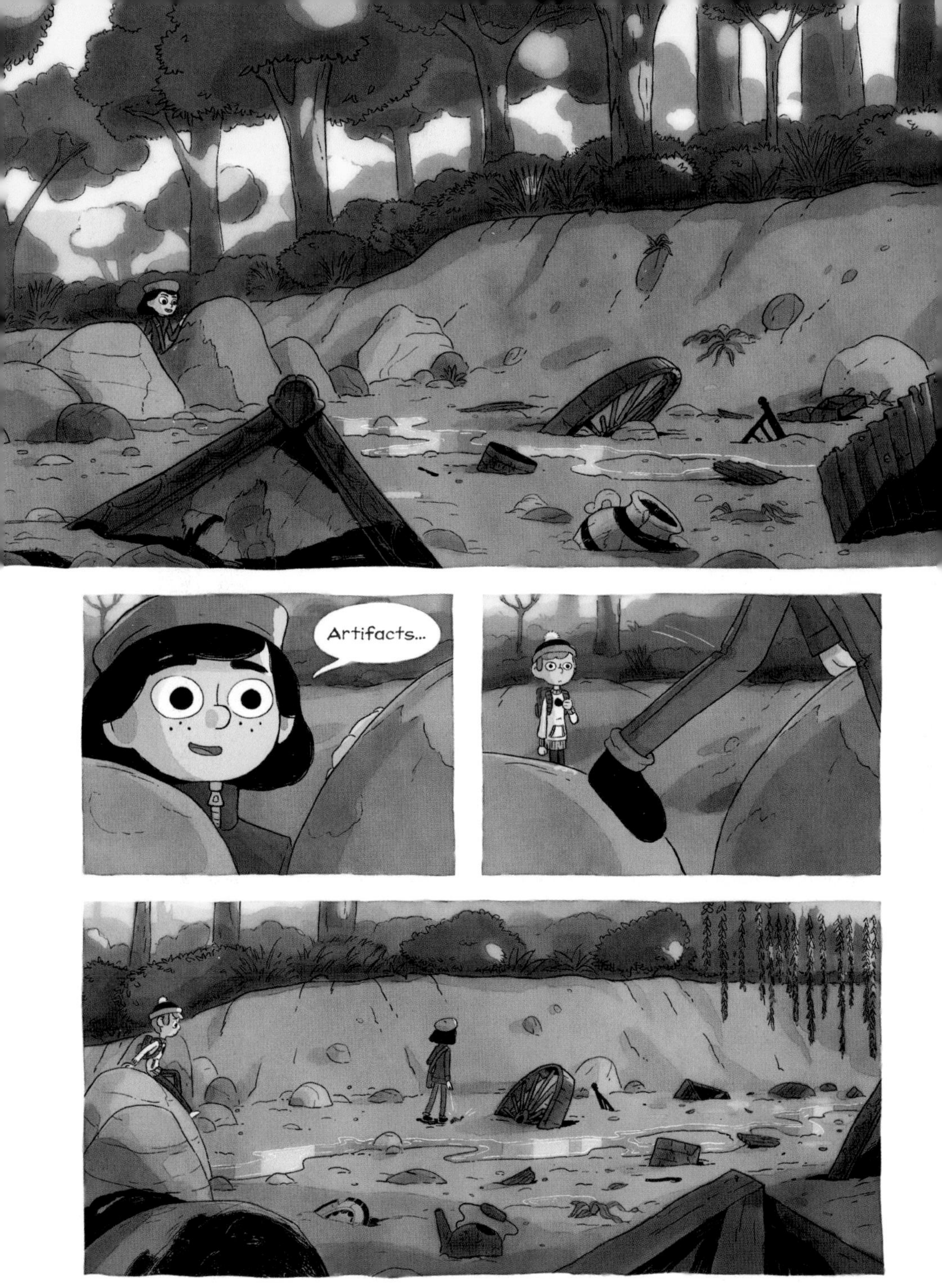
Artifacts...

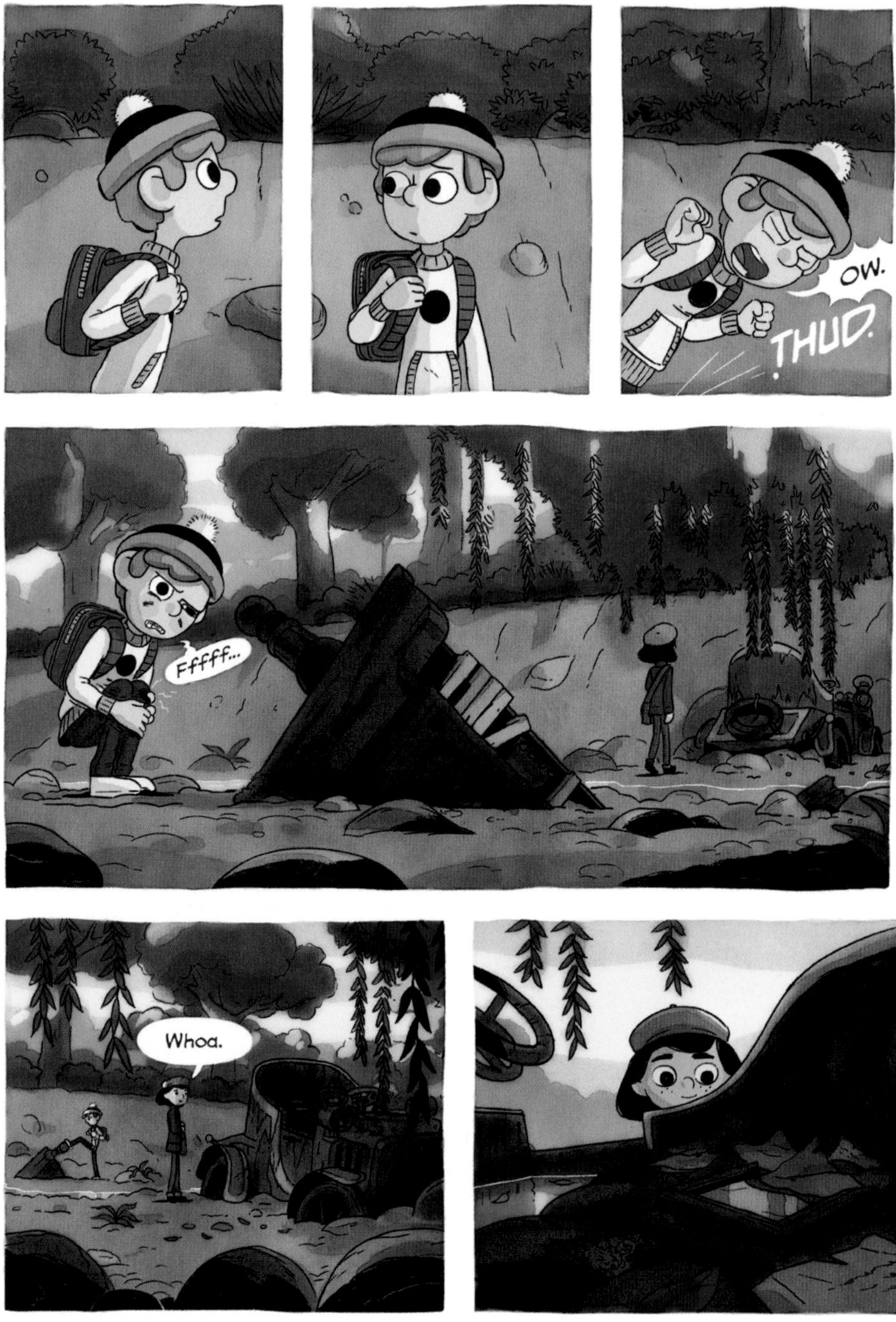
OW.
THUD.
Fffff...
Whoa.

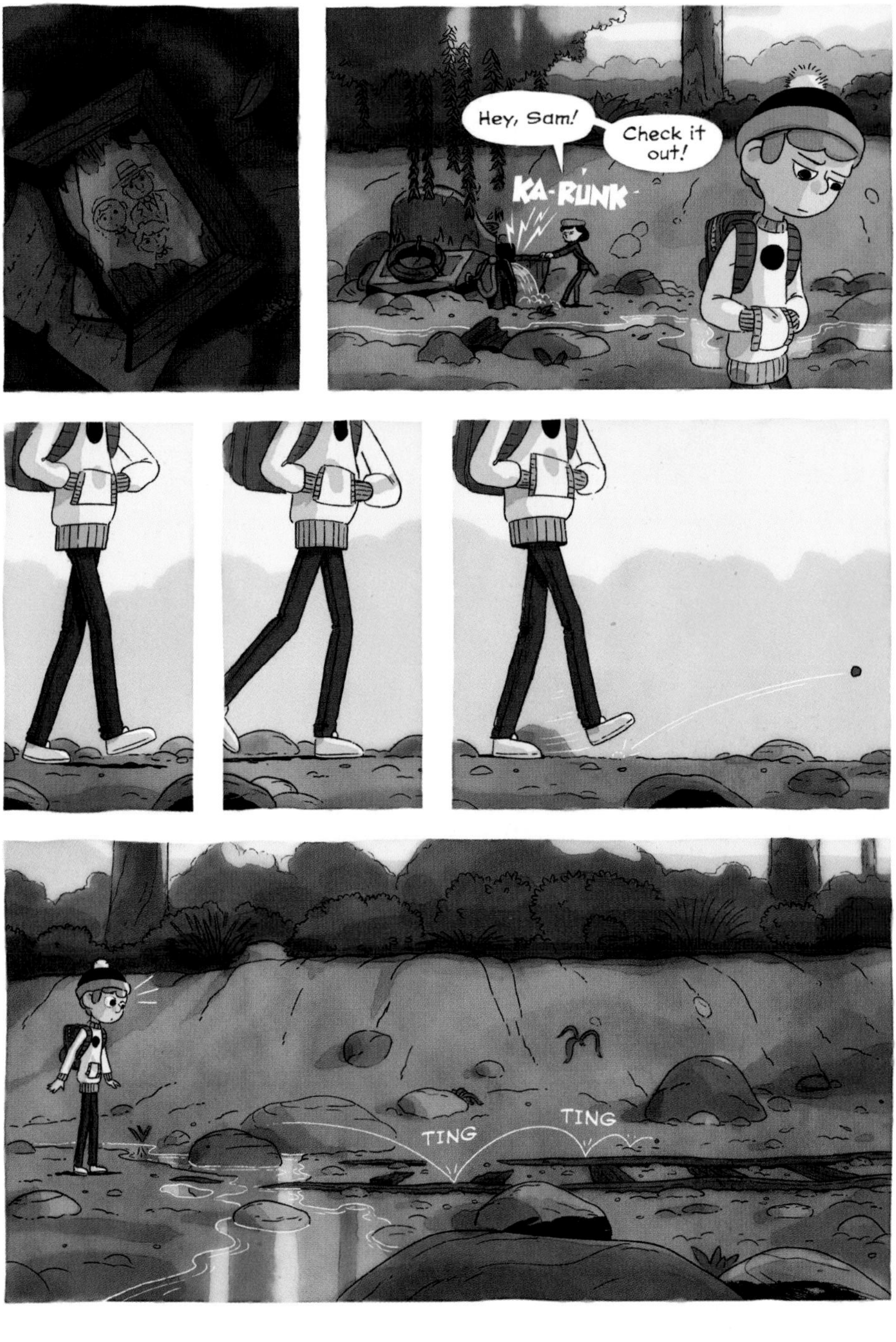
Hey, Sam!
Check it out!
KA-RUNK
TING
TING

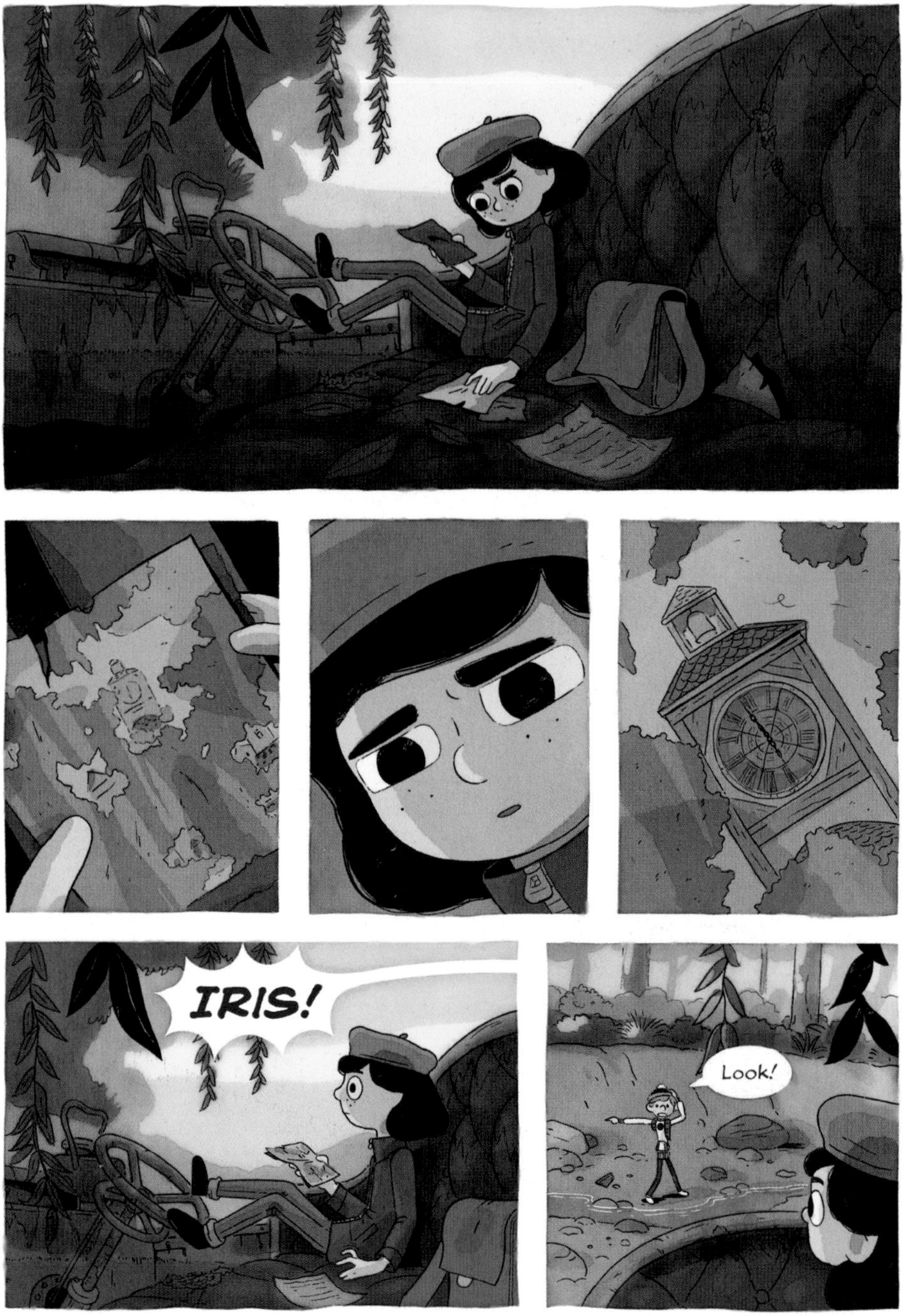
IRIS!
Look!

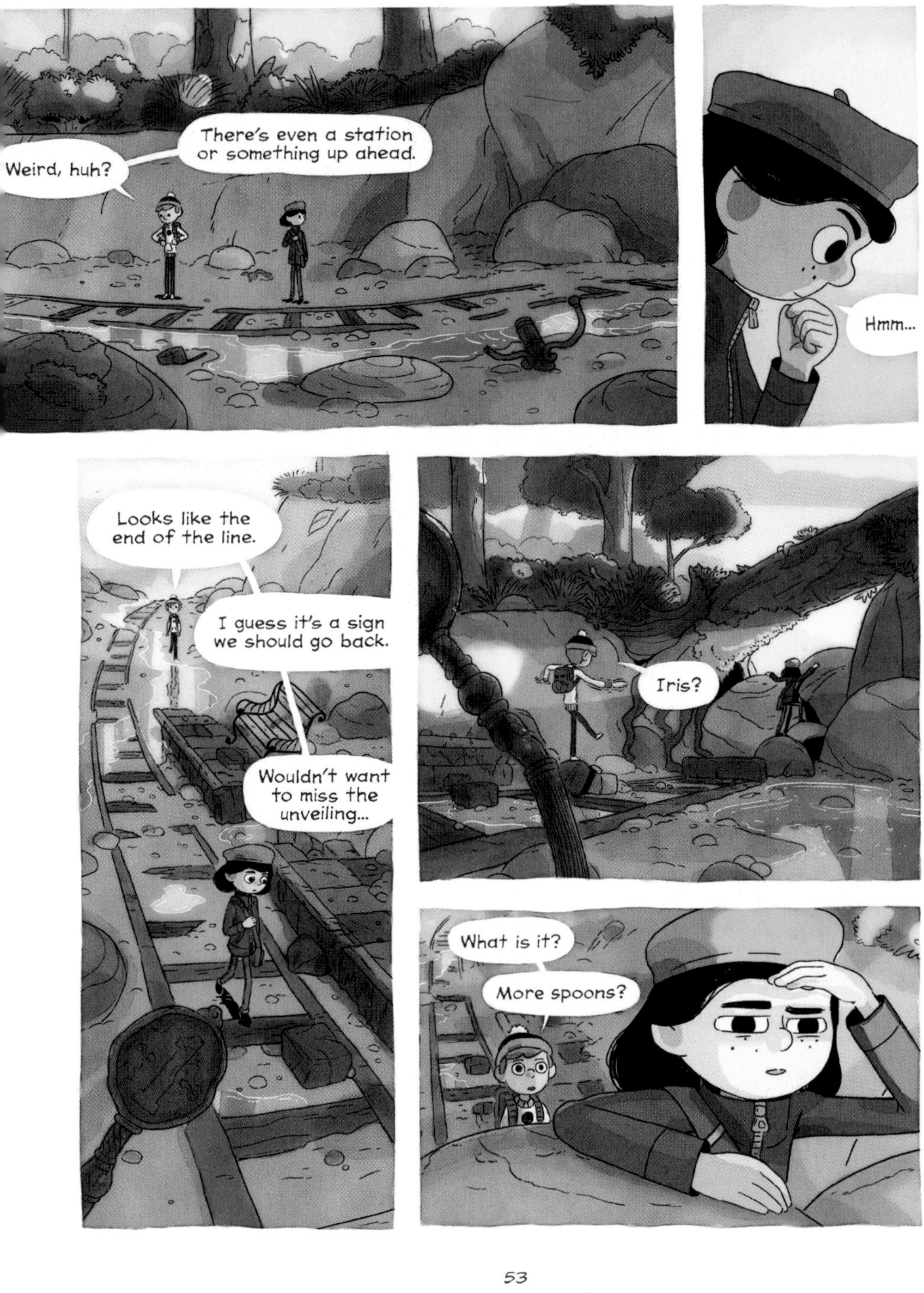
Weird, huh?
There's even a station or something up ahead.
Hmm...
Looks like the end of the line.
I guess it's a sign we should go back.
Wouldn't want to miss the unveiling...
Iris?
What is it?
More spoons?

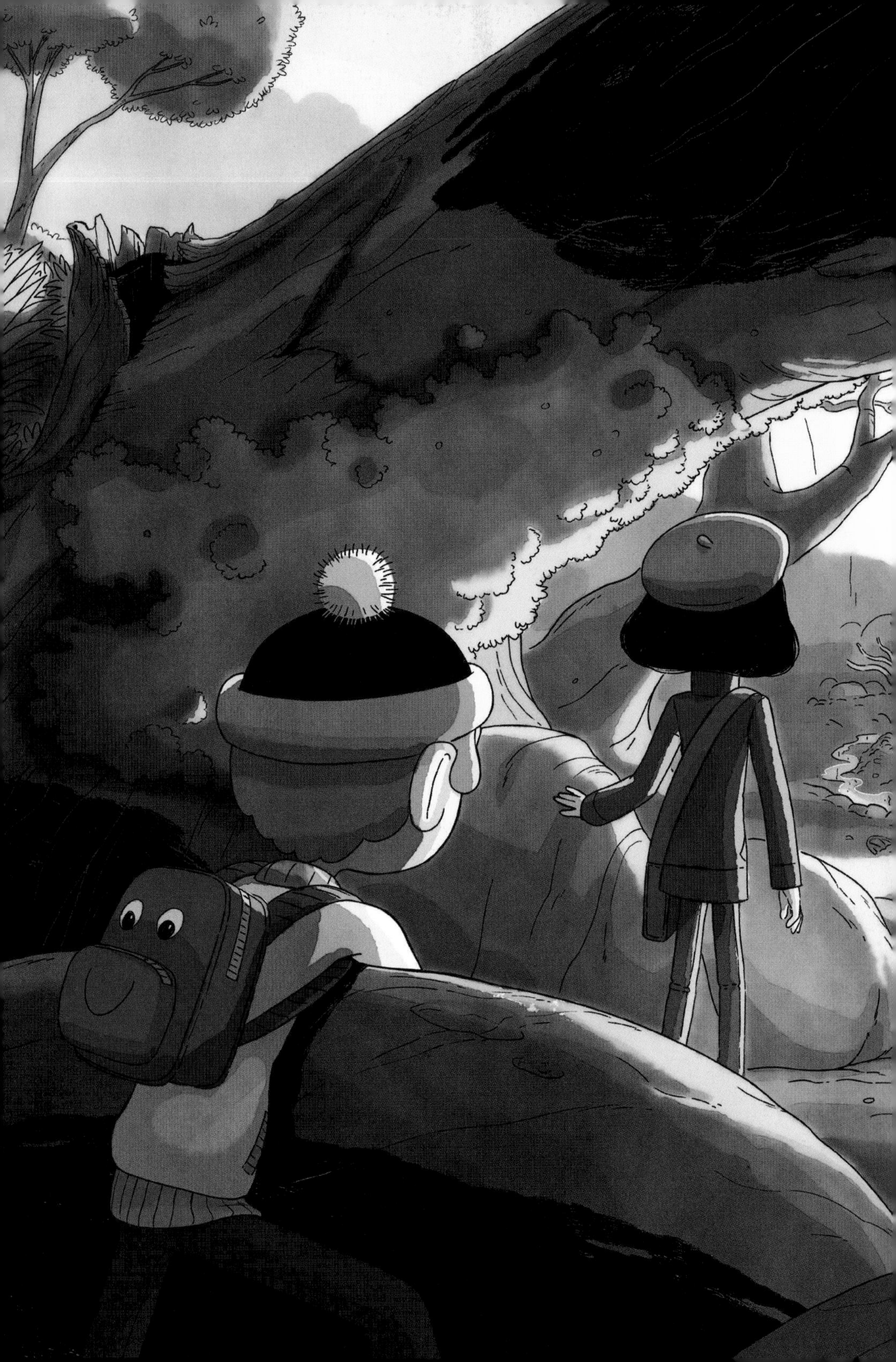

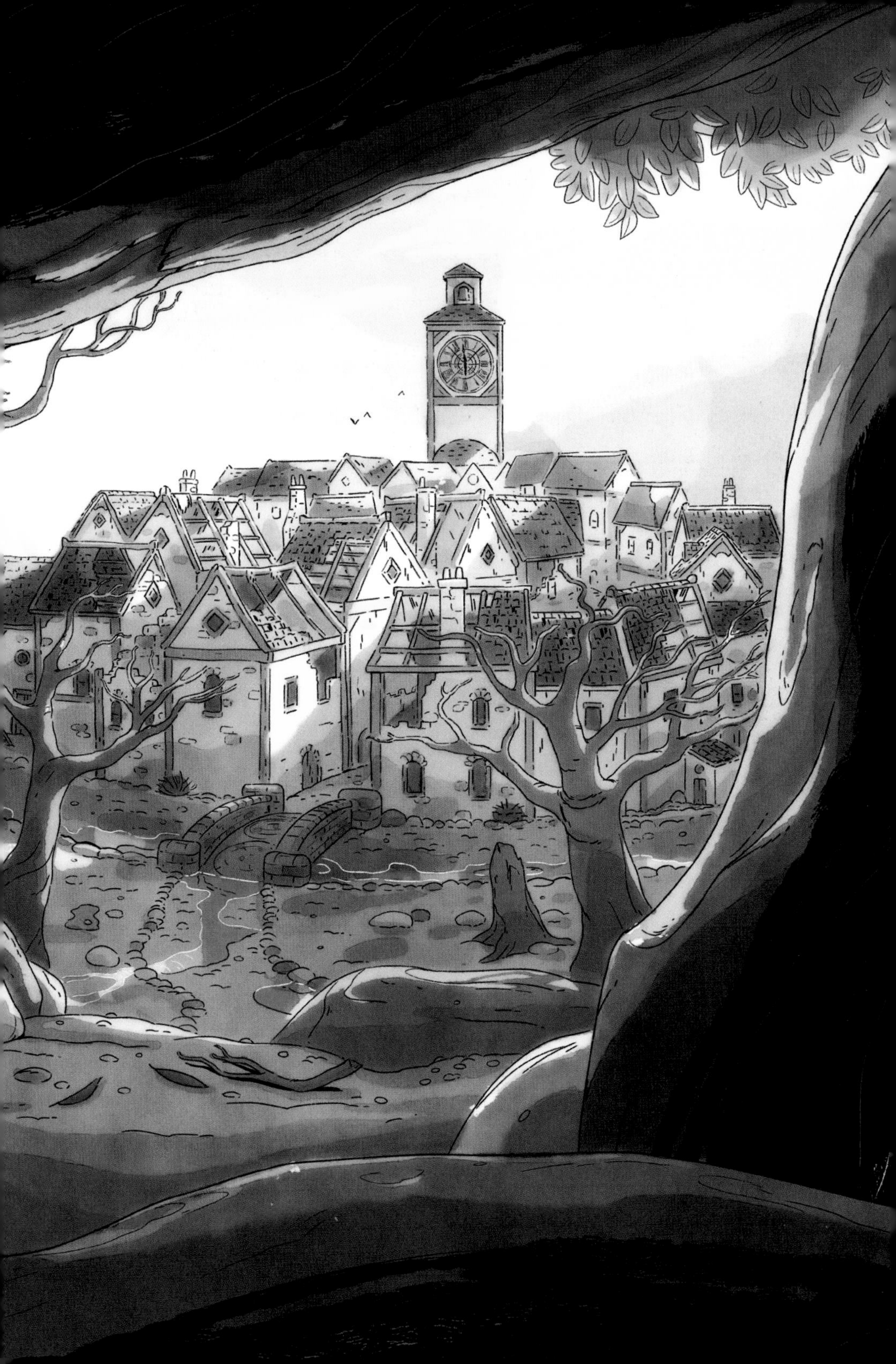

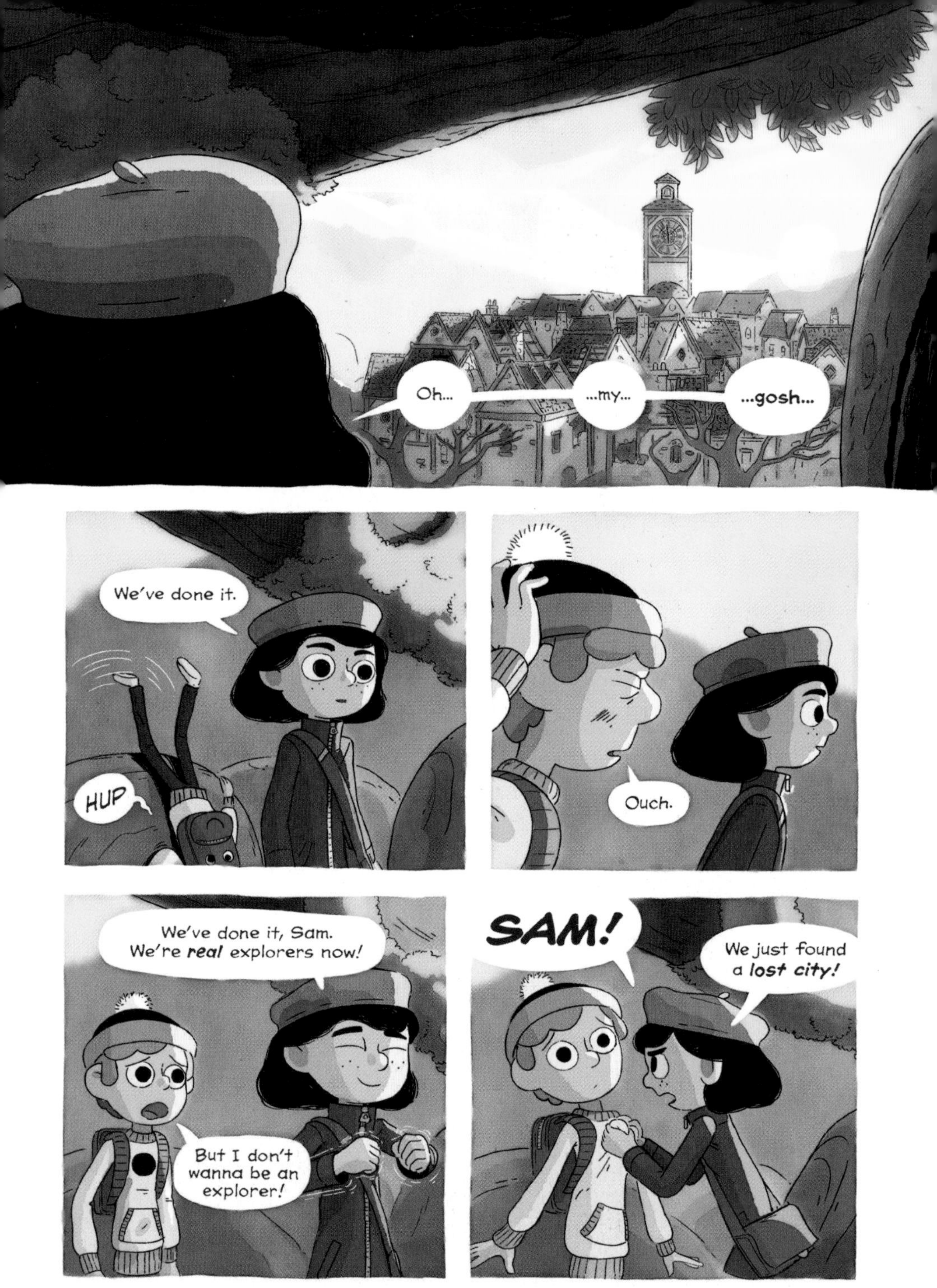
Oh...
...my...
...gosh...
We've done it.
HUP
Ouch.
We've done it, Sam. We're ***real*** explorers now!
But I don't wanna be an explorer!
SAM!
We just found a ***lost city!***

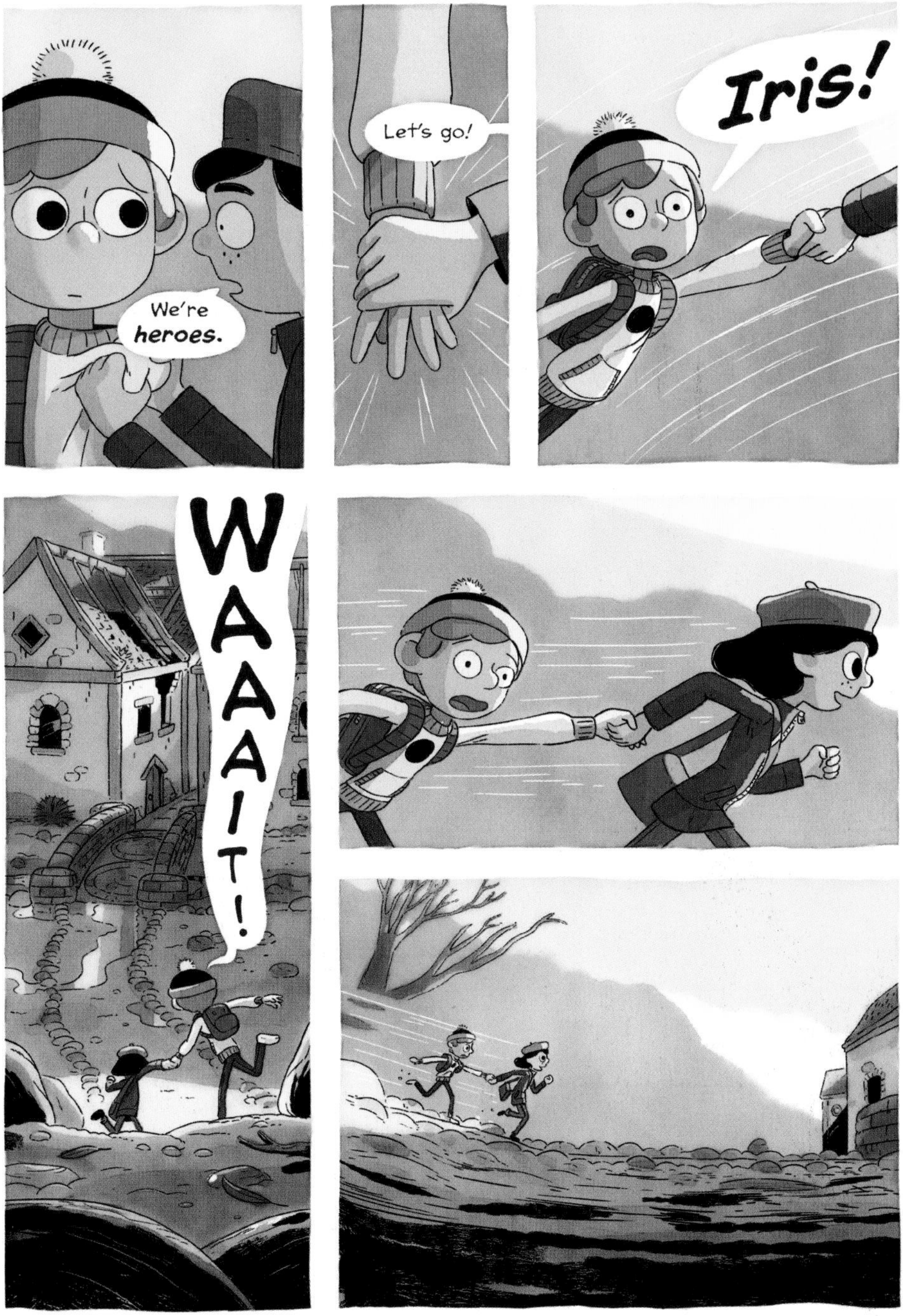
We're **heroes.**
Let's go!
Iris!
WAAAIT!

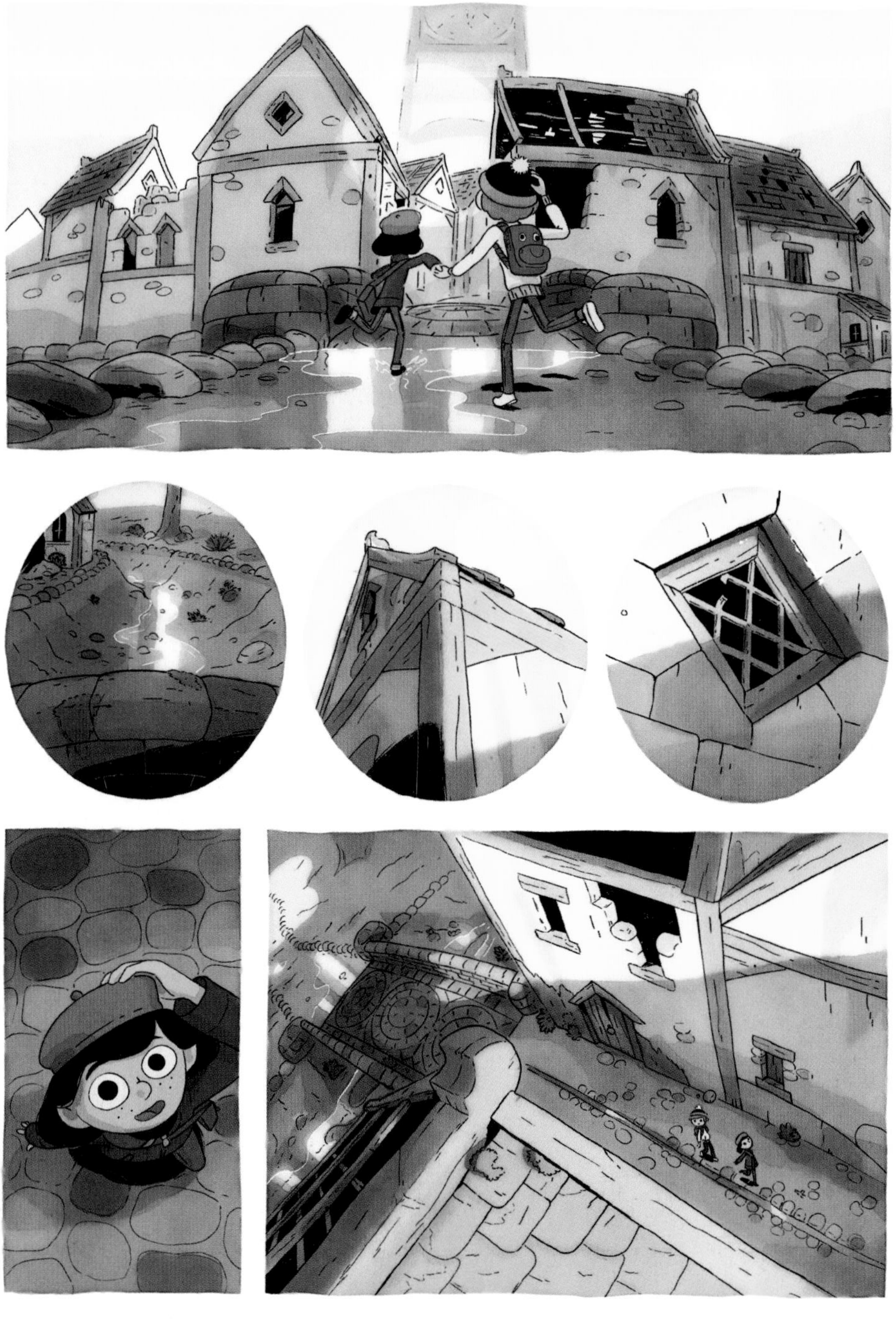

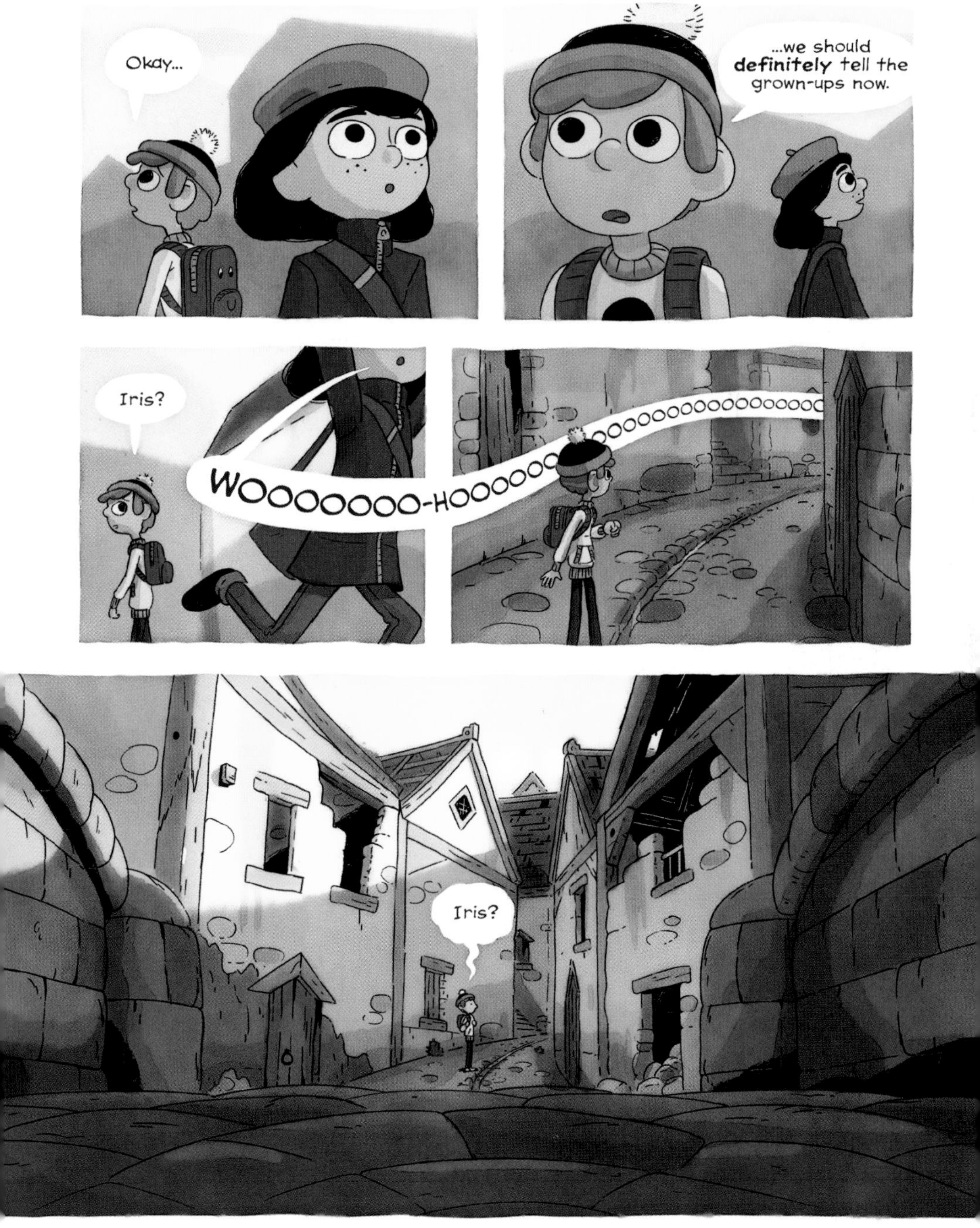
Okay...
...we should **definitely** tell the grown-ups now.
Iris?
WOOOOOOOO-HOOOOOOOOOOOOOOOOOOOOOOOOOO
Iris?

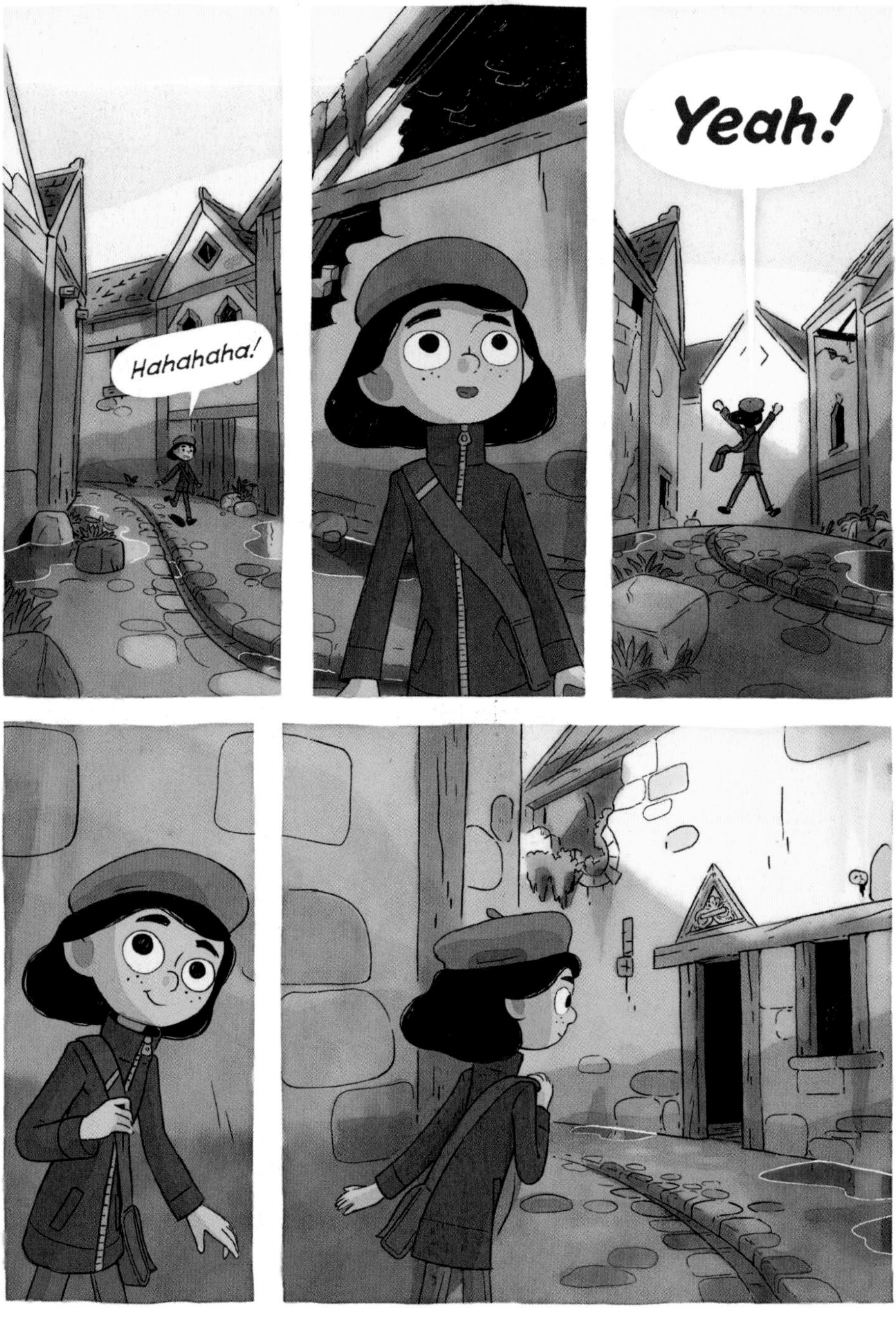
Hahahaha!
Yeah!

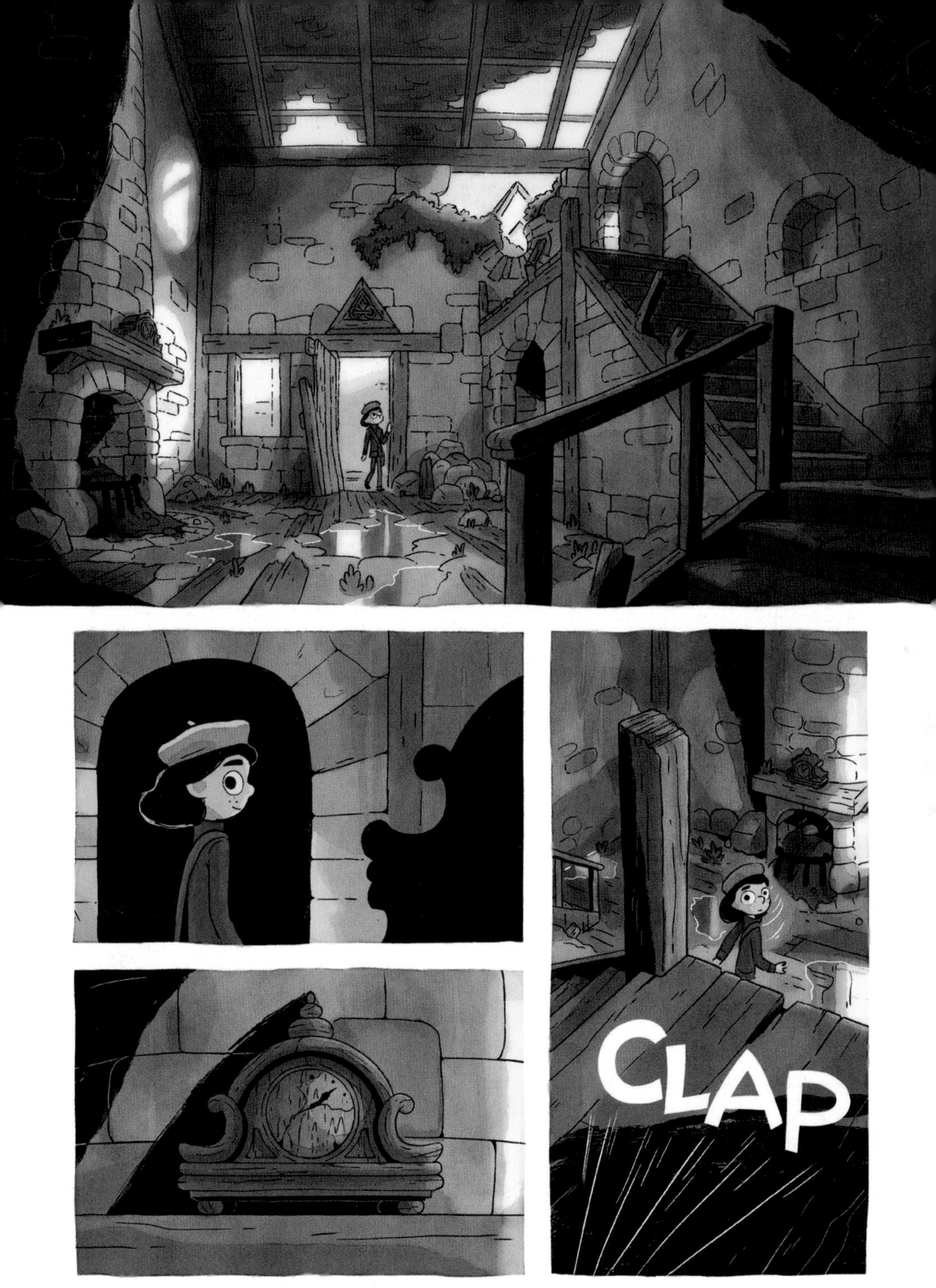
CLAP

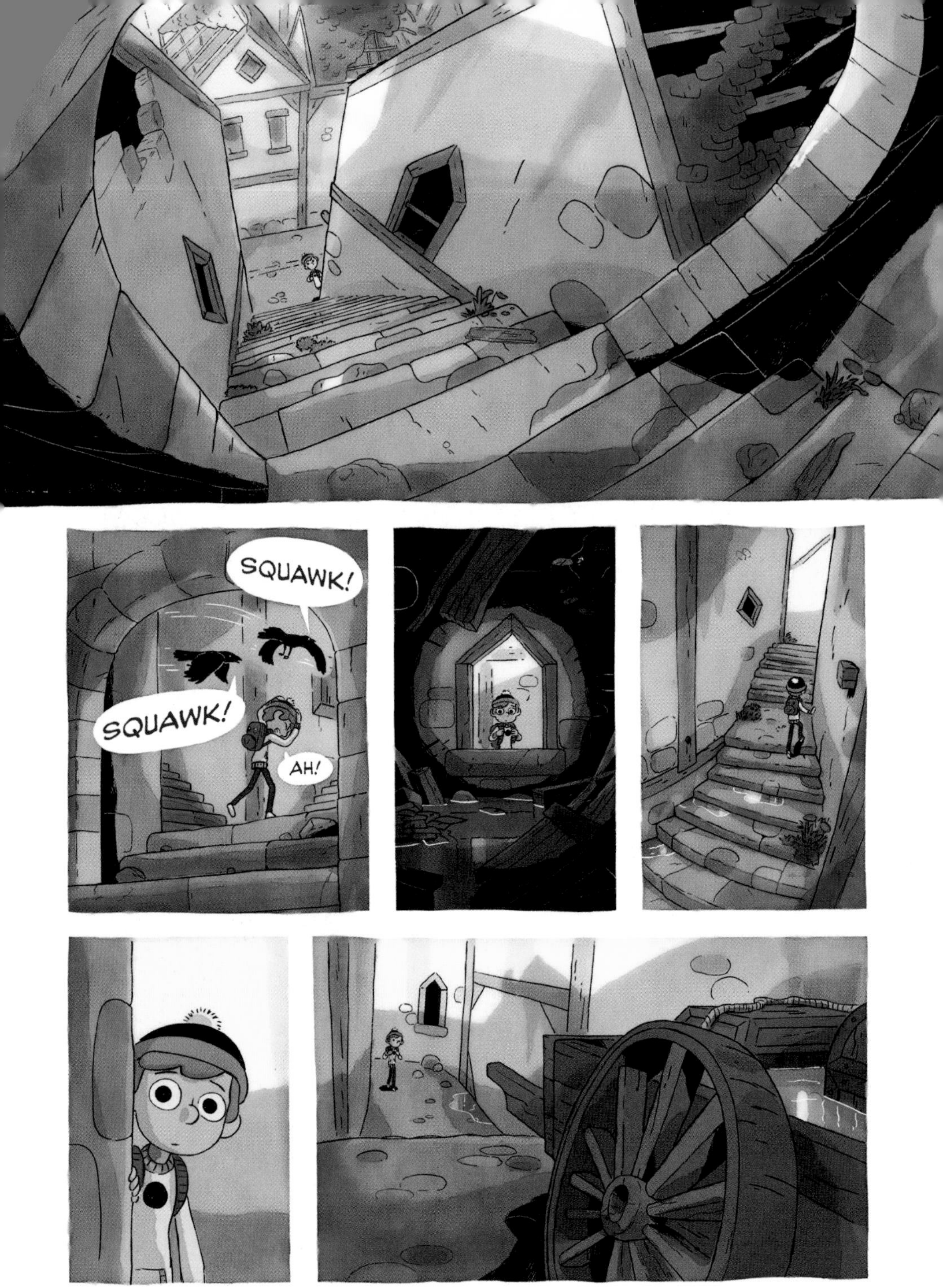
SQUAWK!
SQUAWK!
AH!

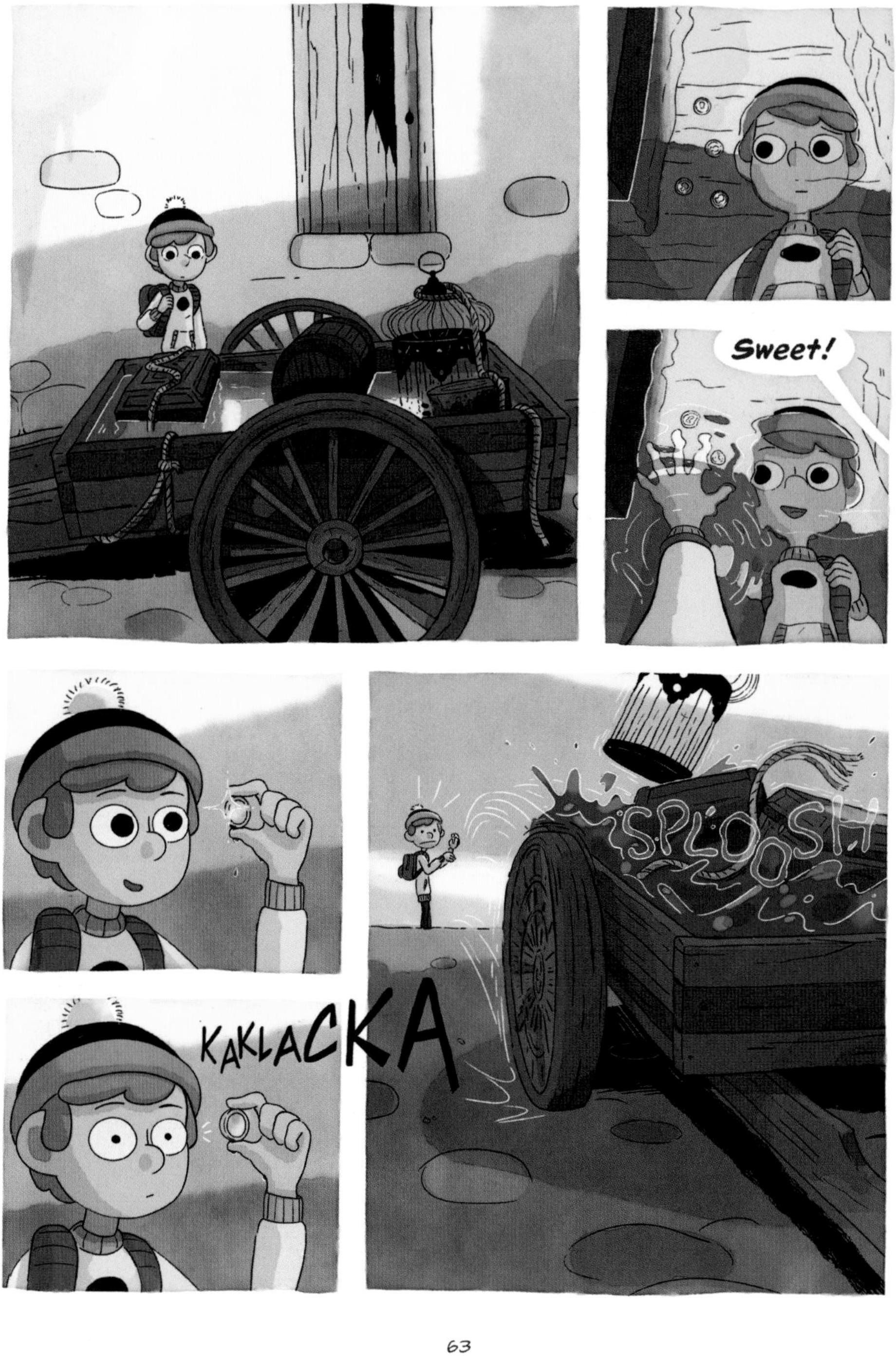
Sweet!
SPLOOSH
KAKLACKA

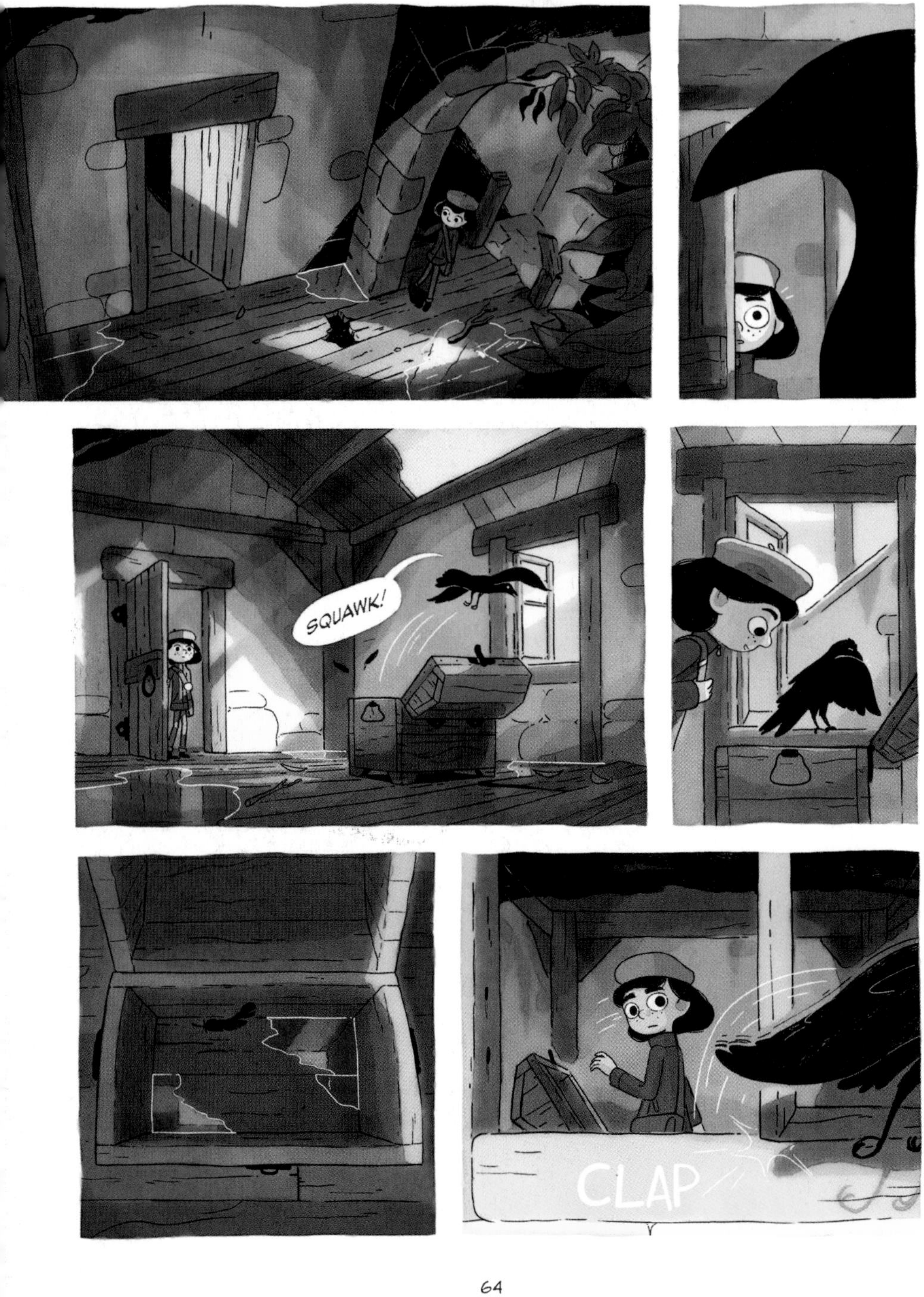
SQUAWK!
CLAP

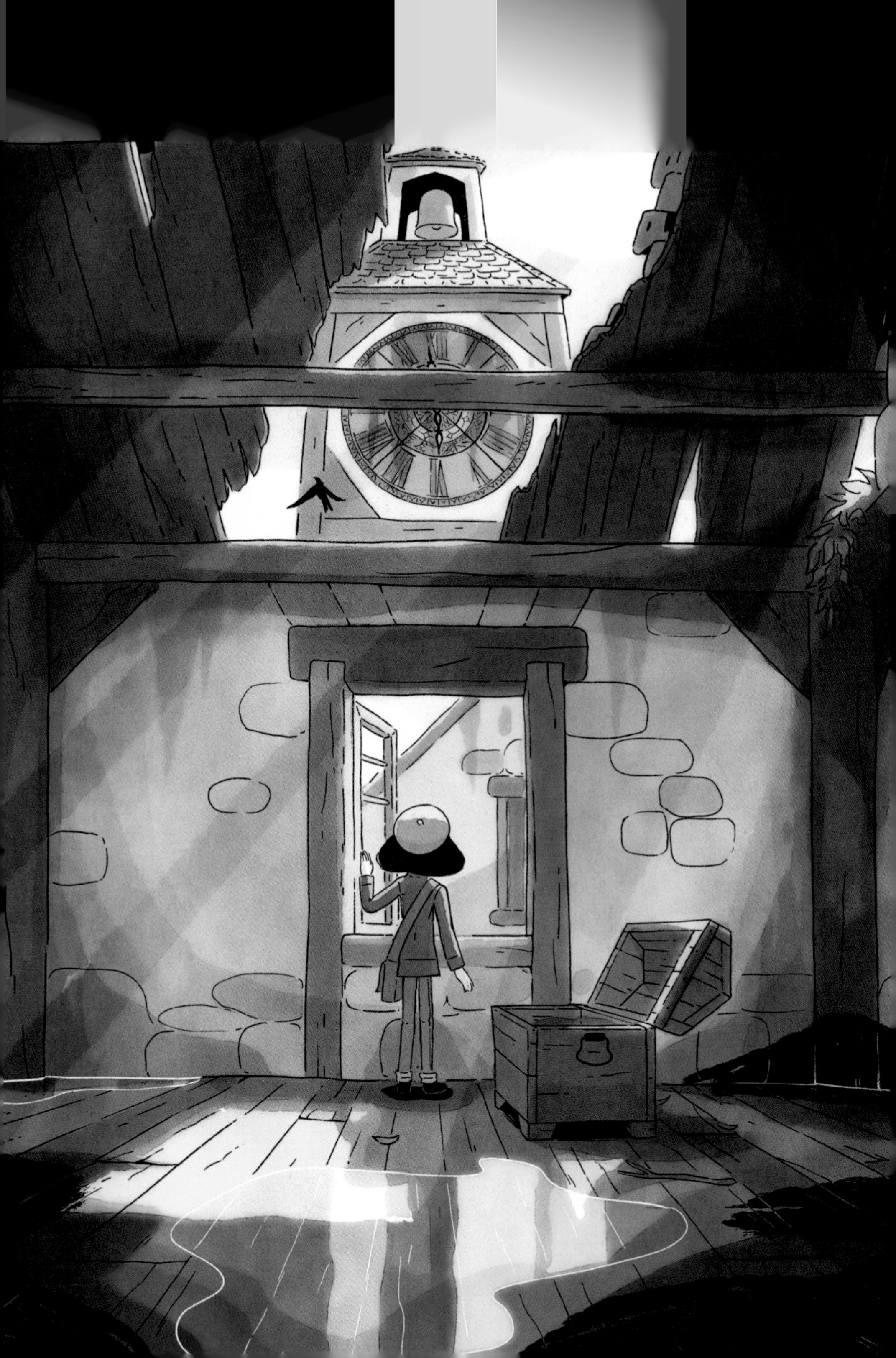

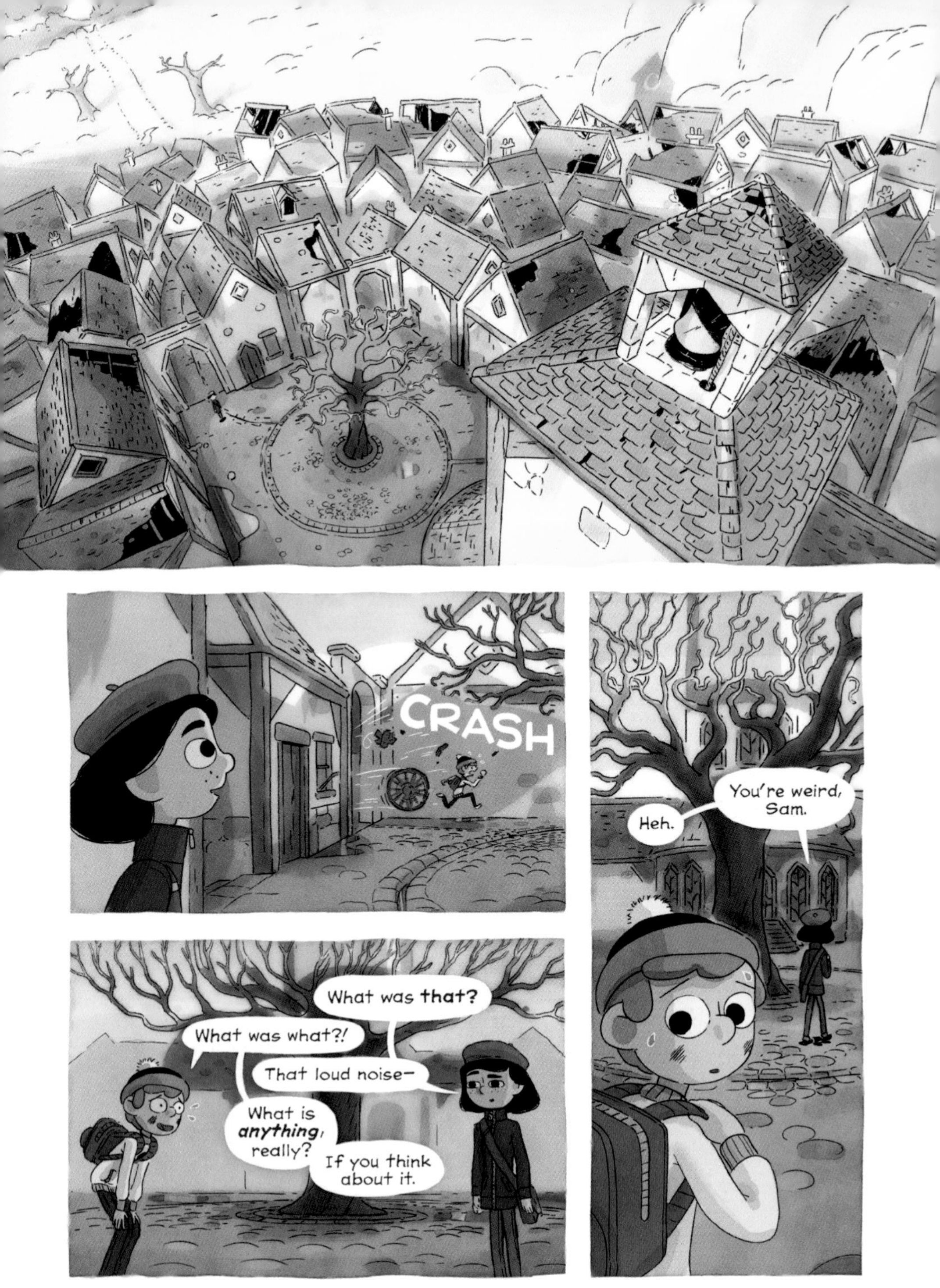
CRASH
What was that?
What was what?!
That loud noise—
What is anything, really?
If you think about it.
You're weird, Sam.
Heh.

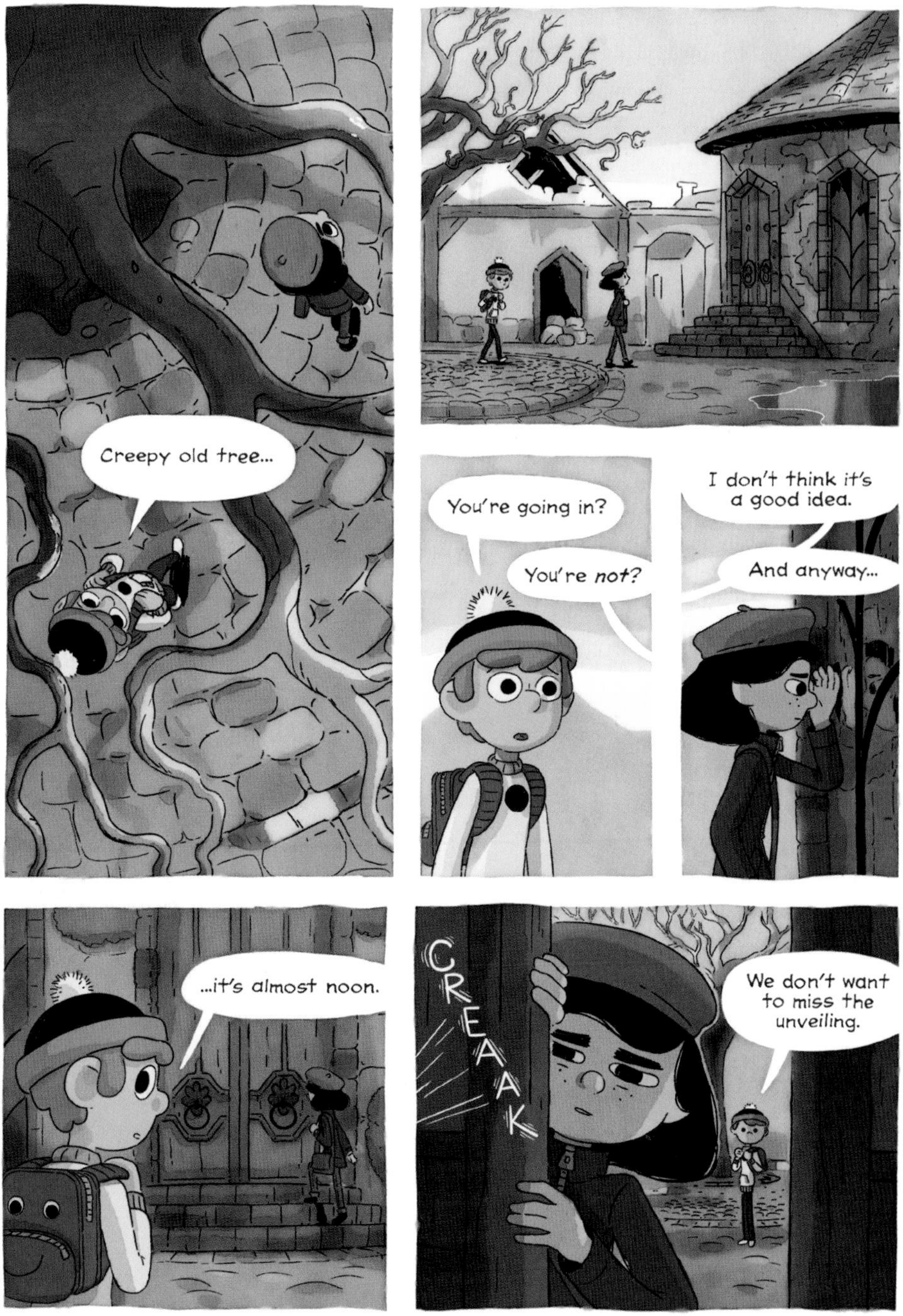
Creepy old tree...
You're going in?
You're *not?*
I don't think it's a good idea.
And anyway...
...it's almost noon.
CREAAK
We don't want to miss the unveiling.

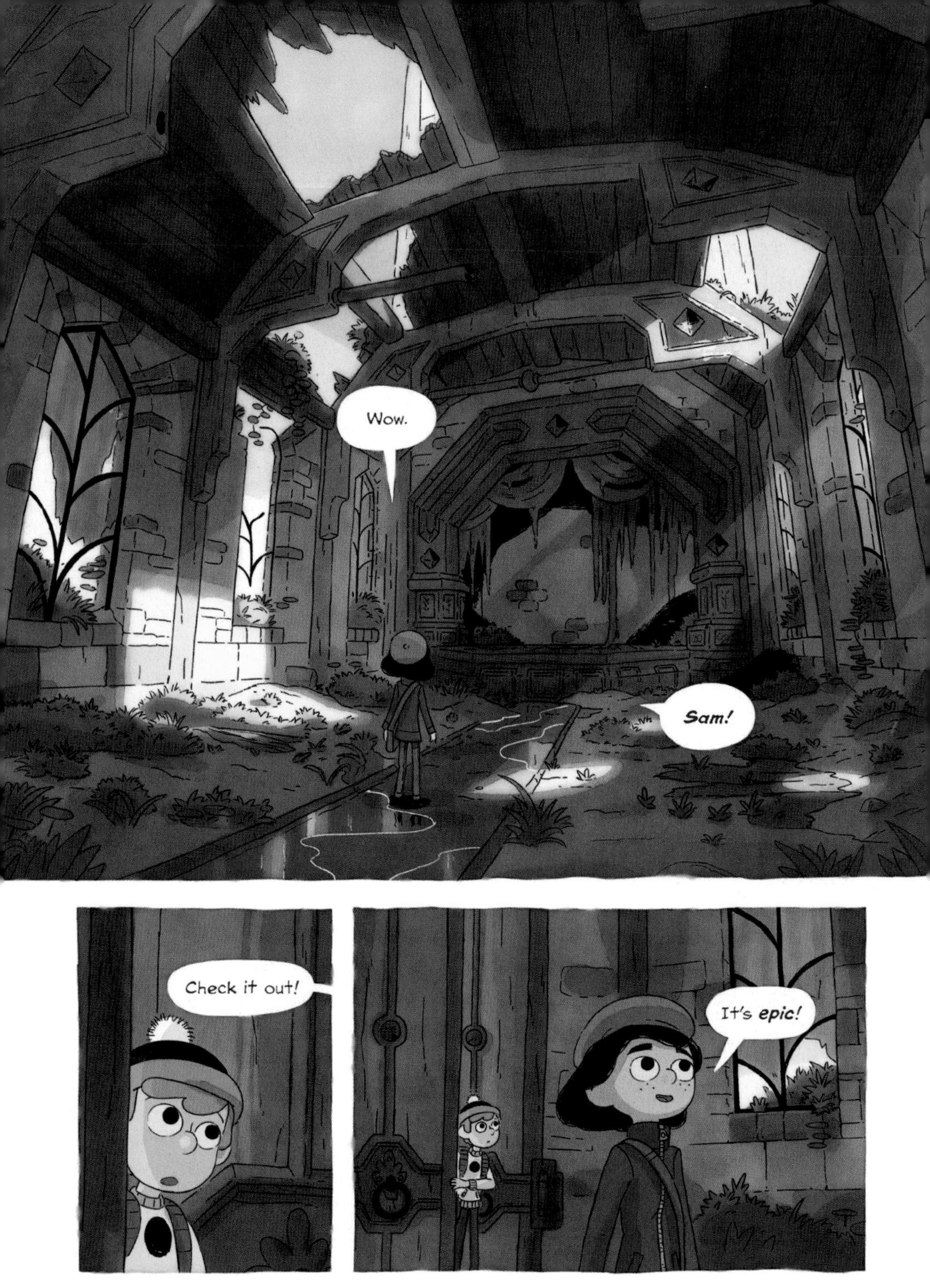
Wow.
Sam!
Check it out!
It's *epic!*

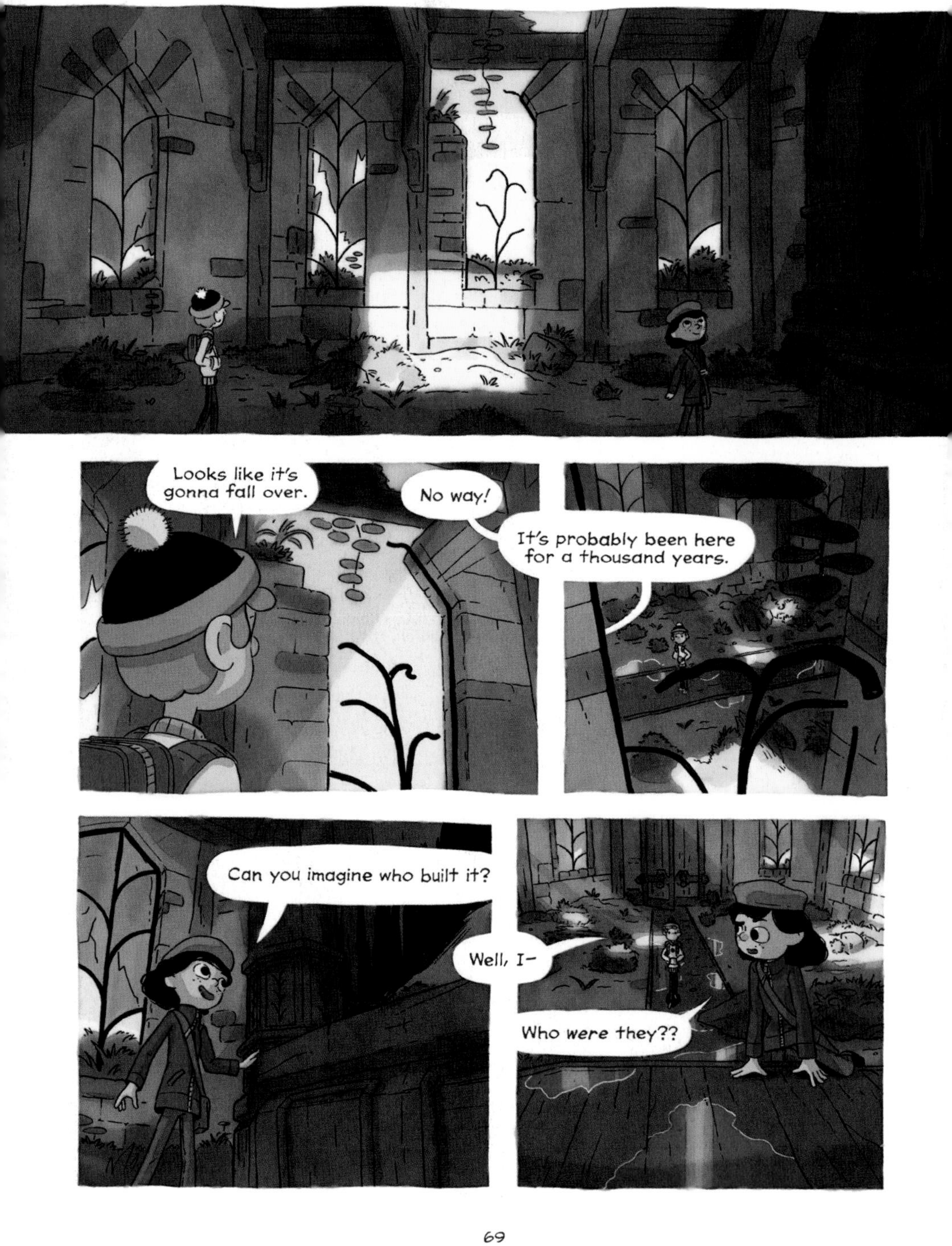
Looks like it's gonna fall over.
No way!
It's probably been here for a thousand years.
Can you imagine who built it?
Well, I-
Who were they??

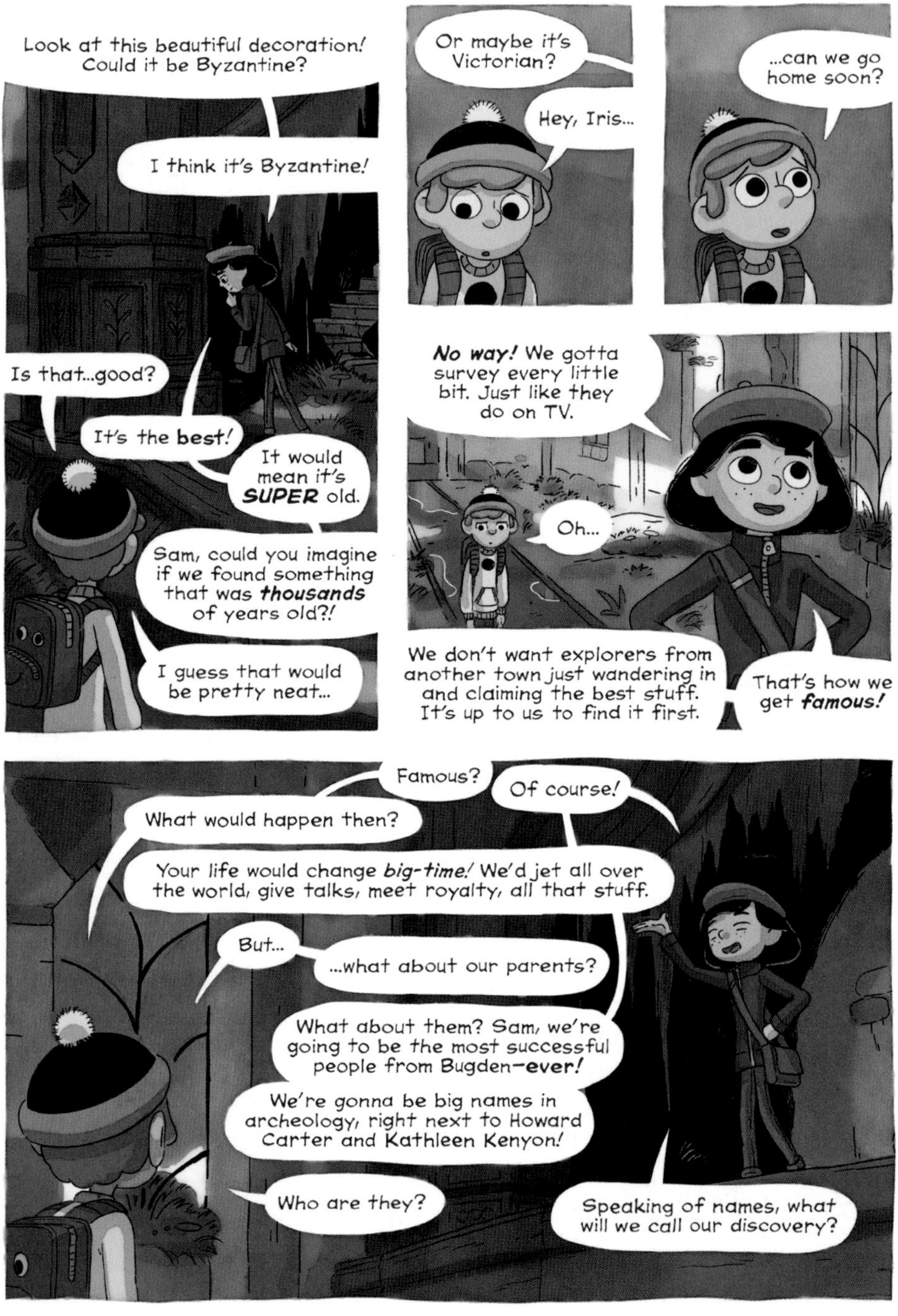
Look at this beautiful decoration! Could it be Byzantine?
I think it's Byzantine!
Is that...good?
It's the **best!**
It would mean it's **SUPER** old.
Sam, could you imagine if we found something that was ***thousands*** of years old?!
I guess that would be pretty neat...
Or maybe it's Victorian?
Hey, Iris...
...can we go home soon?
No way! We gotta survey every little bit. Just like they do on TV.
Oh...
We don't want explorers from another town just wandering in and claiming the best stuff. It's up to us to find it first.
That's how we get ***famous!***
Famous?
What would happen then?
Of course!
Your life would change ***big-time!*** We'd jet all over the world, give talks, meet royalty, all that stuff.
But...
...what about our parents?
What about them? Sam, we're going to be the most successful people from Bugden—**ever!**
We're gonna be big names in archeology, right next to Howard Carter and Kathleen Kenyon!
Who are they?
Speaking of names, what will we call our discovery?

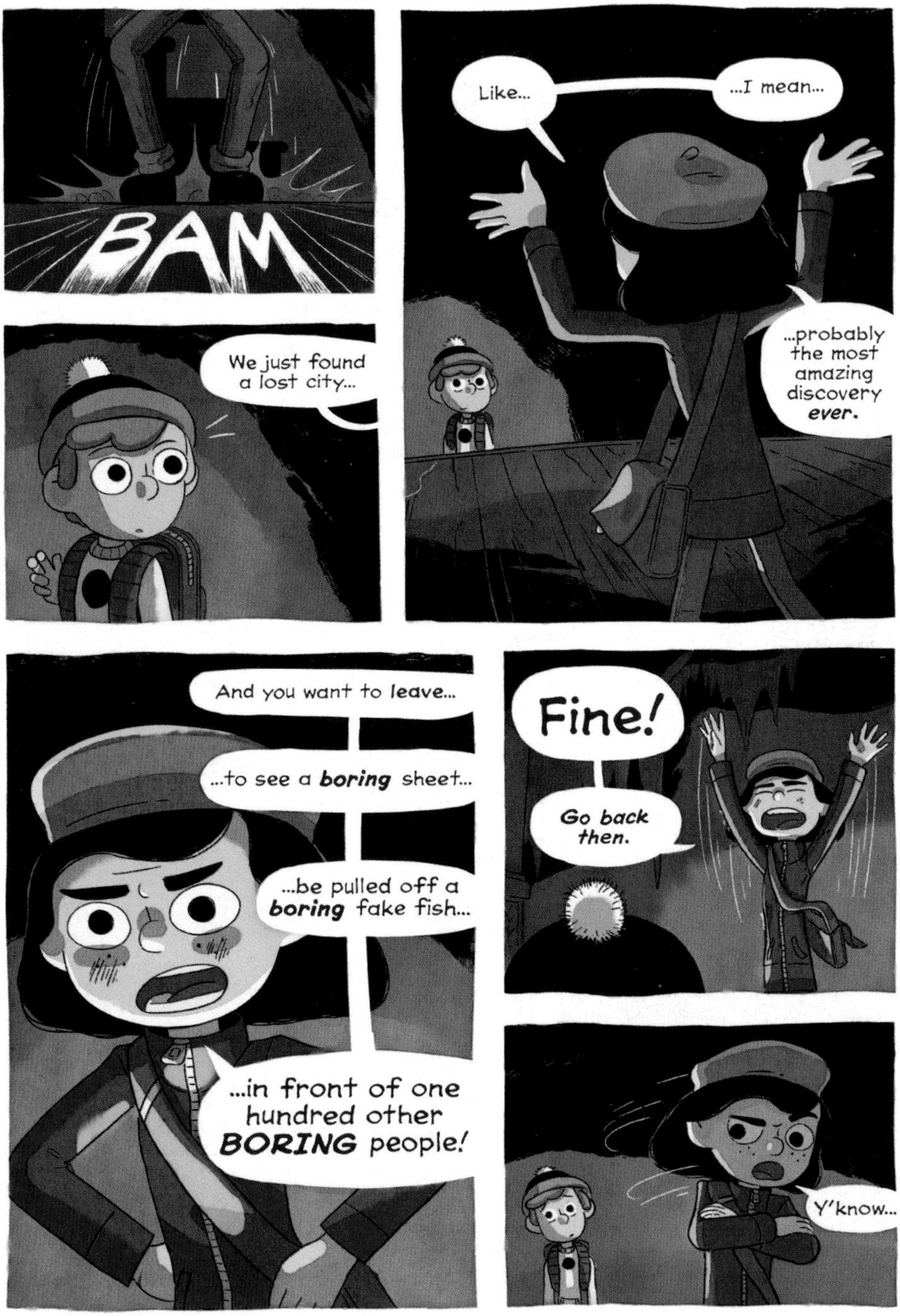
BAM
Like...
...I mean...
We just found a lost city...
...probably the most amazing discovery ever.
And you want to leave...
...to see a boring sheet...
...be pulled off a boring fake fish...
...in front of one hundred other BORING people!
Fine!
Go back then.
Y'know...

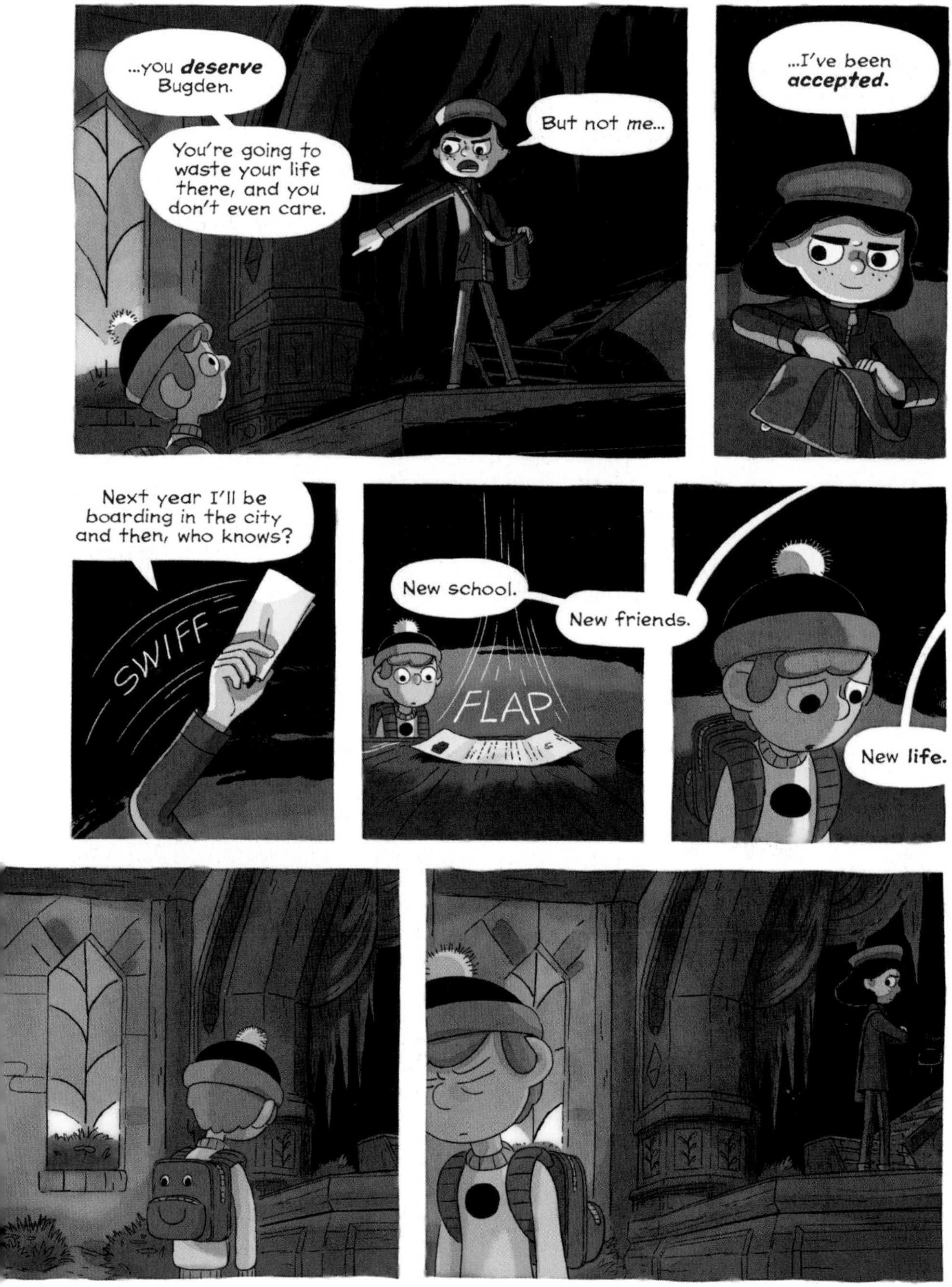
...you **deserve** Bugden.
You're going to waste your life there, and you don't even care.
But not *me*...
...I've been **accepted.**
Next year I'll be boarding in the city and then, who knows?
SWIFF
New school.
New friends.
FLAP
New **life.**

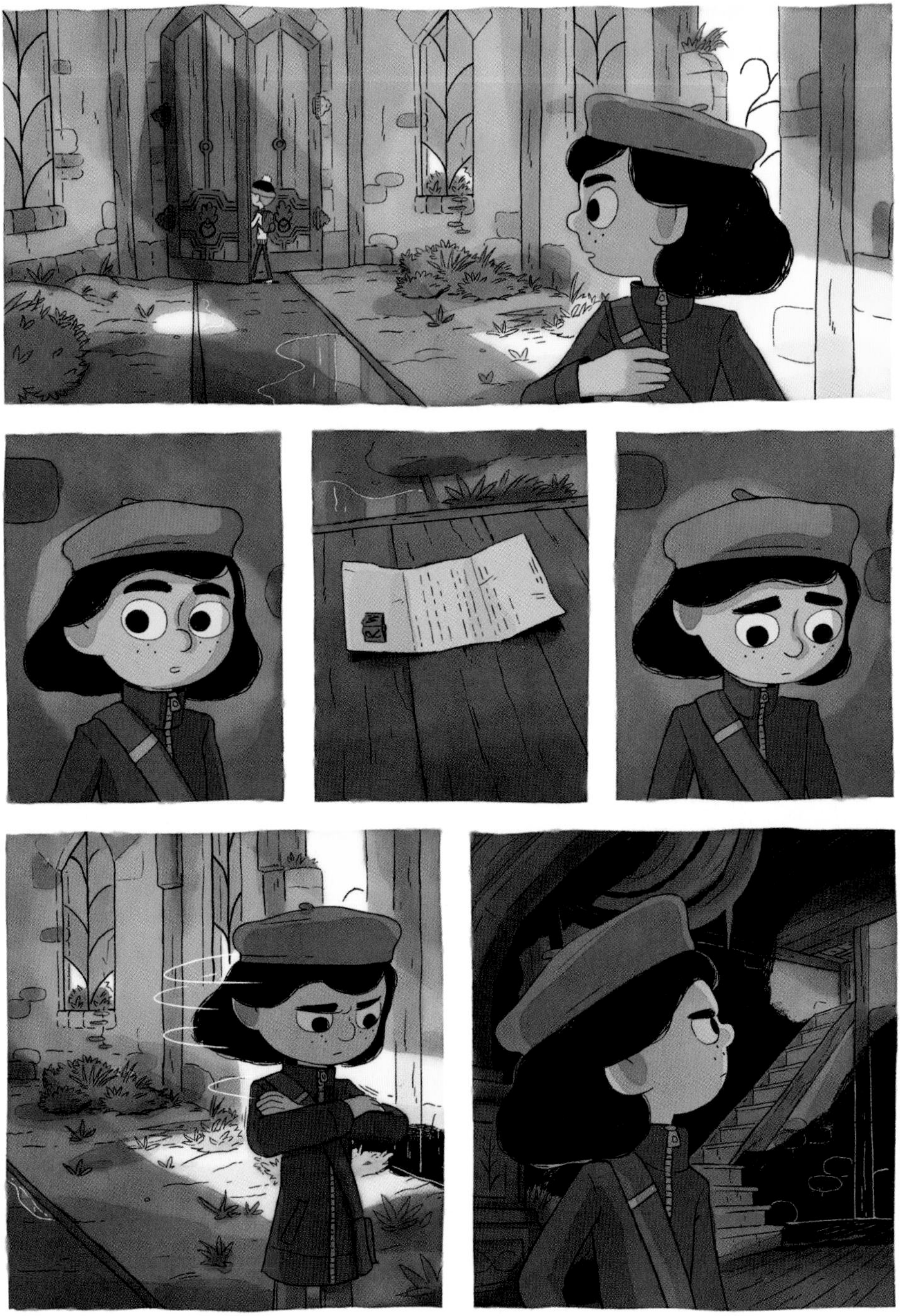

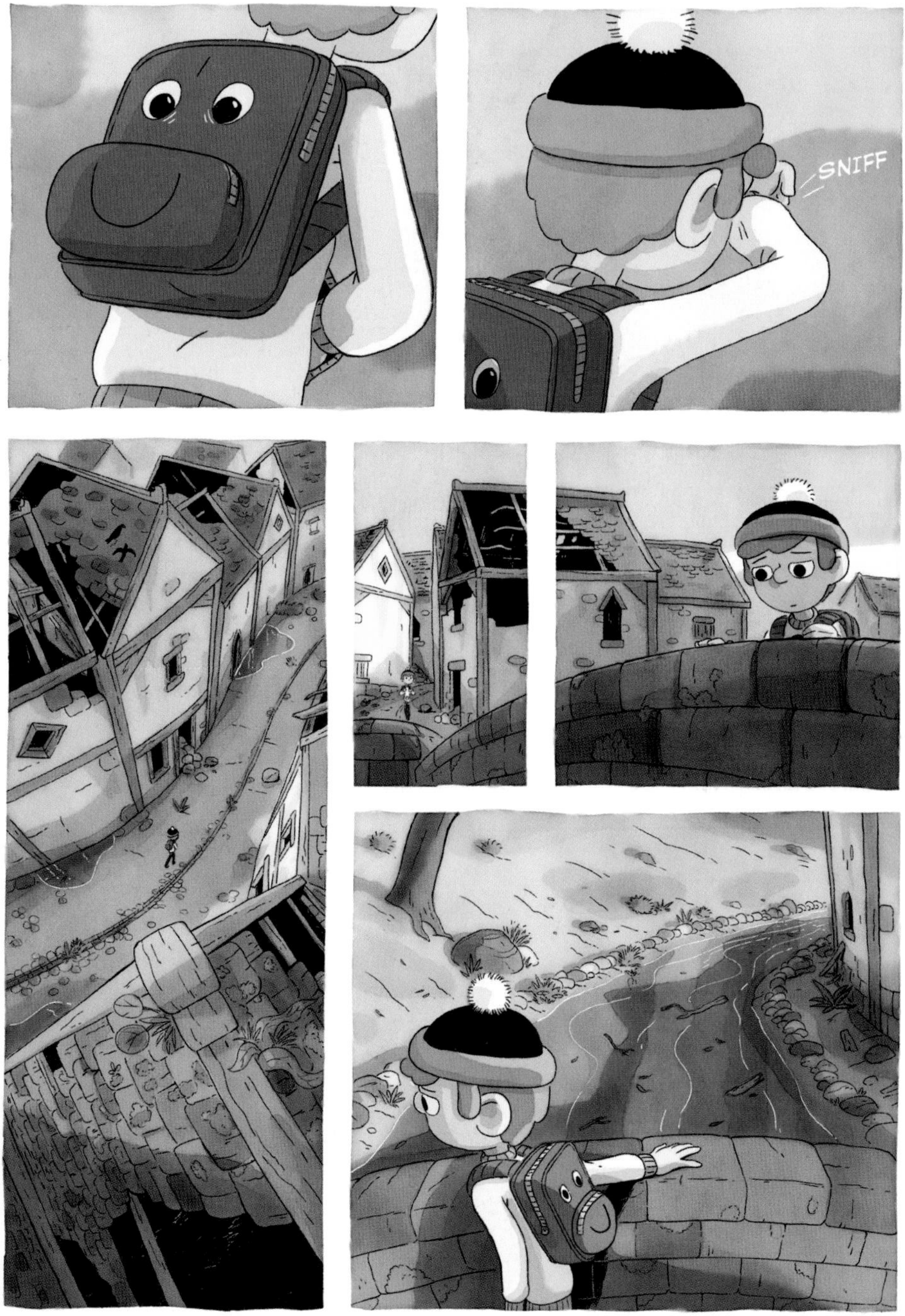
SNIFF

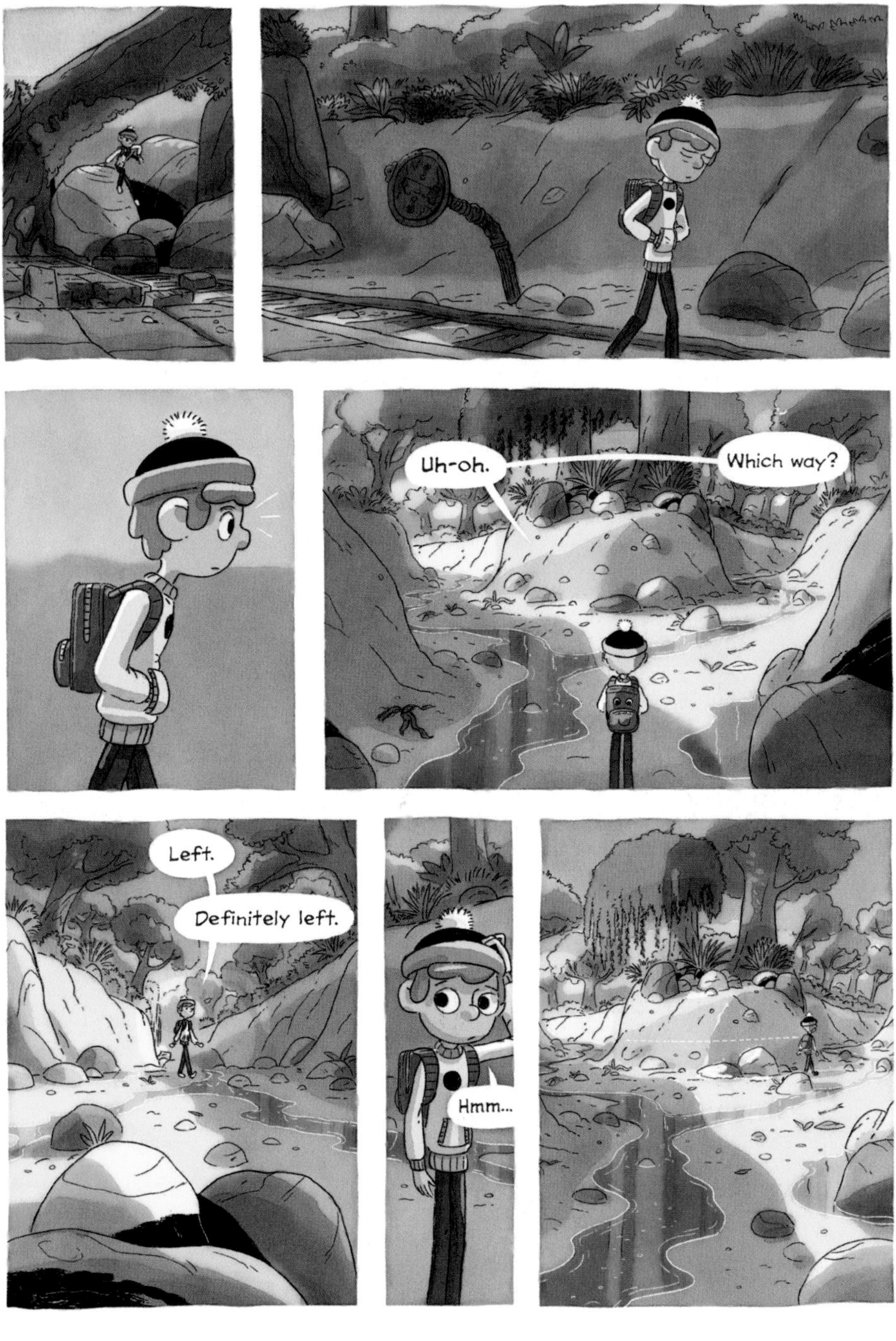
Uh-oh.
Which way?
Left.
Definitely left.
Hmm...

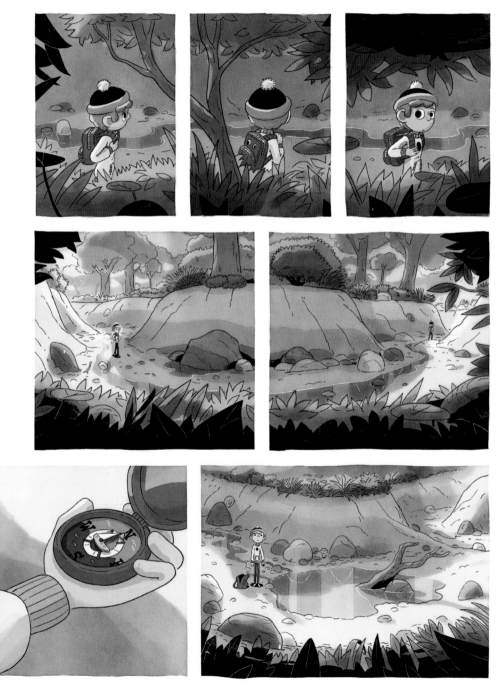

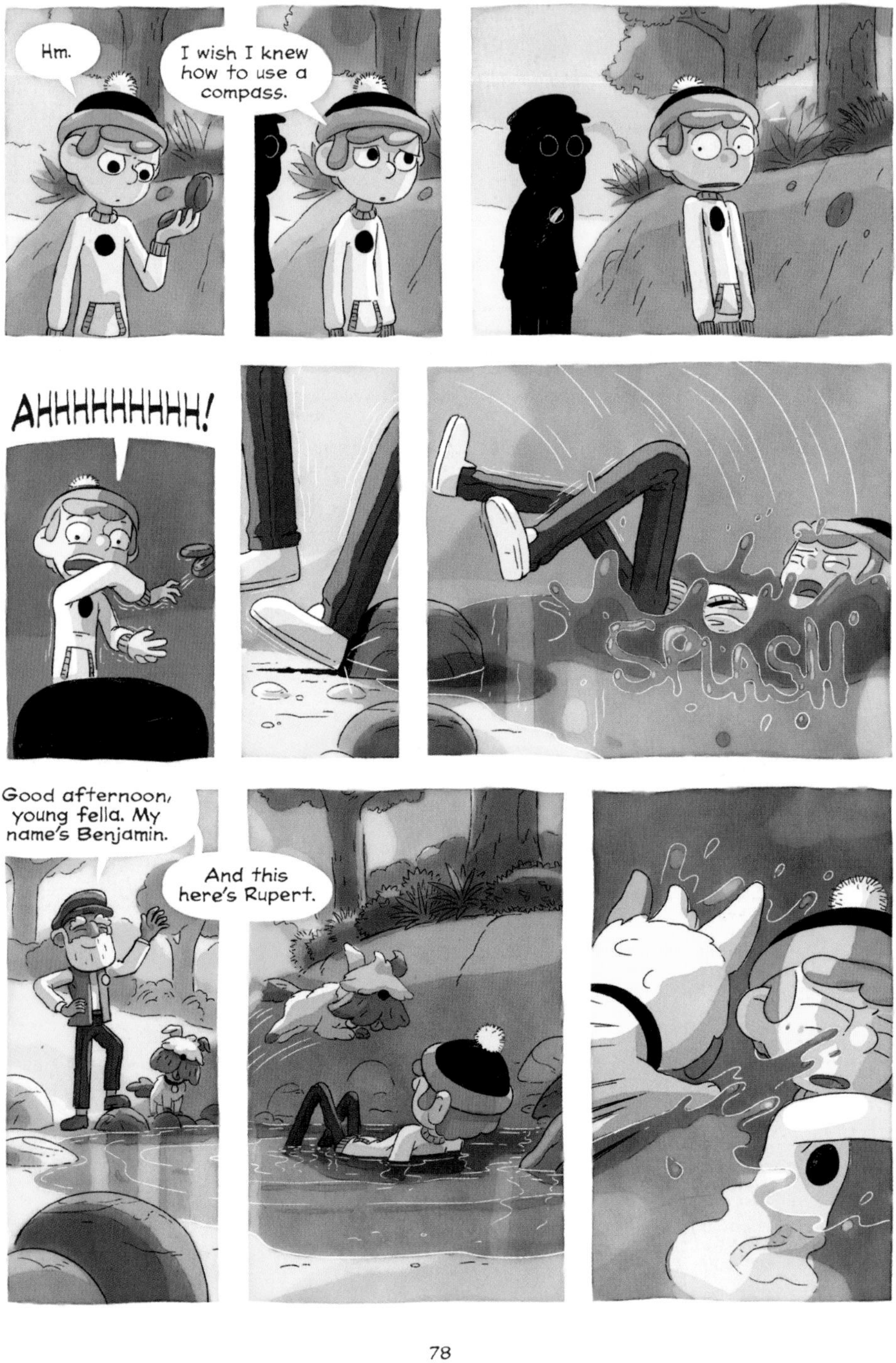
Hm.
I wish I knew how to use a compass.
AHHHHHHHHH!
SPLASH
Good afternoon, young fella. My name's Benjamin.
And this here's Rupert.

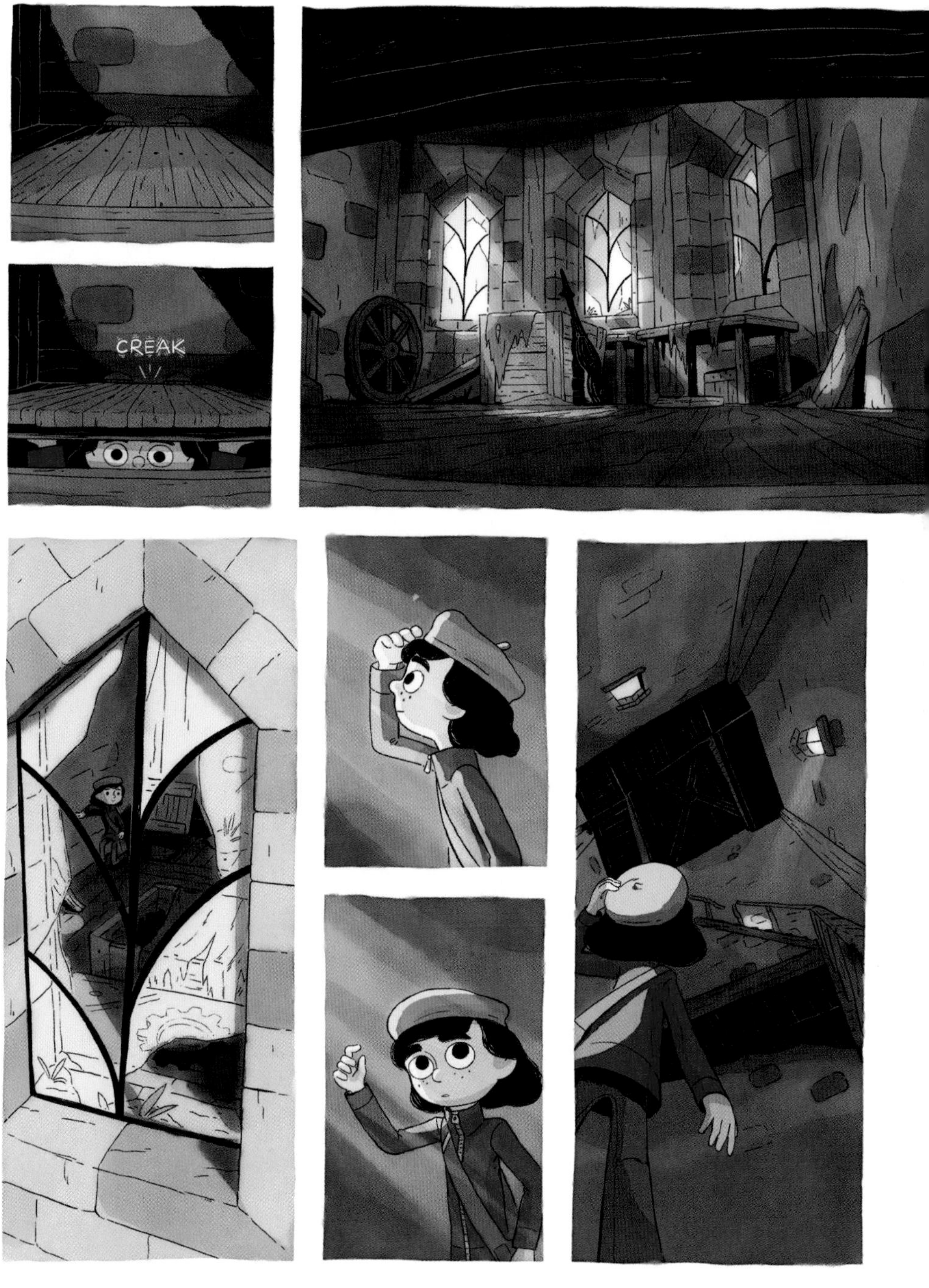
CREAK

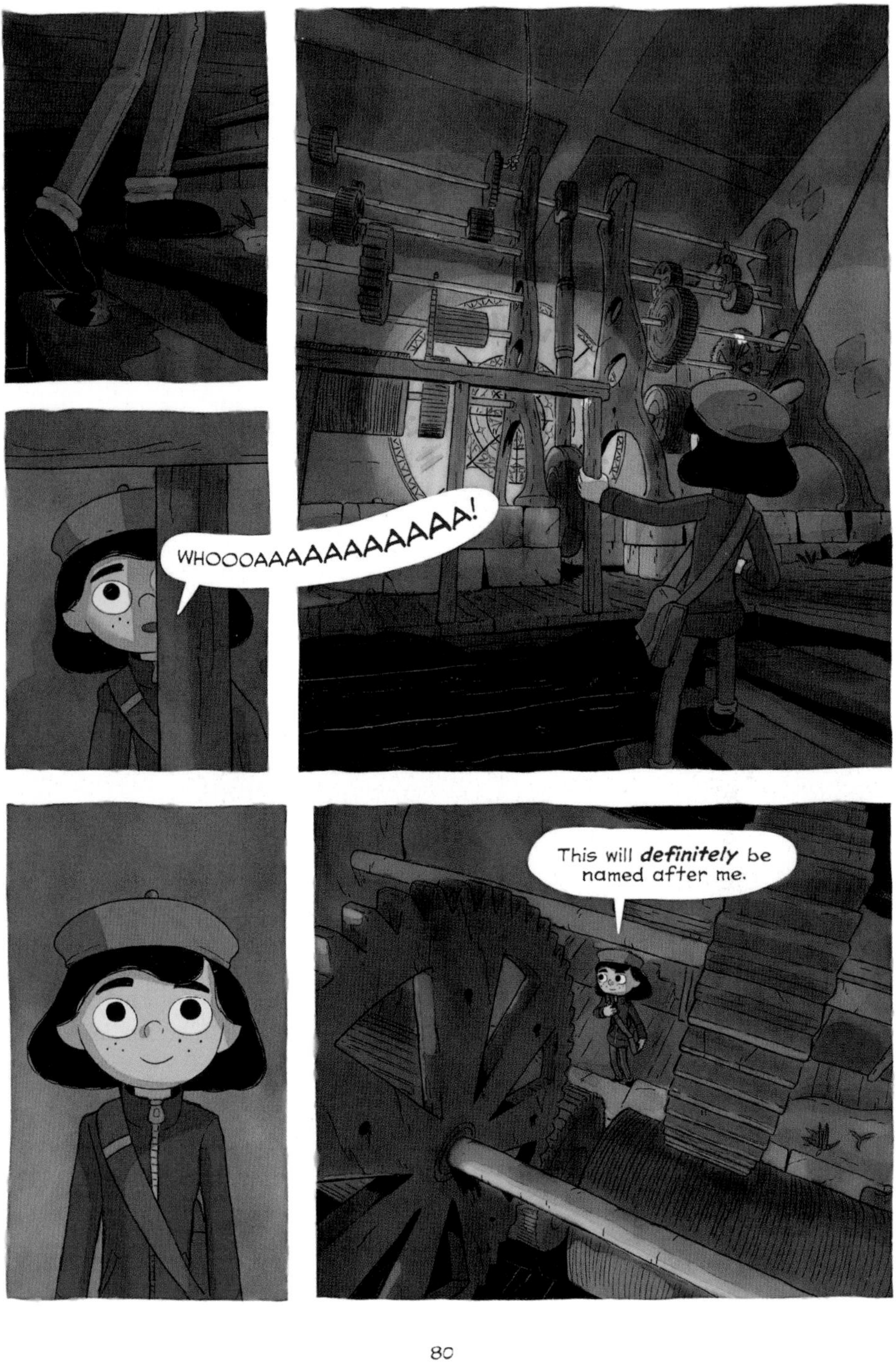
WHOOOAAAAAAAAAAAA!
This will *definitely* be named after me.

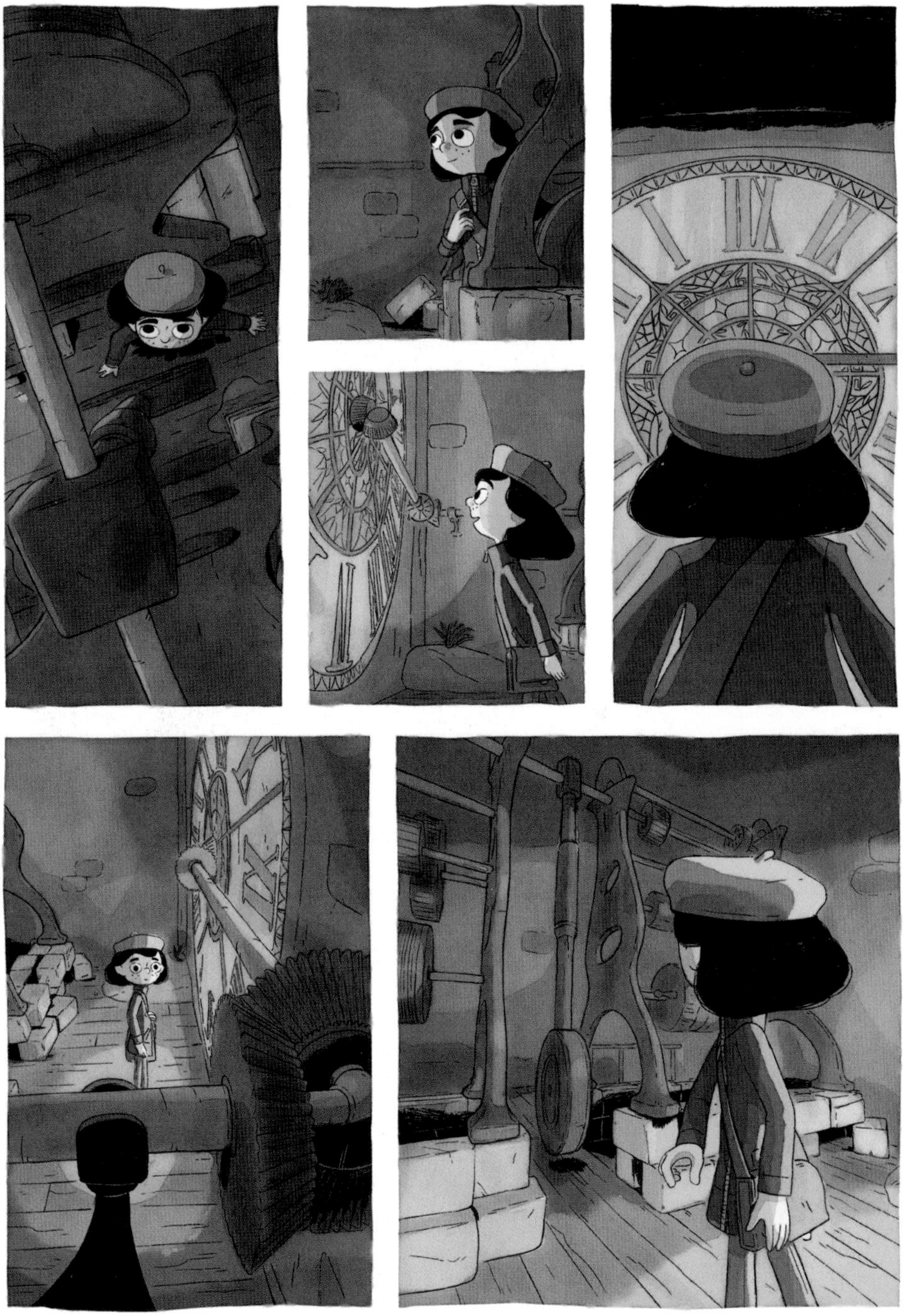

EUGH

EEEEEEE

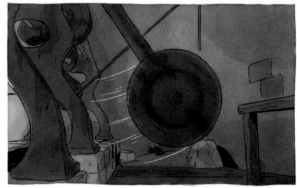

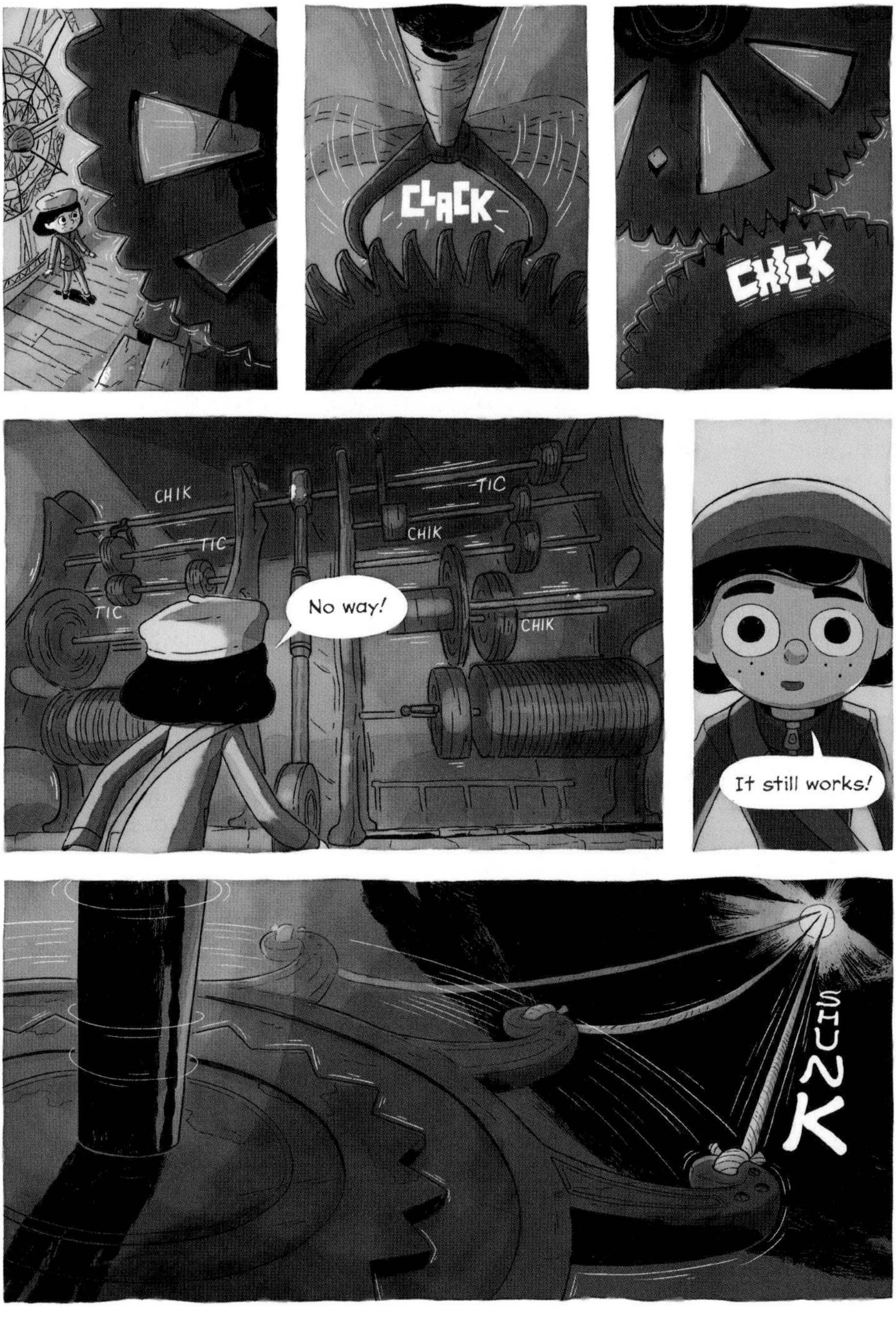
CLACK
CHICK
CHIK
TIC
TIC
TIC
CHIK
CHIK
No way!
It still works!
SHUNK

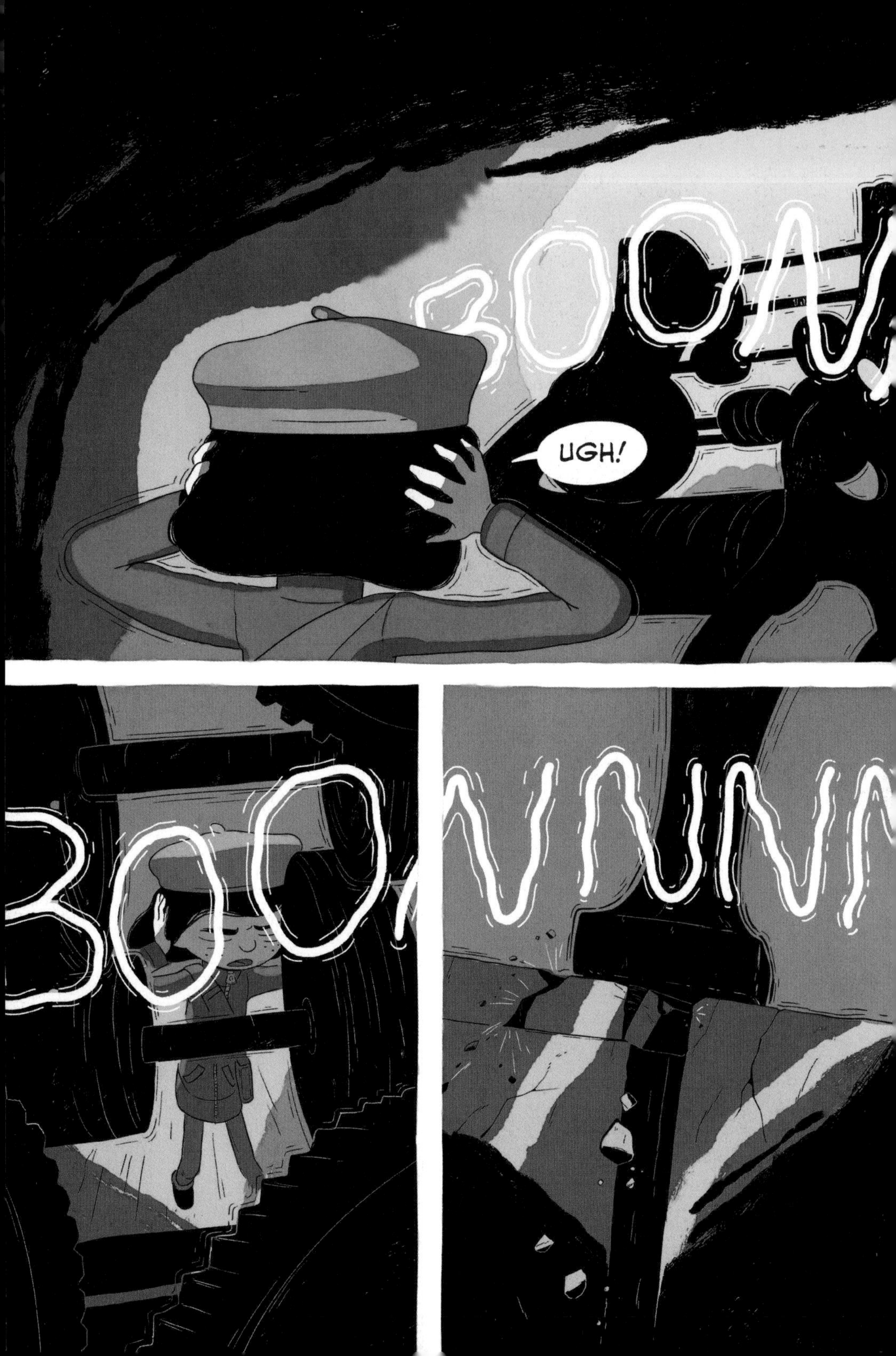
BOO
UGH!
BOO

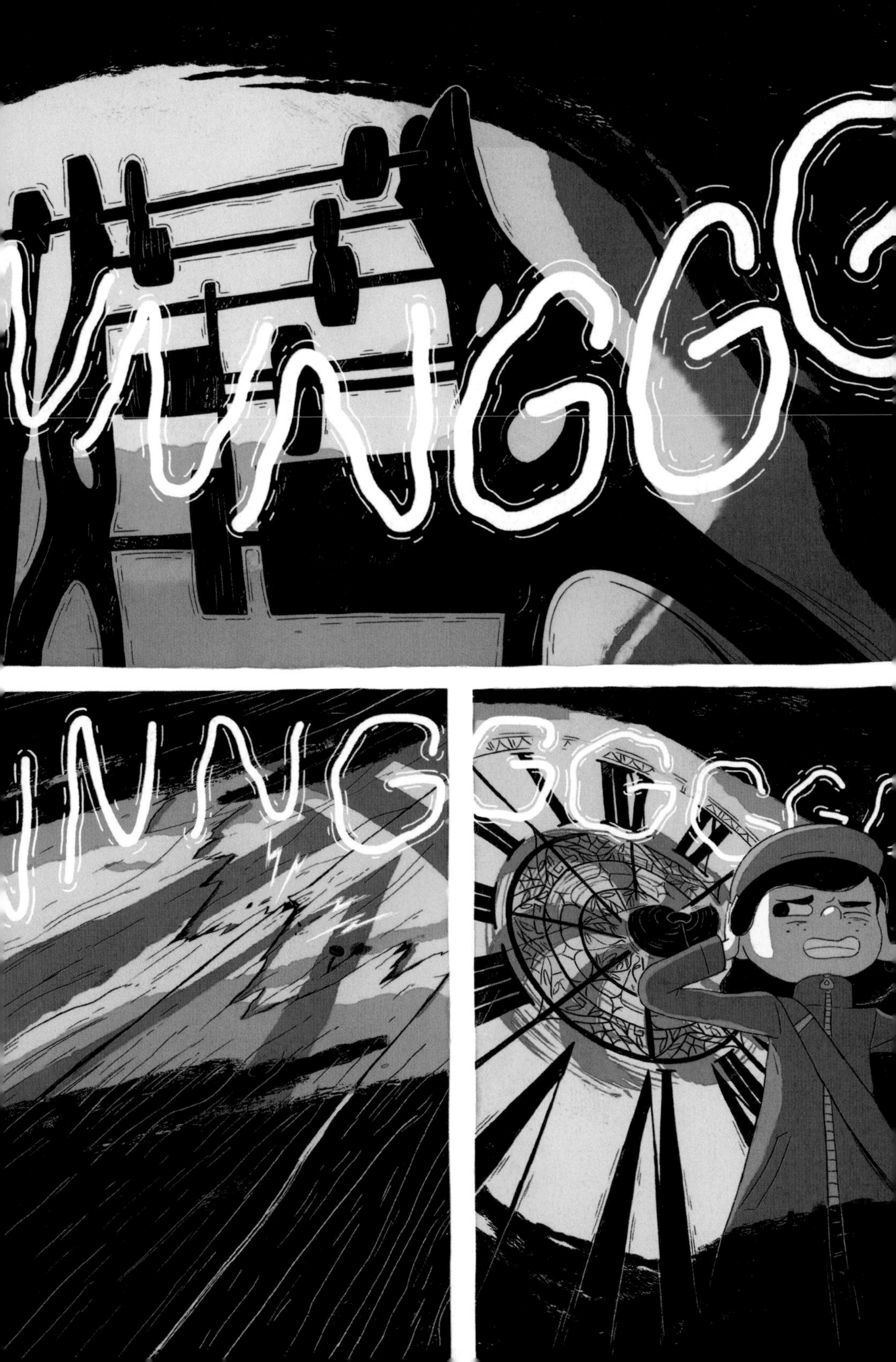

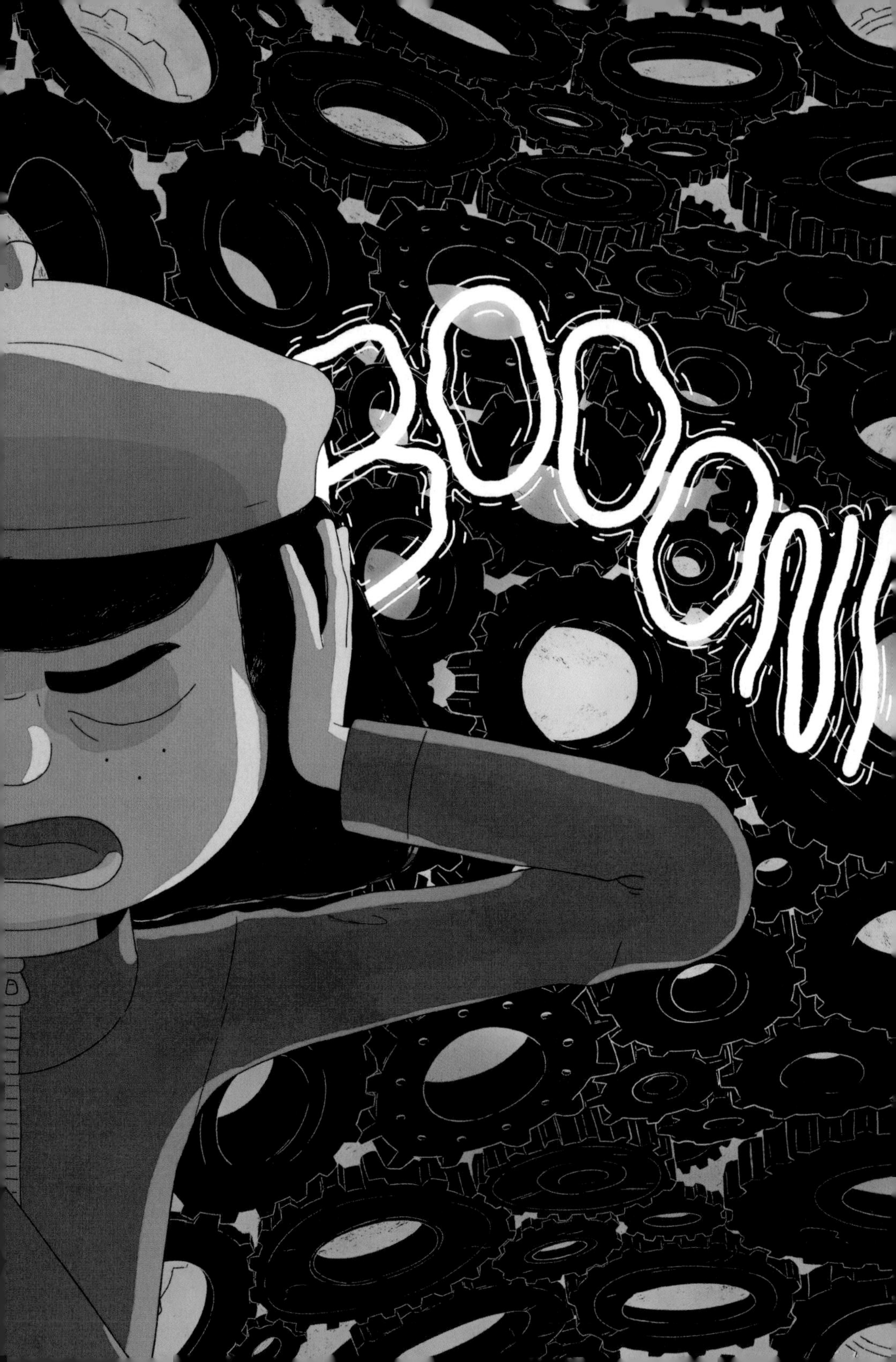
BOOO

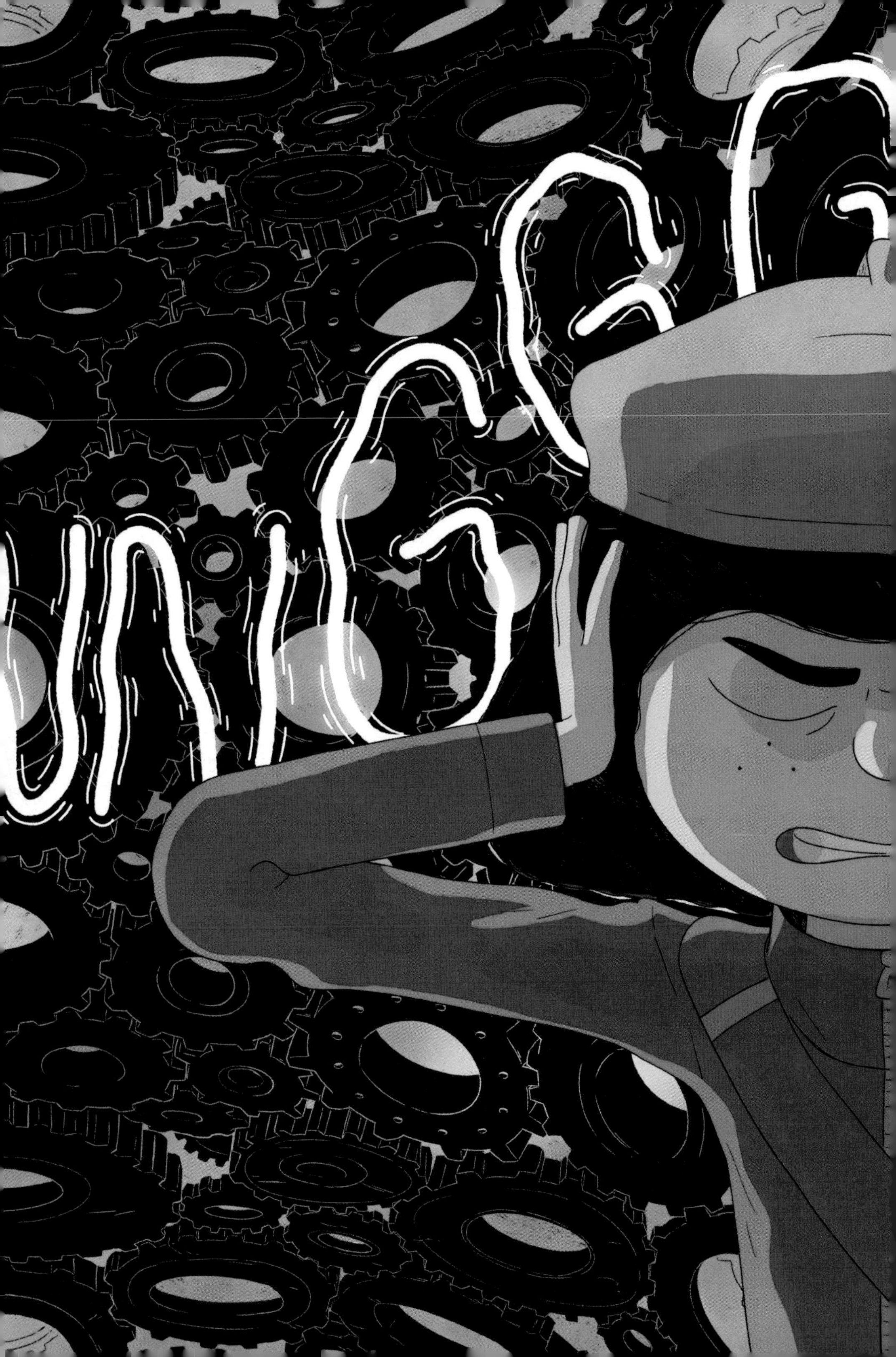

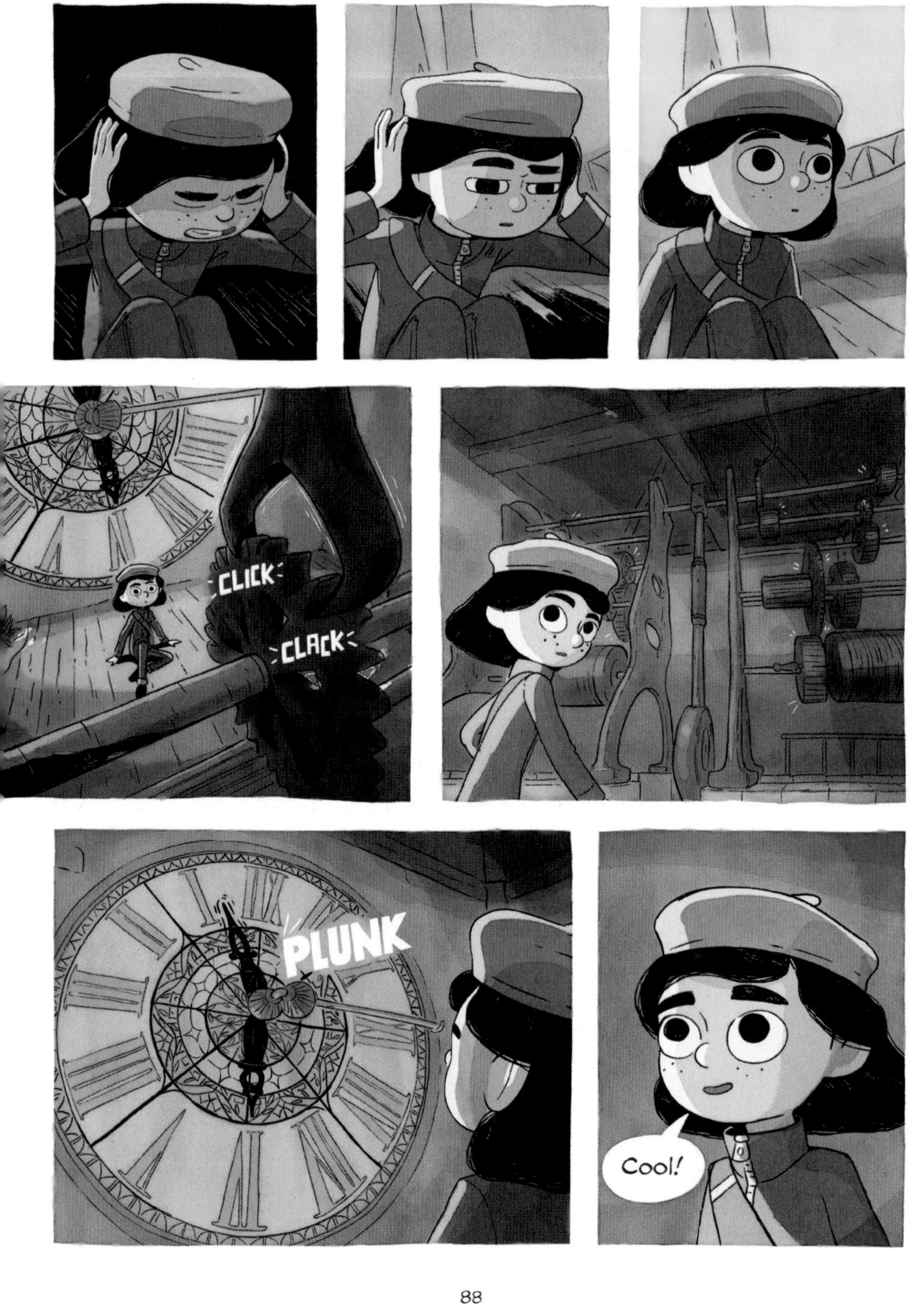
CLICK
CLACK
PLUNK
Cool!

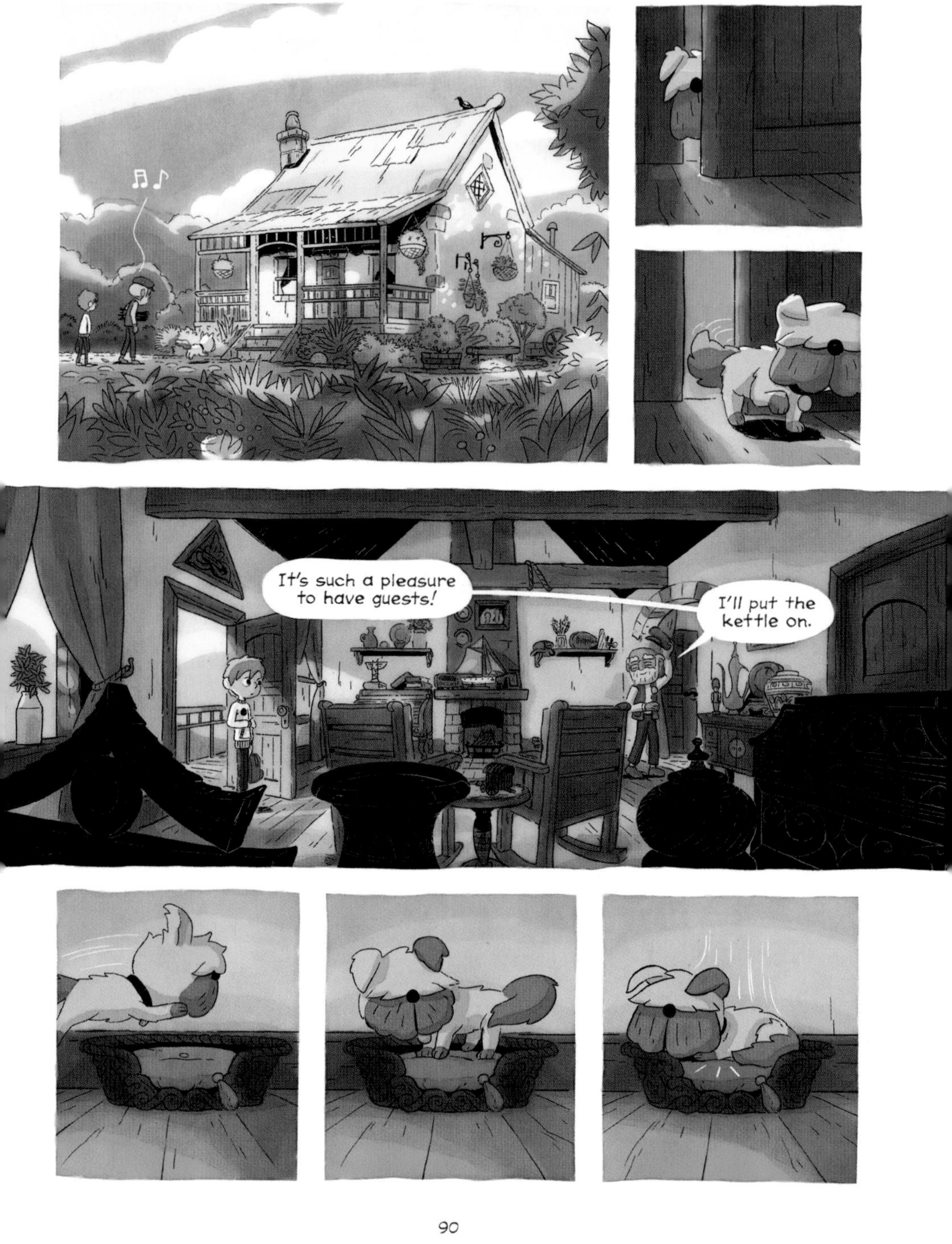
It's such a pleasure to have guests!
I'll put the kettle on.

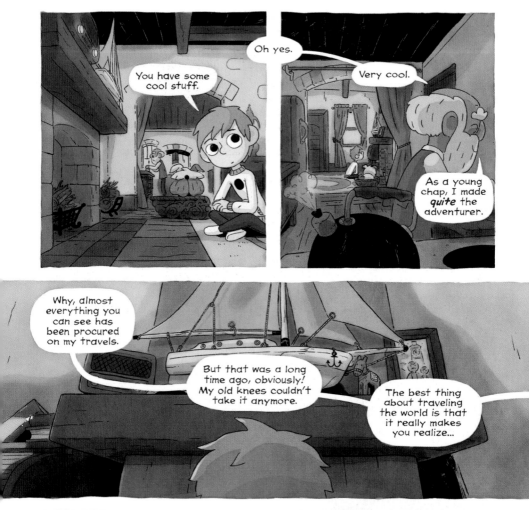

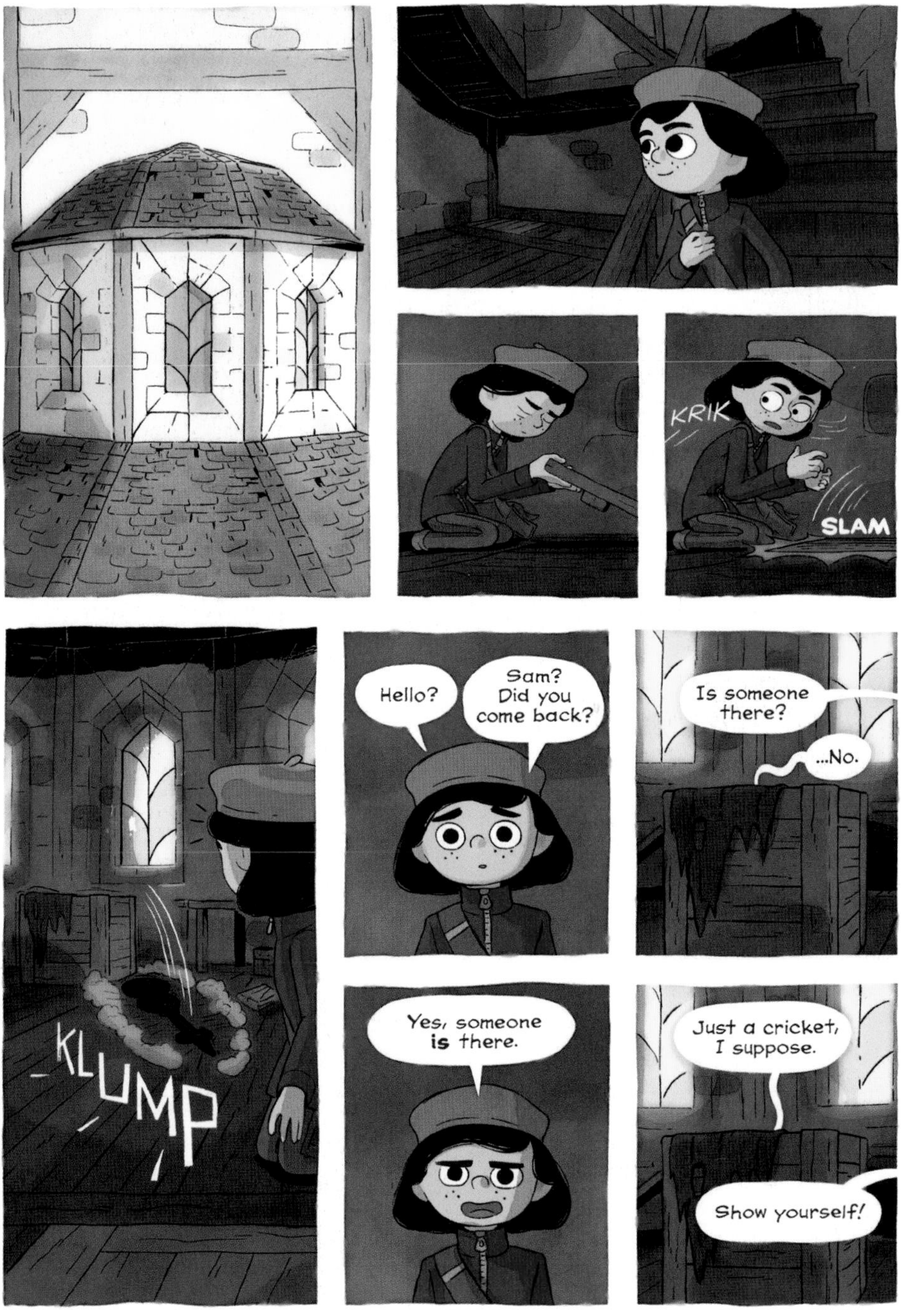

KRIK
SLAM
KLUMP
Hello?
Sam? Did you come back?
Is someone there?
...No.
Yes, someone **is** there.
Just a cricket, I suppose.
Show yourself!

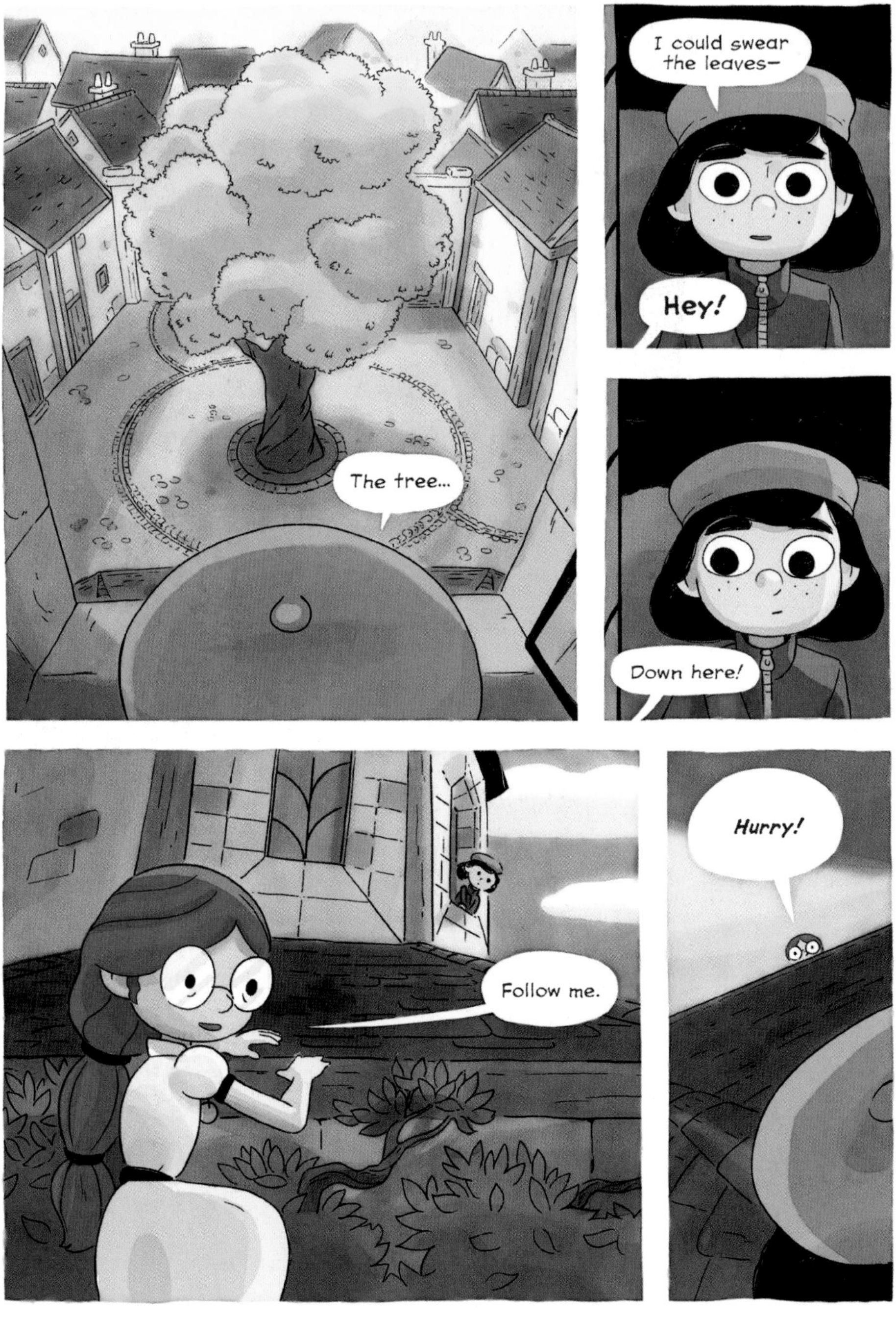
The tree...
I could swear the leaves—
Hey!
Down here!
Follow me.
Hurry!

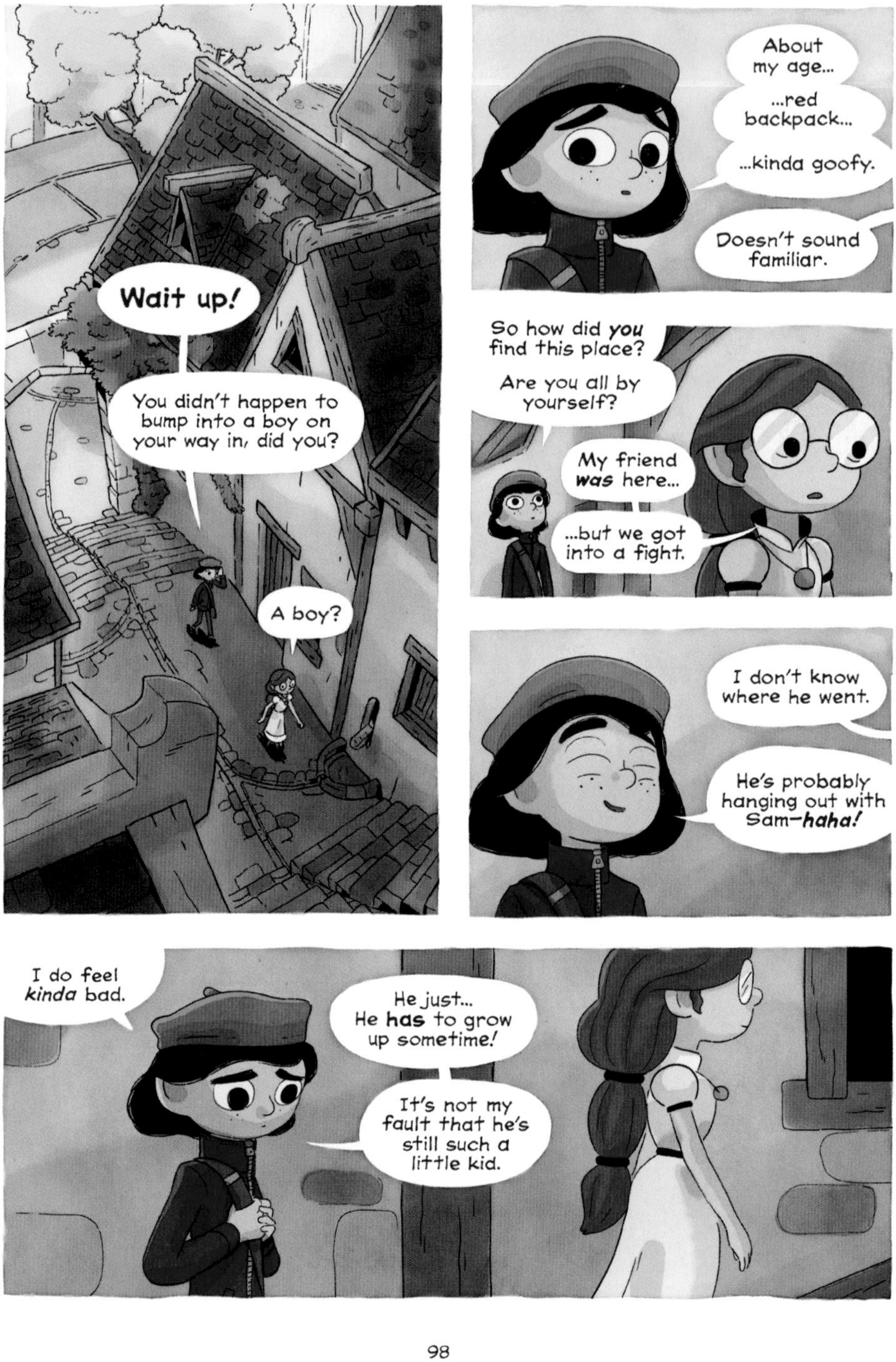
Wait up!
You didn't happen to bump into a boy on your way in, did you?
A boy?
About my age...
...red backpack...
...kinda goofy.
Doesn't sound familiar.
So how did *you* find this place?
Are you all by yourself?
My friend *was* here...
...but we got into a fight.
I don't know where he went.
He's probably hanging out with Sam—*haha!*
I do feel *kinda* bad.
He just... He **has** to grow up sometime!
It's not my fault that he's still such a little kid.

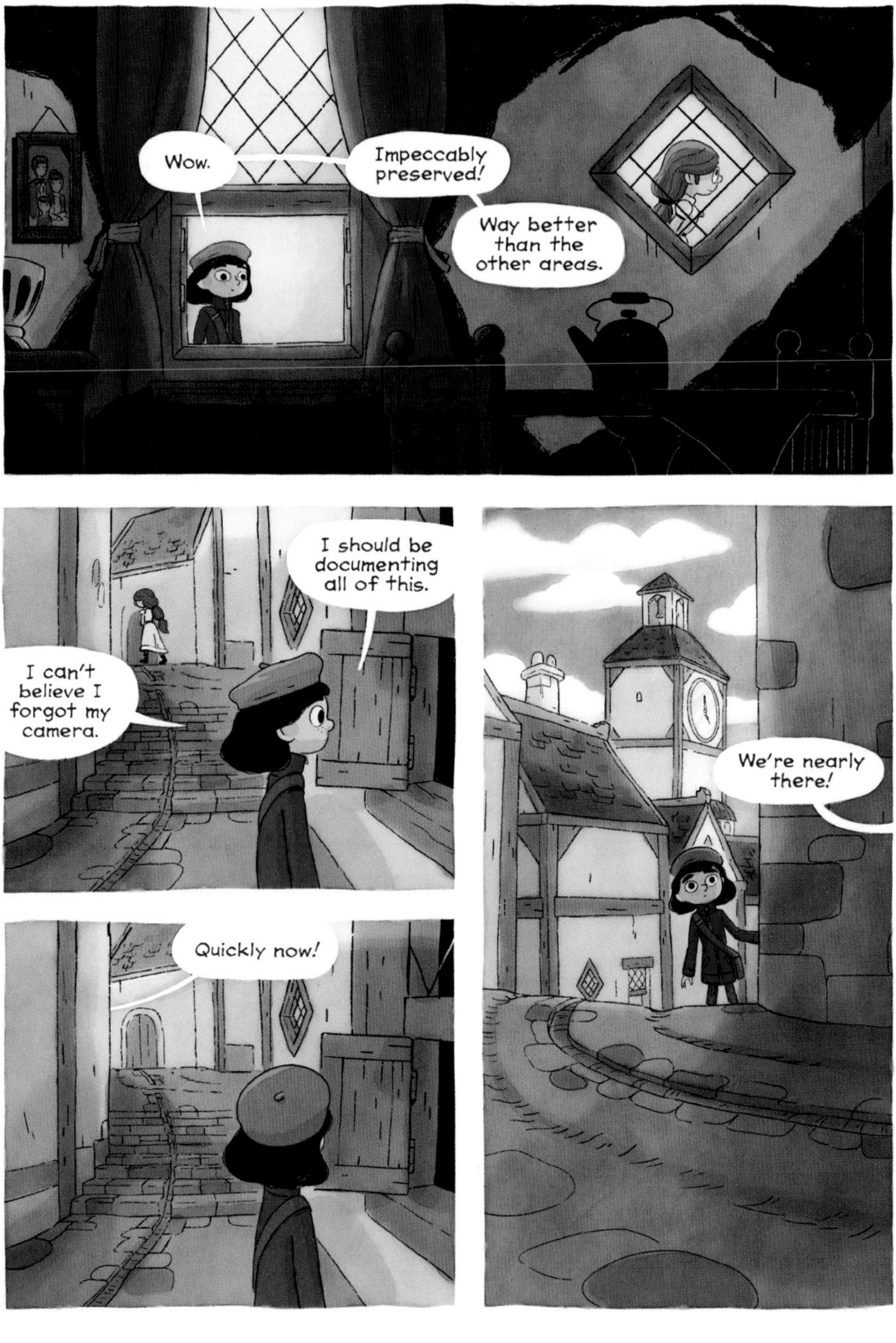
Wow.
Impeccably preserved!
Way better than the other areas.
I should be documenting all of this.
I can't believe I forgot my camera.
We're nearly there!
Quickly now!

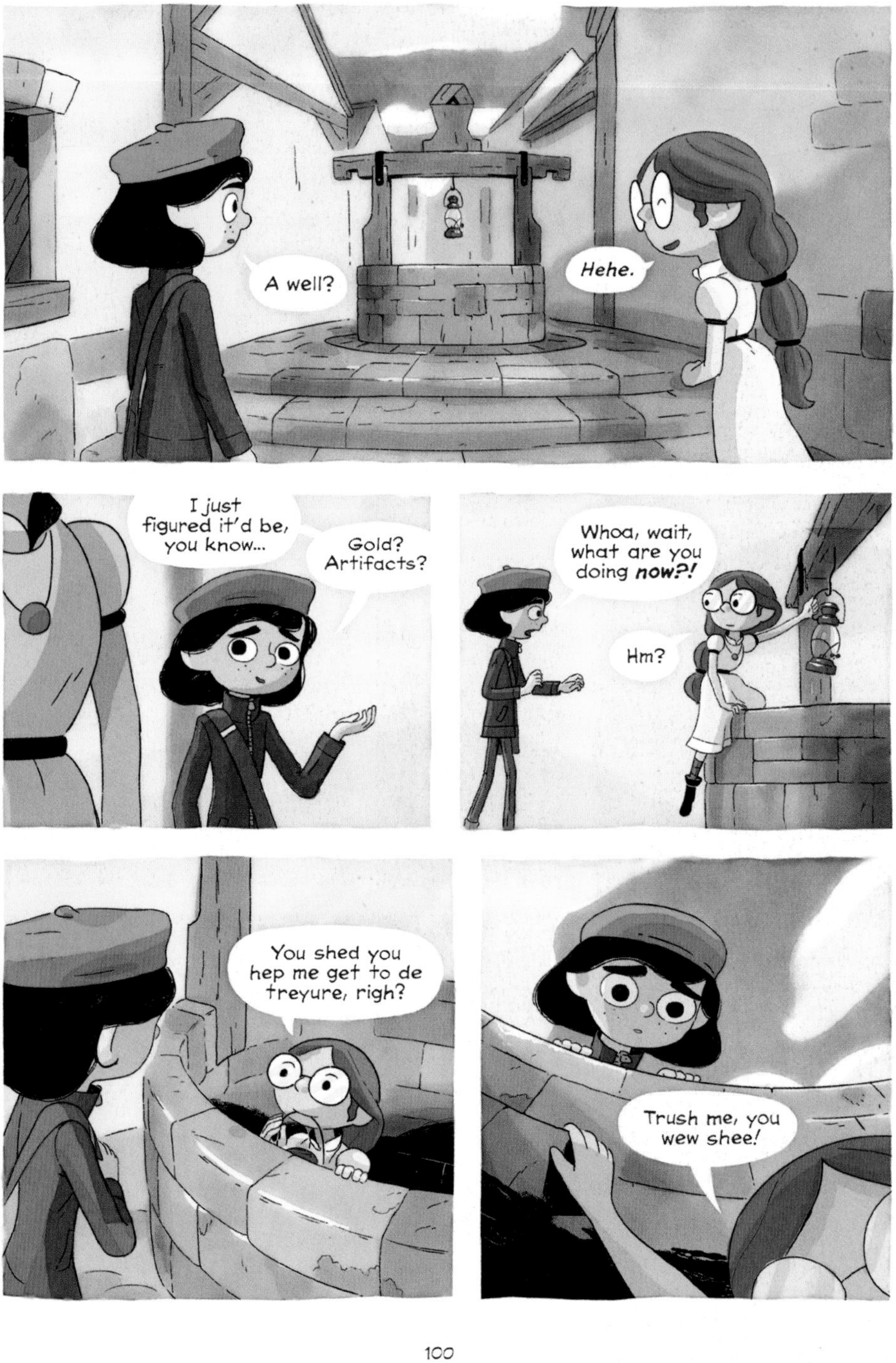
A well?
Hehe.
I just figured it'd be, you know...
Gold? Artifacts?
Whoa, wait, what are you doing **now?!**
Hm?
You shed you hep me get to de treyure, righ?
Trush me, you wew shee!

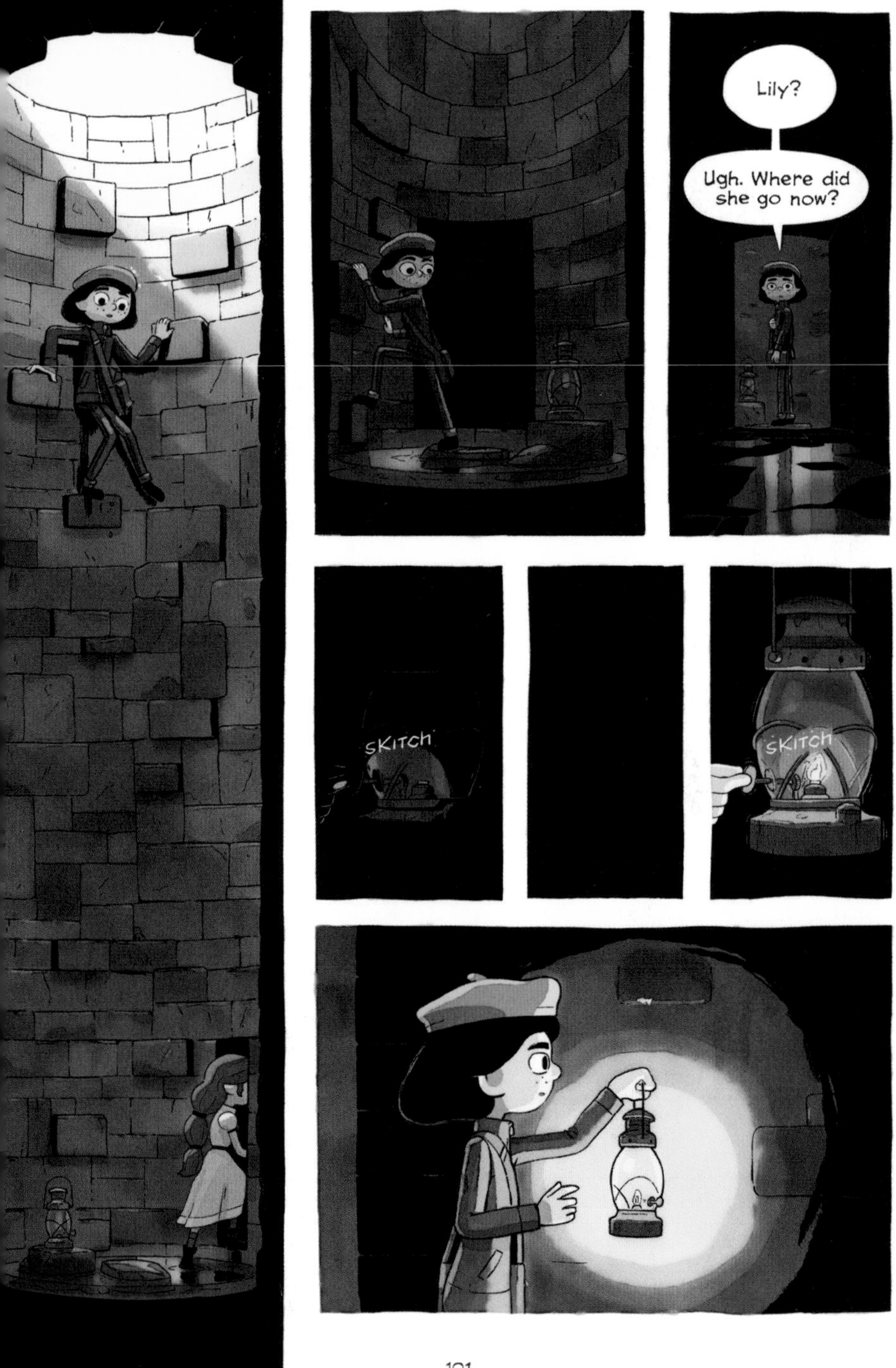
Lily?
Ugh. Where did she go now?
SKITCH
SKITCH

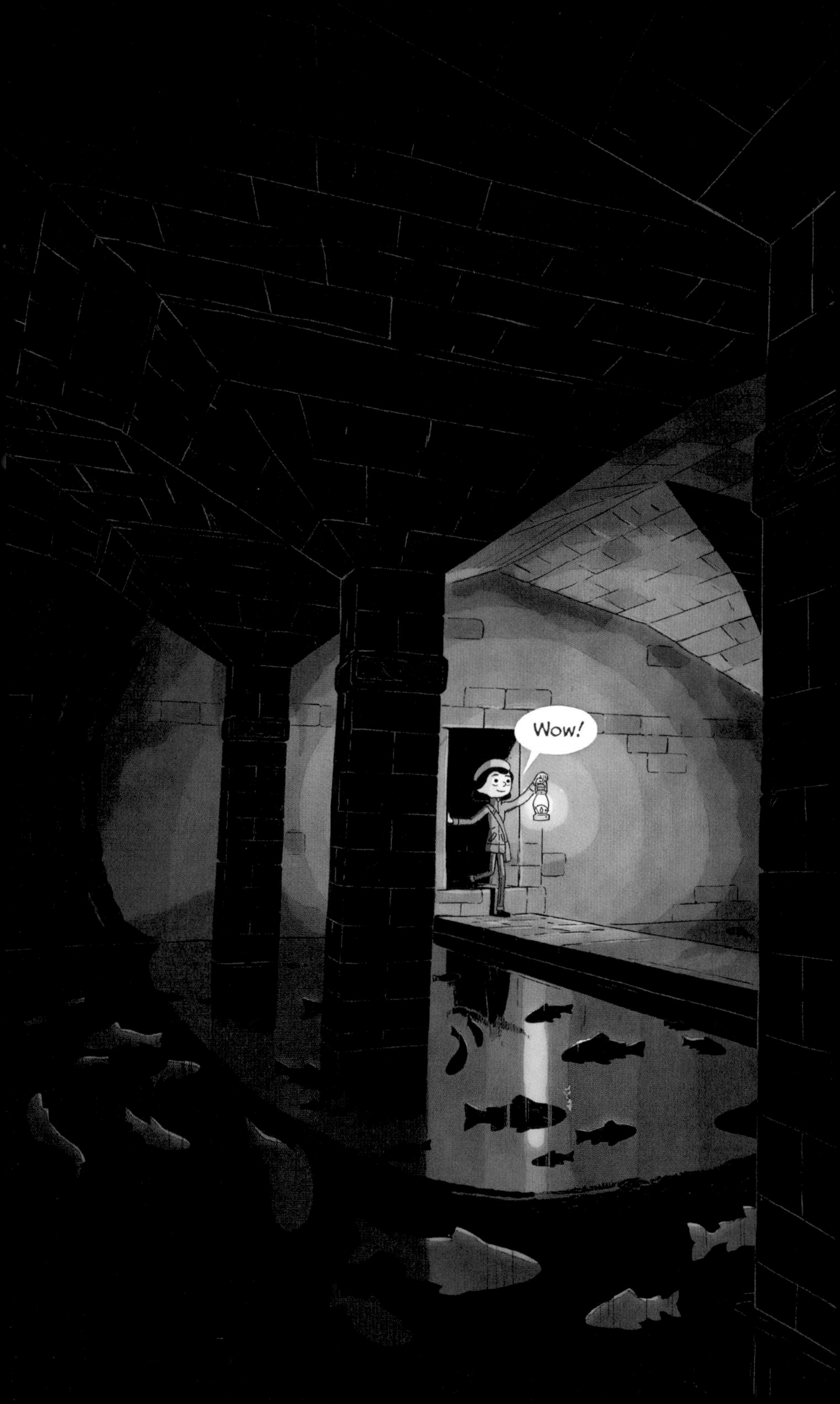
Wow!

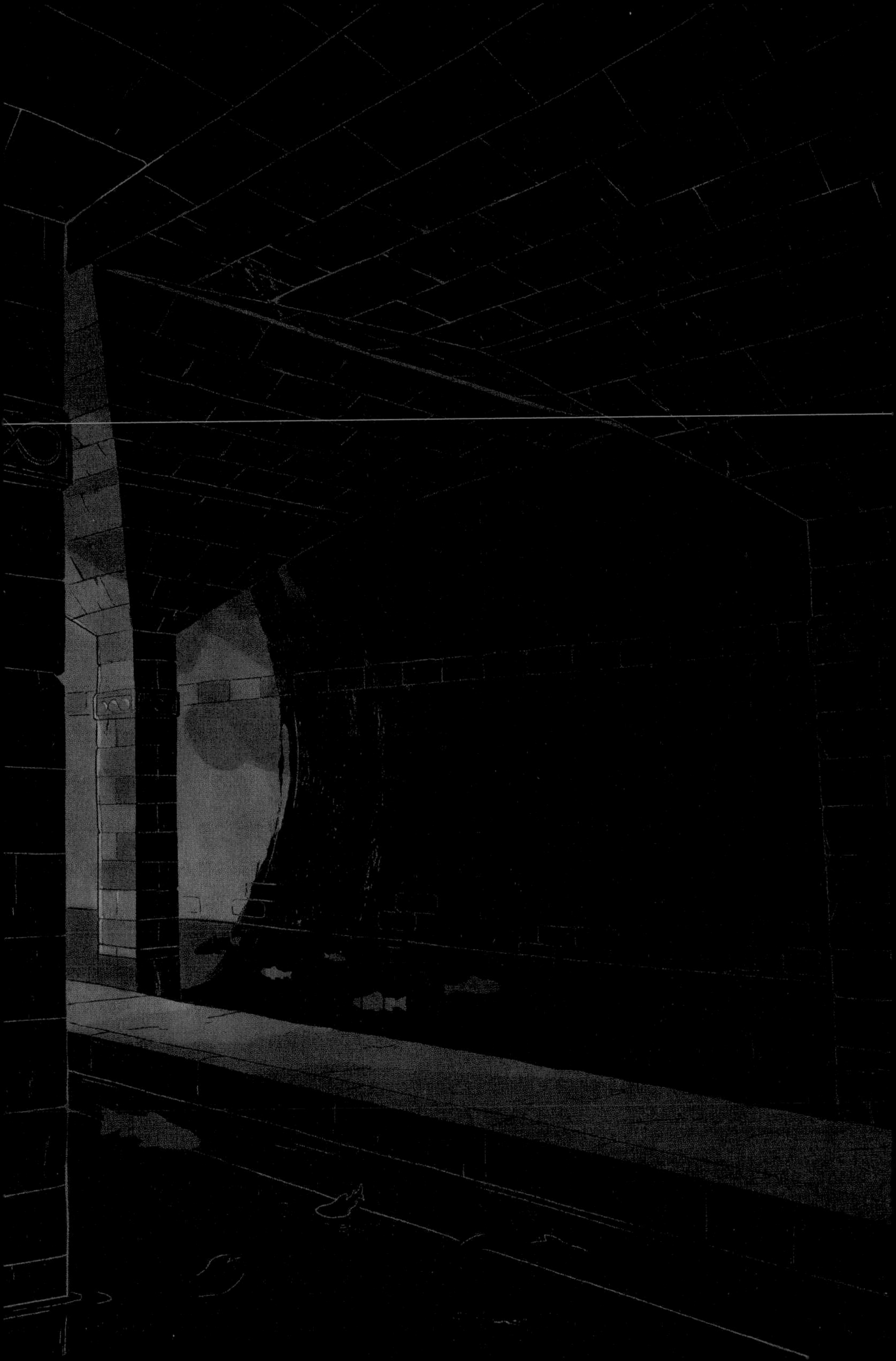

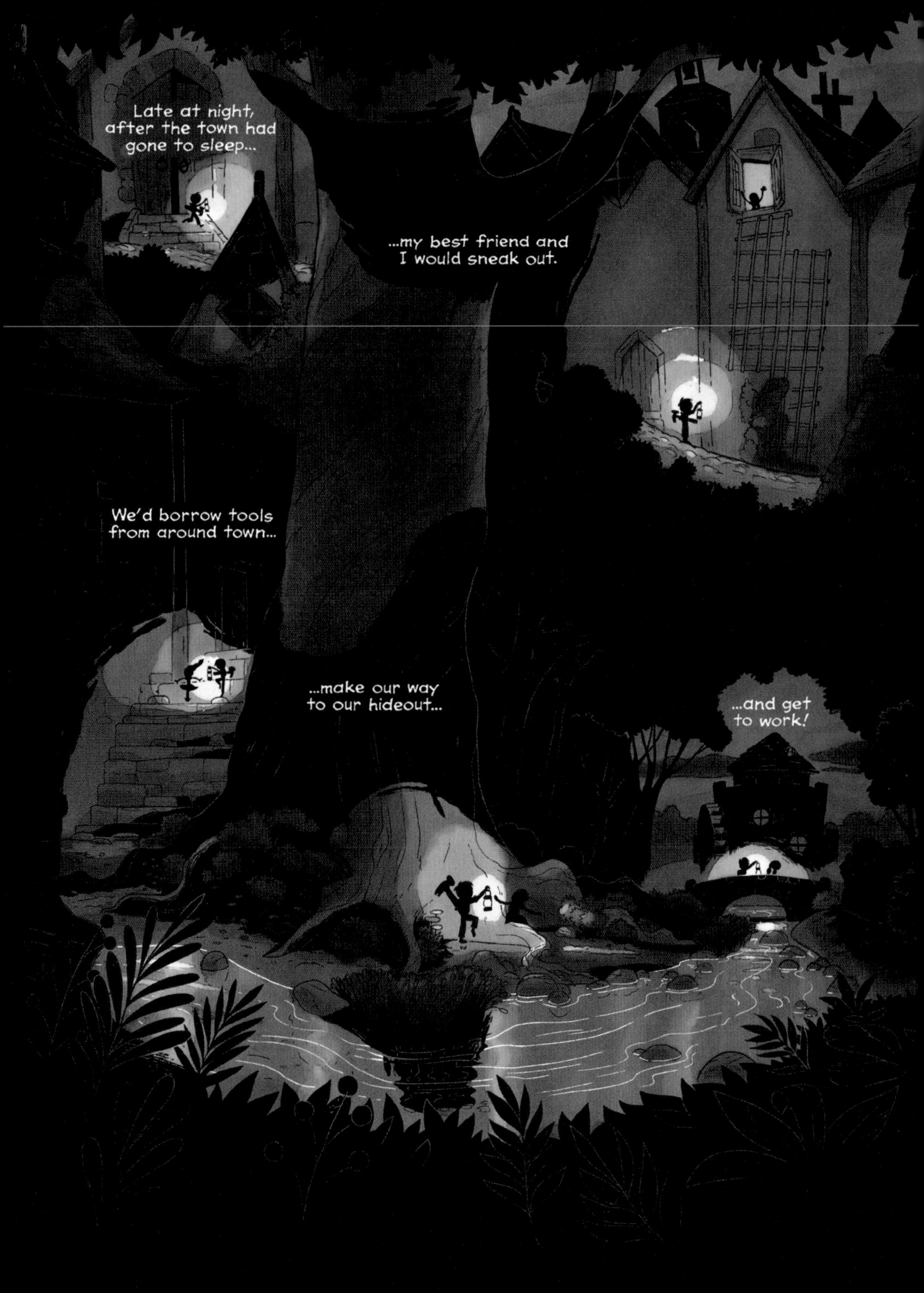
Late at night, after the town had gone to sleep...
...my best friend and I would sneak out.
We'd borrow tools from around town...
...make our way to our hideout...
...and get to work!

Work?
Doing what?

And on this particular night, it was the ship you see sitting proudly on my mantelpiece.

Adding to our kingdom!

Months in the making!

She pleaded with me to wait...

...but we had finished!

The water was unusually rough that day, however.

"It's blowing a gale! We should take it out in fairer weather," she said.

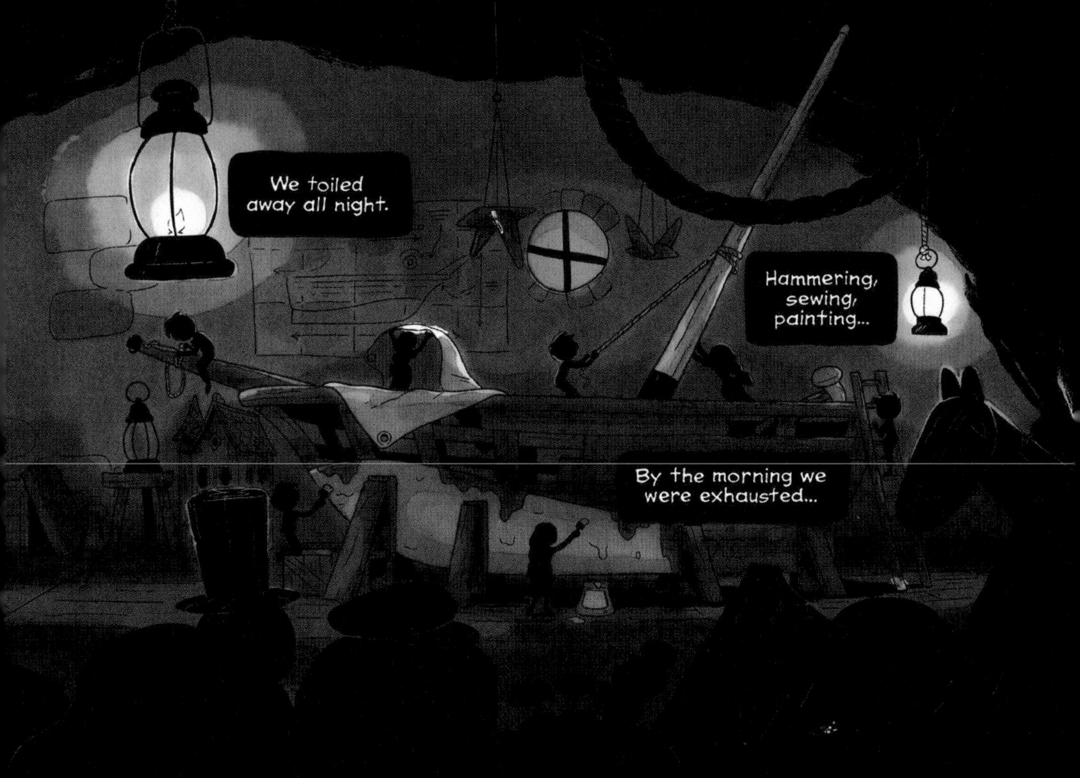
We toiled away all night.
Hammering, sewing, painting...
By the morning we were exhausted...

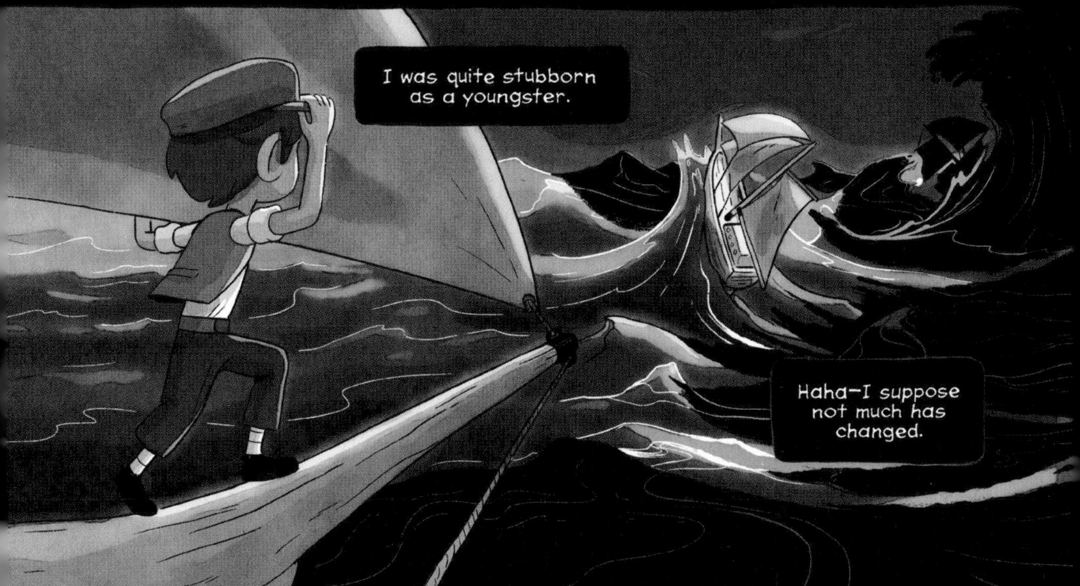
I was quite stubborn as a youngster.
Haha—I suppose not much has changed.

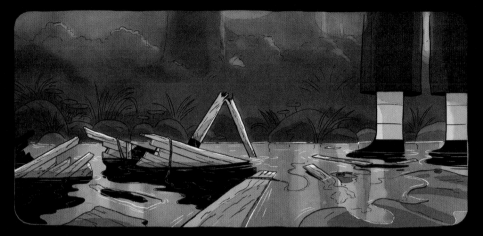

Your friend was mad, huh?

FURIOUS!

And she never spoke to you ever again?

I certainly thought that would be true, but, well...

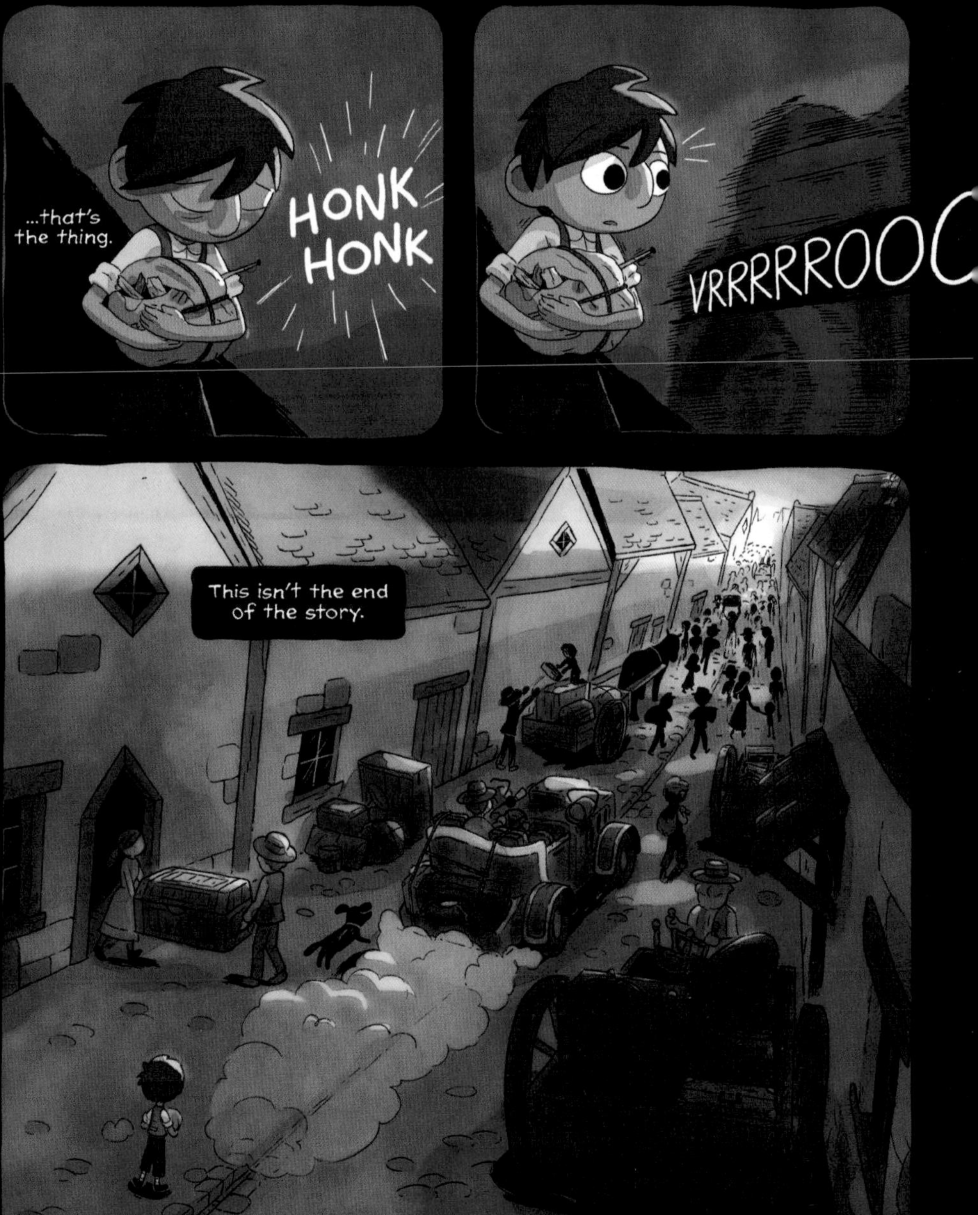
...that's the thing.
HONK HONK
VRRRRROOO
This isn't the end of the story.

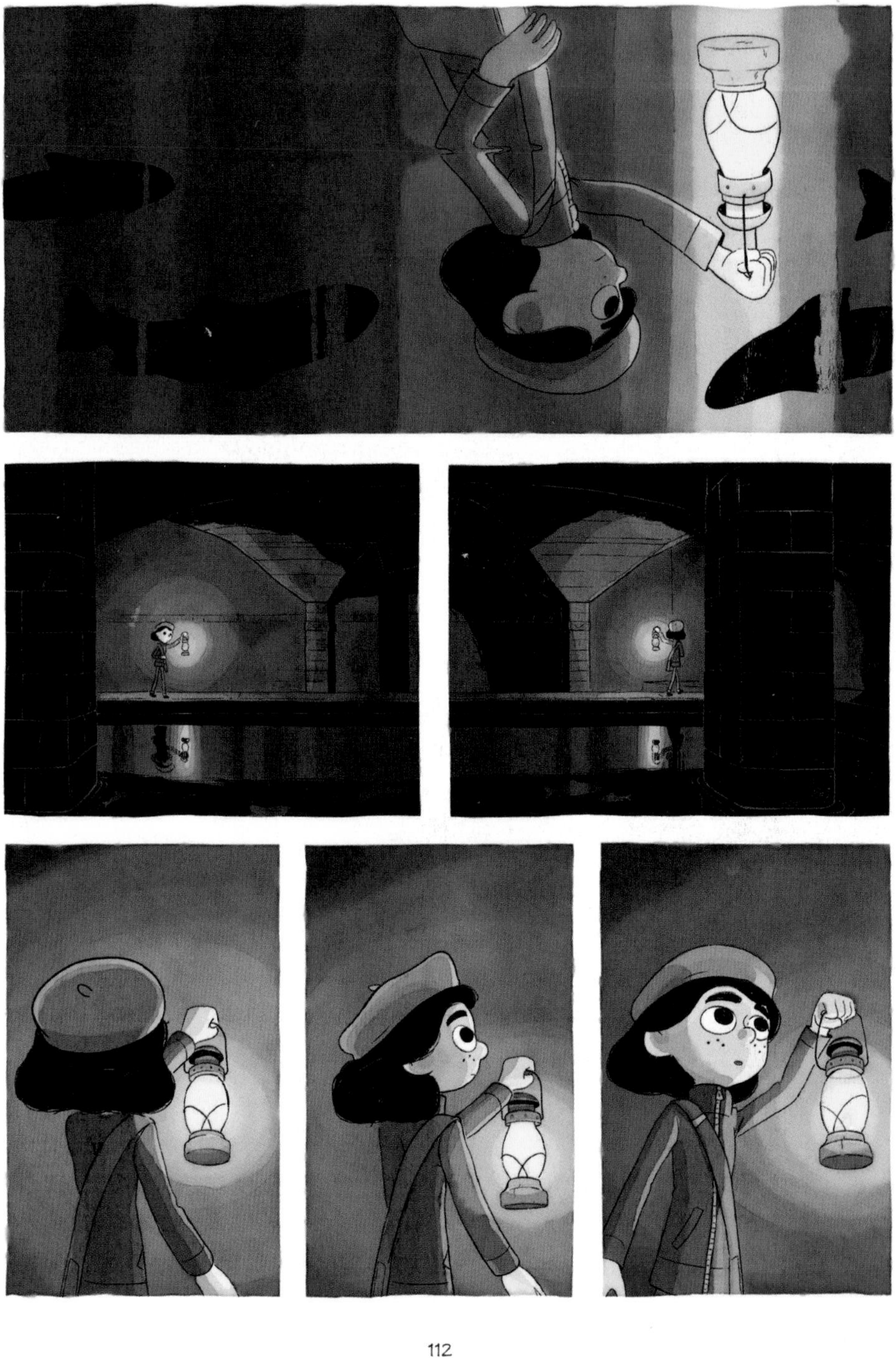

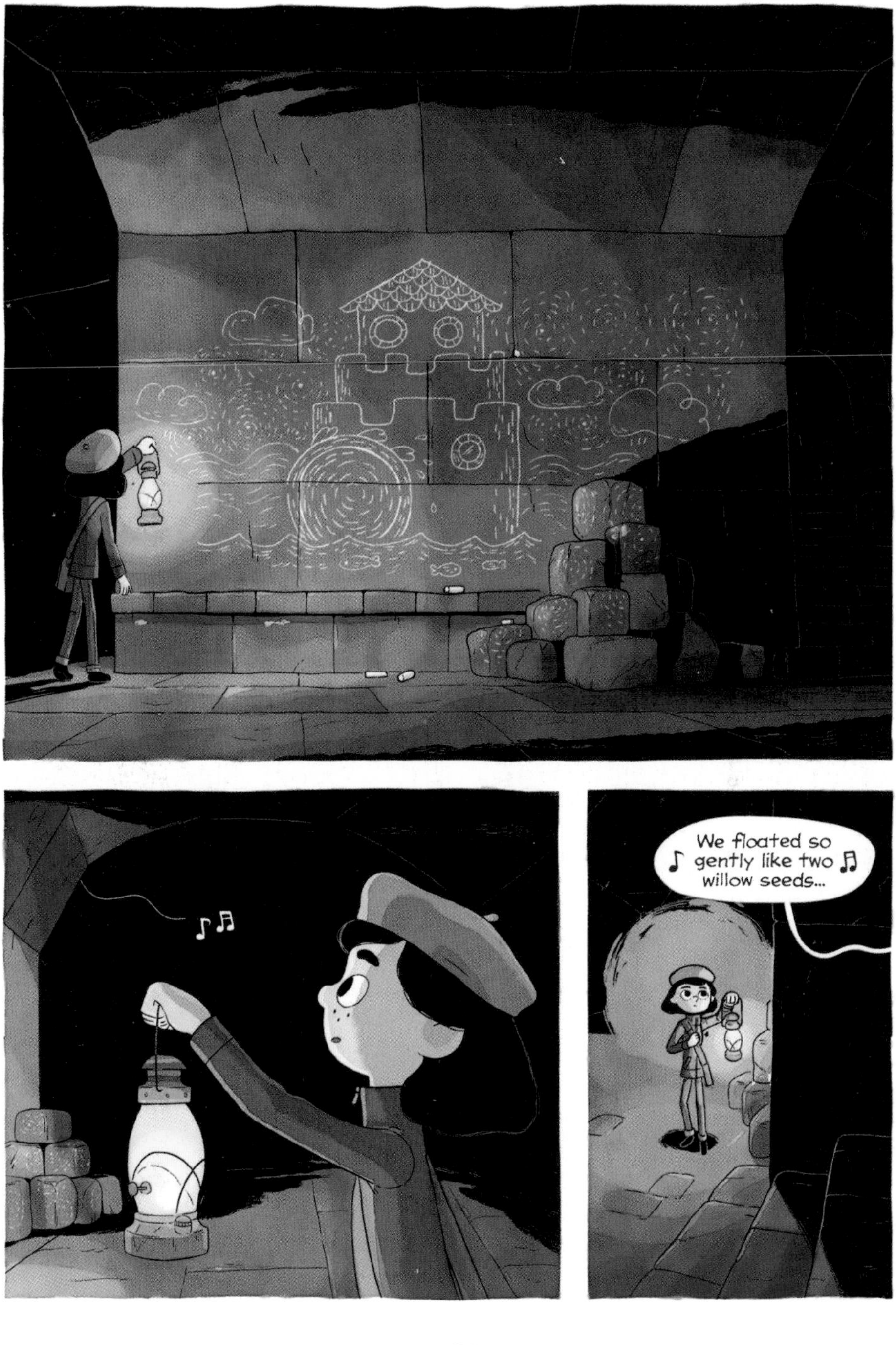
We floated so gently like two willow seeds...

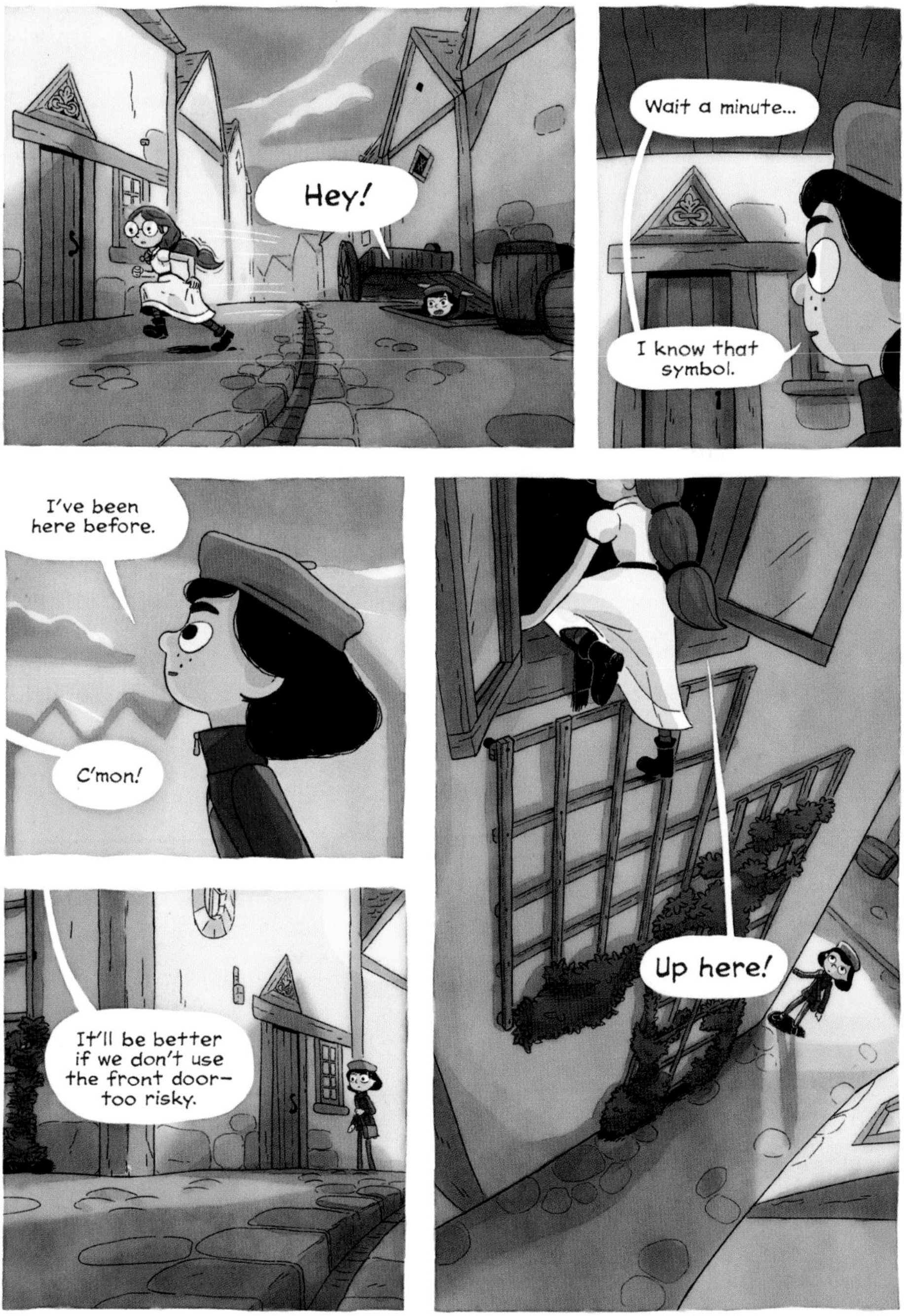
Hey!
Wait a minute...
I know that symbol.
I've been here before.
C'mon!
It'll be better if we don't use the front door—too risky.
Up here!

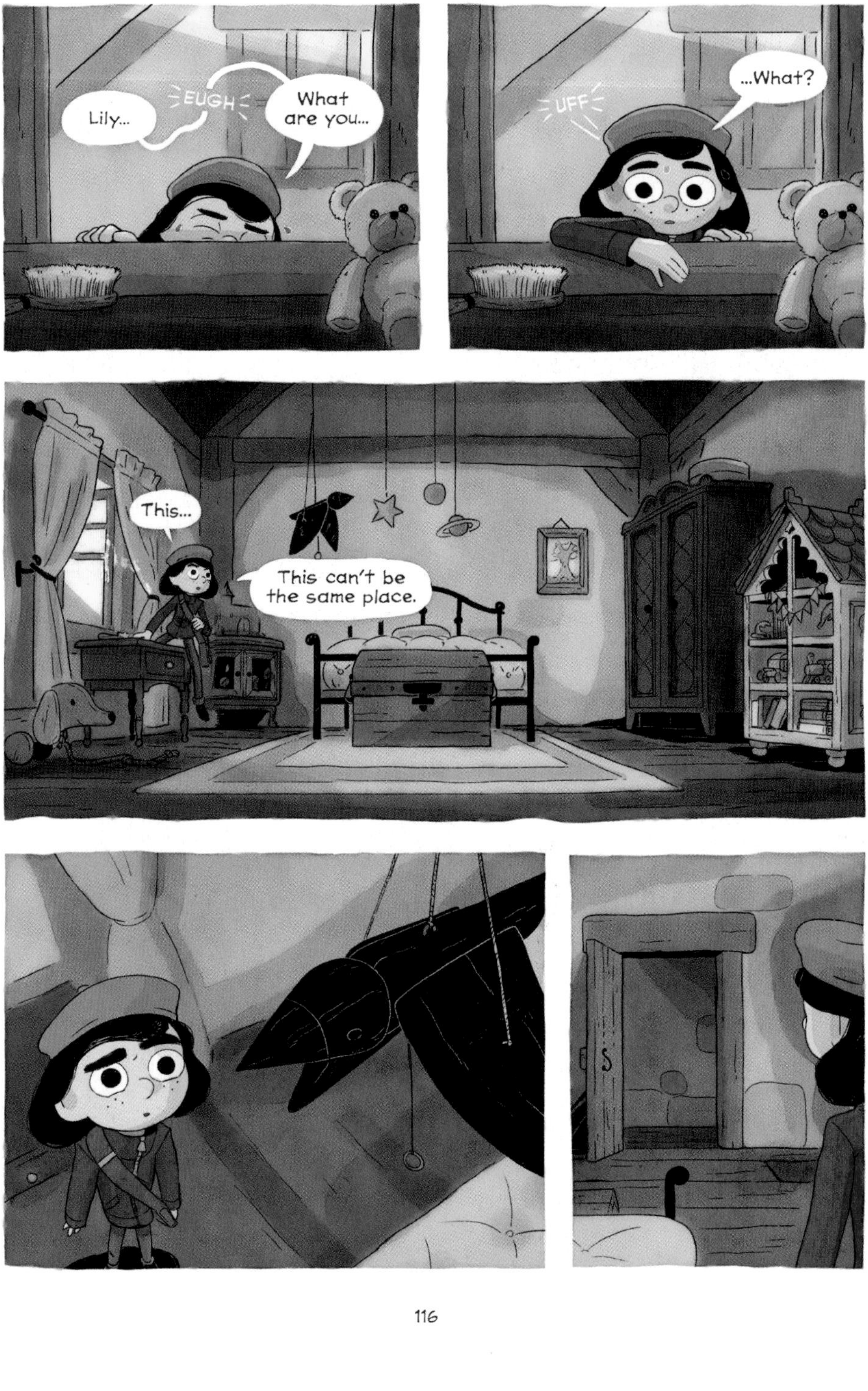
Lily...
EUGH
What are you...
UFF
...What?
This...
This can't be the same place.

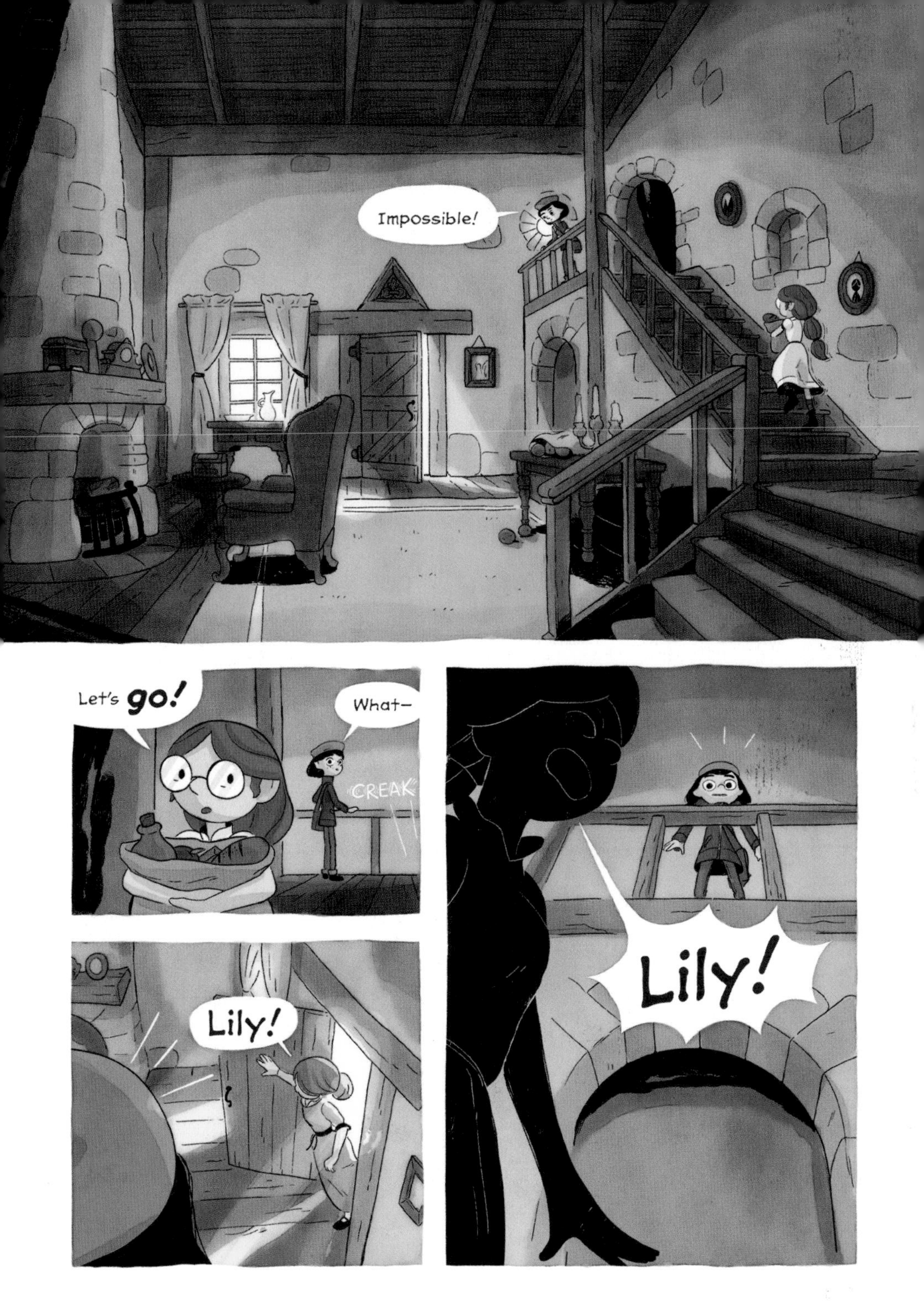

Impossible!
Let's go!
What–
CREAK
Lily!
Lily!

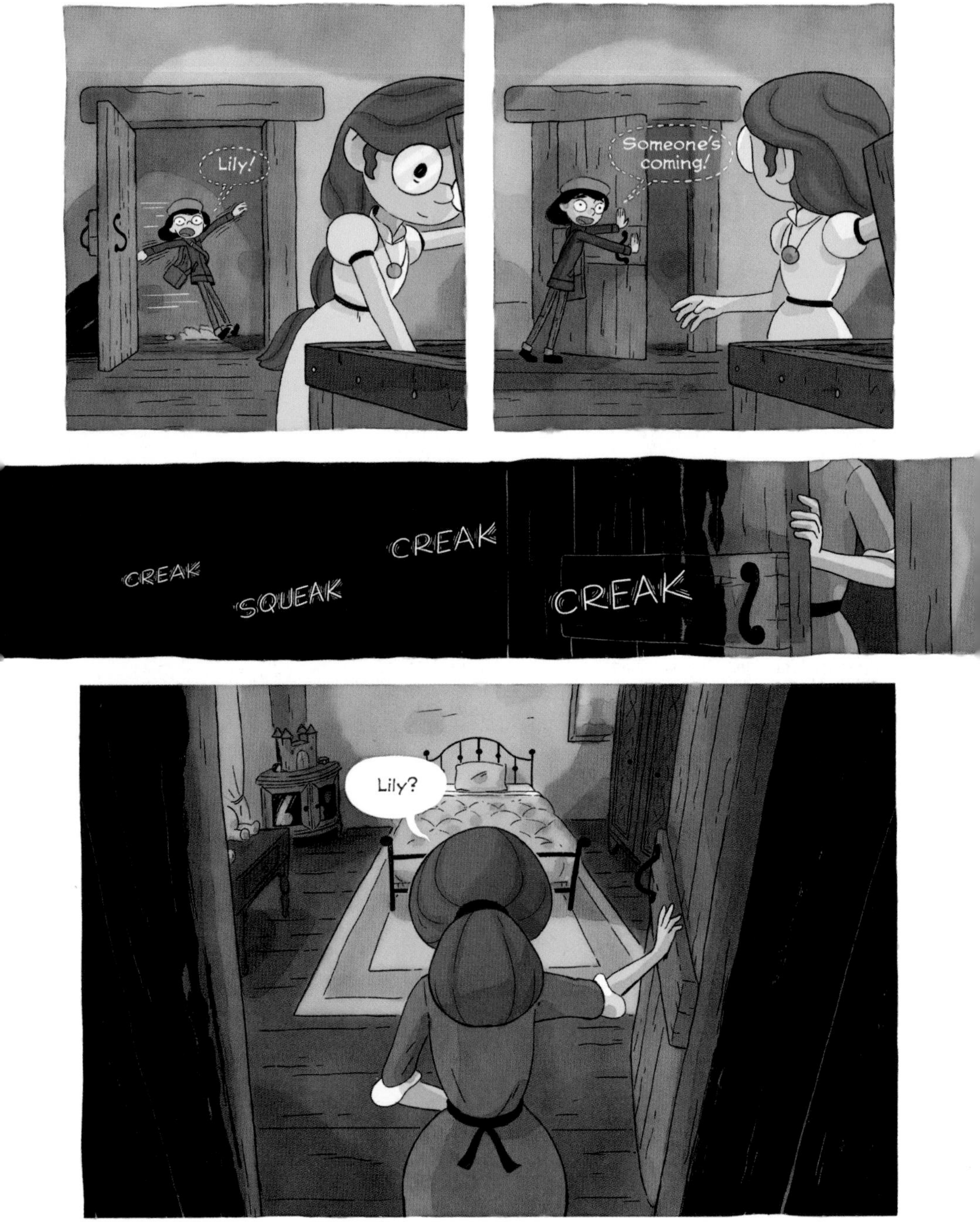

Lily!
Someone's coming!
CREAK
SQUEAK
CREAK
CREAK
Lily?

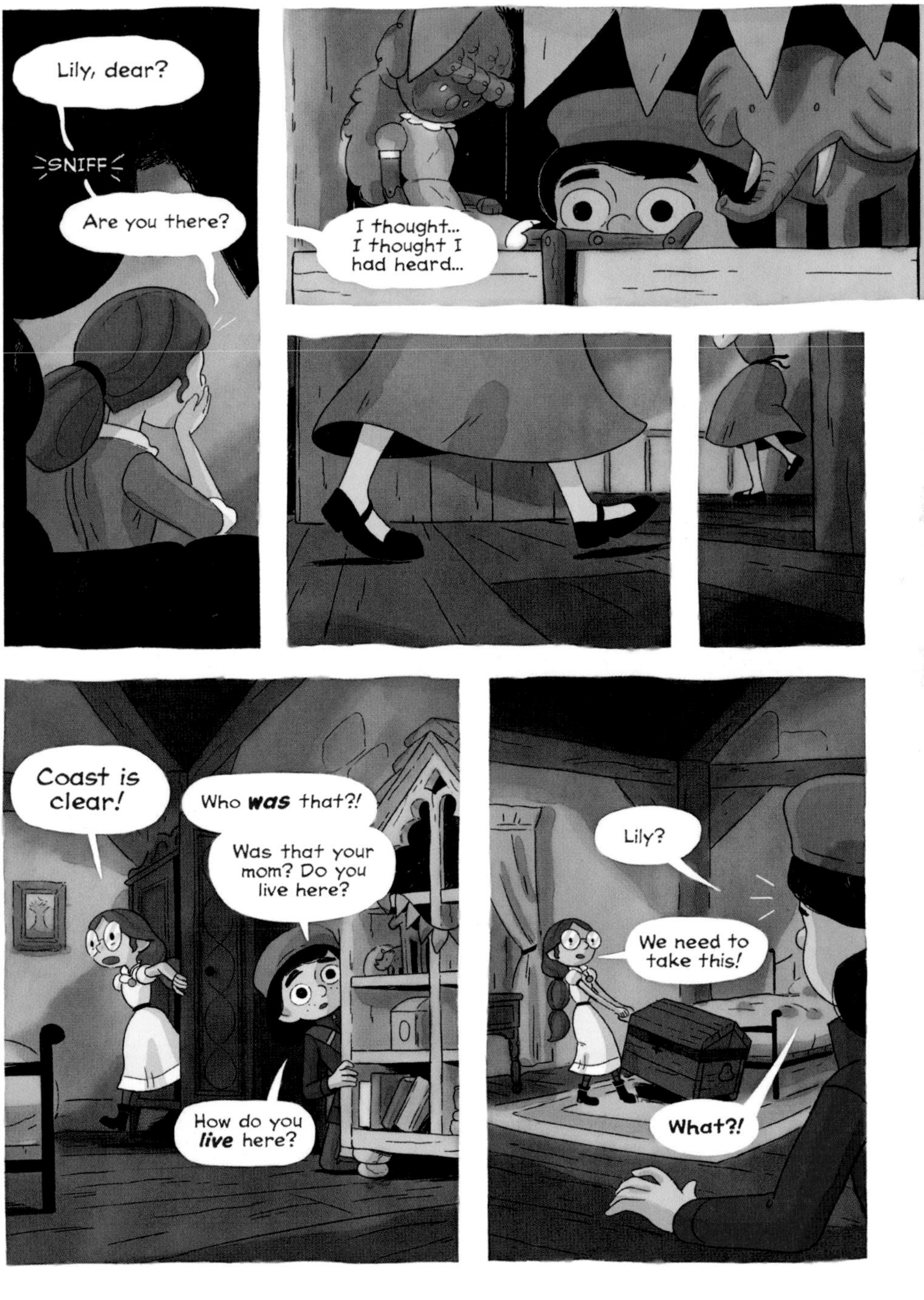
Lily, dear?
SNIFF
Are you there?
I thought... I thought I had heard...
Coast is clear!
Who **was** that?!
Was that your mom? Do you live here?
How do you **live** here?
Lily?
We need to take this!
What?!

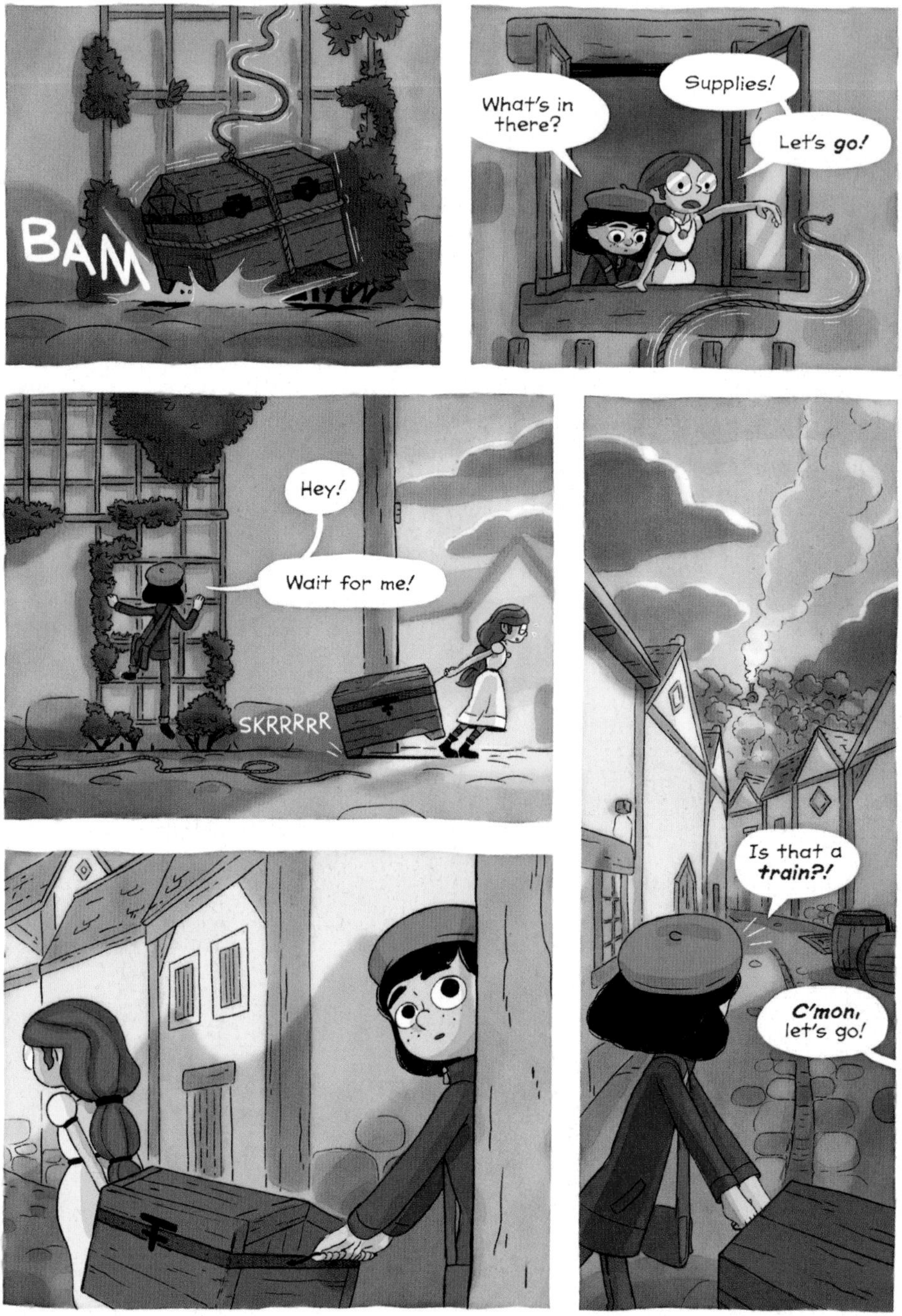
BAM
What's in there?
Supplies!
Let's **go!**
Hey!
Wait for me!
SKRRRRR
Is that a **train?!**
C'mon, let's go!

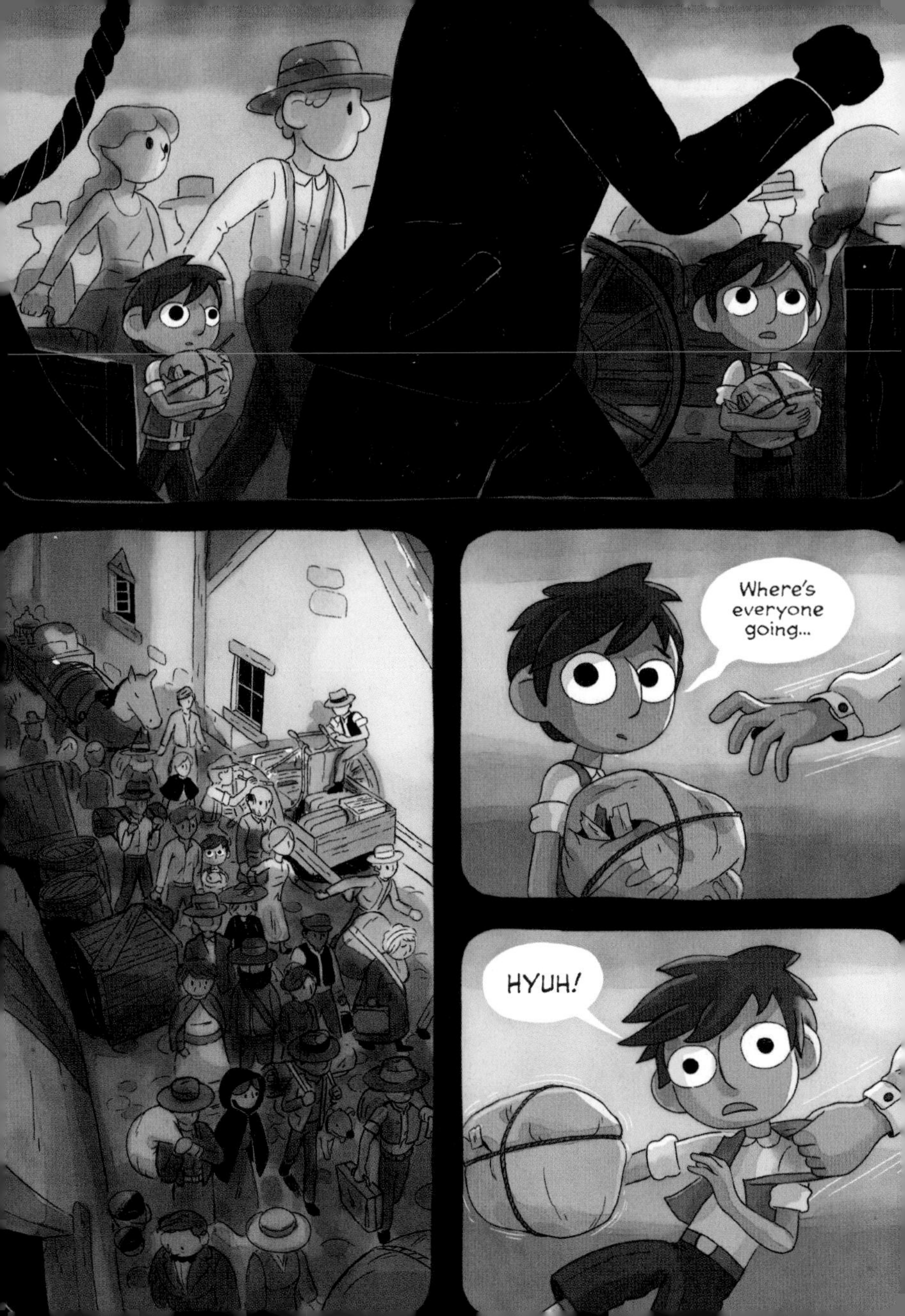
Where's everyone going...
HYUH!

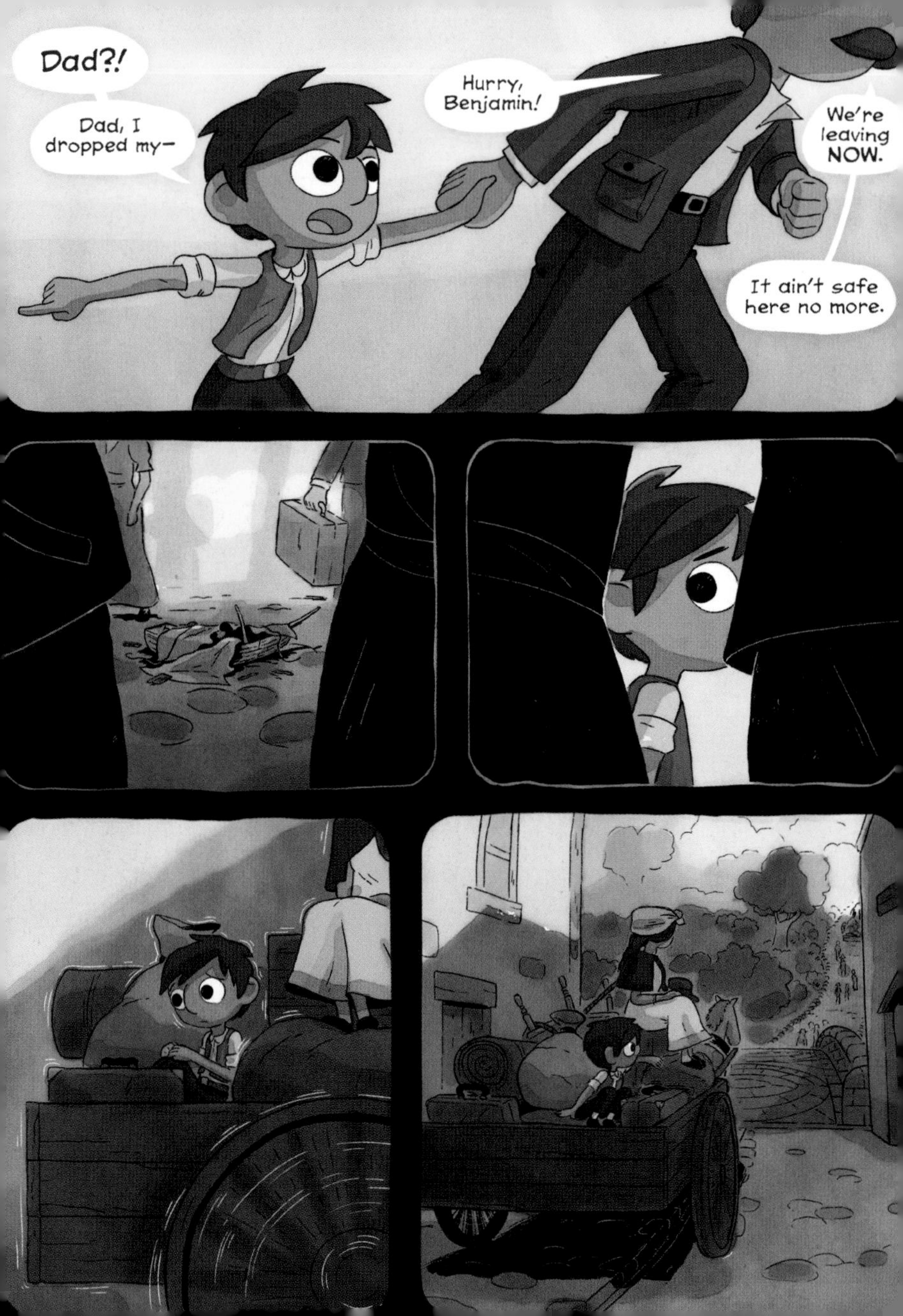
Dad?!
Dad, I dropped my—
Hurry, Benjamin!
We're leaving NOW.
It ain't safe here no more.

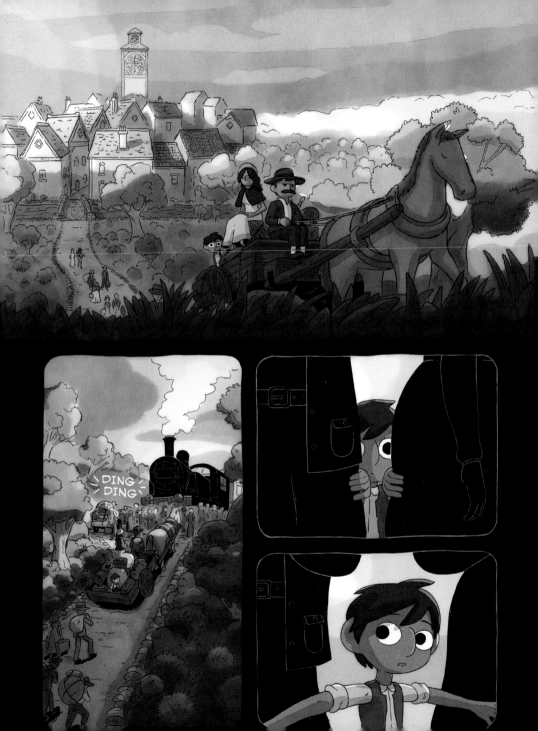

DING
DING

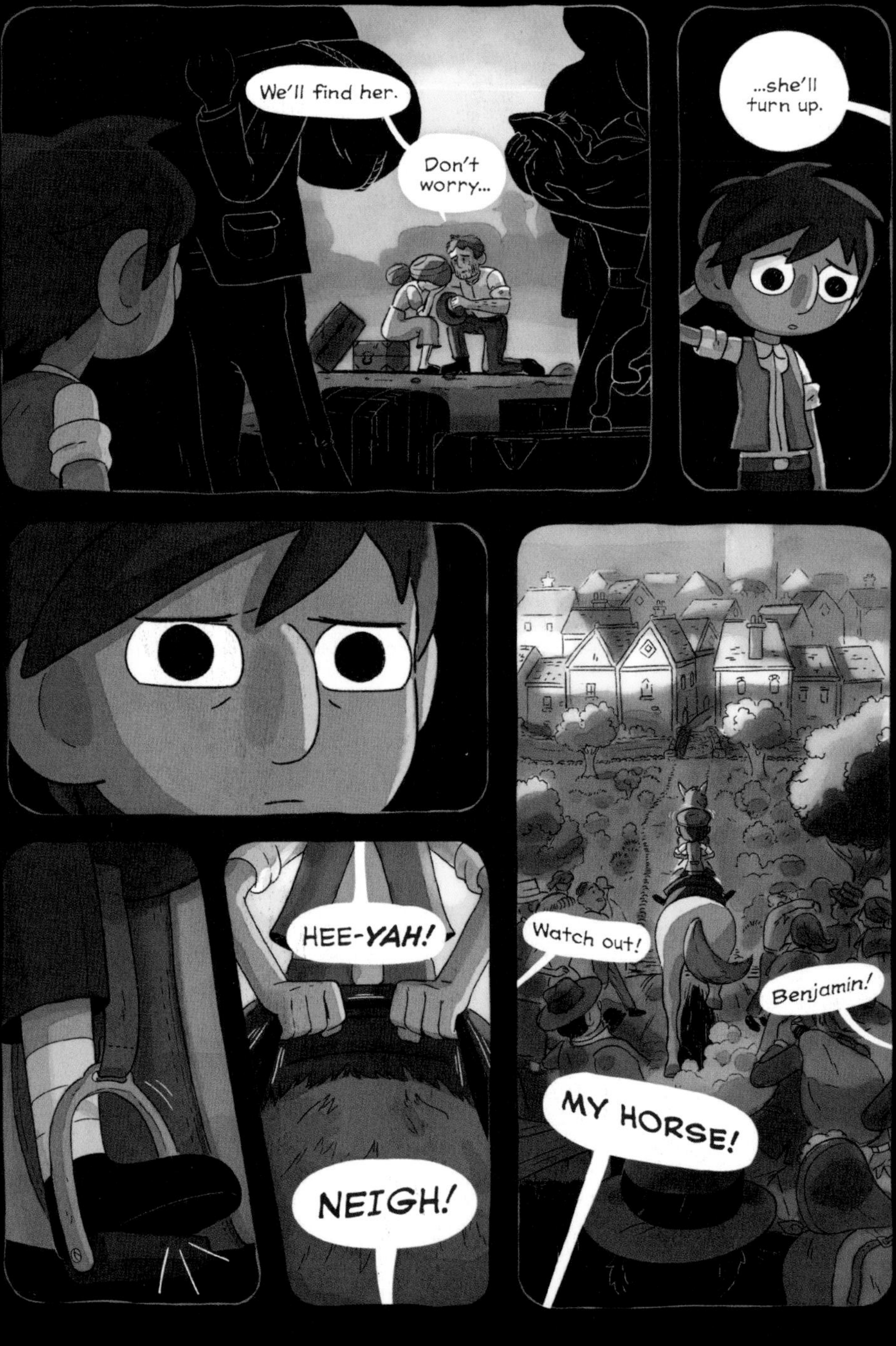
We'll find her.
Don't worry...
...she'll turn up.
HEE-YAH!
NEIGH!
Watch out!
Benjamin!
MY HORSE!

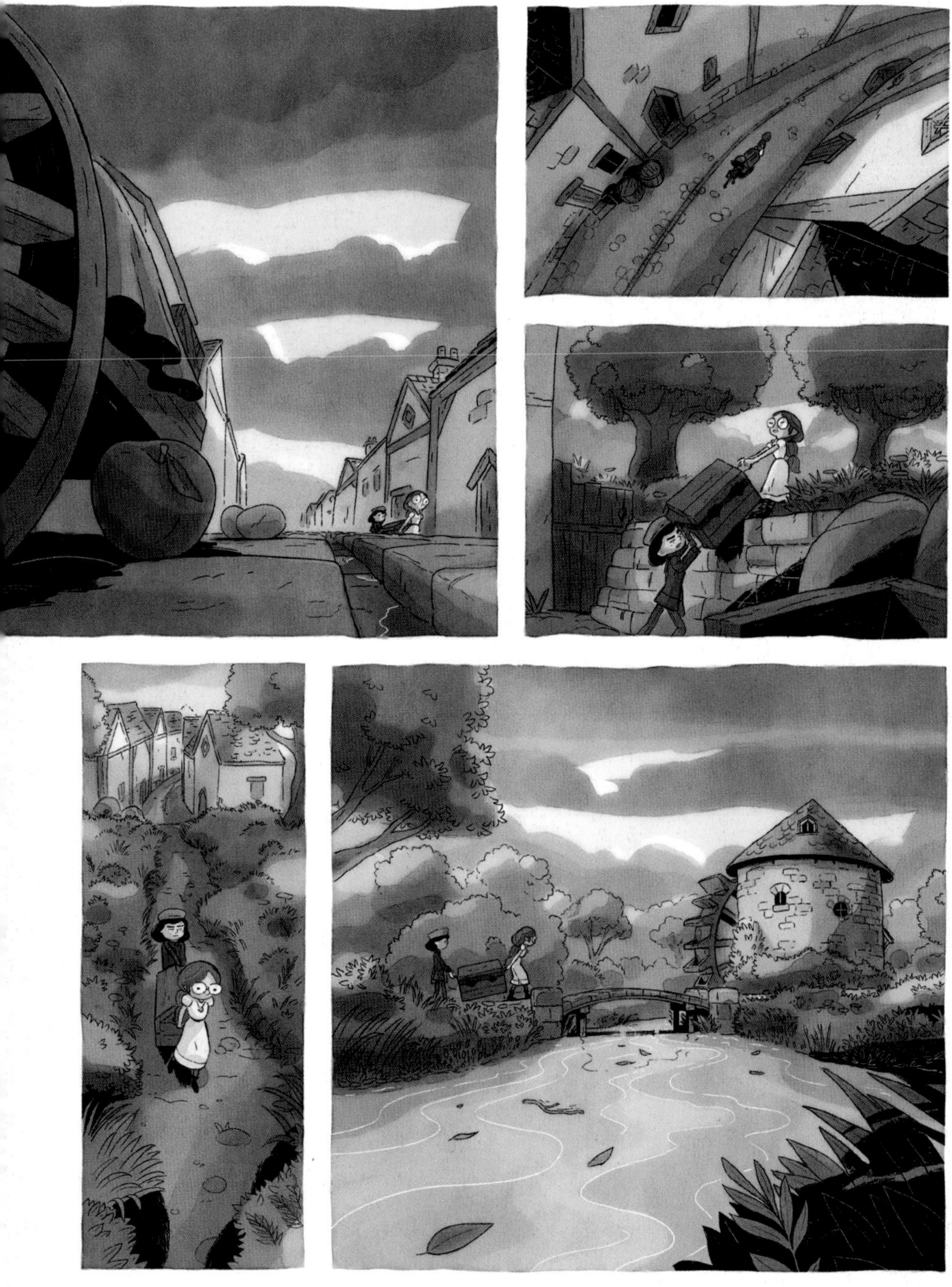

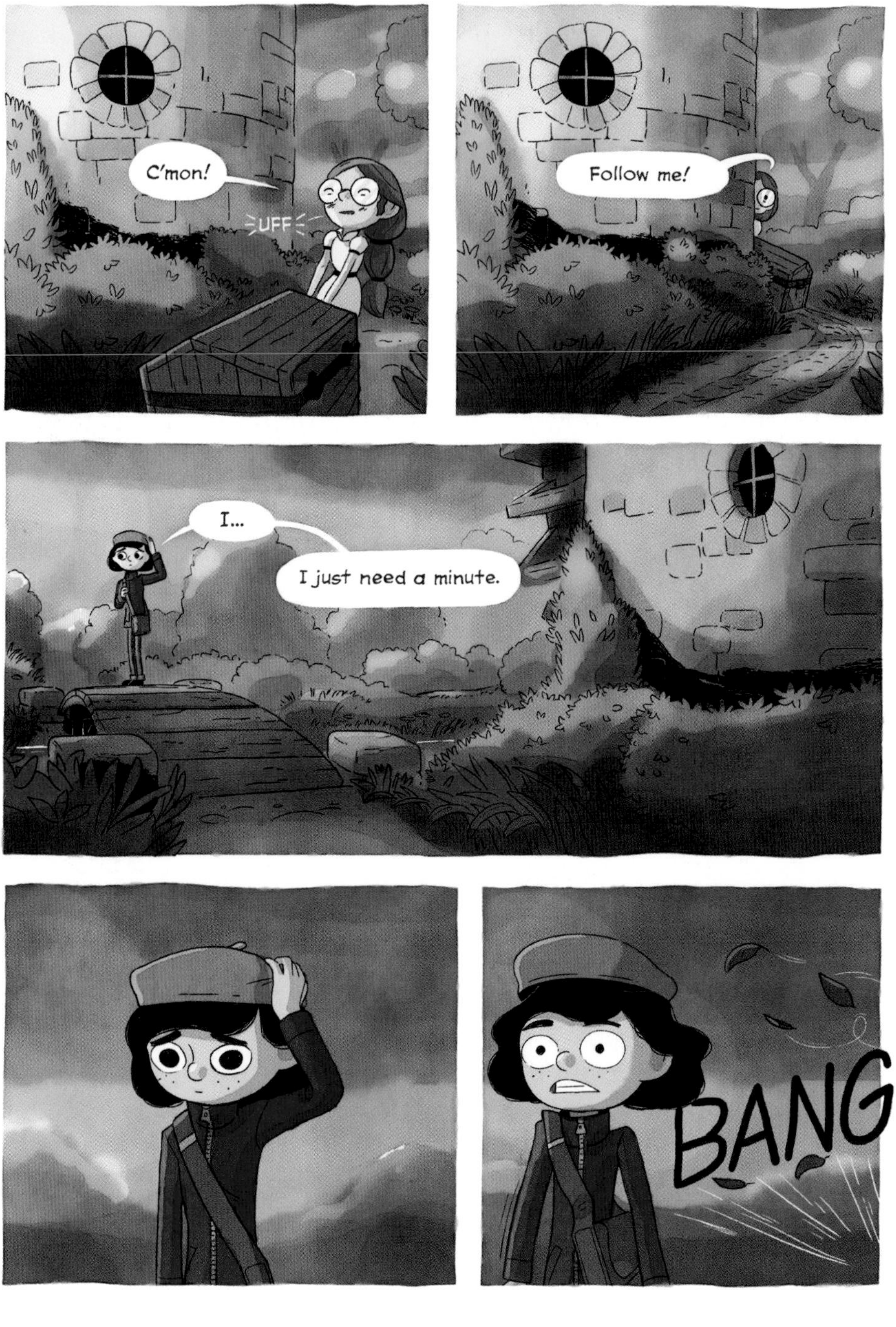

C'mon!
UFF
Follow me!
I...
I just need a minute.
BANG

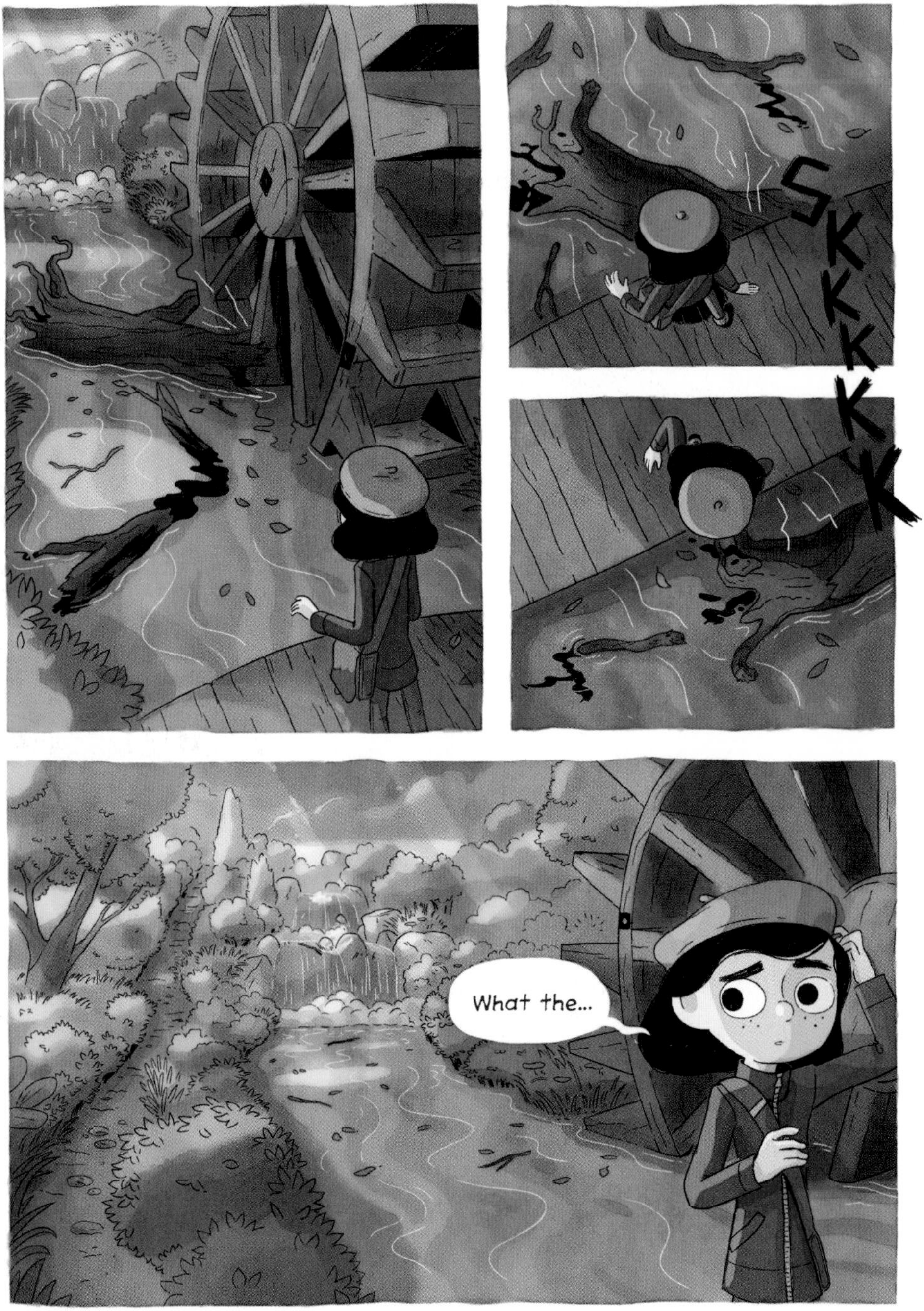
SKKKKK
What the...

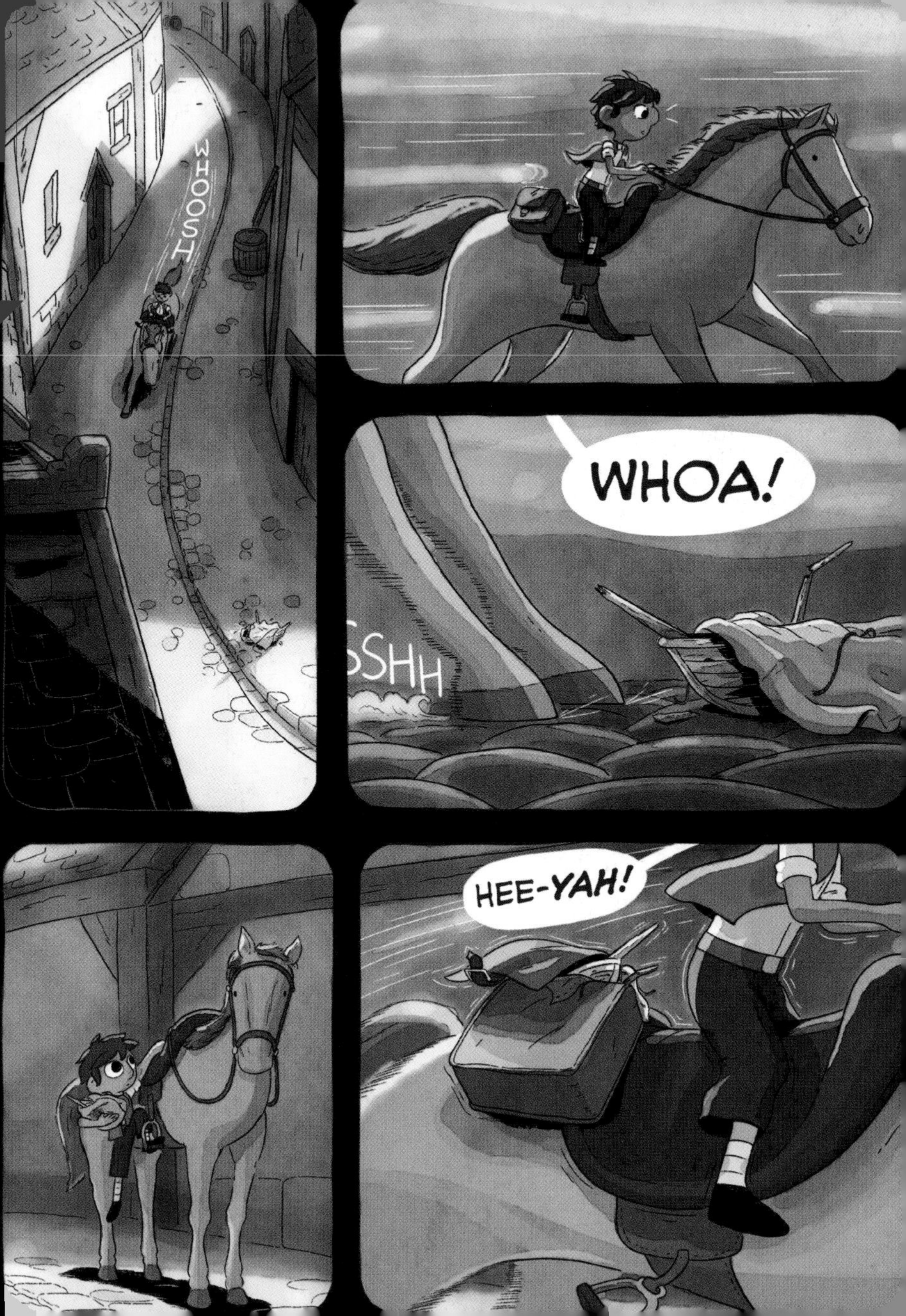
WHOOSH
WHOA!
SSHH
HEE-YAH!

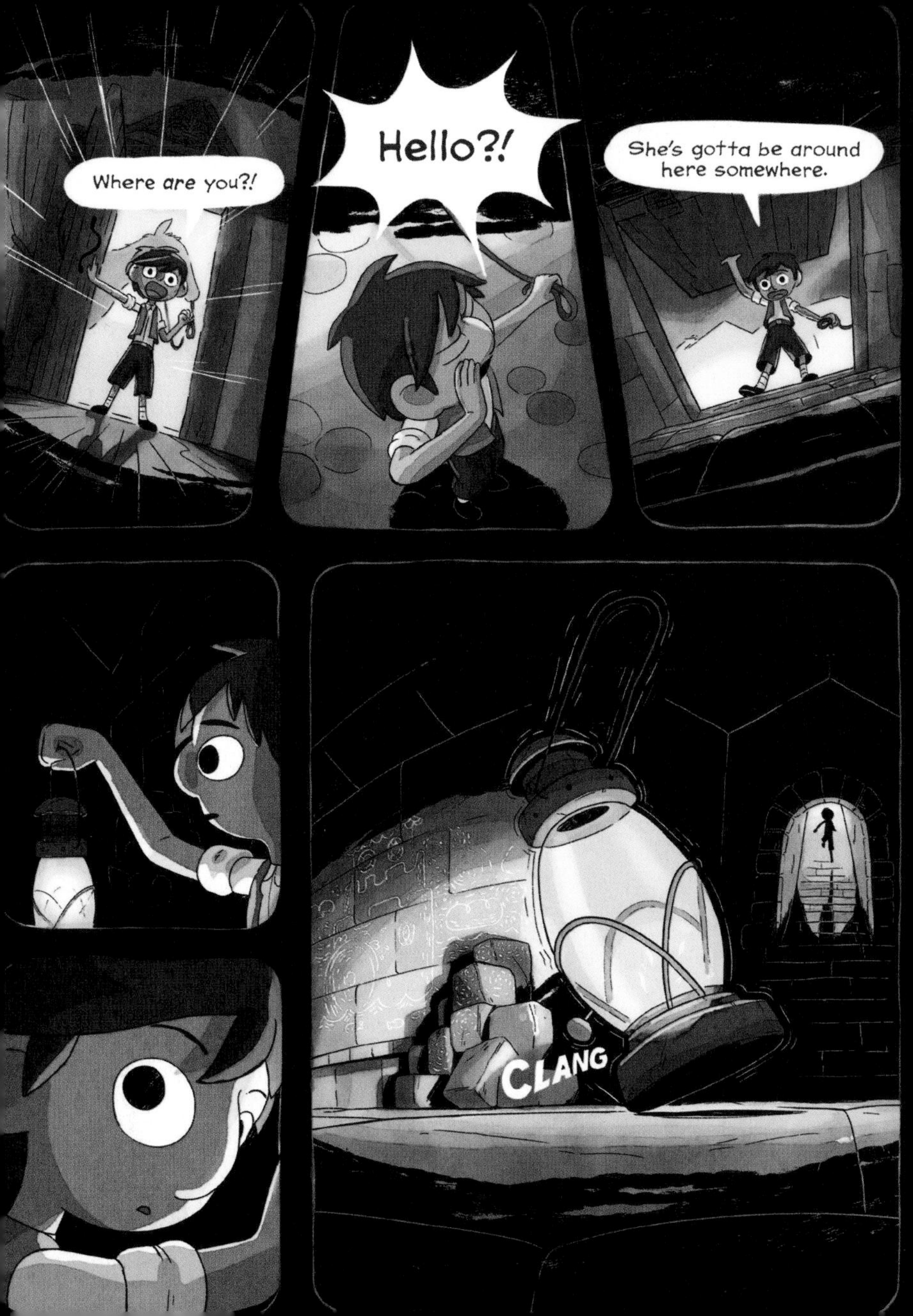
Where are you?!
Hello?!
She's gotta be around here somewhere.
CLANG

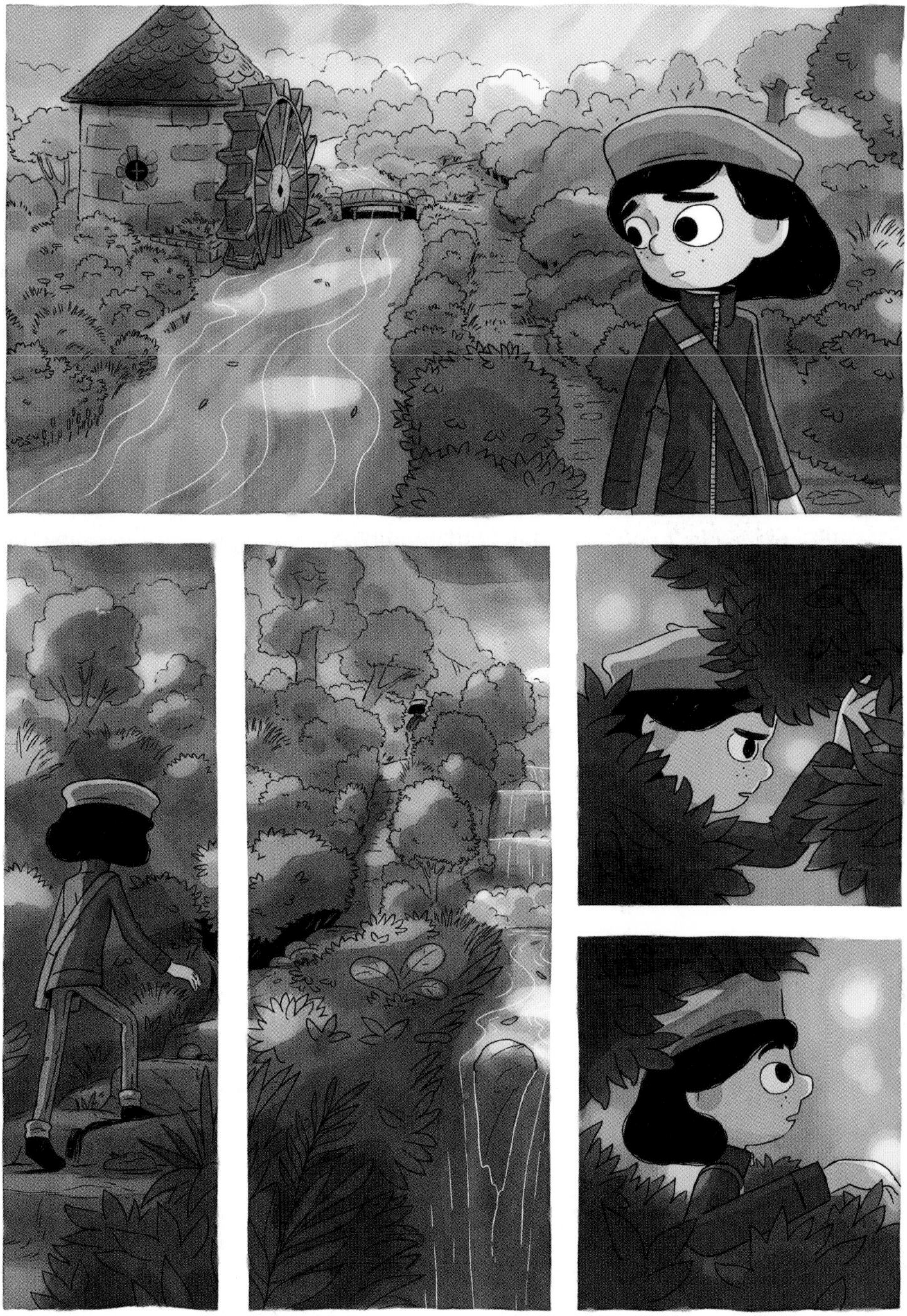

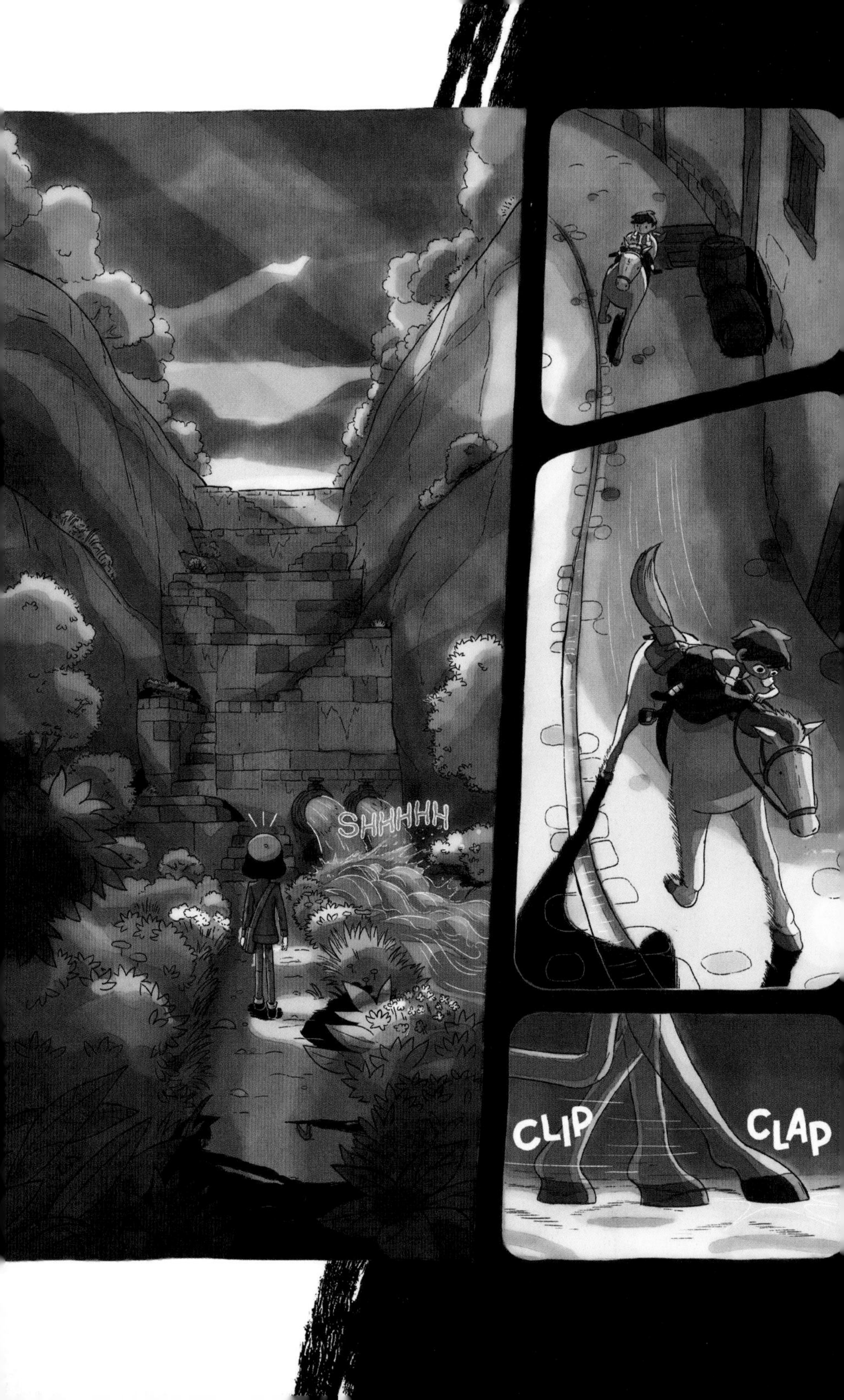
SHHHHH
CLIP
CLAP

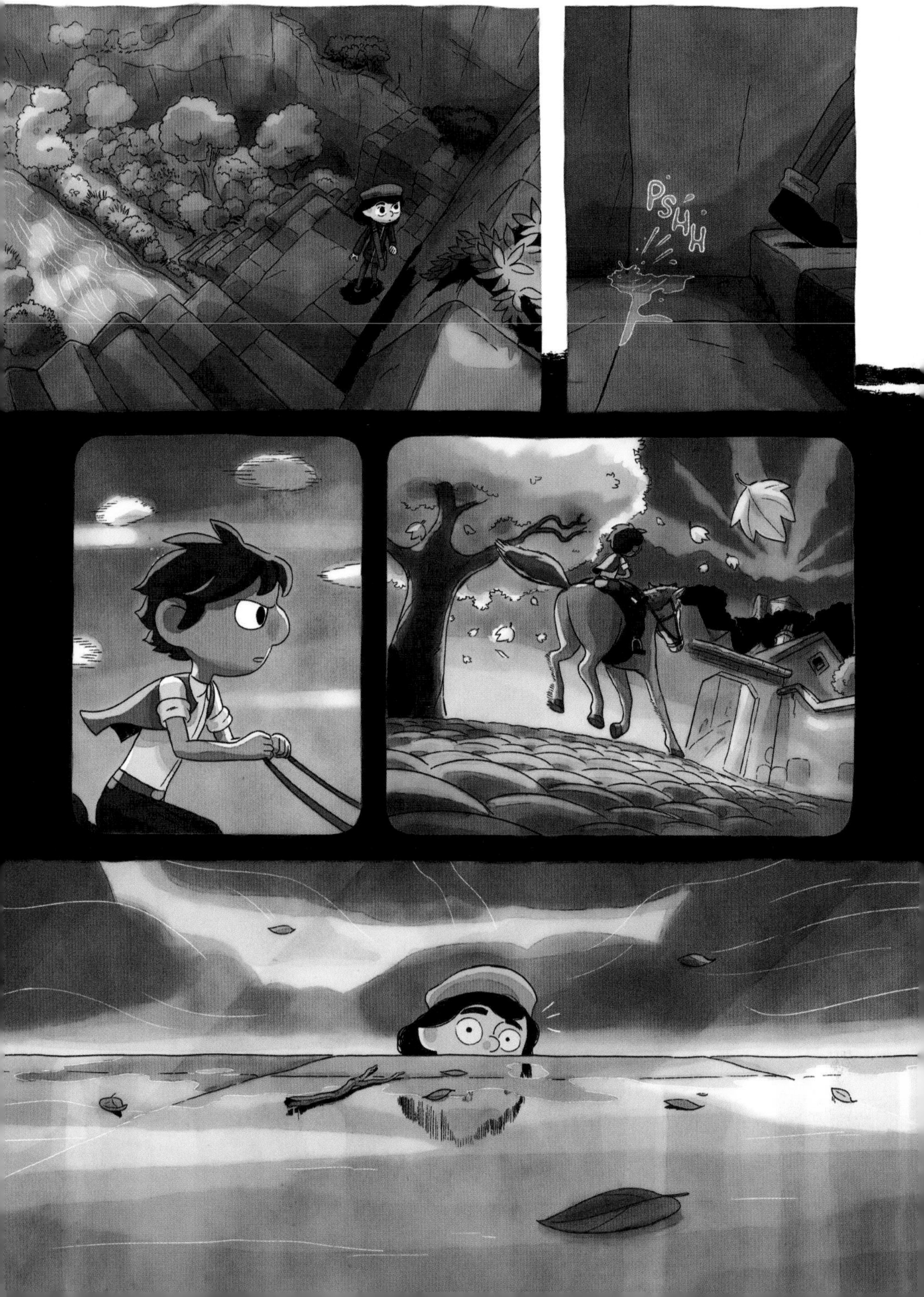
PSHH

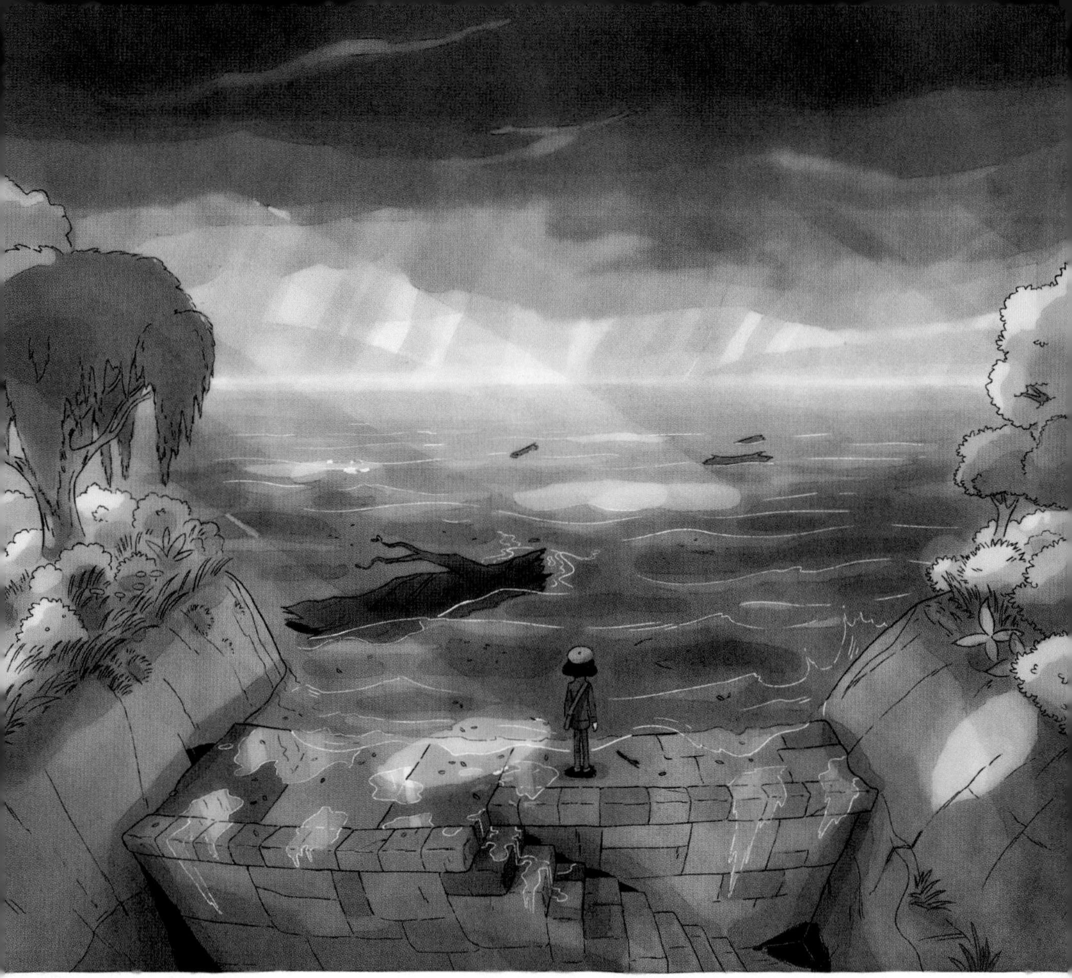

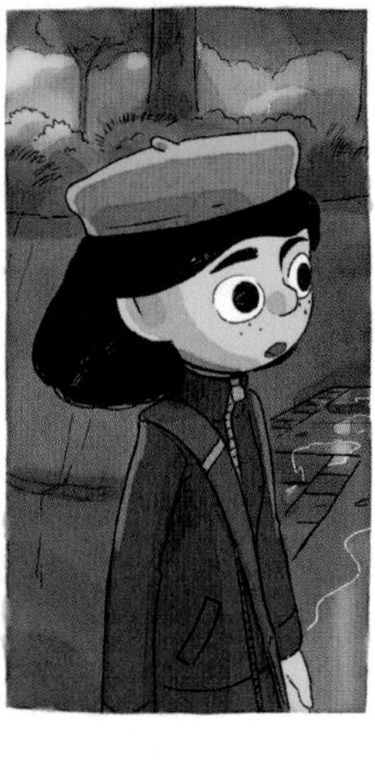

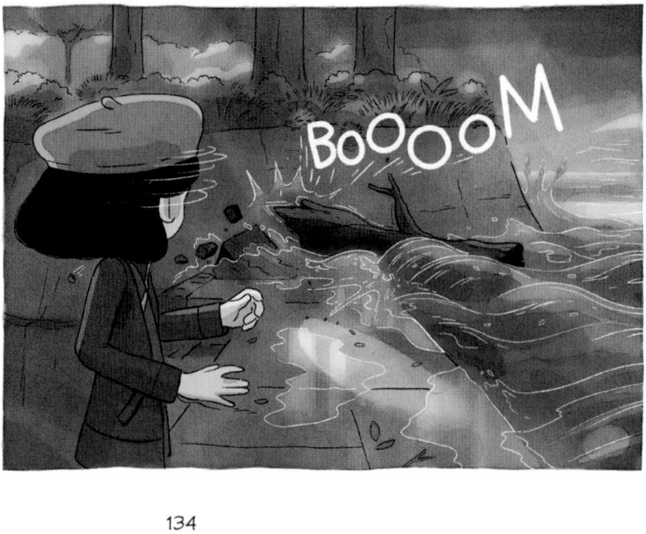
BOOOOM

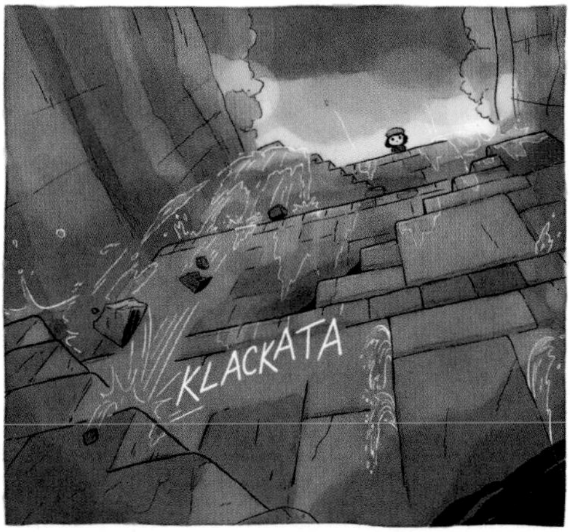
KLACKATA

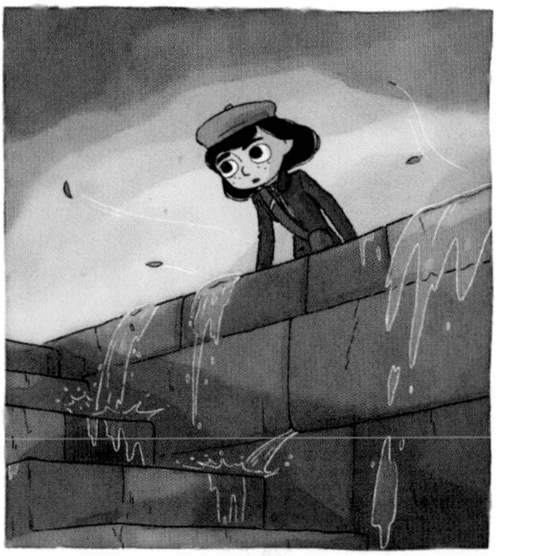

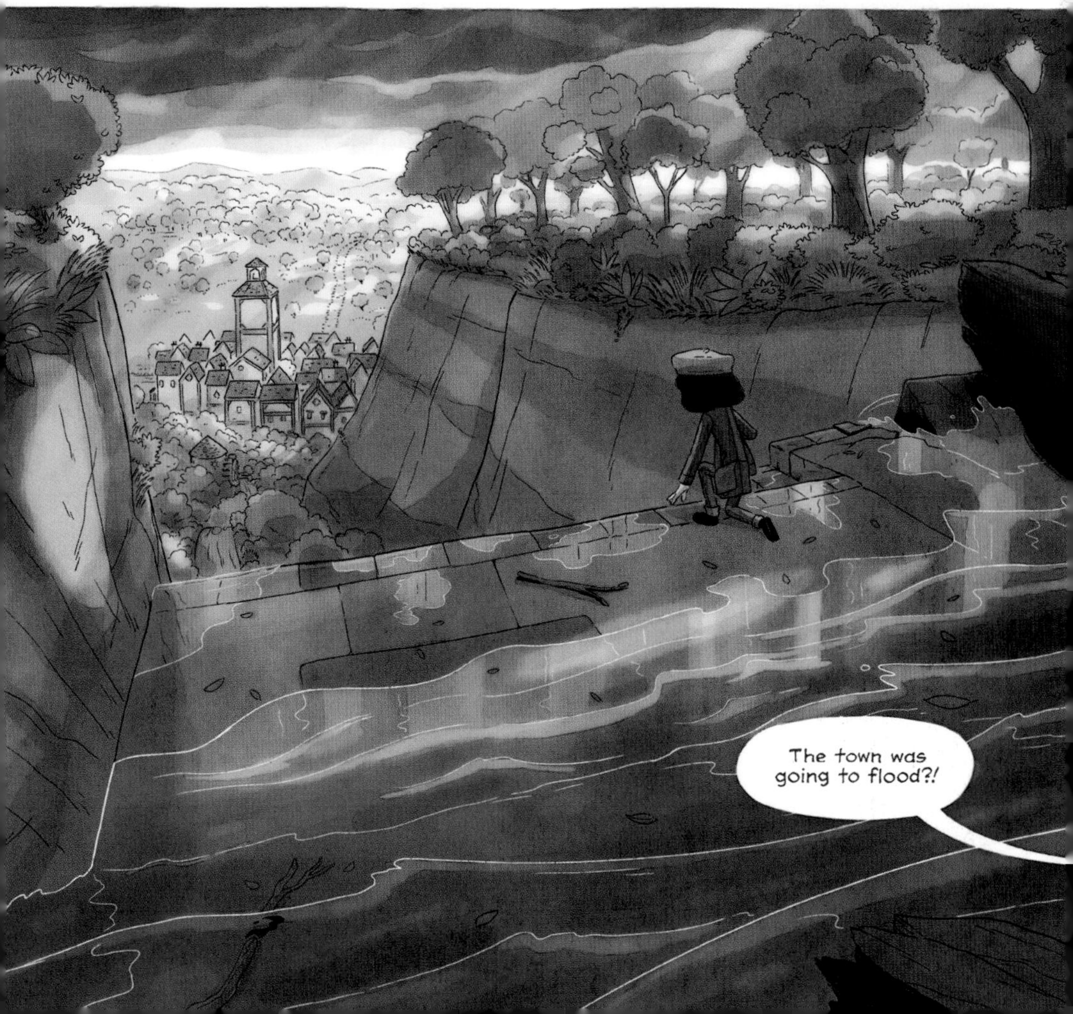
The town was
going to flood?!

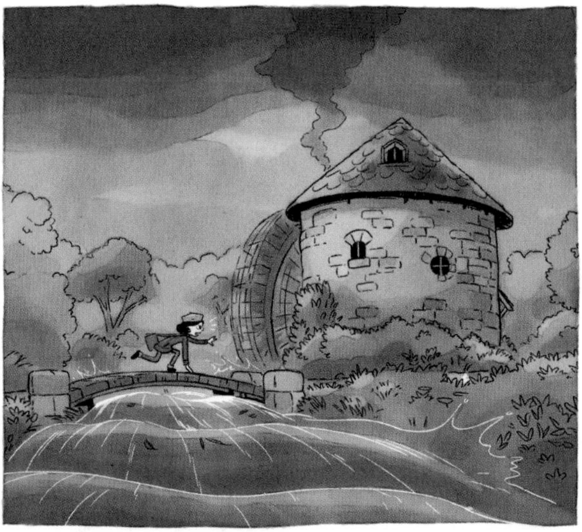

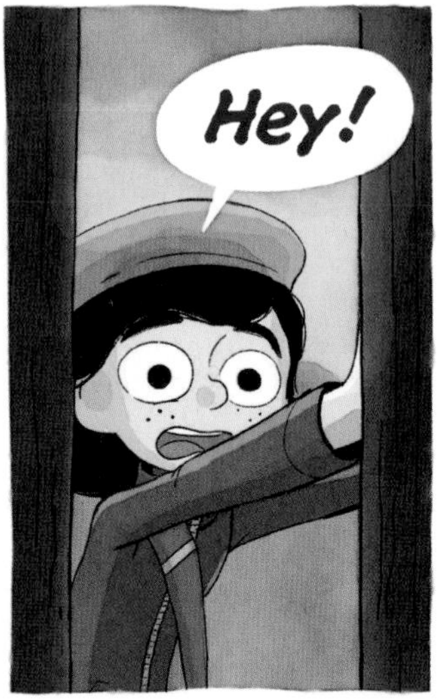
Hey!

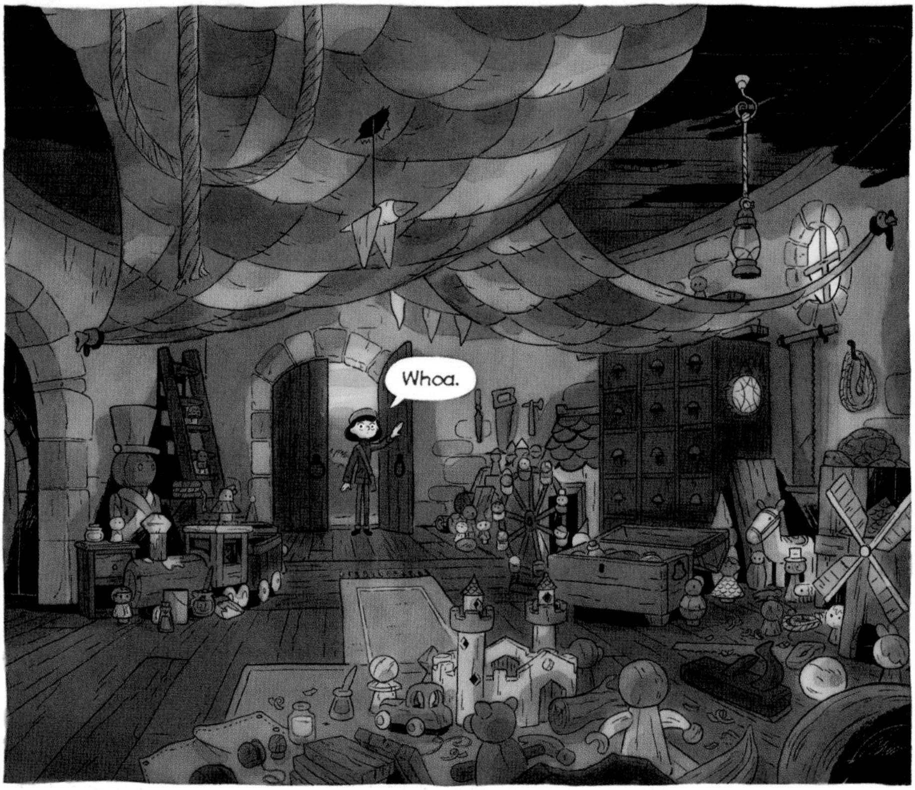
Whoa.

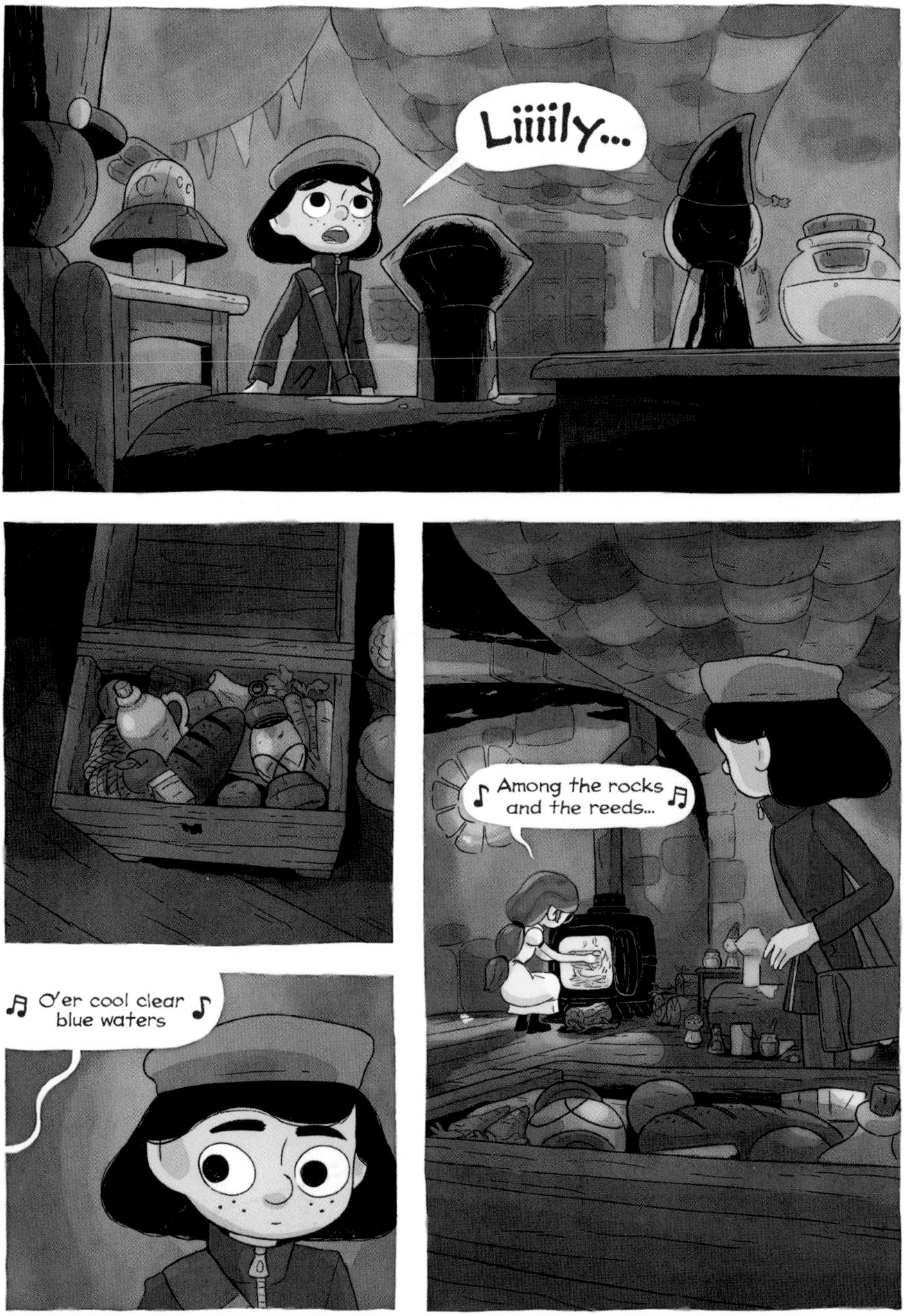
Liiiily...
O'er cool clear blue waters
Among the rocks and the reeds...

140

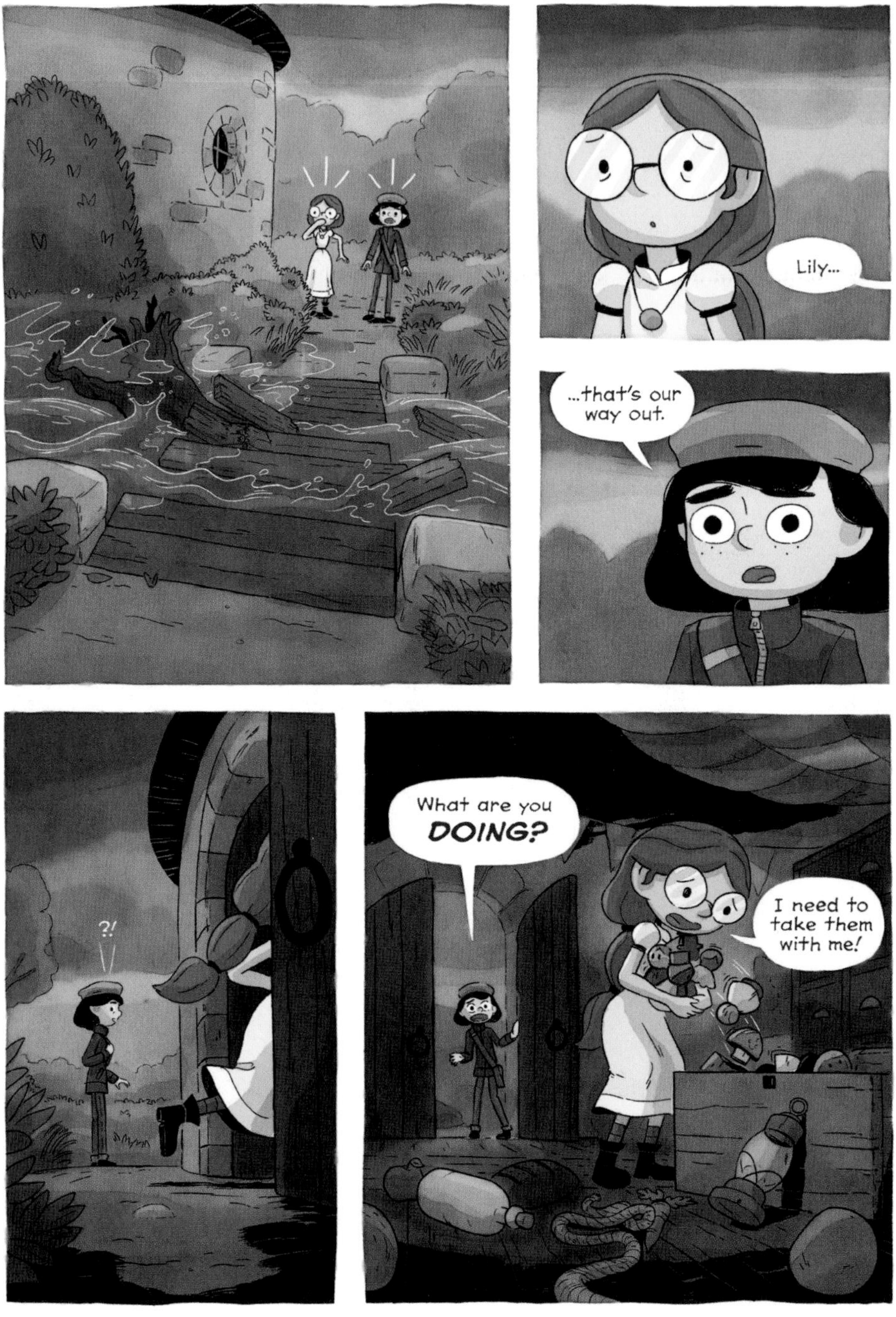

Lily...
...that's our way out.
?!
What are you DOING?
I need to take them with me!

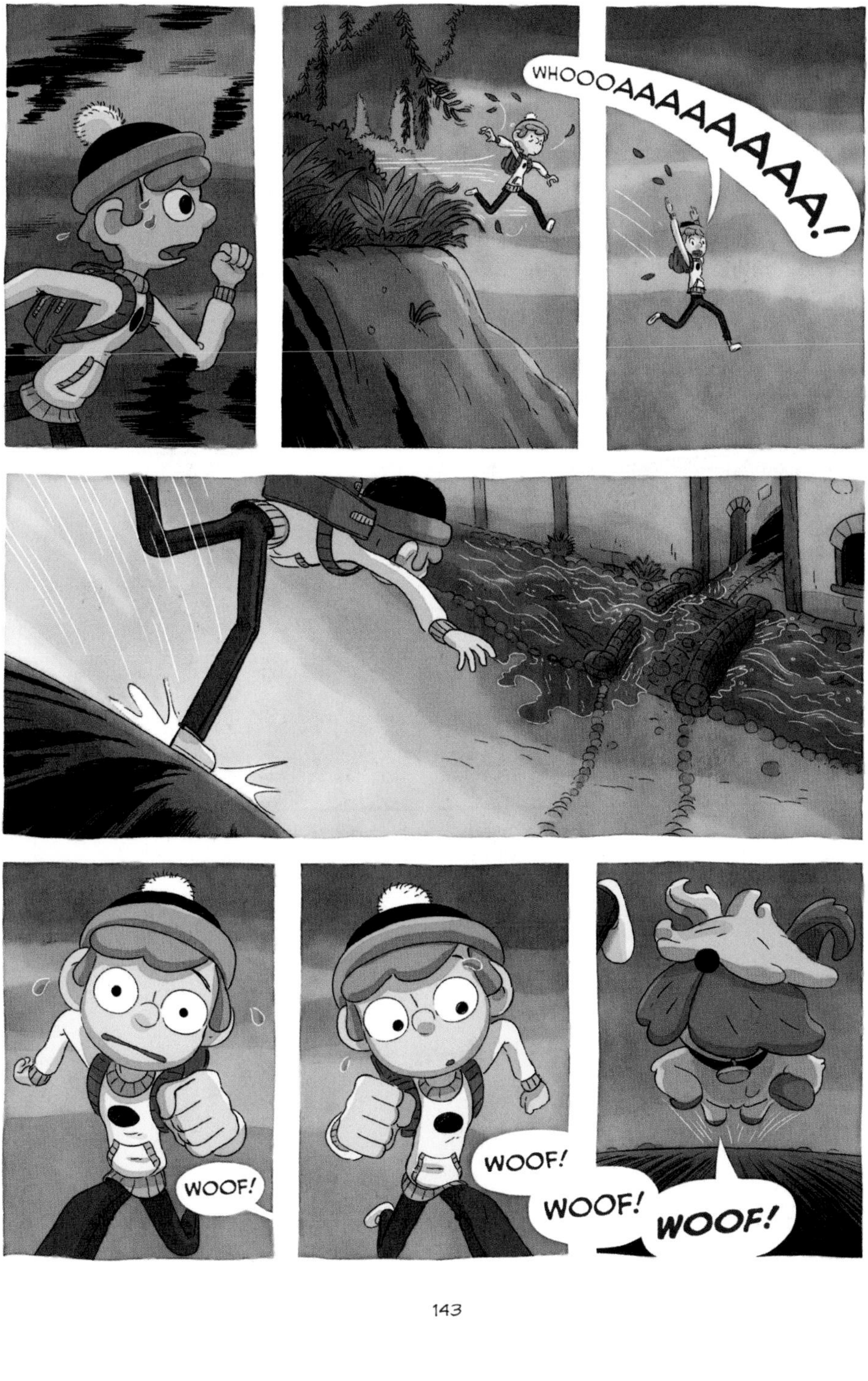
WHOOOAAAAAAAAAA!
WOOF!
WOOF!
WOOF!
WOOF!

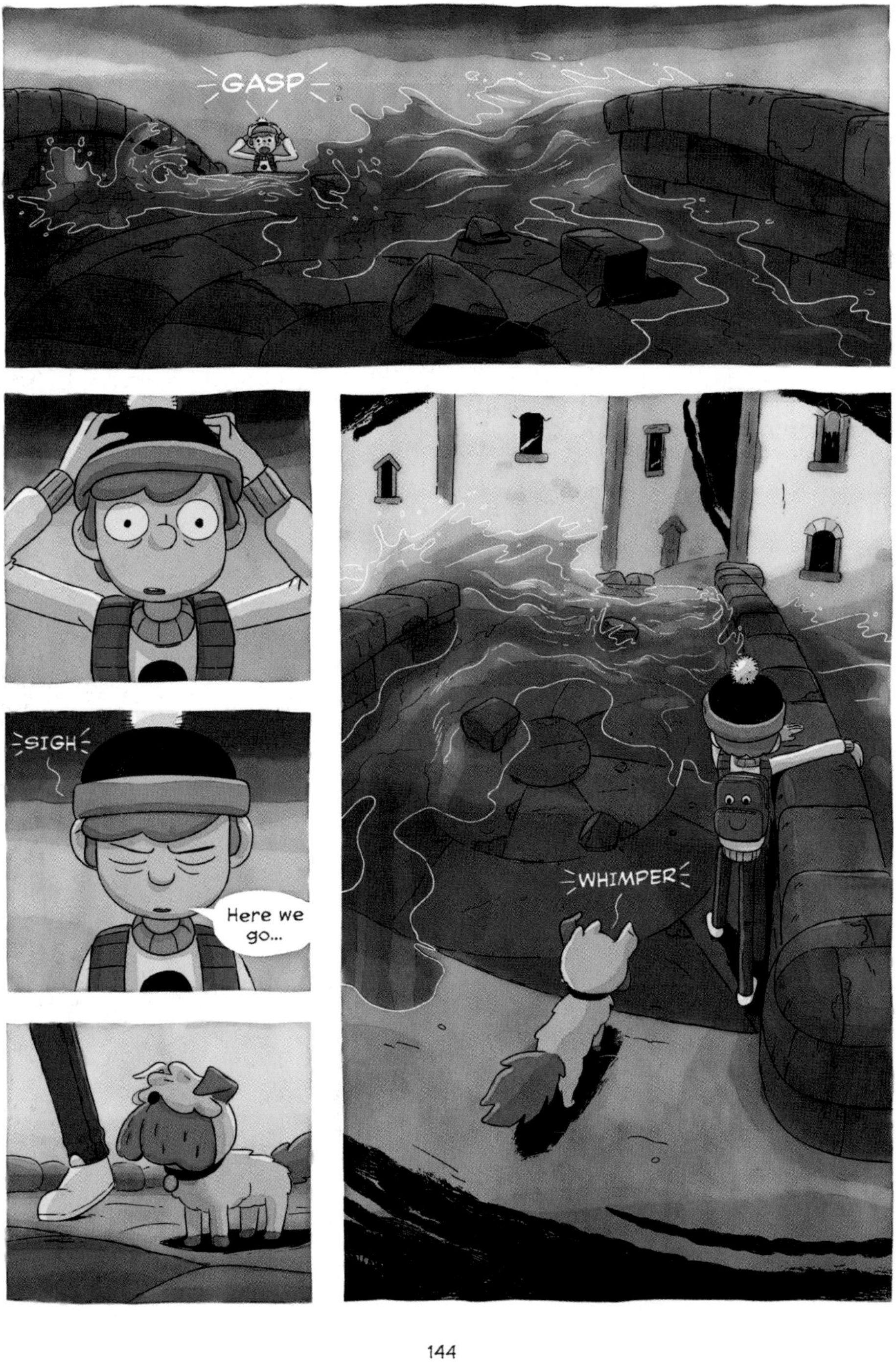
GASP
SIGH
Here we go...
WHIMPER

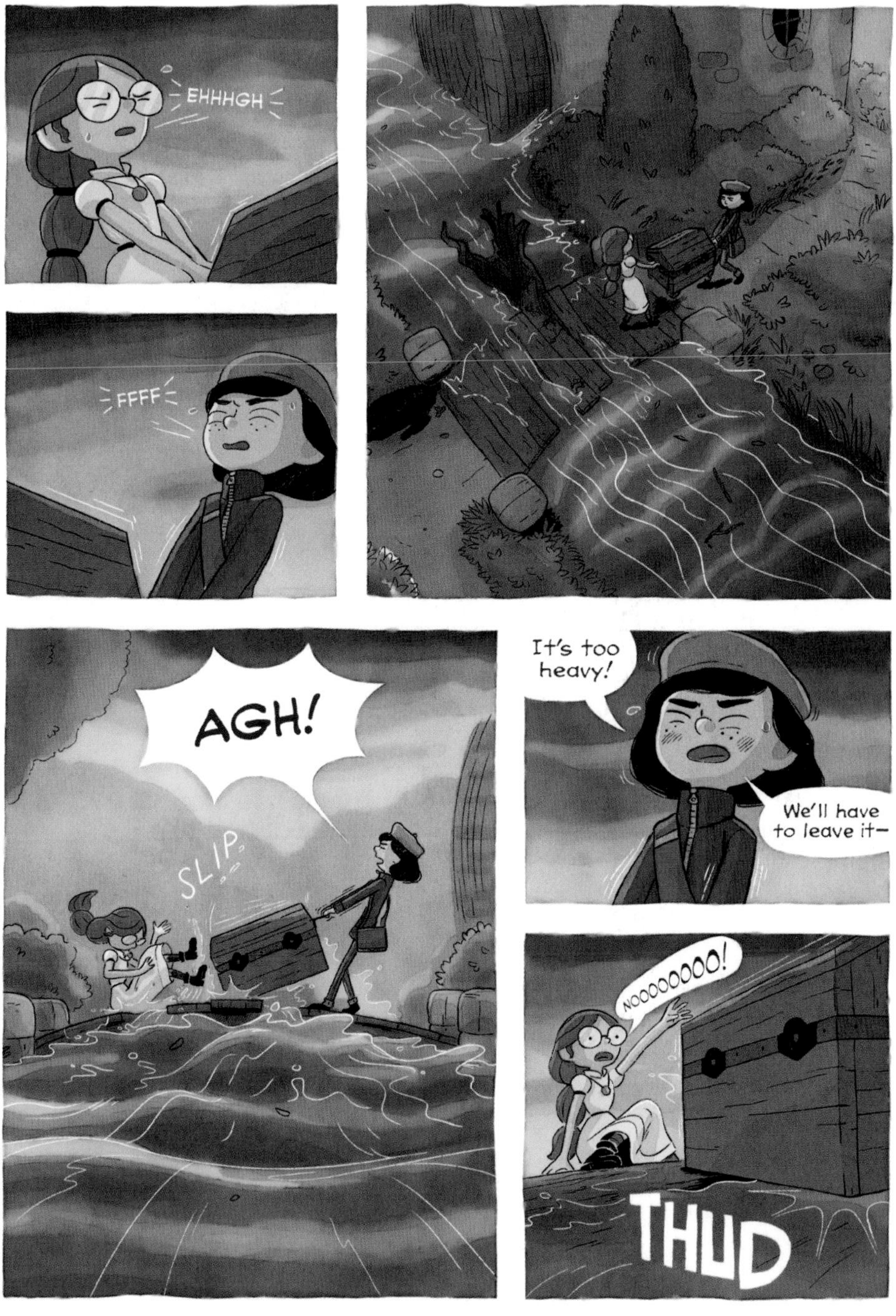
EHHHGH
FFFF
AGH!
SLIP
It's too heavy!
We'll have to leave it—
NOOOOOOOO!
THUD

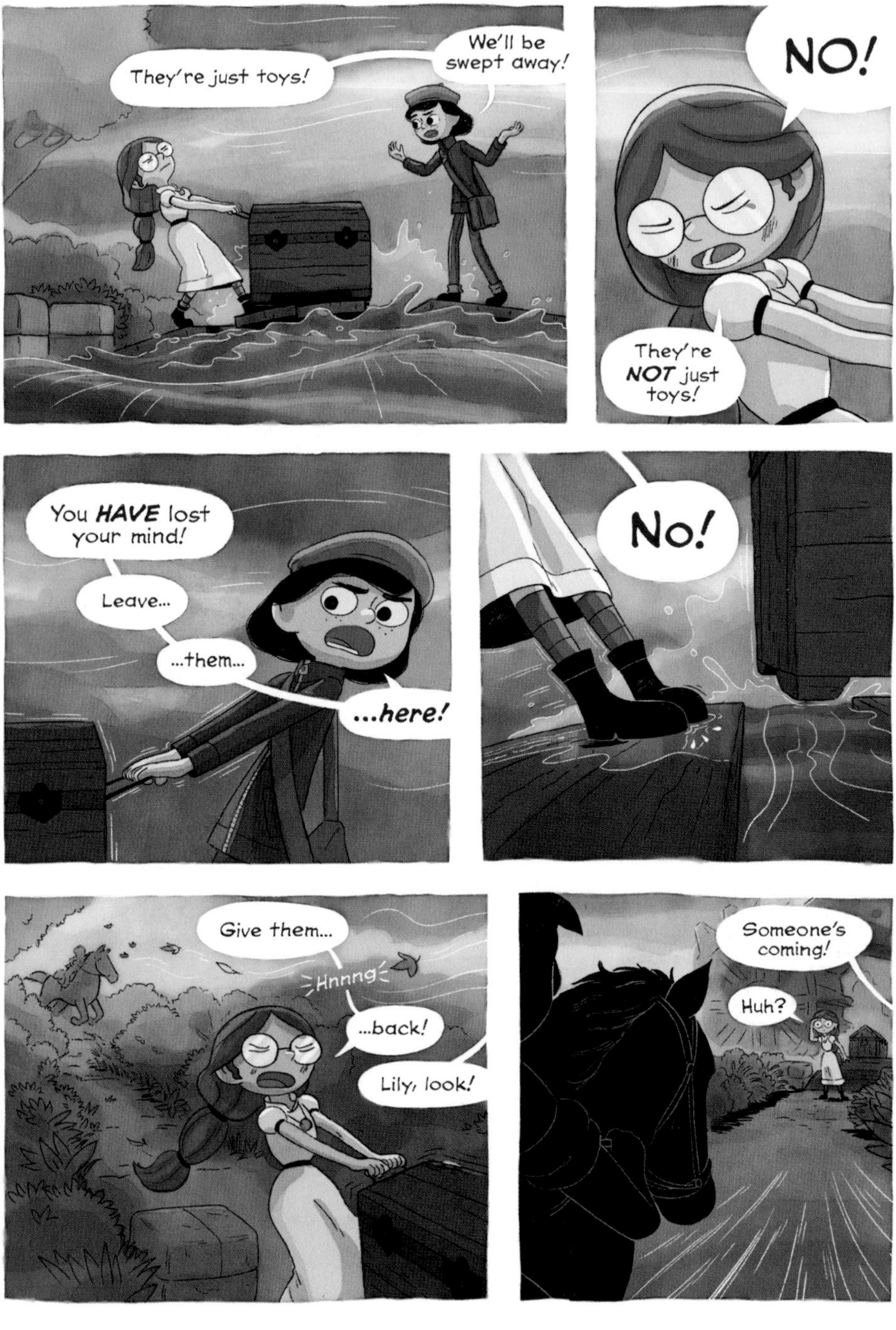
They're just toys!
We'll be swept away!
NO!
They're NOT just toys!
You HAVE lost your mind!
Leave...
...them...
...here!
No!
Give them...
Hnnng
...back!
Lily, look!
Someone's coming!
Huh?

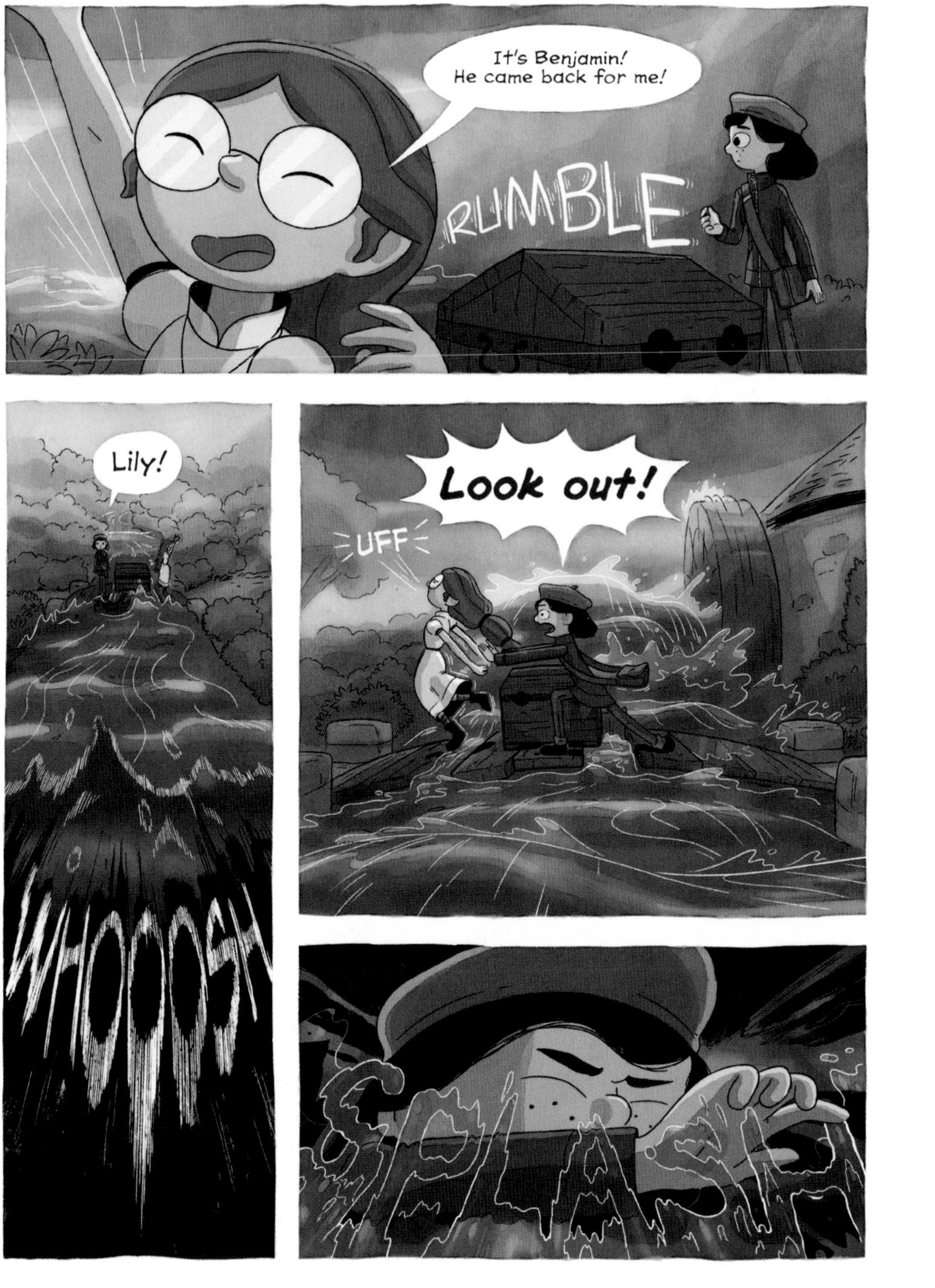
It's Benjamin! He came back for me!
RUMBLE
Lily!
WHOOSH
Look out!
UFF
SPLASH

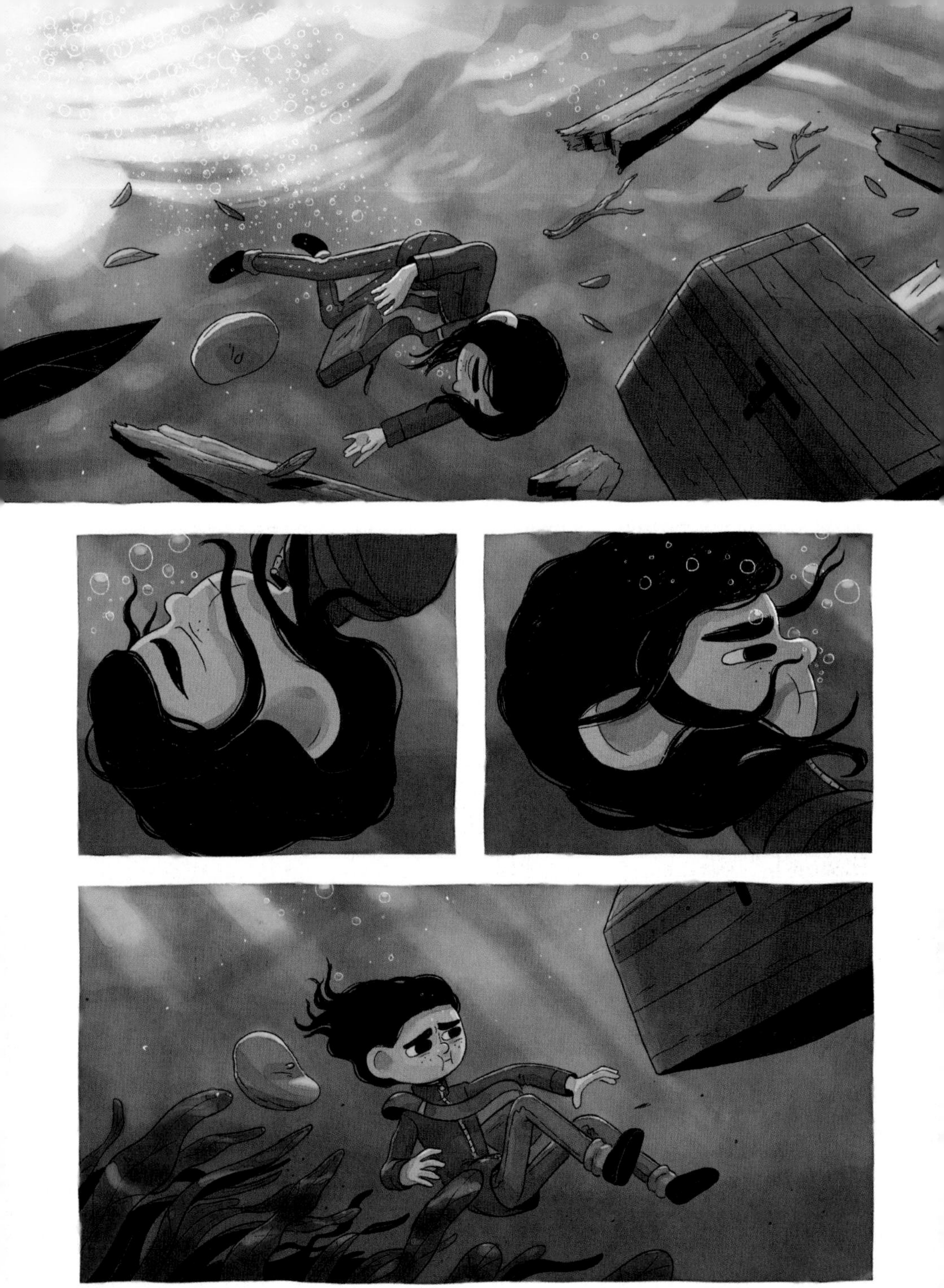

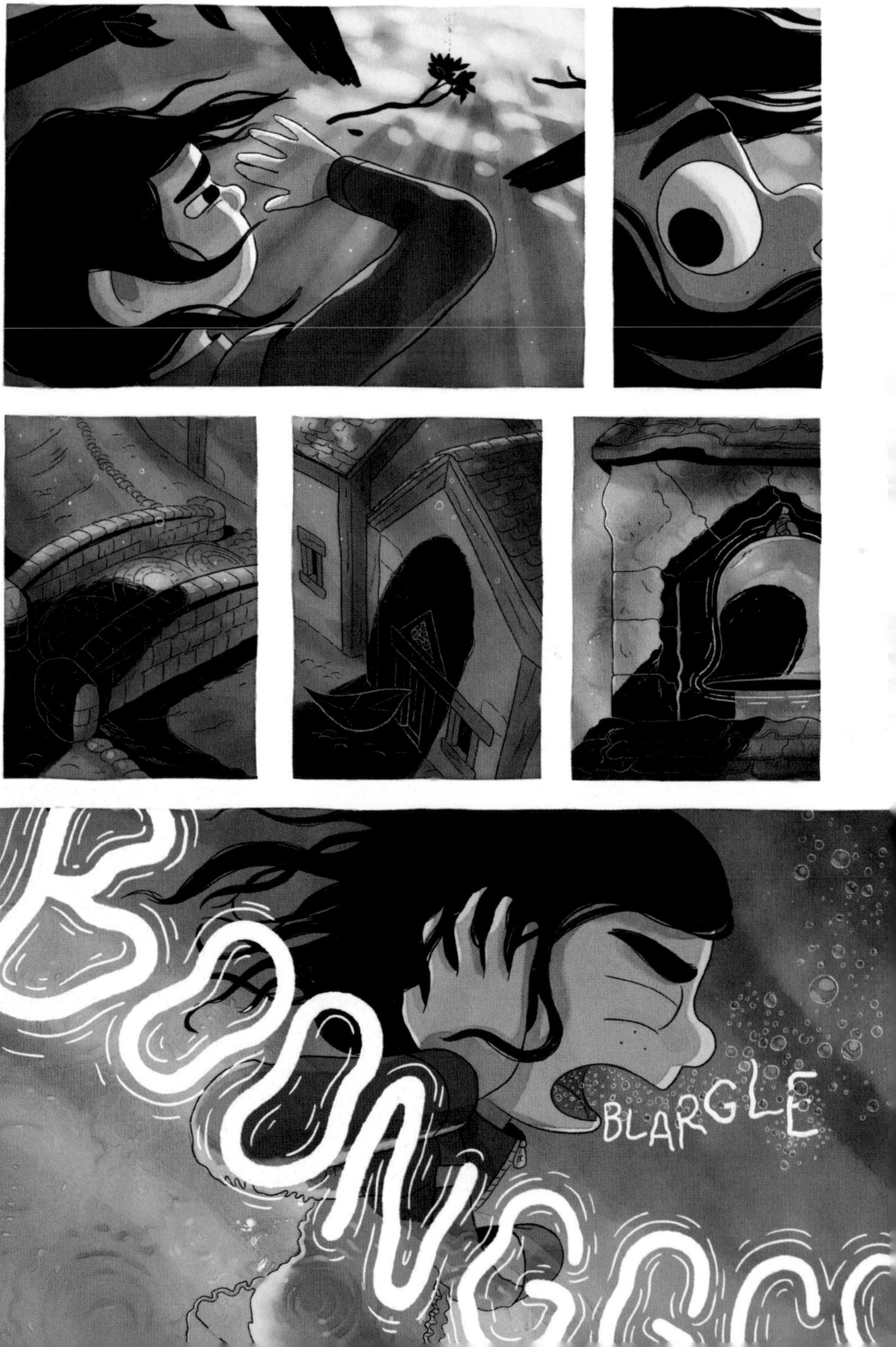
BLARGLE

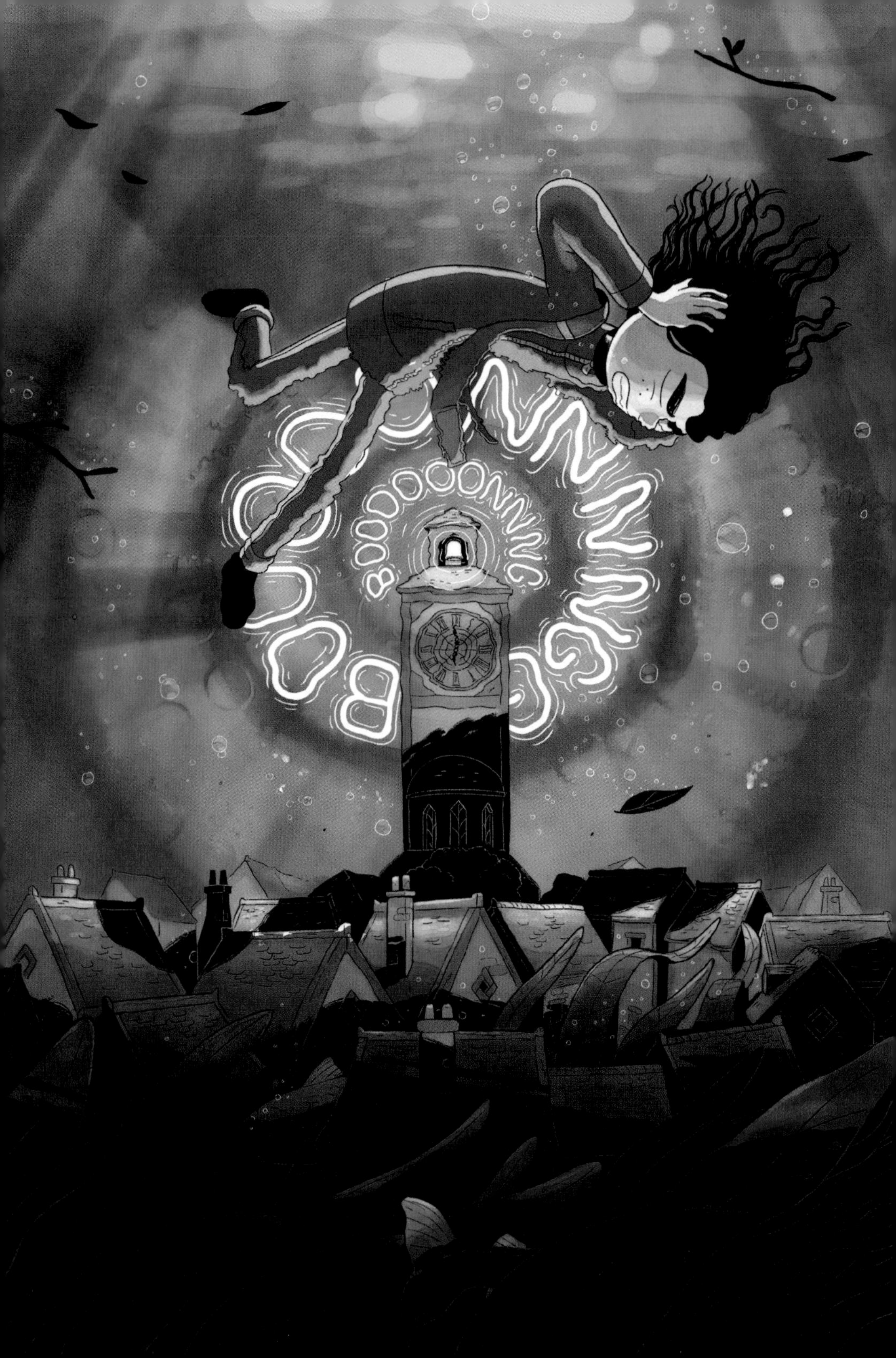
BOOOONNNNG
BOOOOONNNG

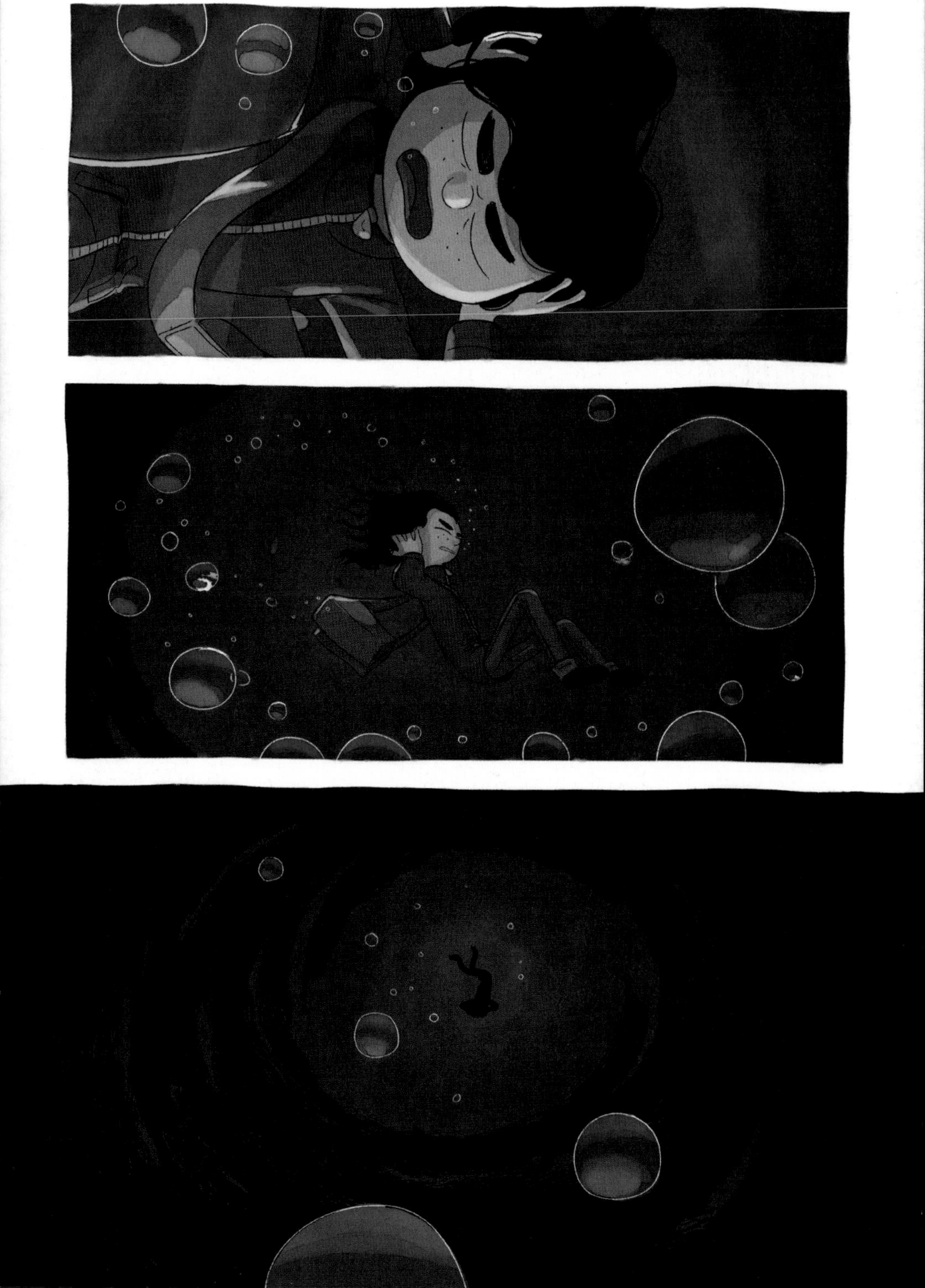

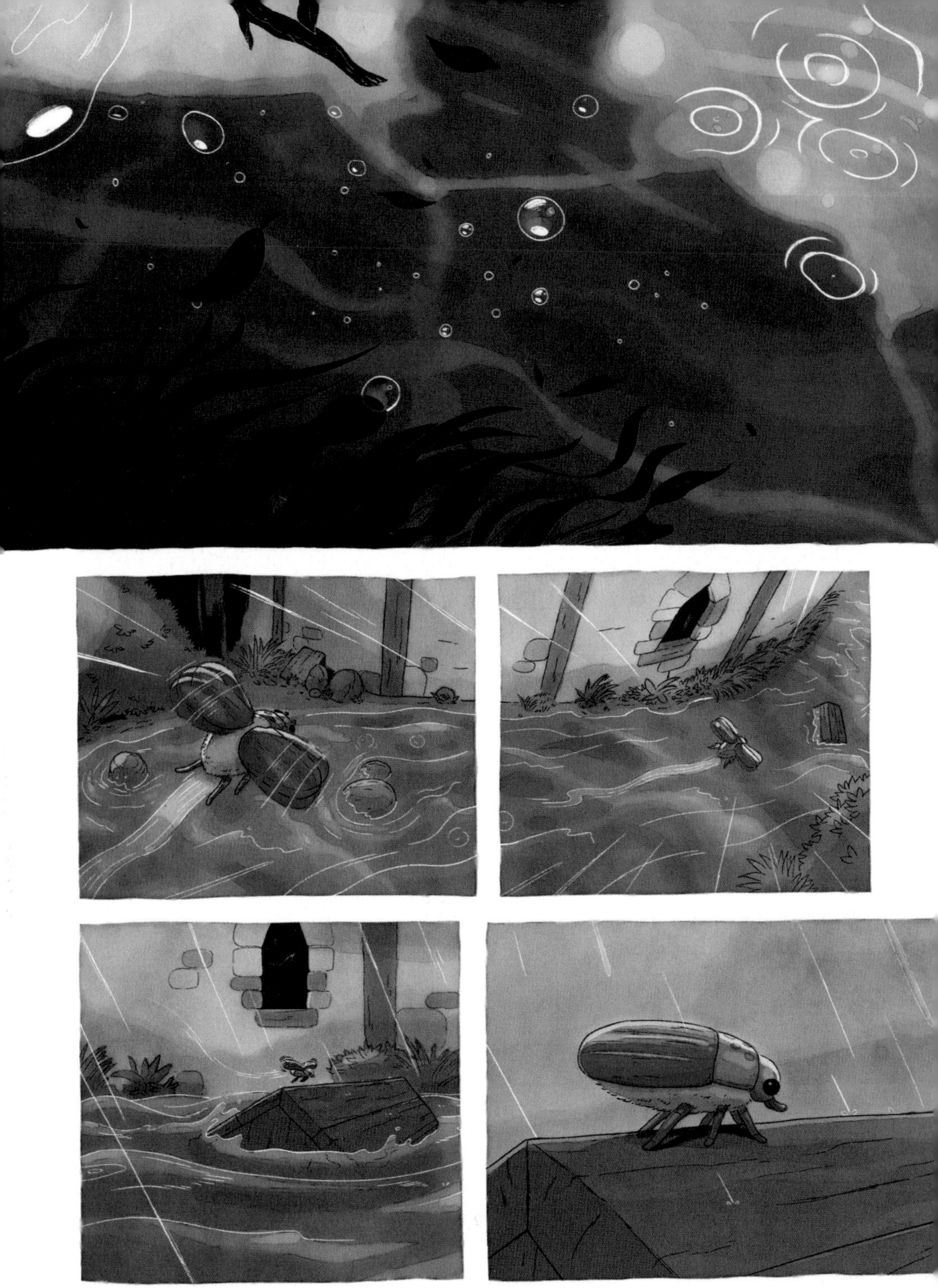

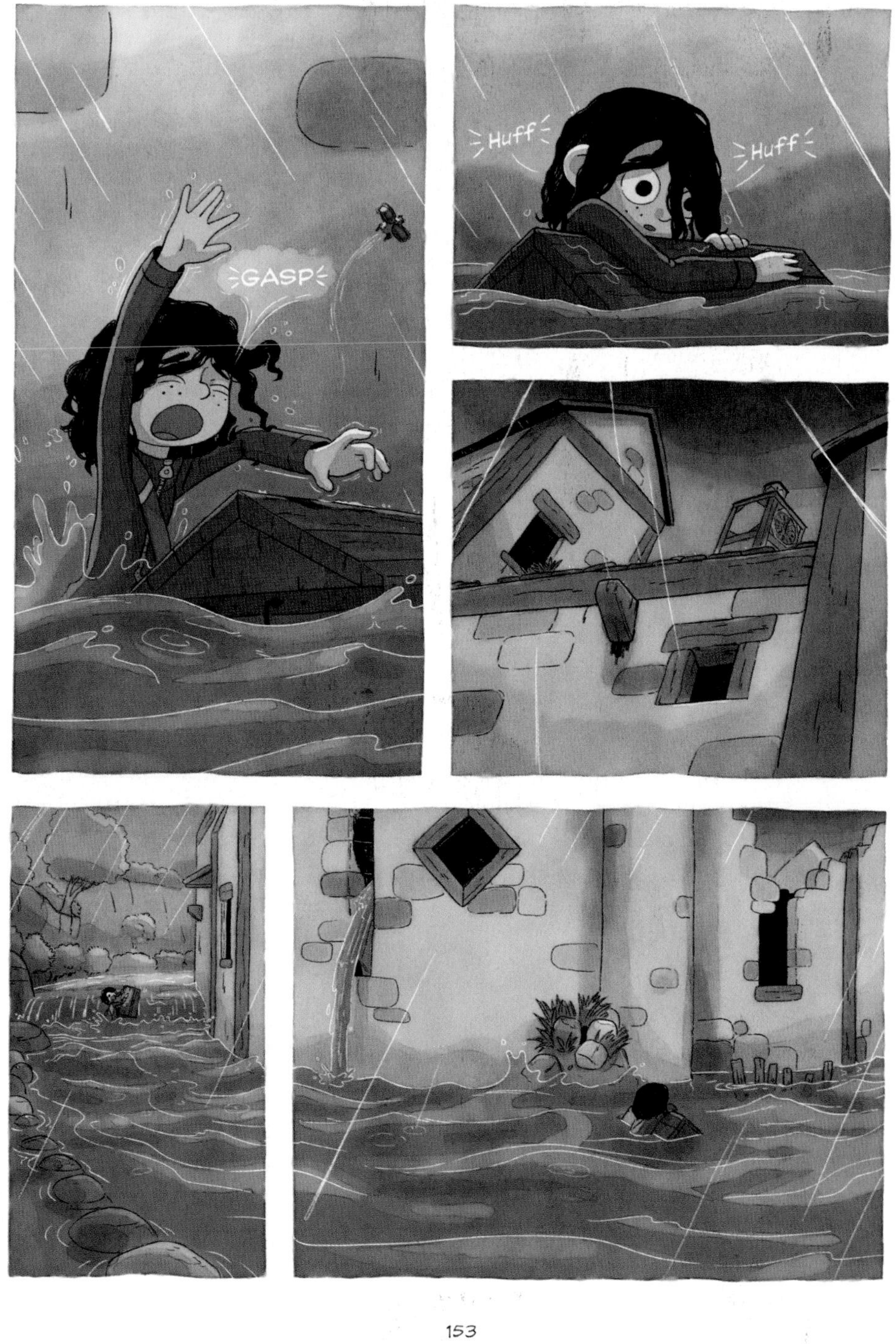
GASP
Huff
Huff

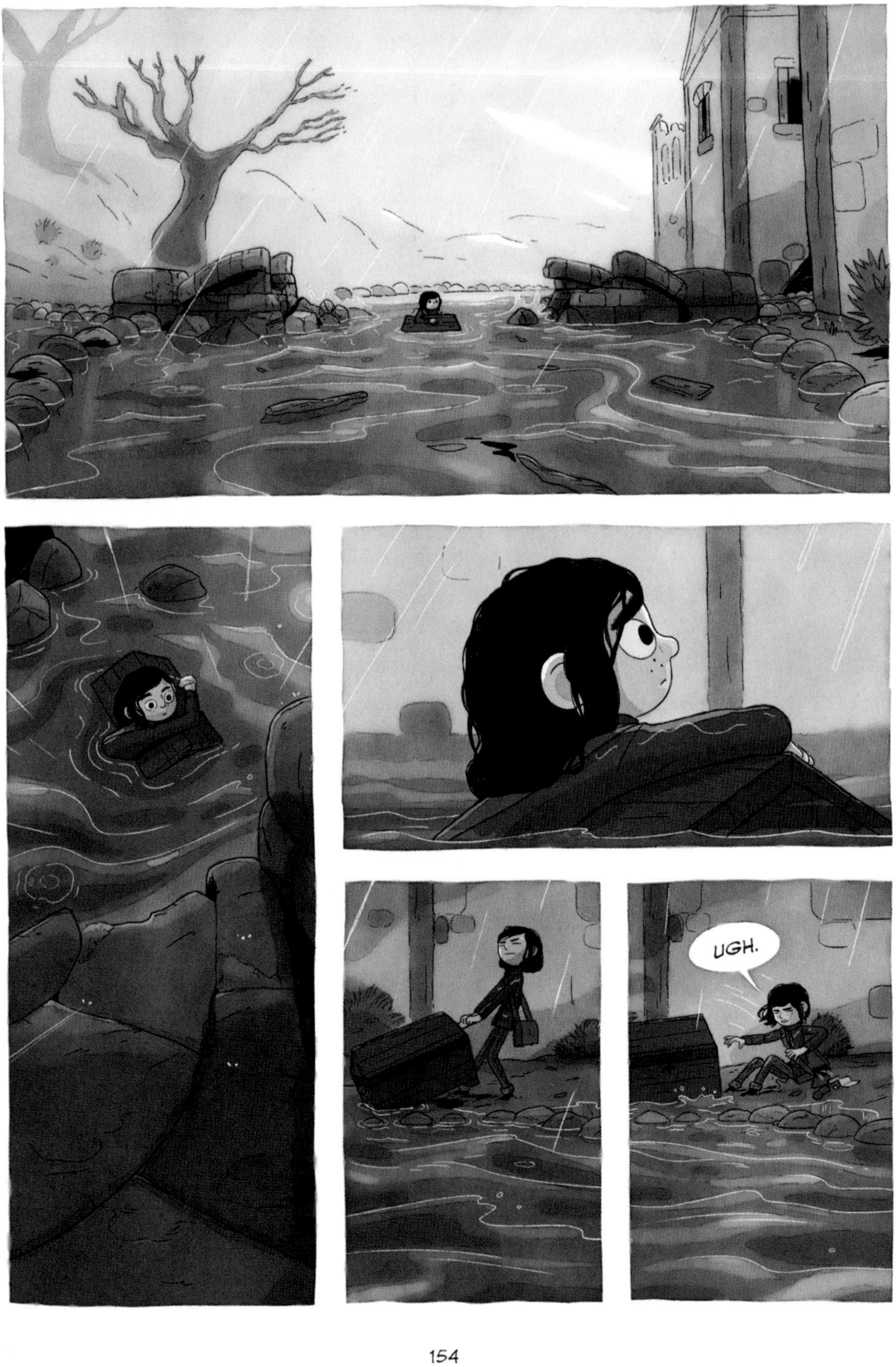
UGH.

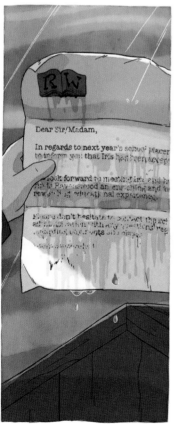

Hm?

Dear Sir/Madam,

In regards to next year's school placement to inform you that Iris has been accepted

look forward to meeting Iris and to ip to Ravenswood an enriching and rewarding educational experience.

Please don't hesitate to contact the administration with any questions regarding your spot as a student

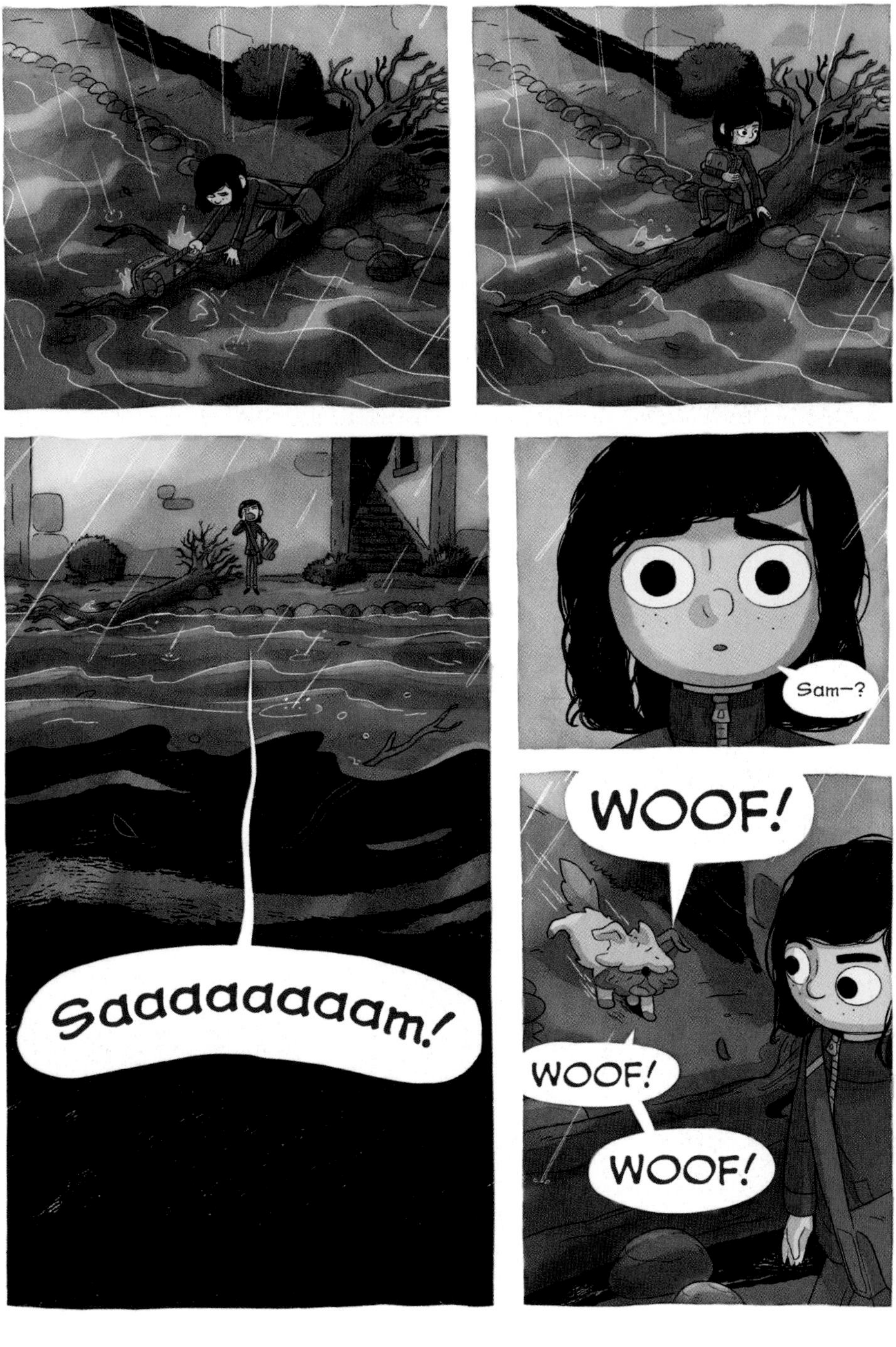
Saaaaaaaam!
Sam—?
WOOF!
WOOF!
WOOF!

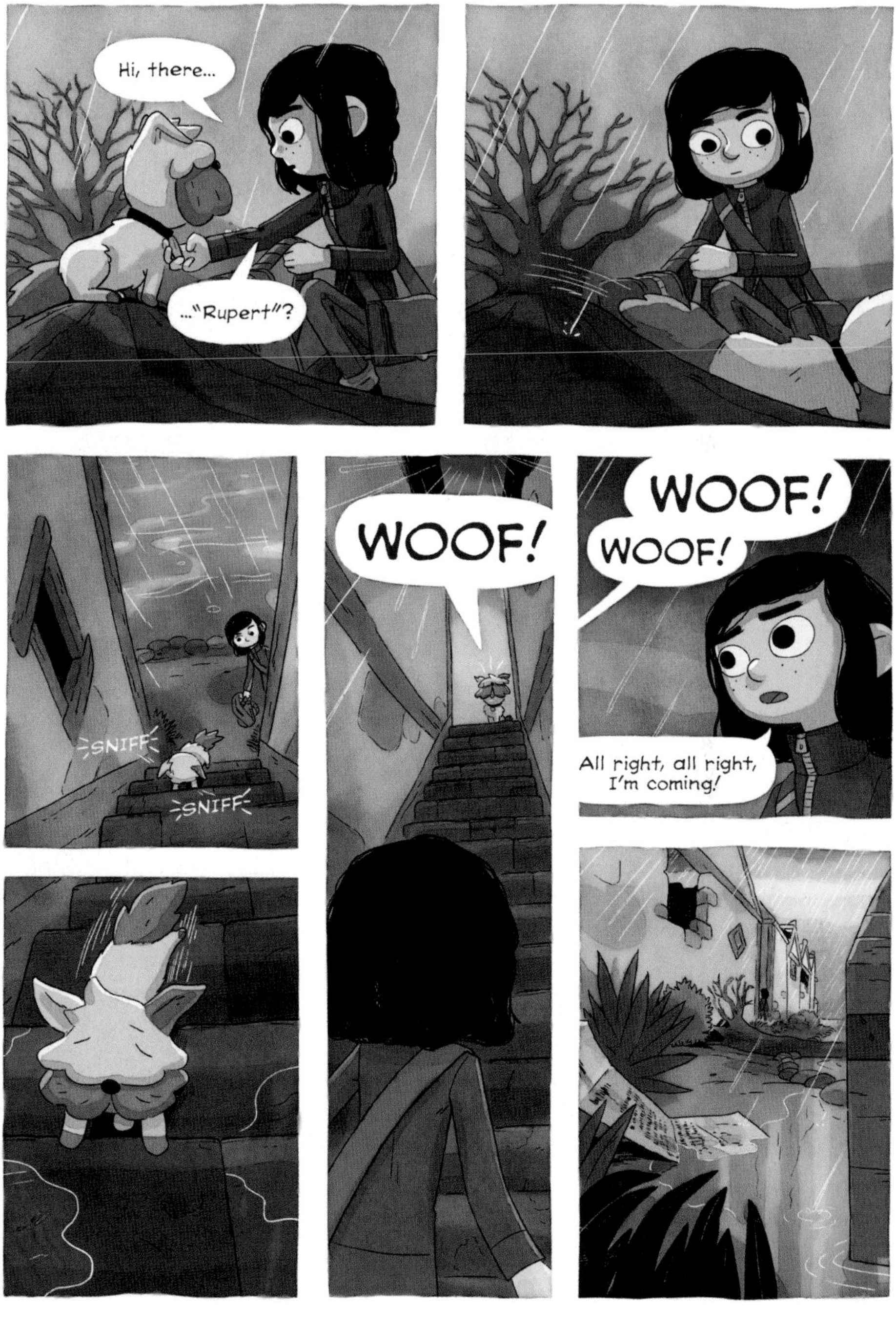
Hi, there...
..."Rupert"?
SNIFF
SNIFF
WOOF!
WOOF!
WOOF!
All right, all right, I'm coming!

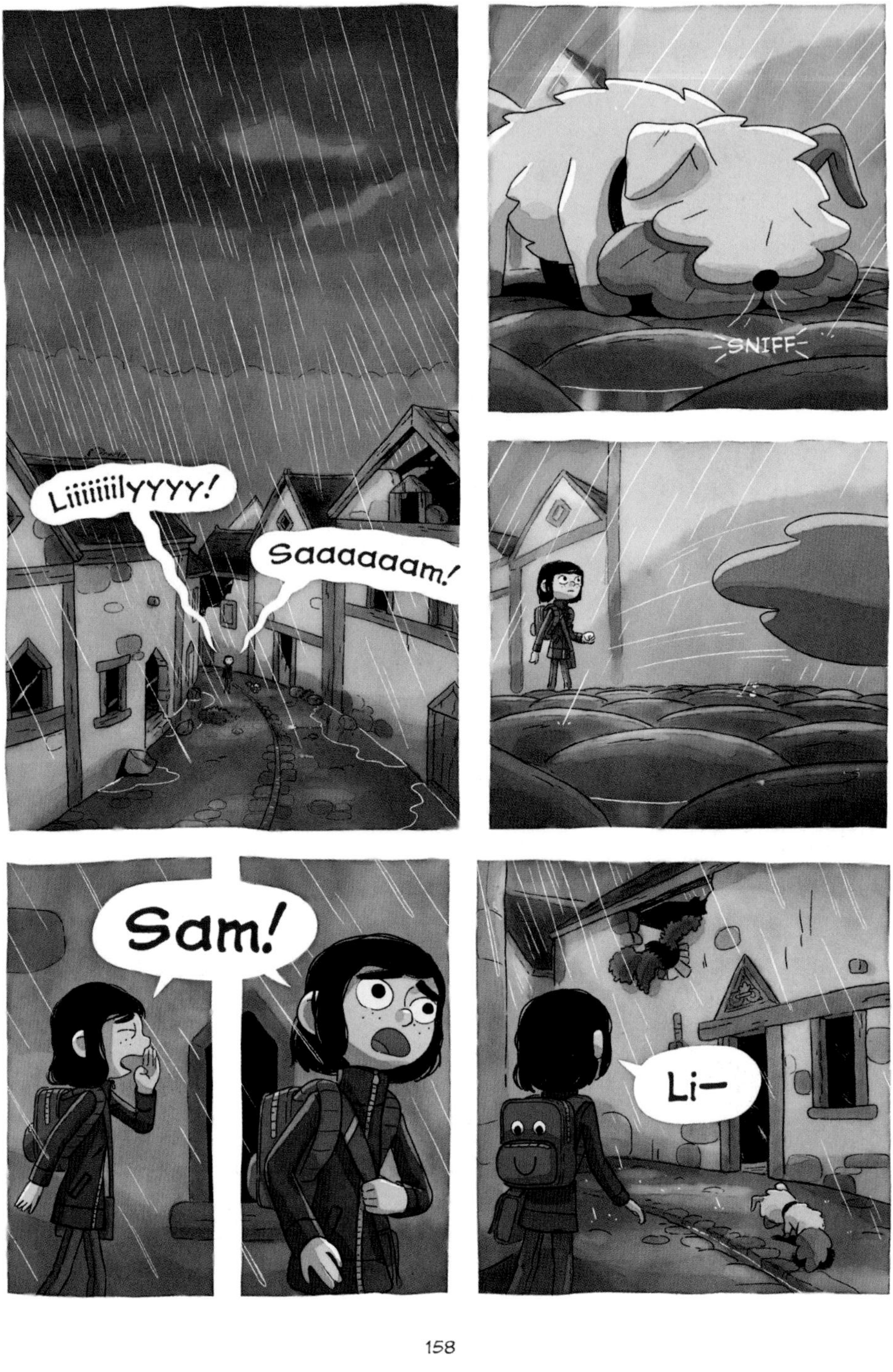
Liiiiiiilyyyy!
Saaaaaam!
SNIFF
Sam!
Li—

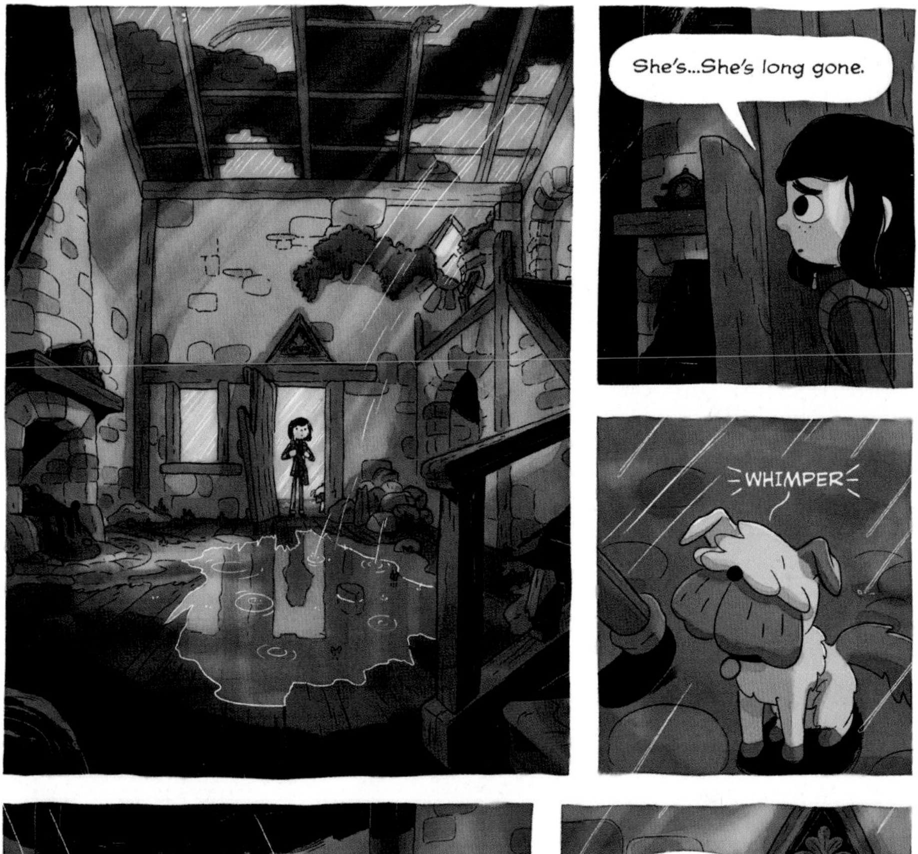
She's...She's long gone.
WHIMPER
Have I lost my mind?
! Hey I !
now!
Can
?!
Hmm?

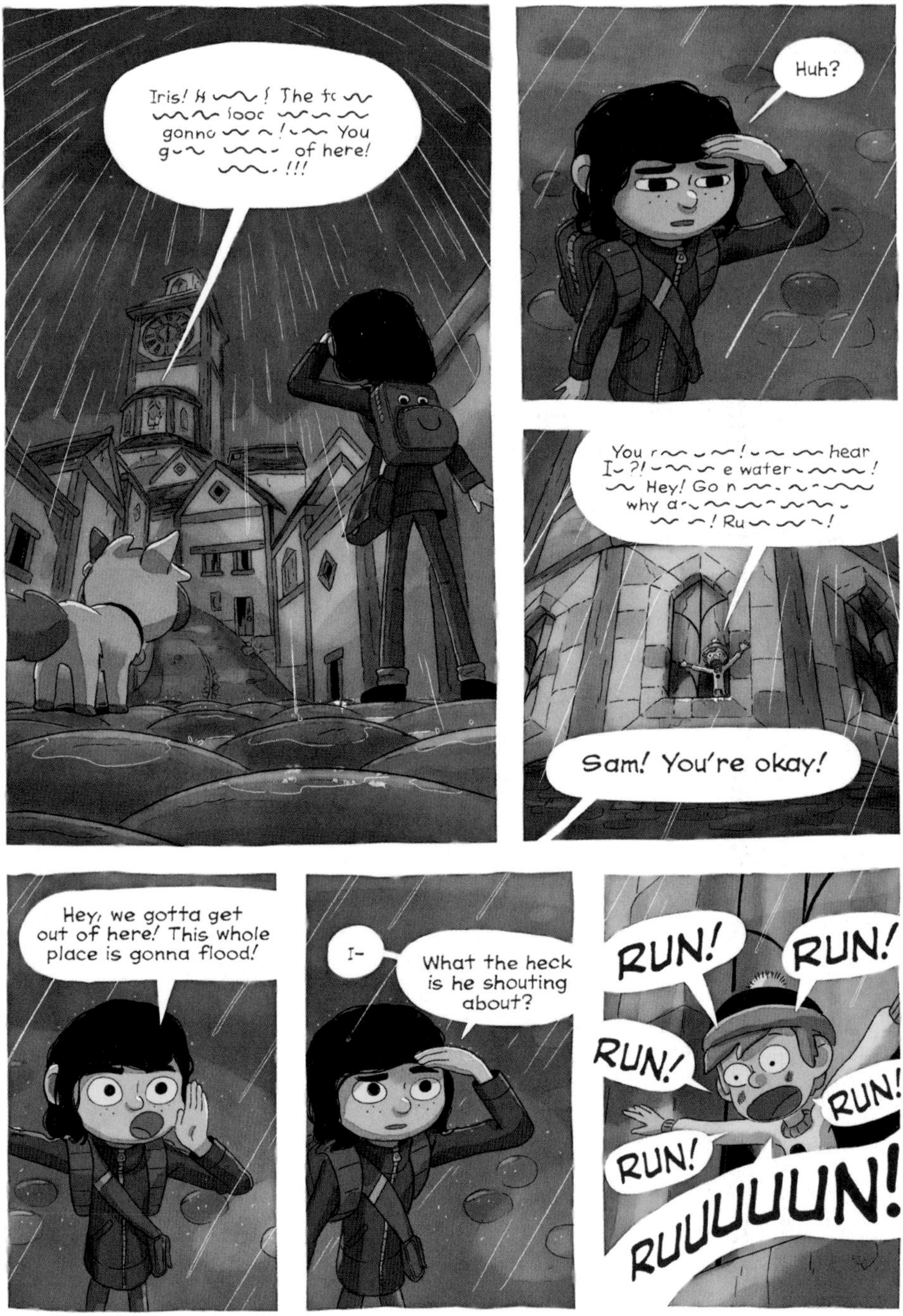
Iris! The
You
of here!
!!!
Huh?
You
hear
e water
Hey! Go
why
! Ru
Sam! You're okay!
Hey, we gotta get out of here! This whole place is gonna flood!
I-
What the heck is he shouting about?
RUN!
RUN!
RUN!
RUN!
RUN!
RUUUUUN!

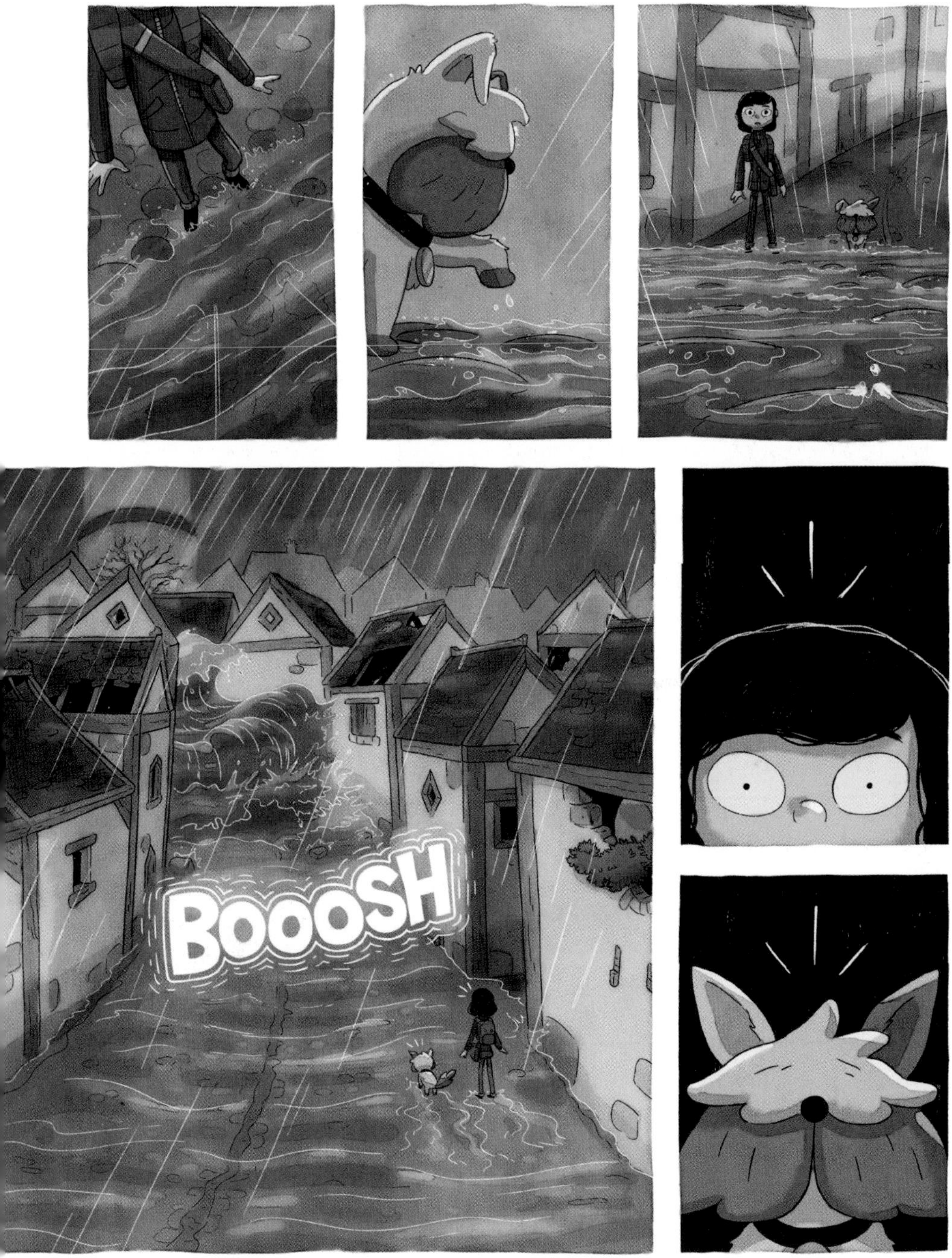
BOOOSH

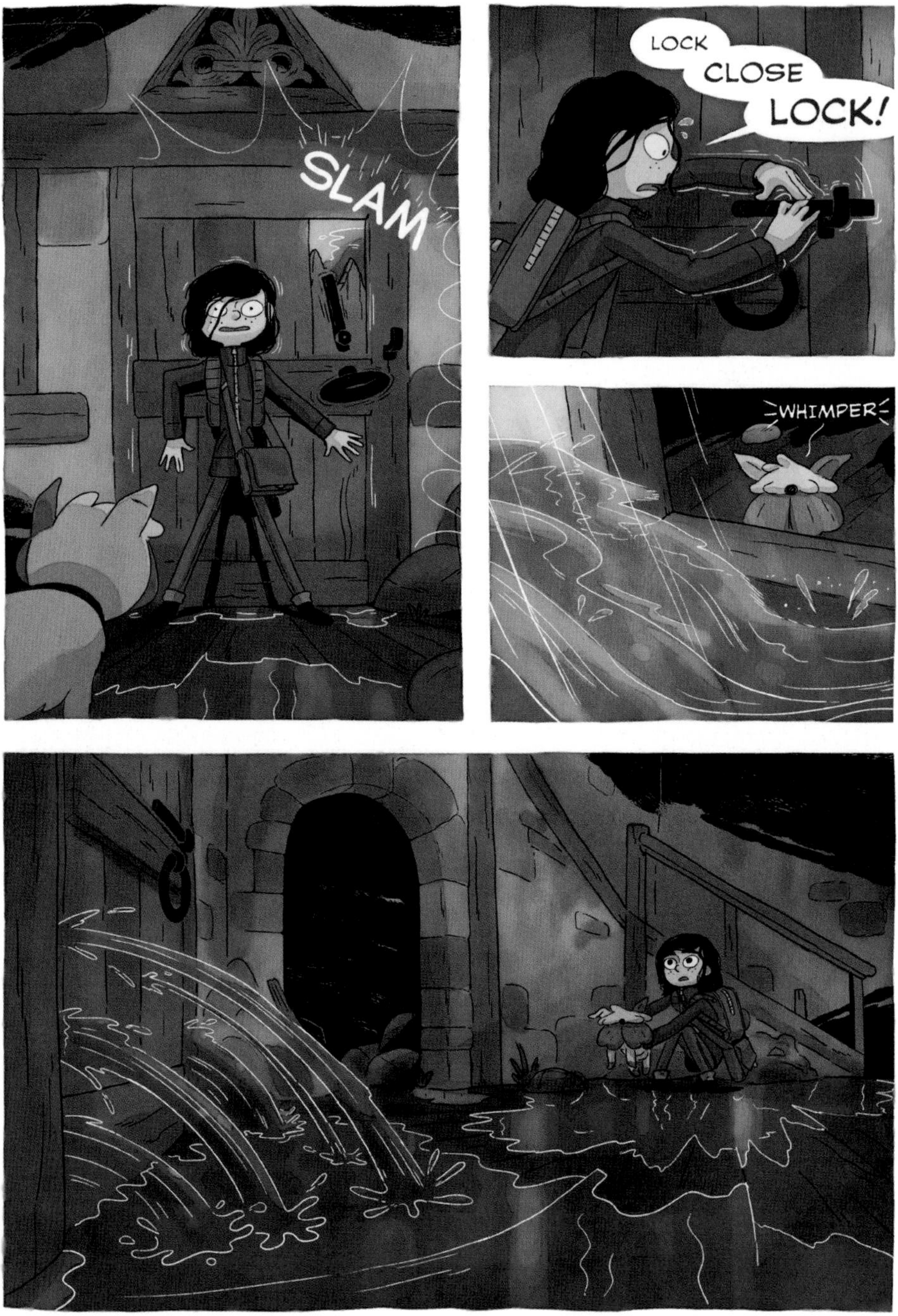
SLAM
LOCK
CLOSE
LOCK!
WHIMPER

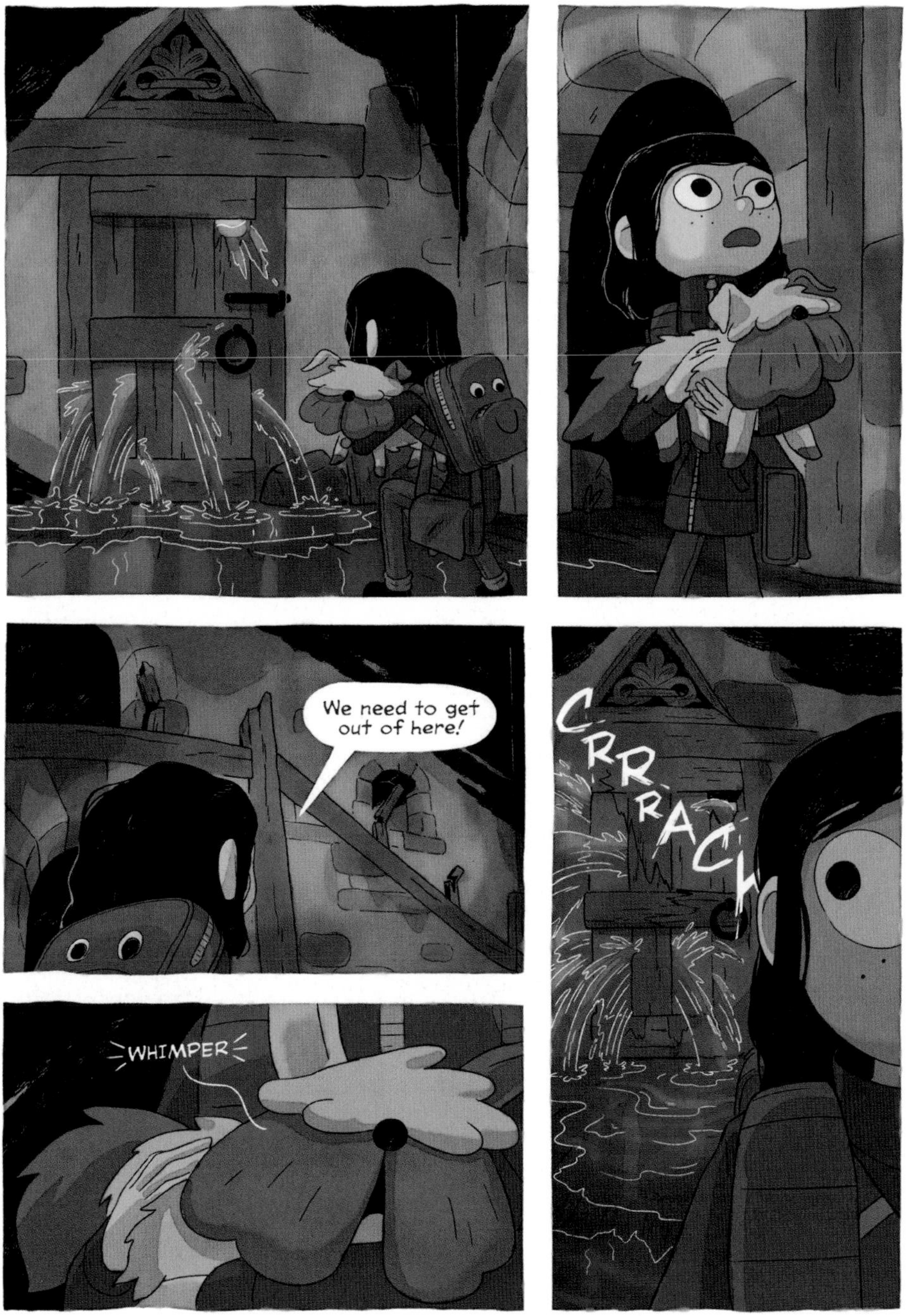
We need to get out of here!
CRRRACH
WHIMPER

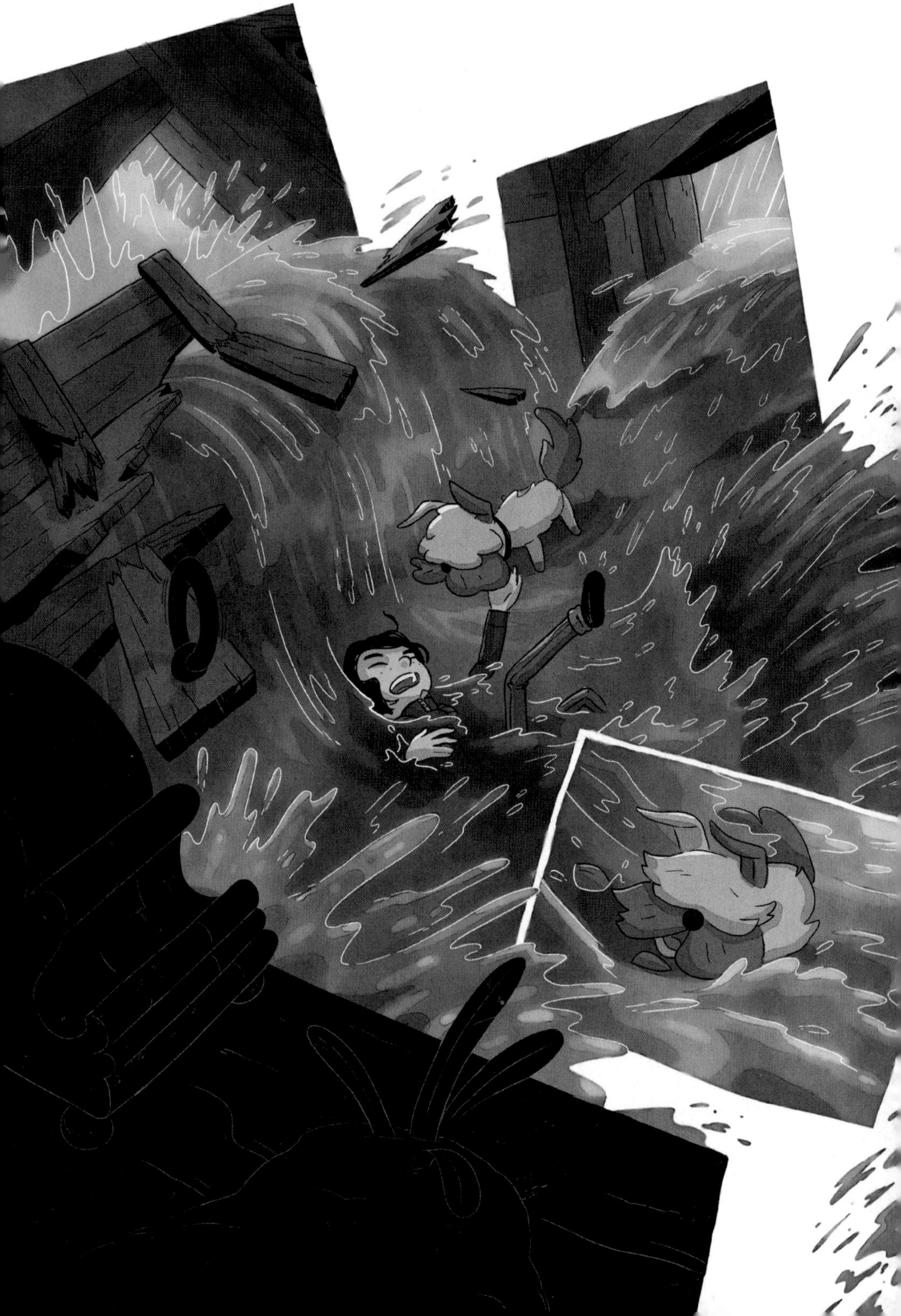

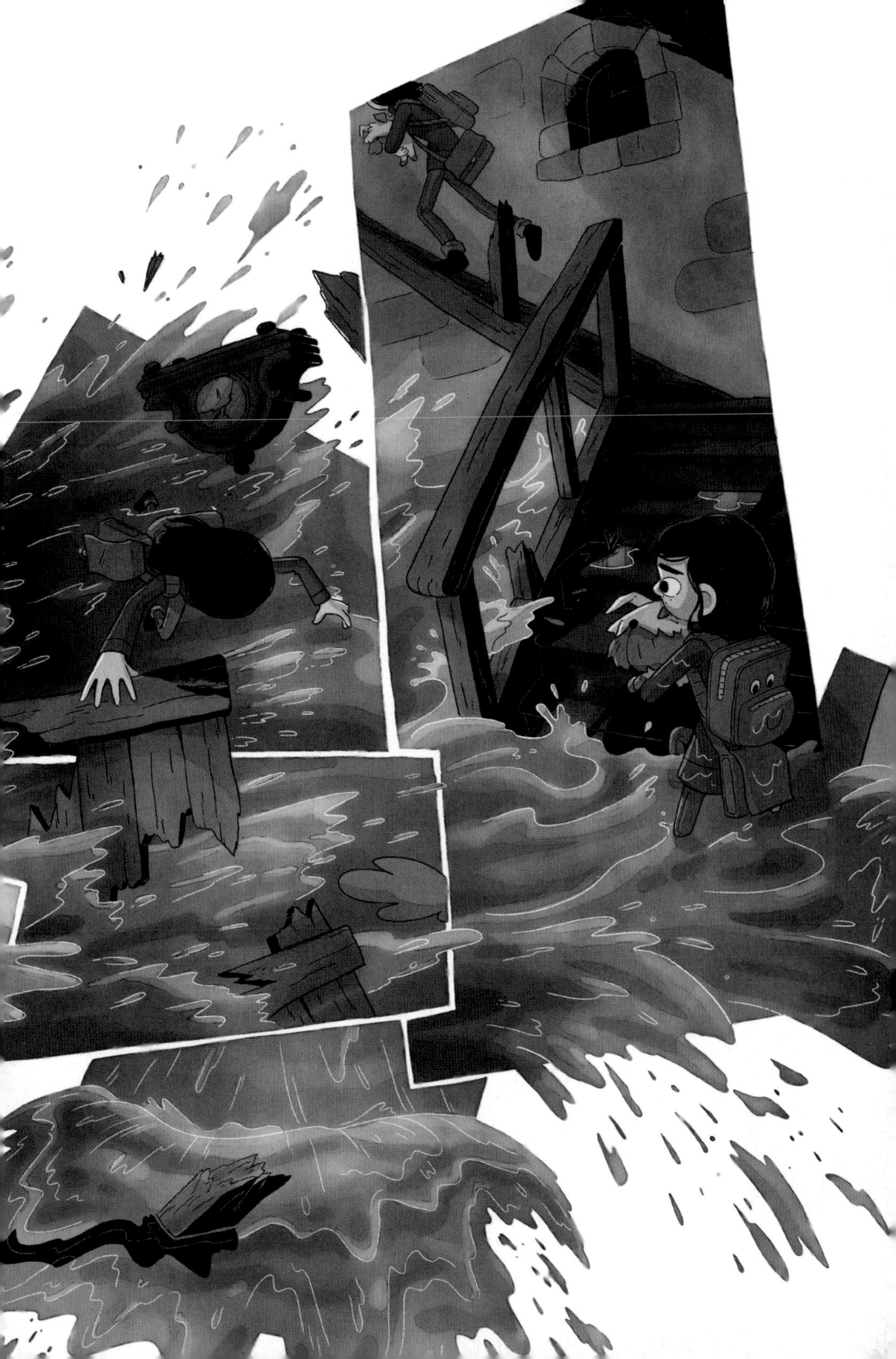

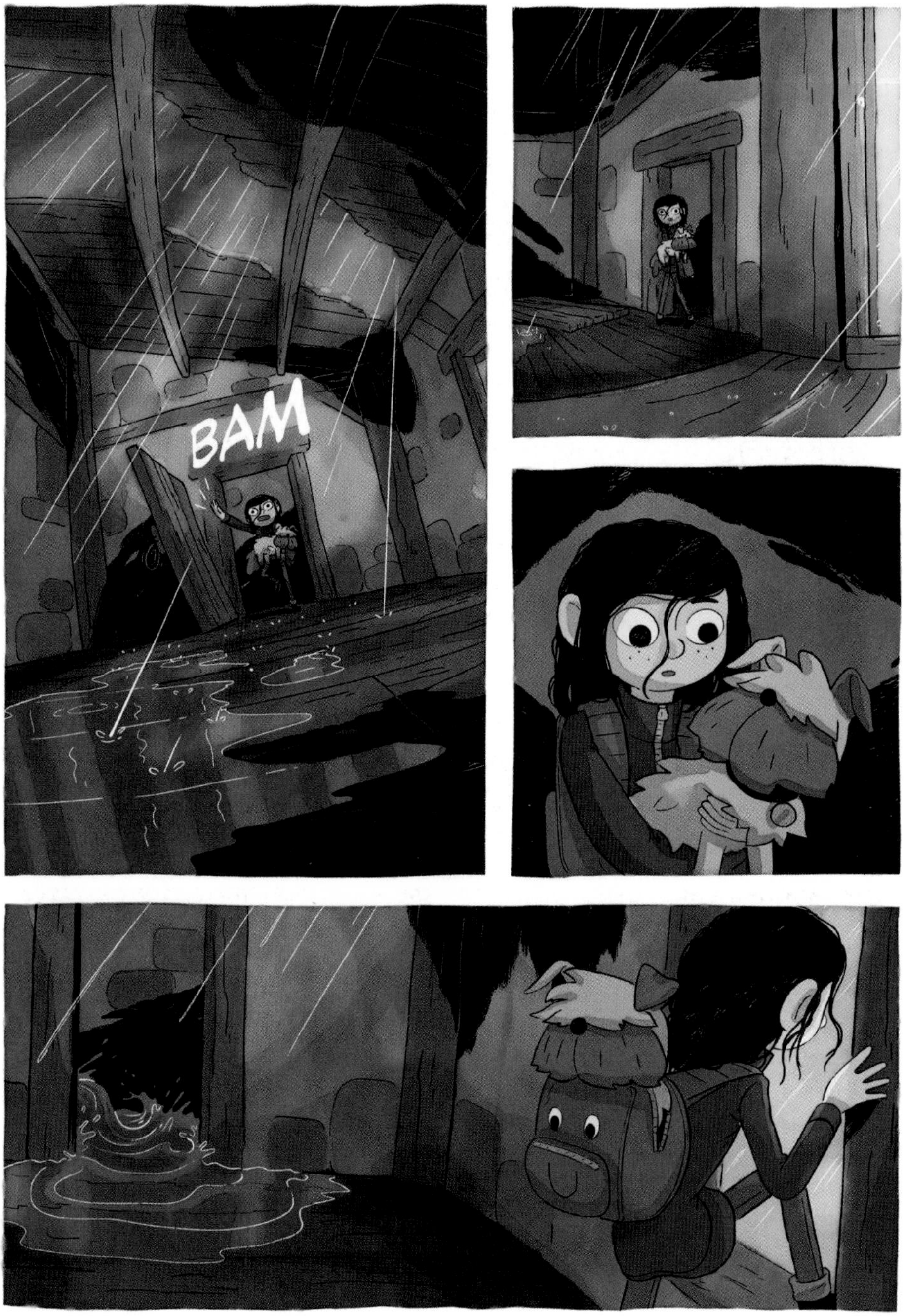
BAM

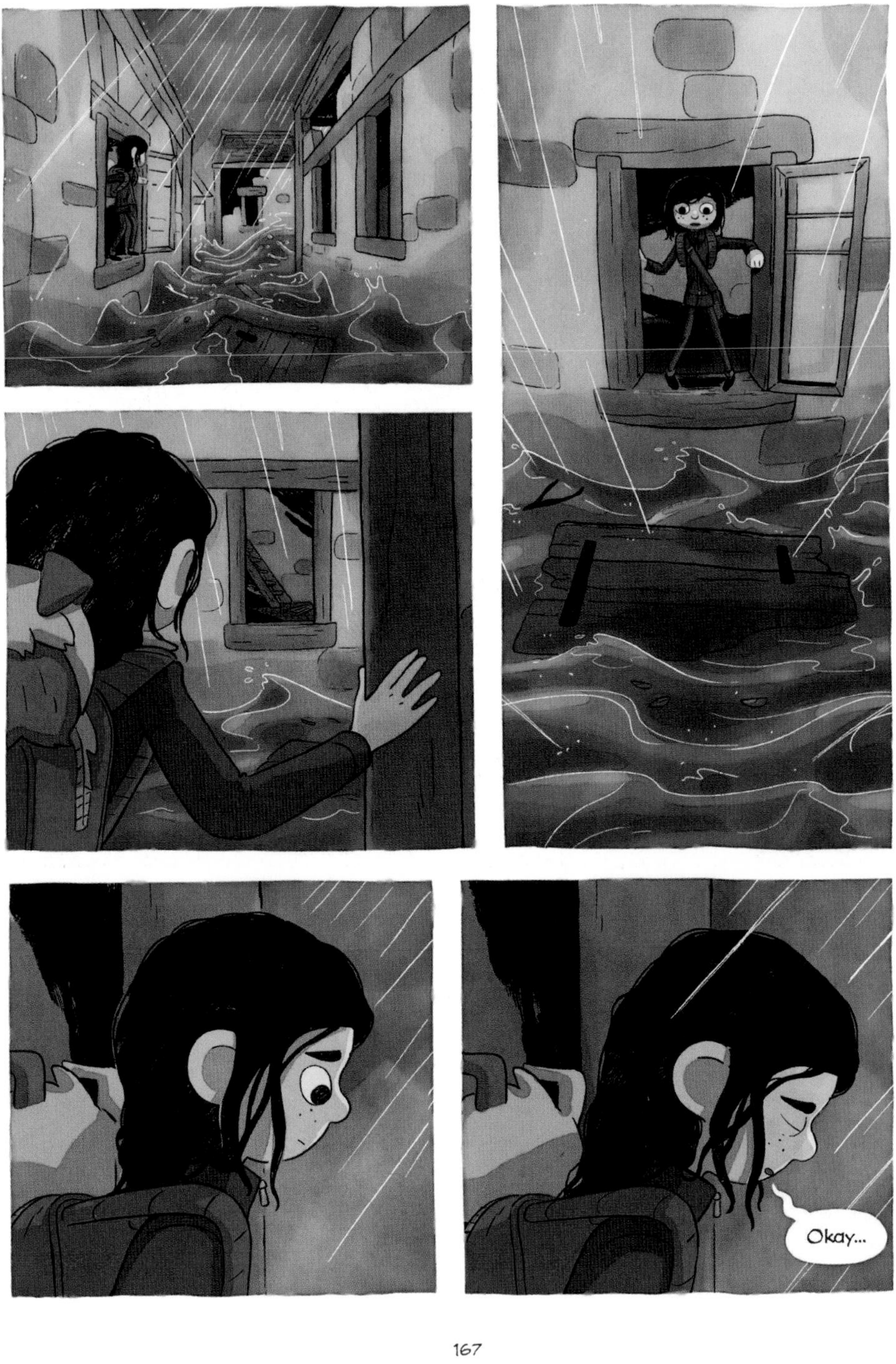
Okay...

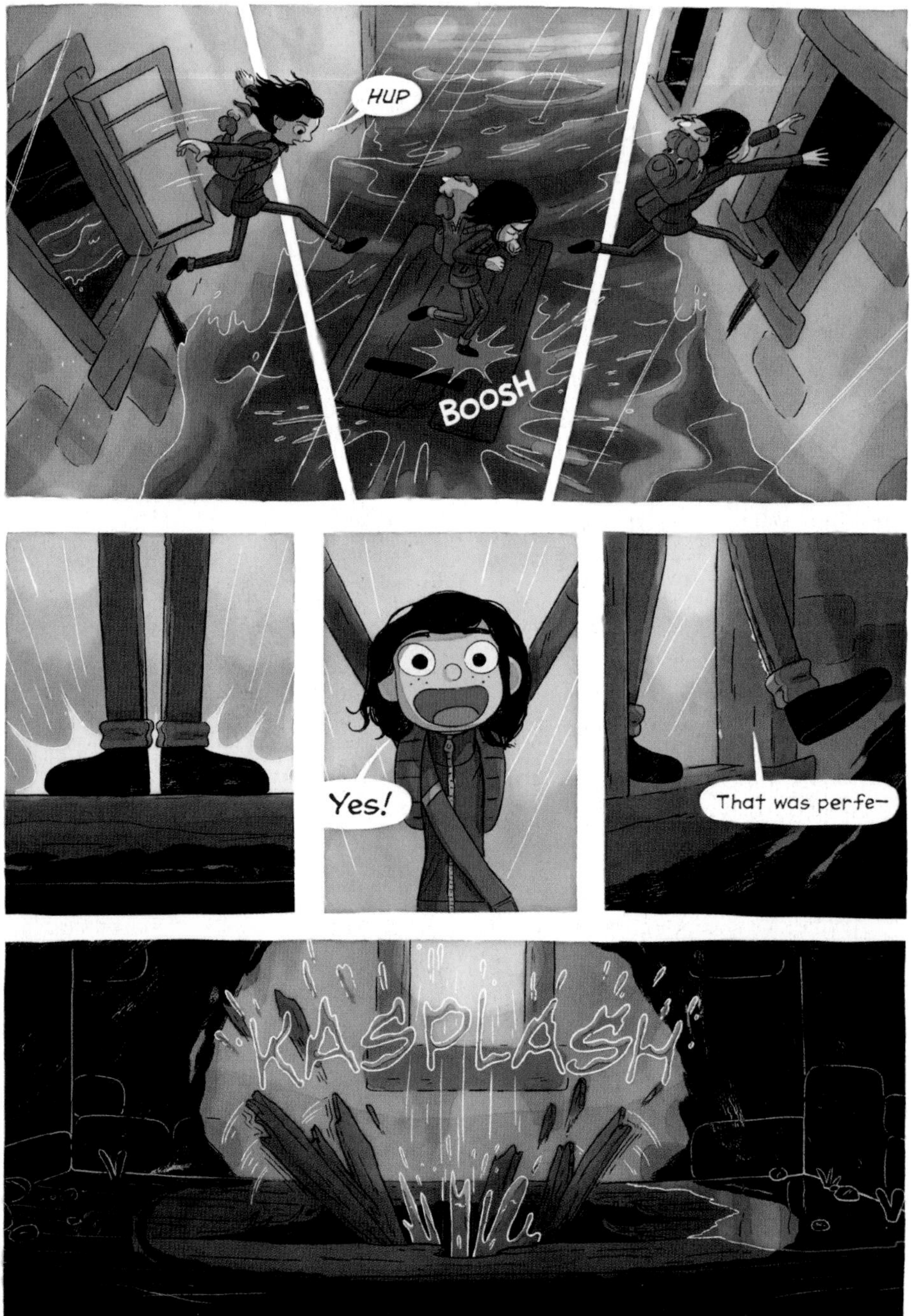
HUP
BOOSH
Yes!
That was perfe—
KASPLASH

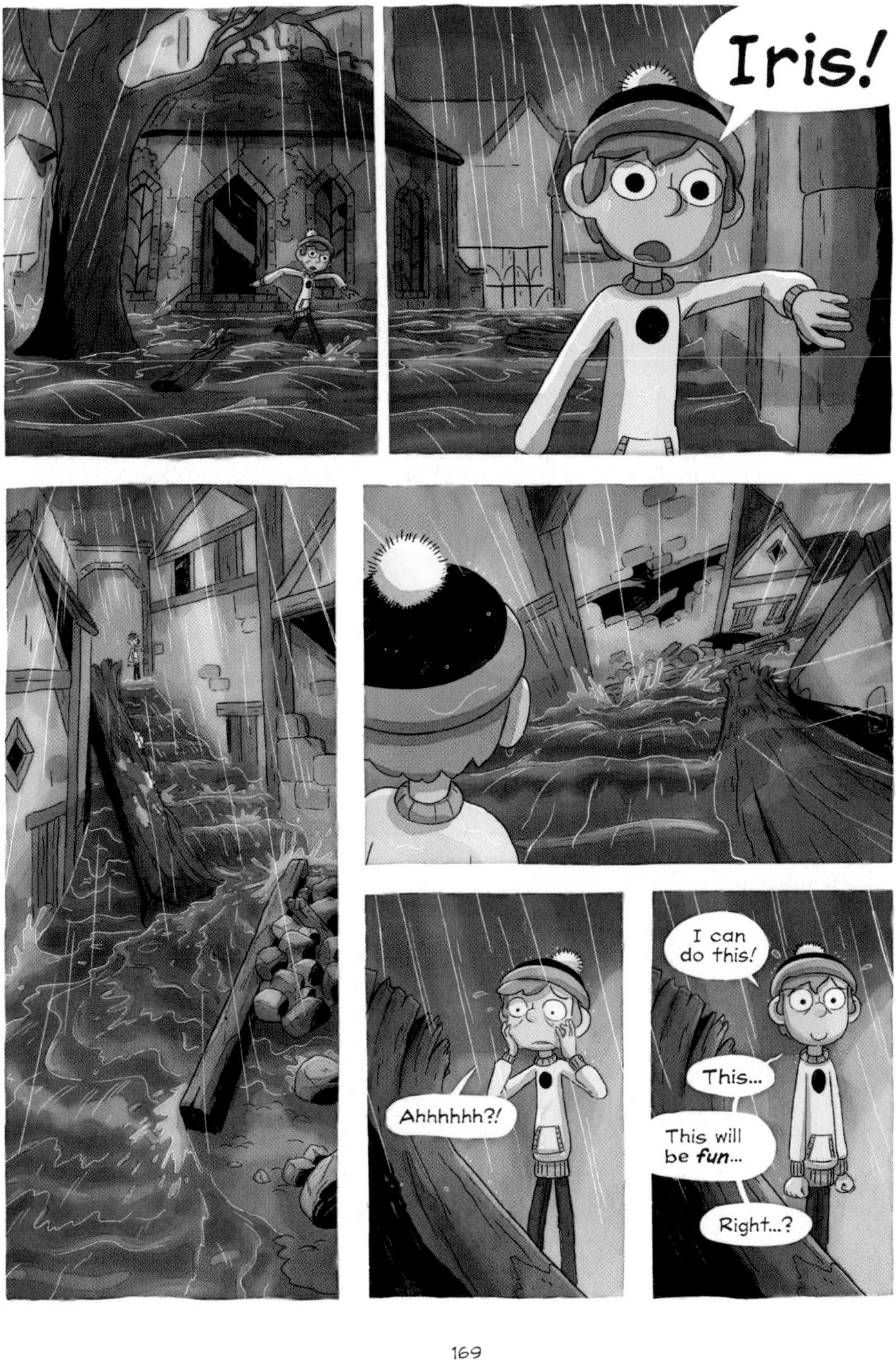
Iris!
Ahhhhhh?!
I can do this!
This...
This will be *fun*...
Right...?

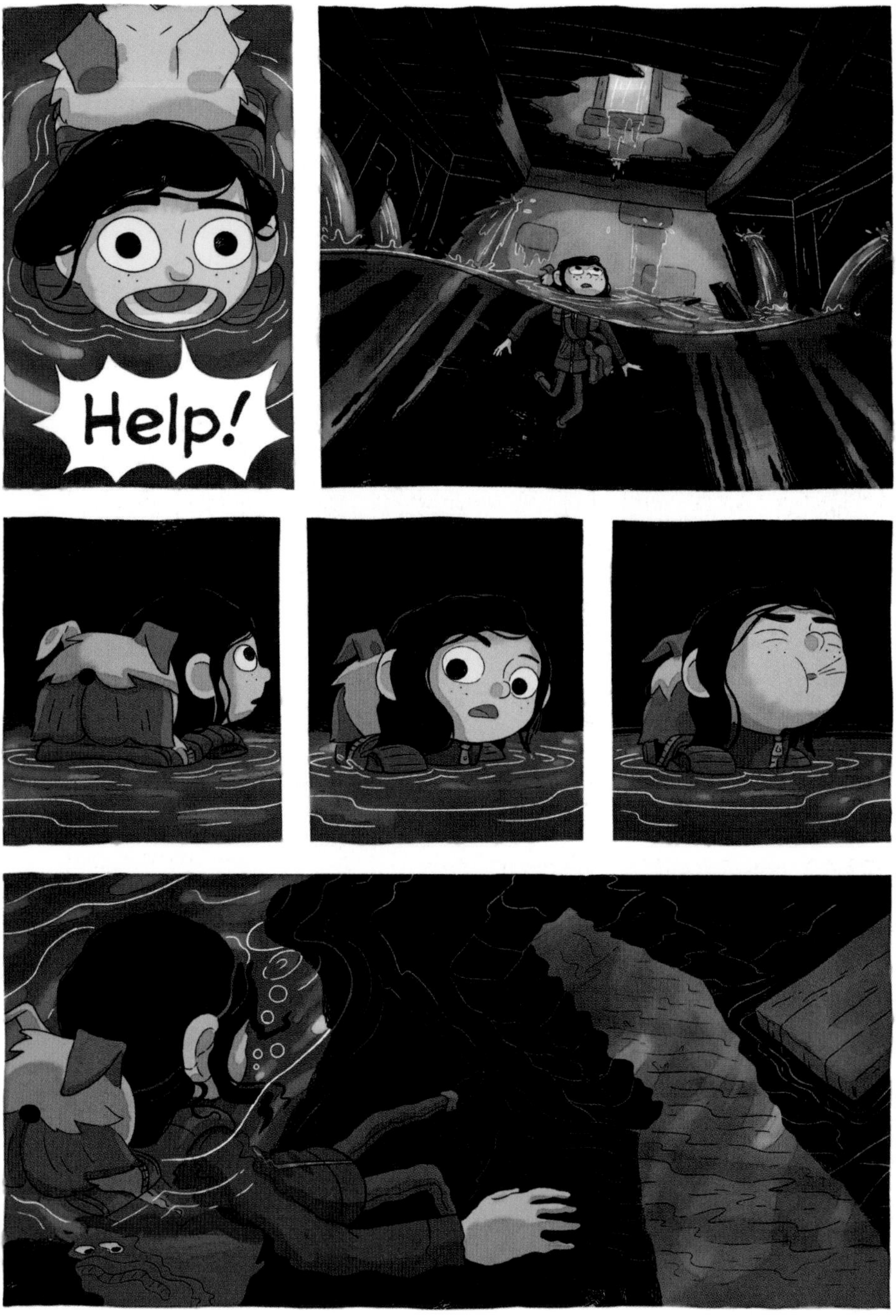
Help!

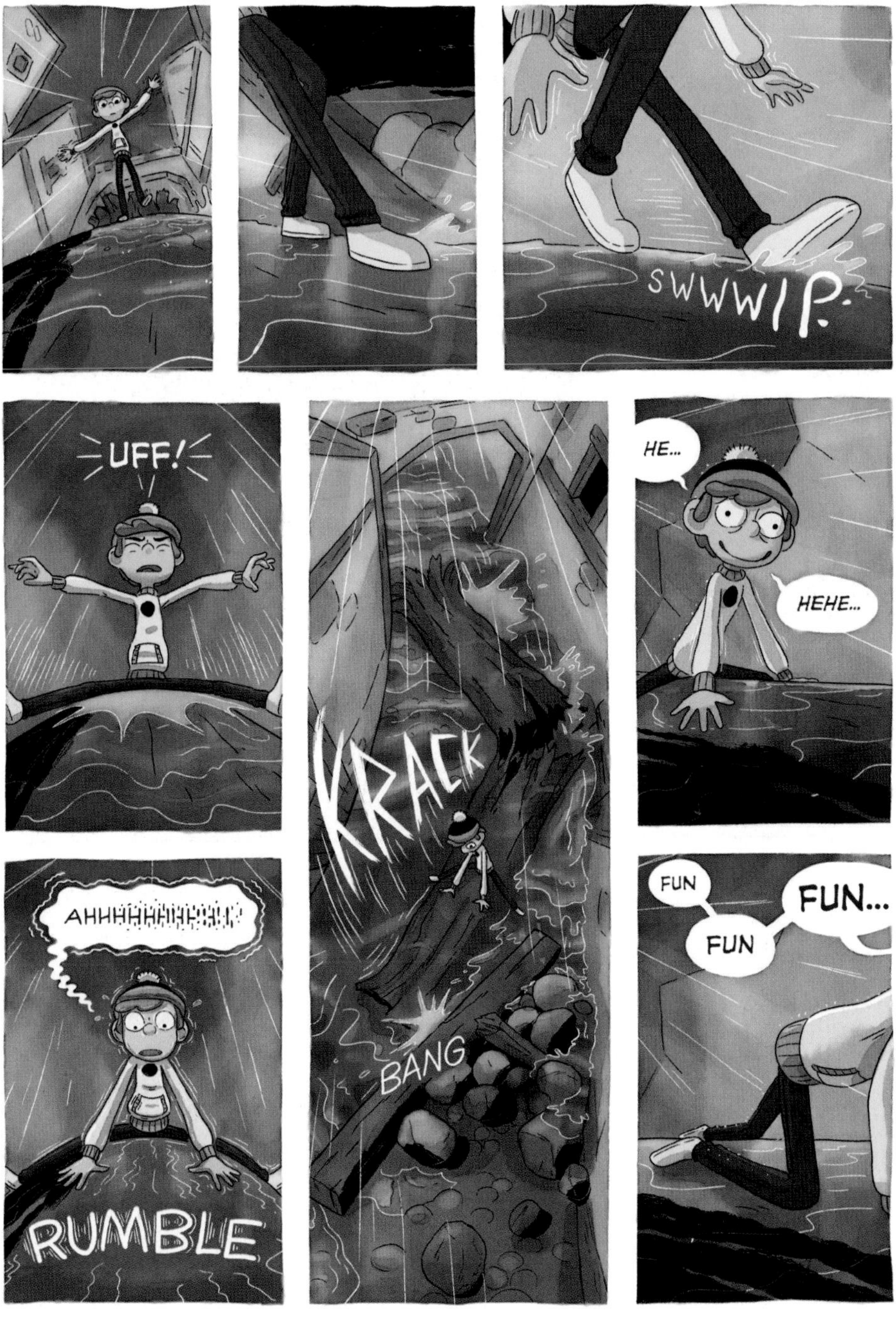
SWWWIP
UFF!
KRACK
BANG
HE...
HEHE...
AHHHHHHHH!!!
RUMBLE
FUN
FUN
FUN...

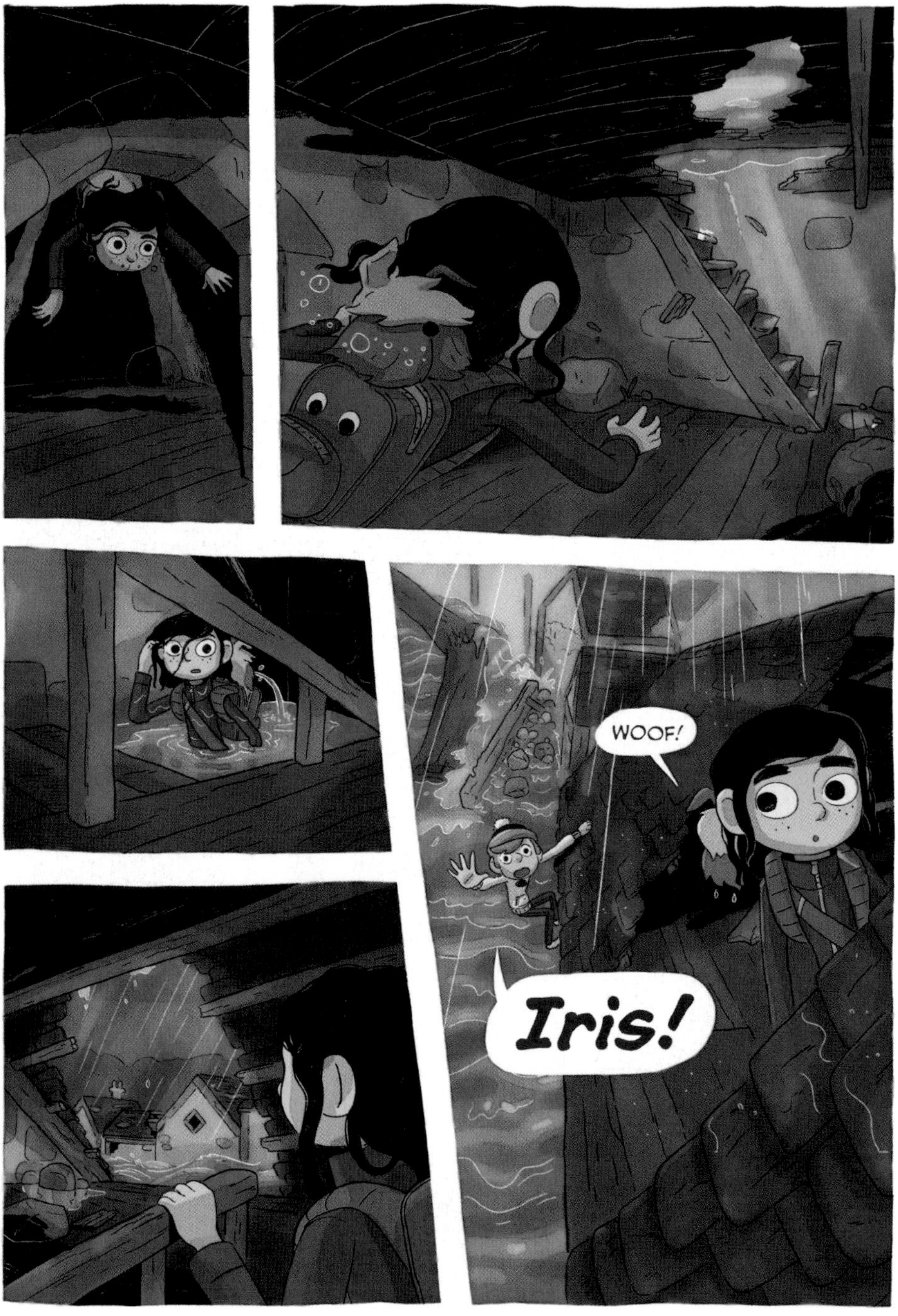
WOOF!
Iris!

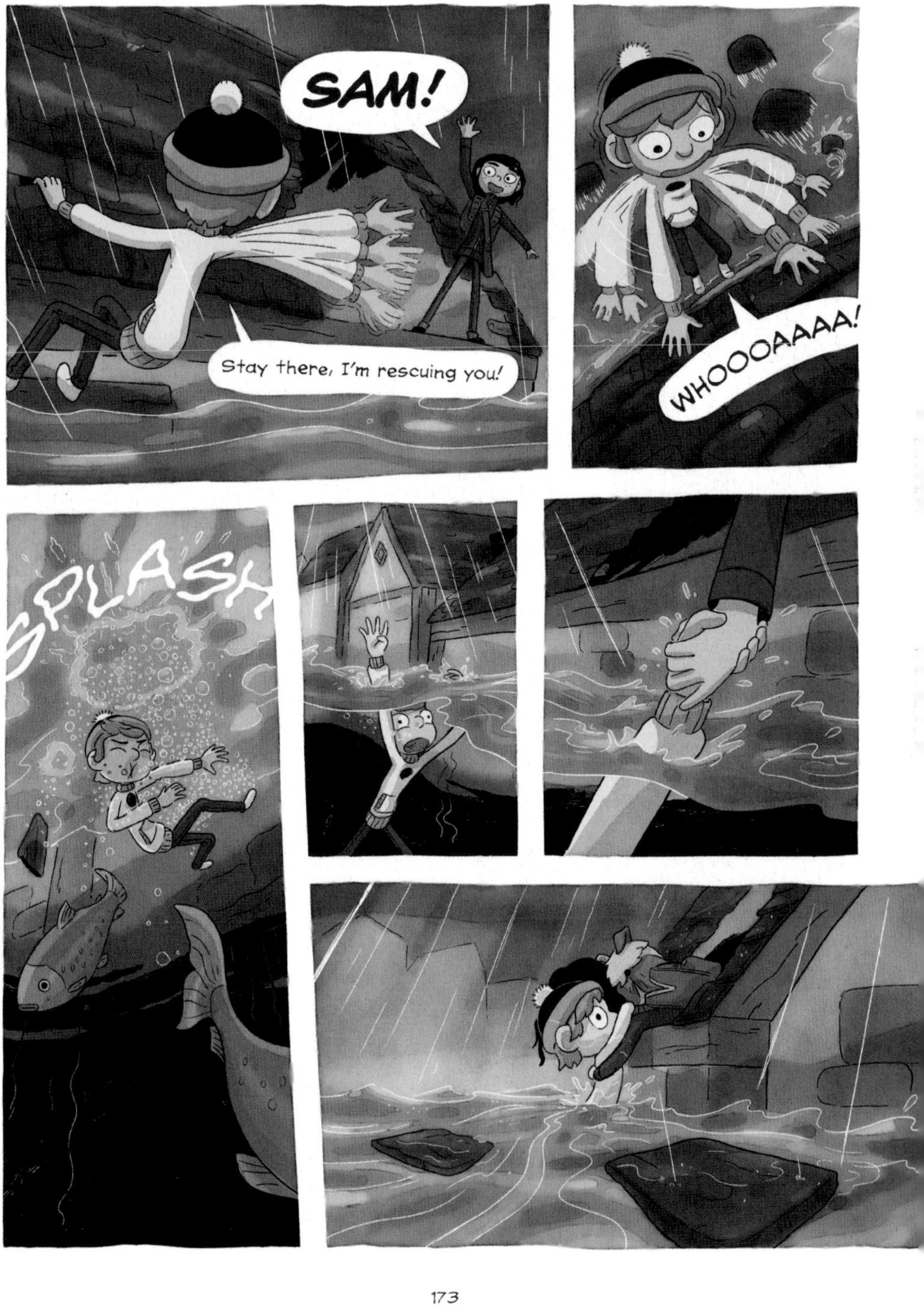
SAM!
Stay there, I'm rescuing you!
WHOOOAAAA!
SPLASH

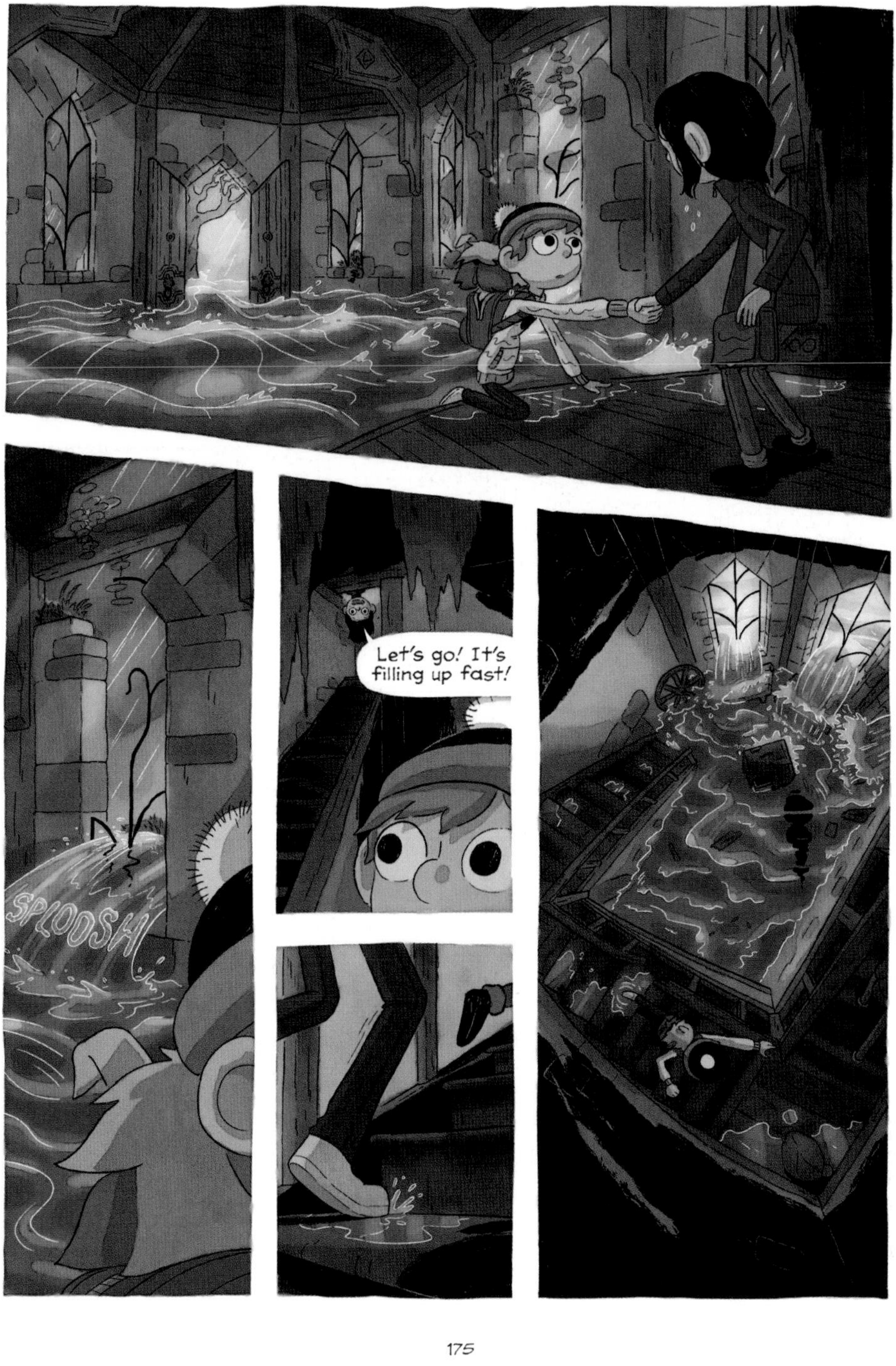
SPLOOSH
Let's go! It's filling up fast!

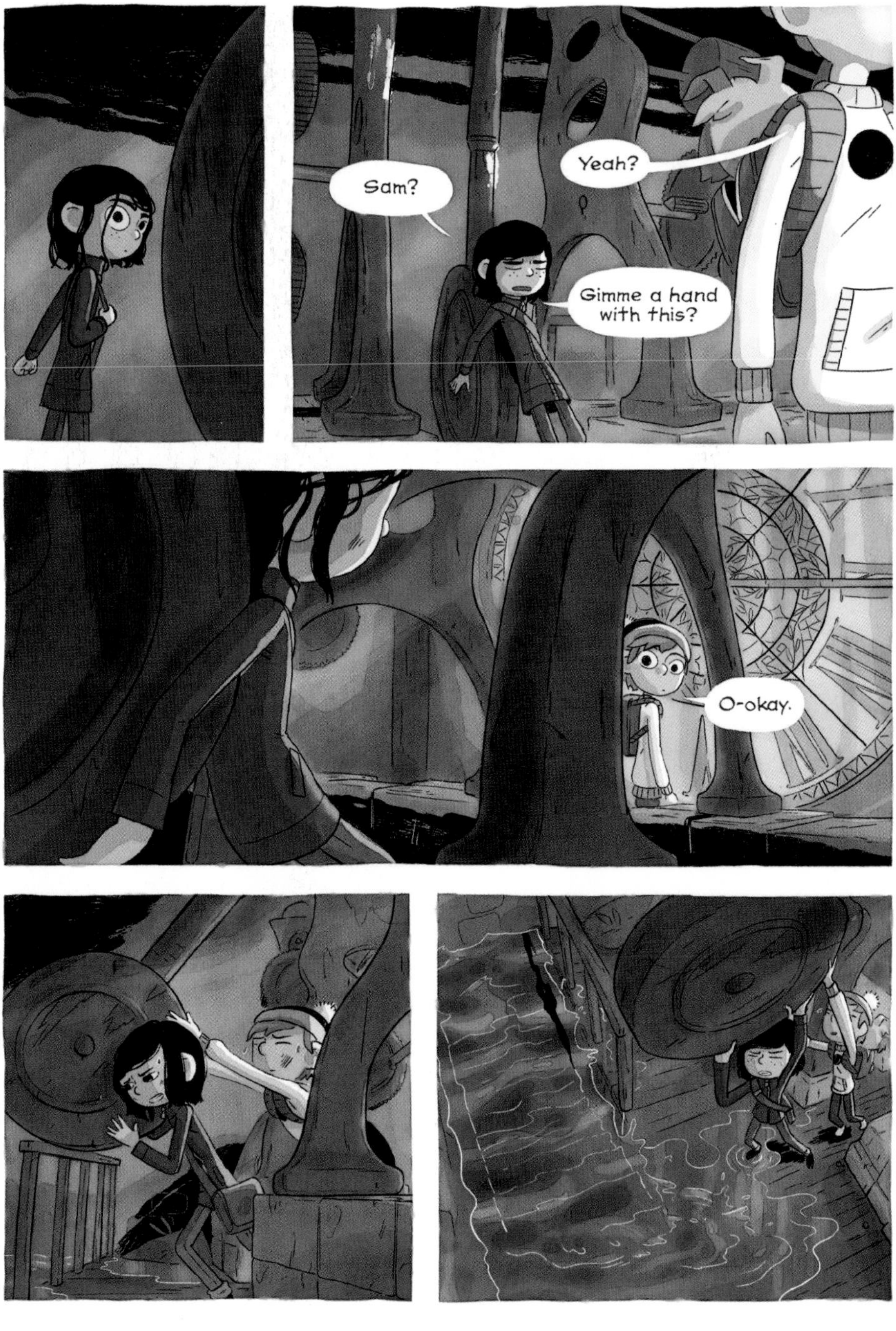
Sam?
Yeah?
Gimme a hand
with this?
O-okay.

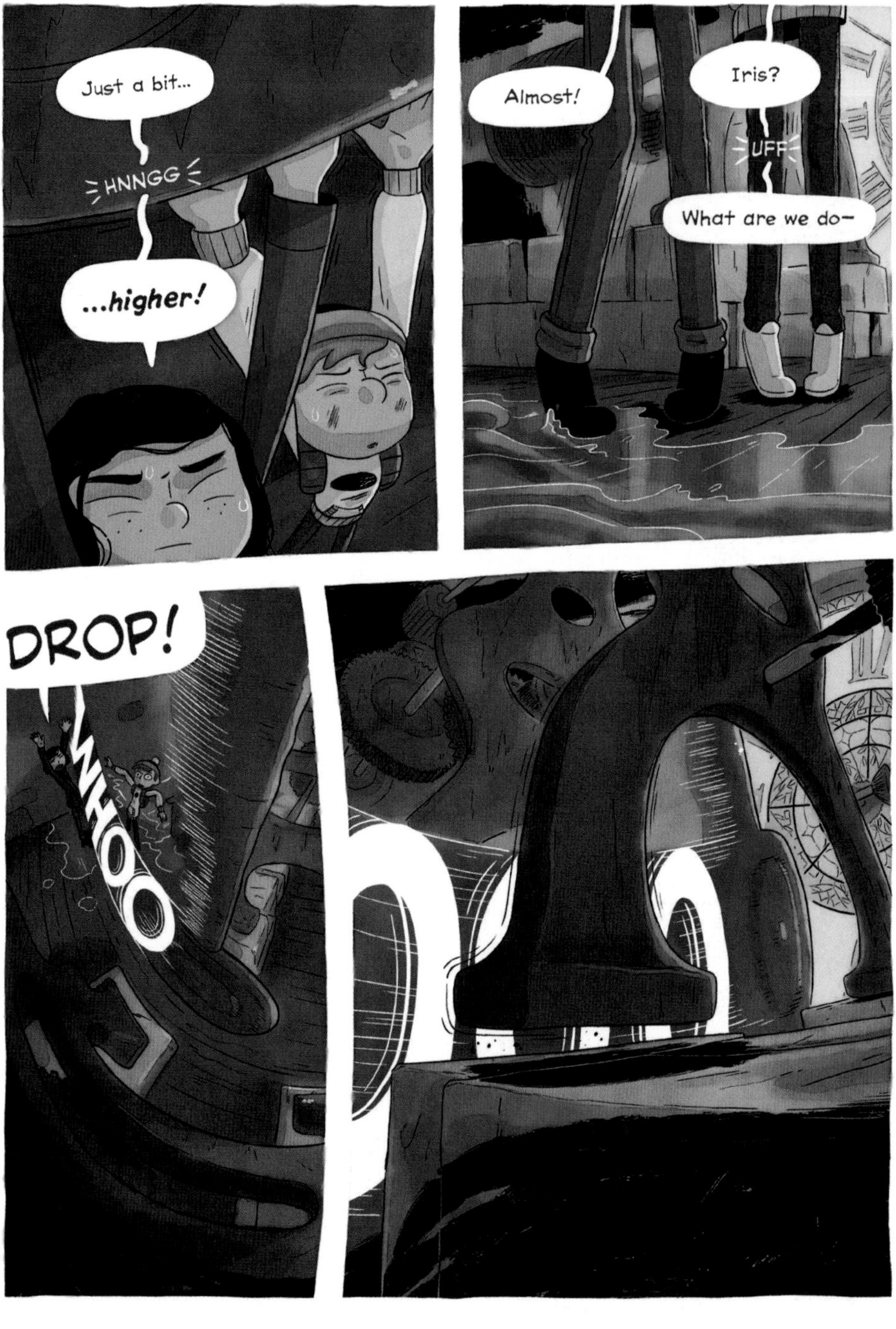

Just a bit...
HNNGG
...higher!
Almost!
Iris?
UFF
What are we do–
DROP!
WHOOO

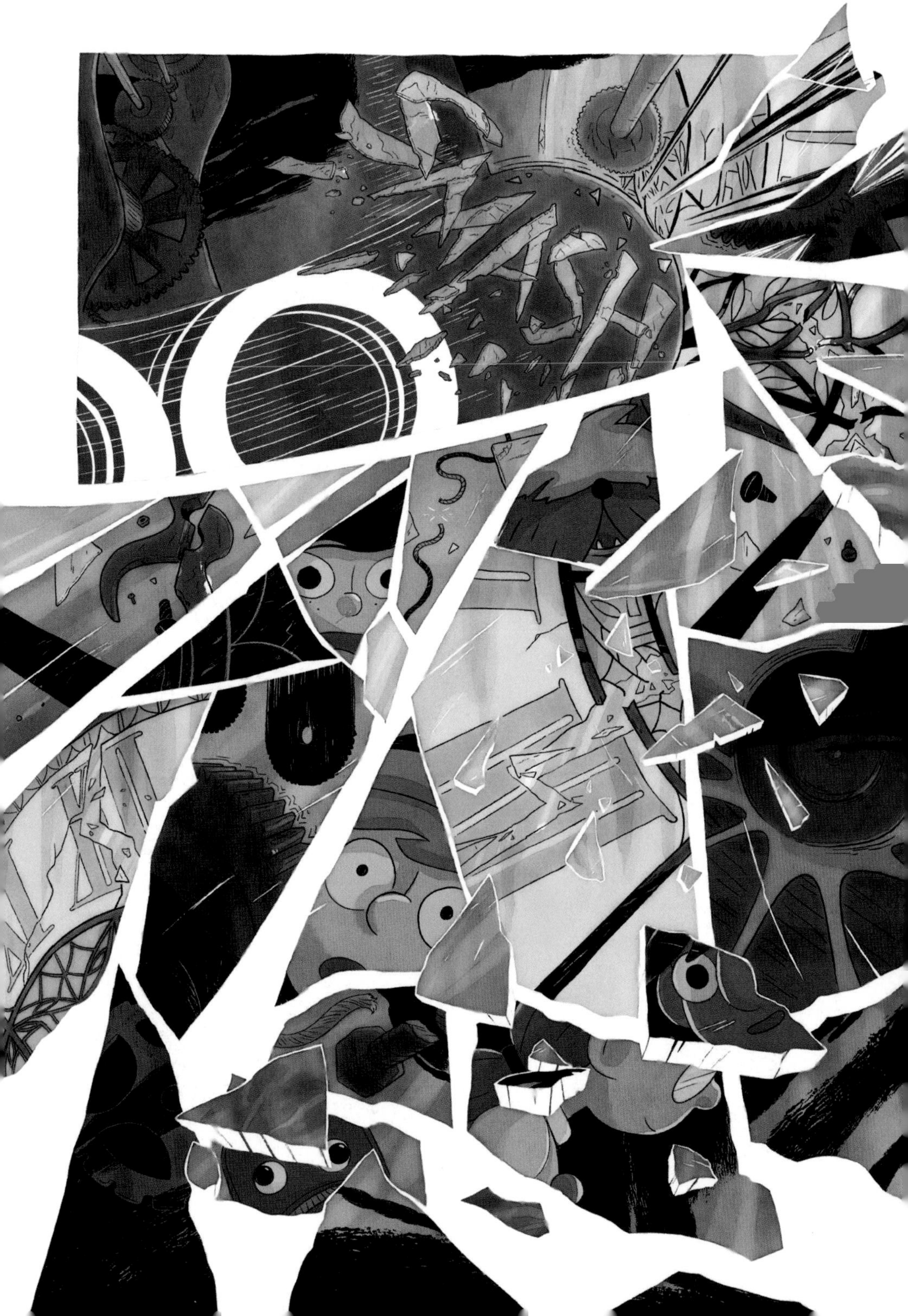

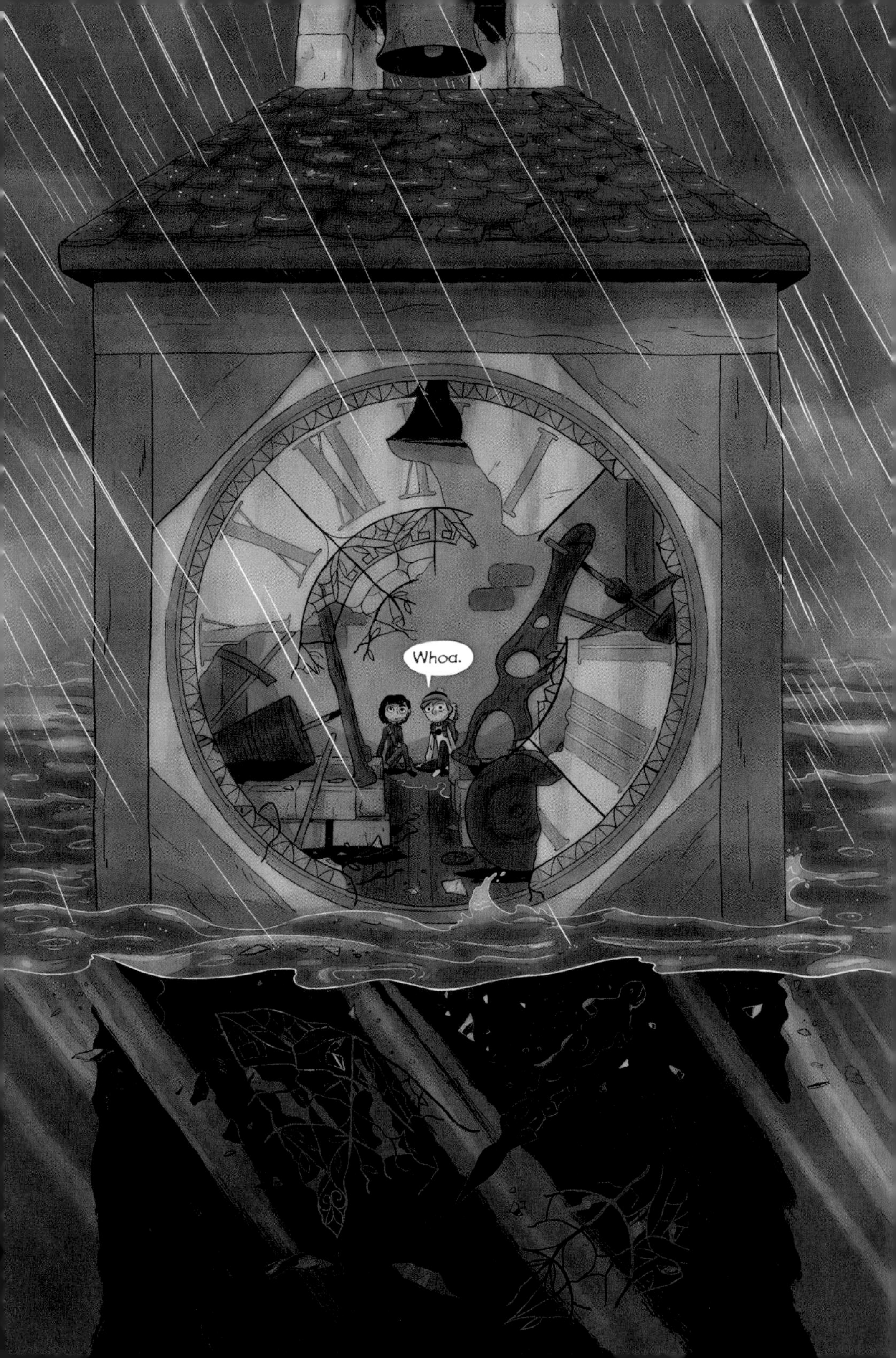
Whoa.

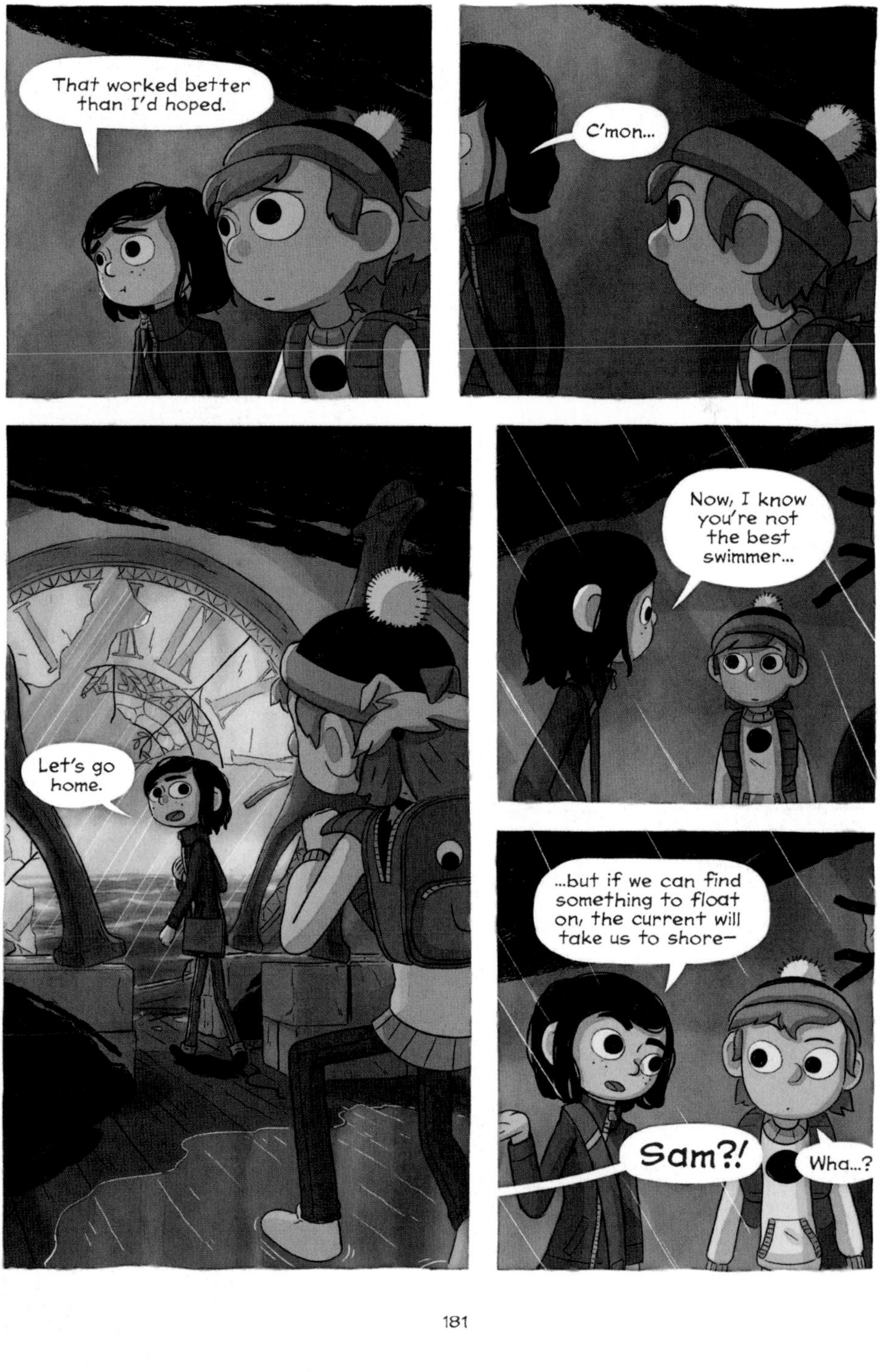
That worked better than I'd hoped.
C'mon...
Let's go home.
Now, I know you're not the best swimmer...
...but if we can find something to float on, the current will take us to shore—
Sam?!
Wha...?

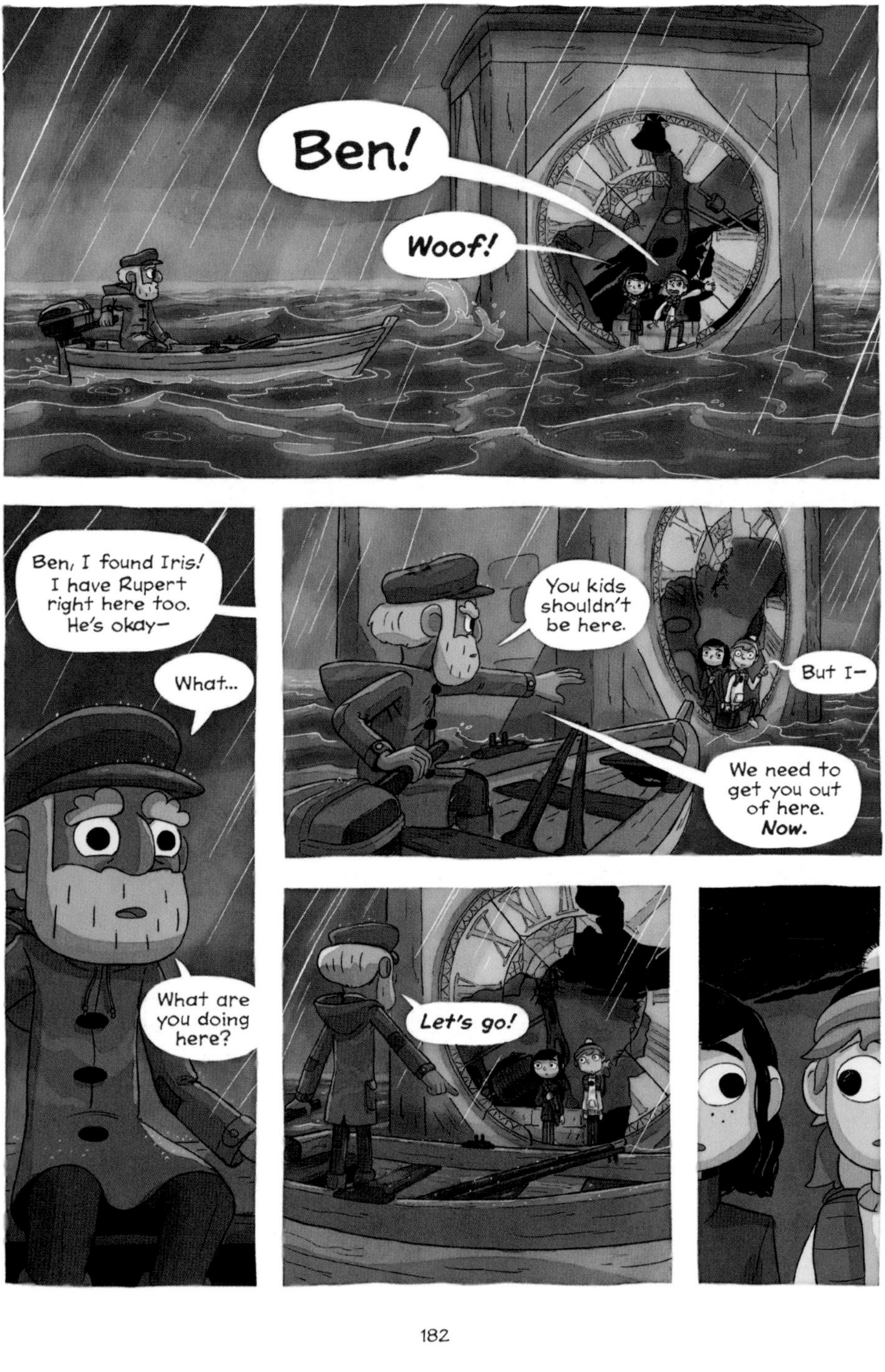
Ben!
Woof!
Ben, I found Iris! I have Rupert right here too. He's okay—
What...
What are you doing here?
You kids shouldn't be here.
But I—
We need to get you out of here. *Now.*
Let's go!

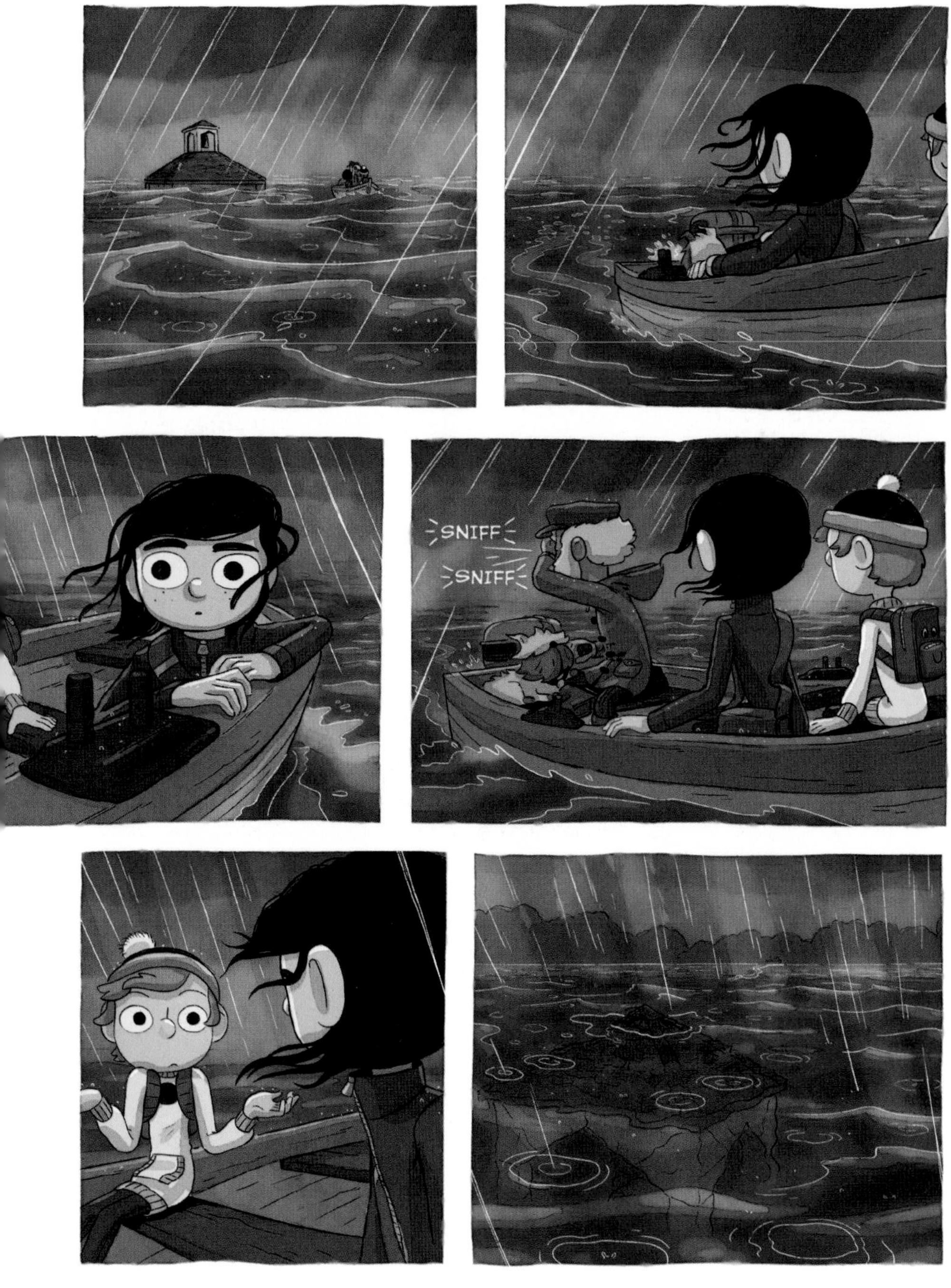
SNIFF
SNIFF

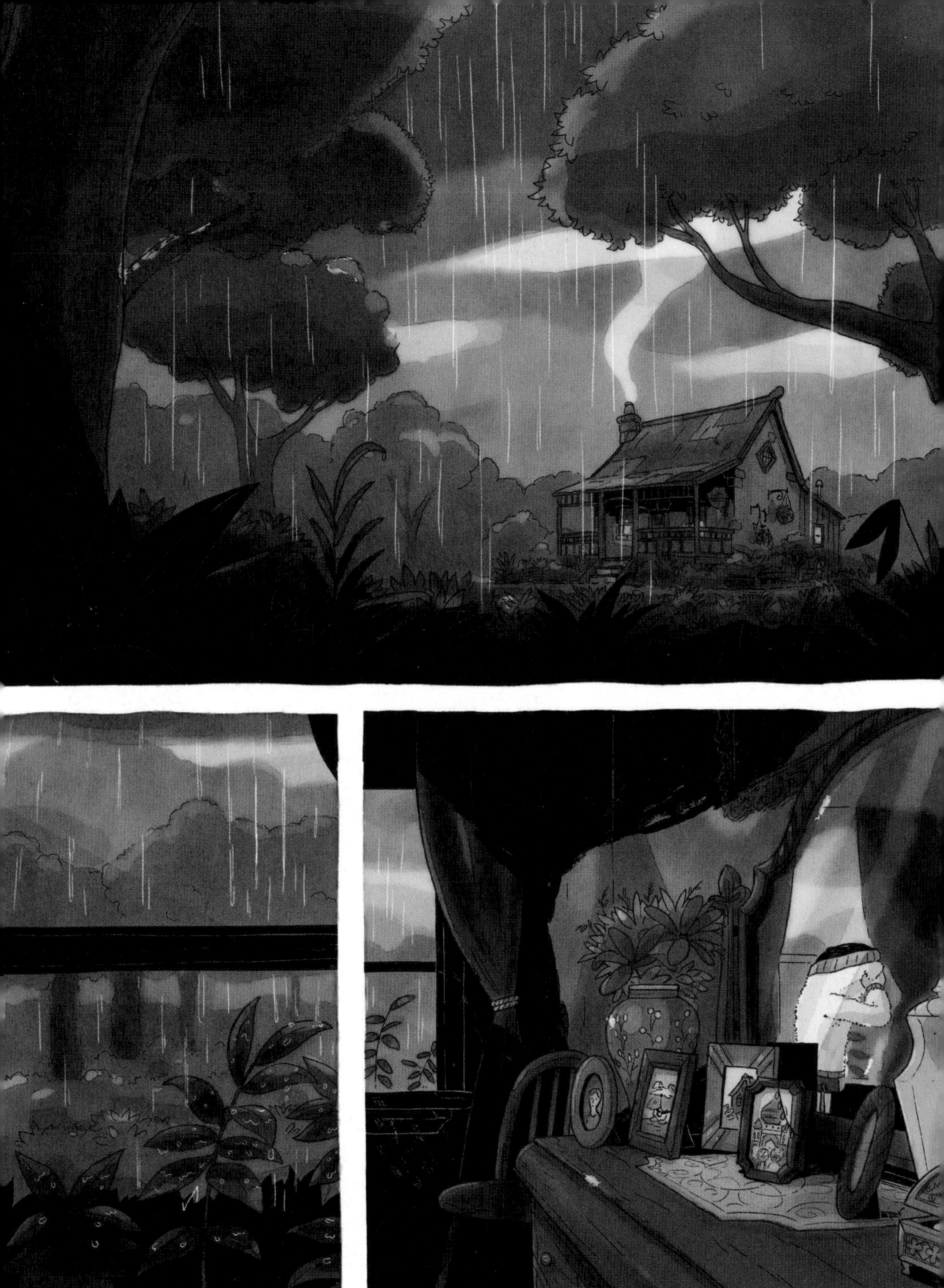

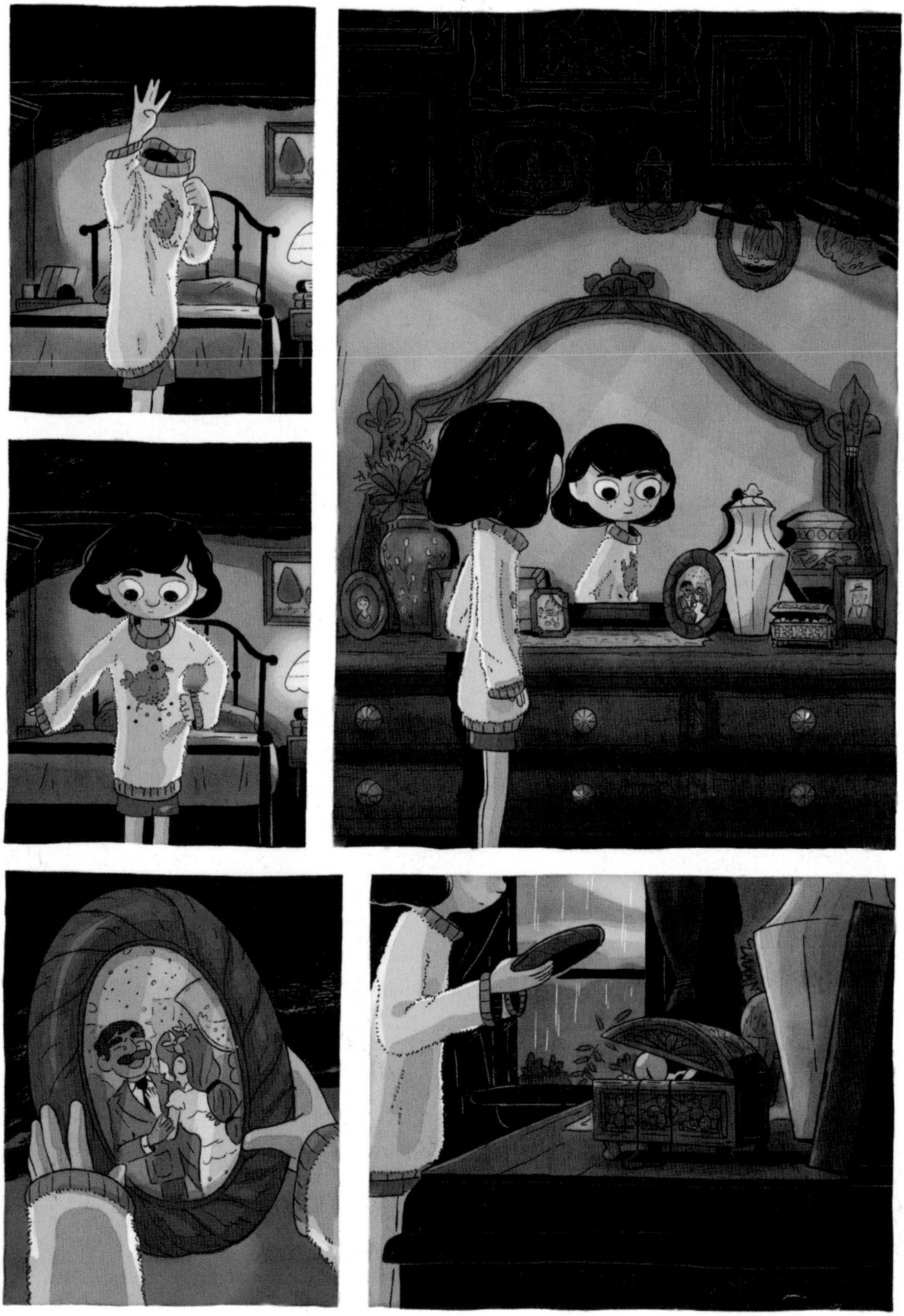

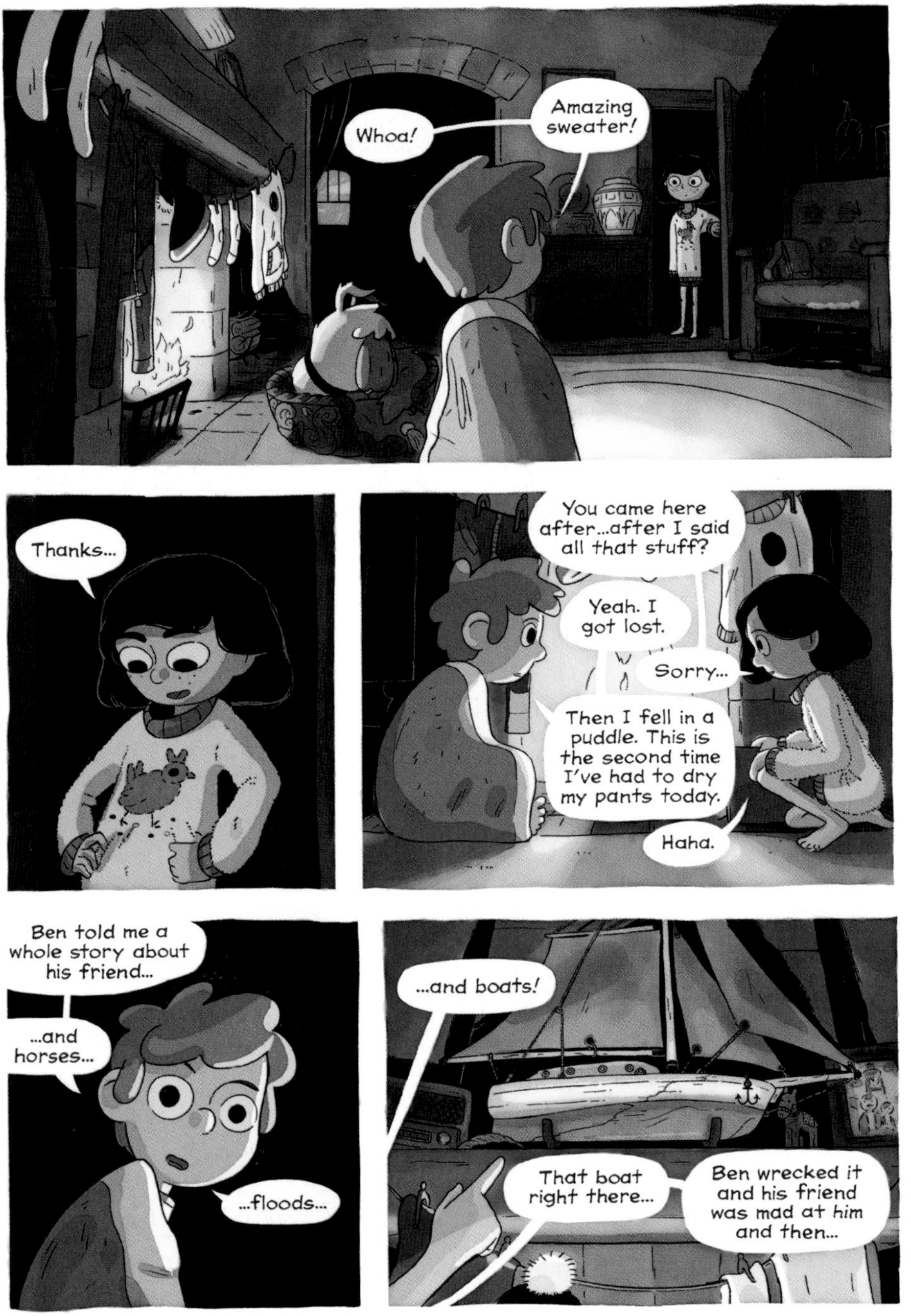
Whoa!
Amazing sweater!
Thanks...
You came here after...after I said all that stuff?
Yeah. I got lost.
Sorry...
Then I fell in a puddle. This is the second time I've had to dry my pants today.
Haha.
Ben told me a whole story about his friend...
...and horses...
...floods...
...and boats!
That boat right there...
Ben wrecked it and his friend was mad at *him* and then...

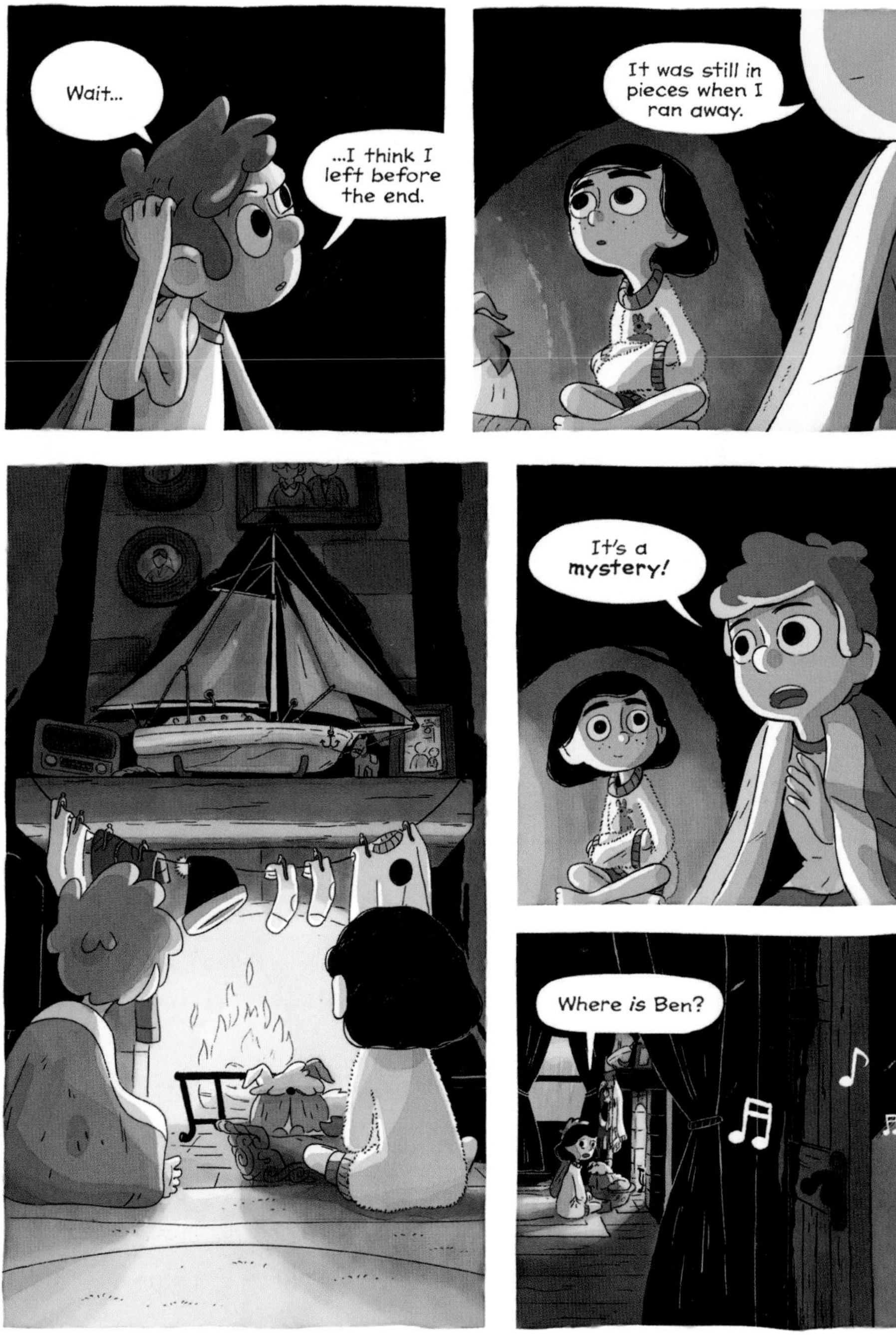
Wait...
...I think I left before the end.
It was still in pieces when I ran away.
It's a **mystery!**
Where *is* Ben?

189

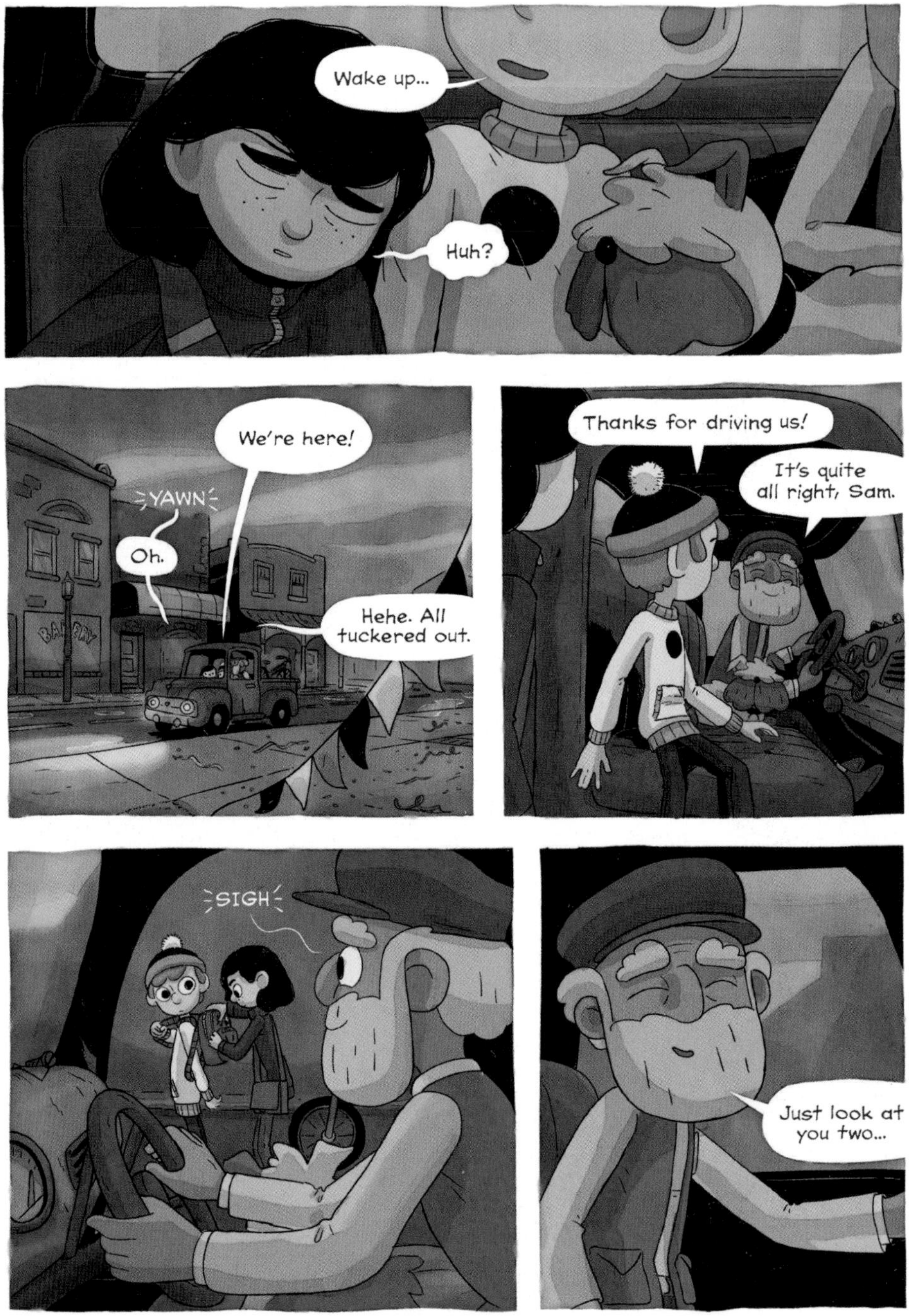
Wake up...
Huh?
YAWN
Oh.
We're here!
Hehe. All tuckered out.
BAKERY
Thanks for driving us!
It's quite all right, Sam.
SIGH
Just look at you two...

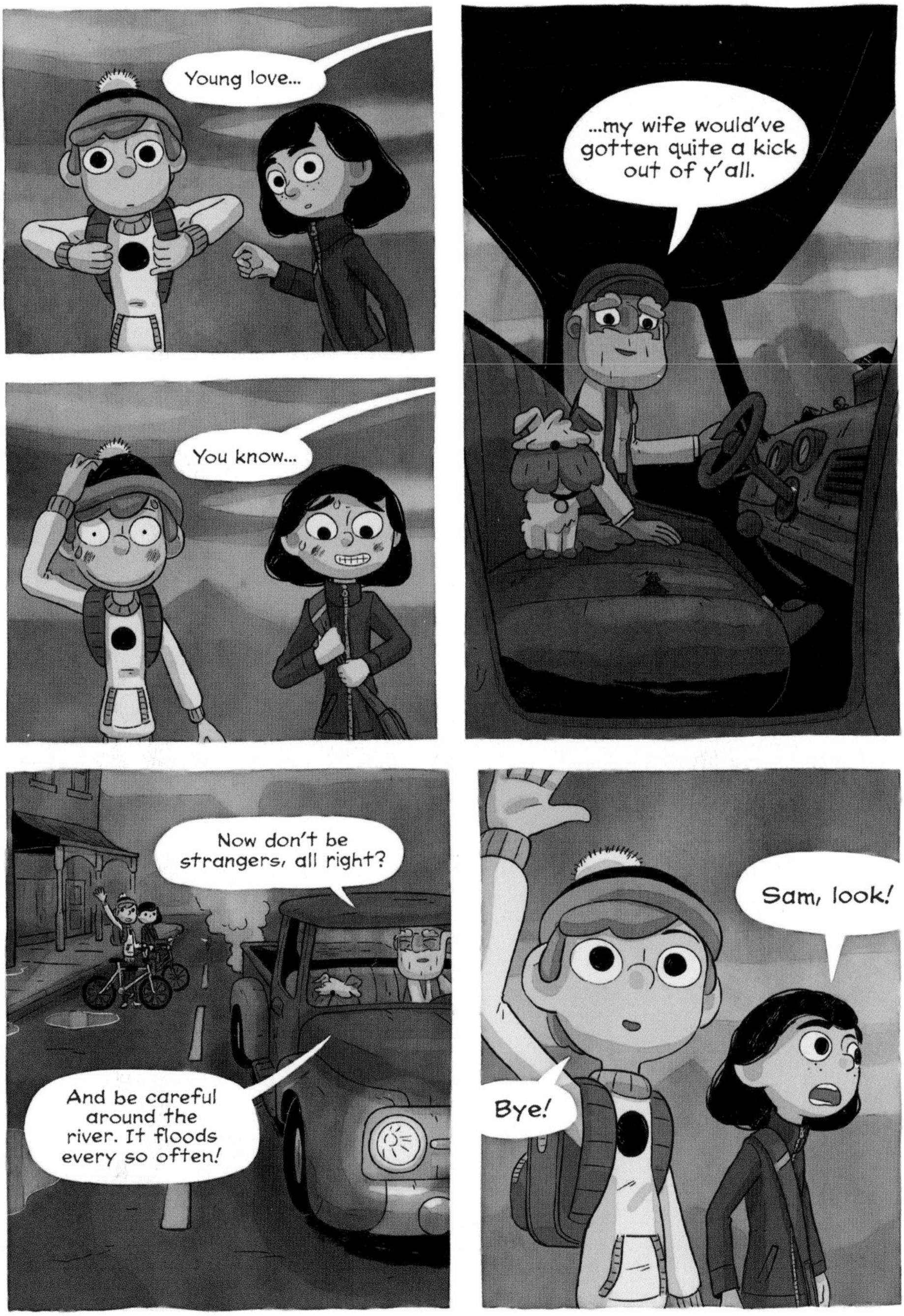
Young love...
...my wife would've gotten quite a kick out of y'all.
You know...
Now don't be strangers, all right?
And be careful around the river. It floods every so often!
Bye!
Sam, look!

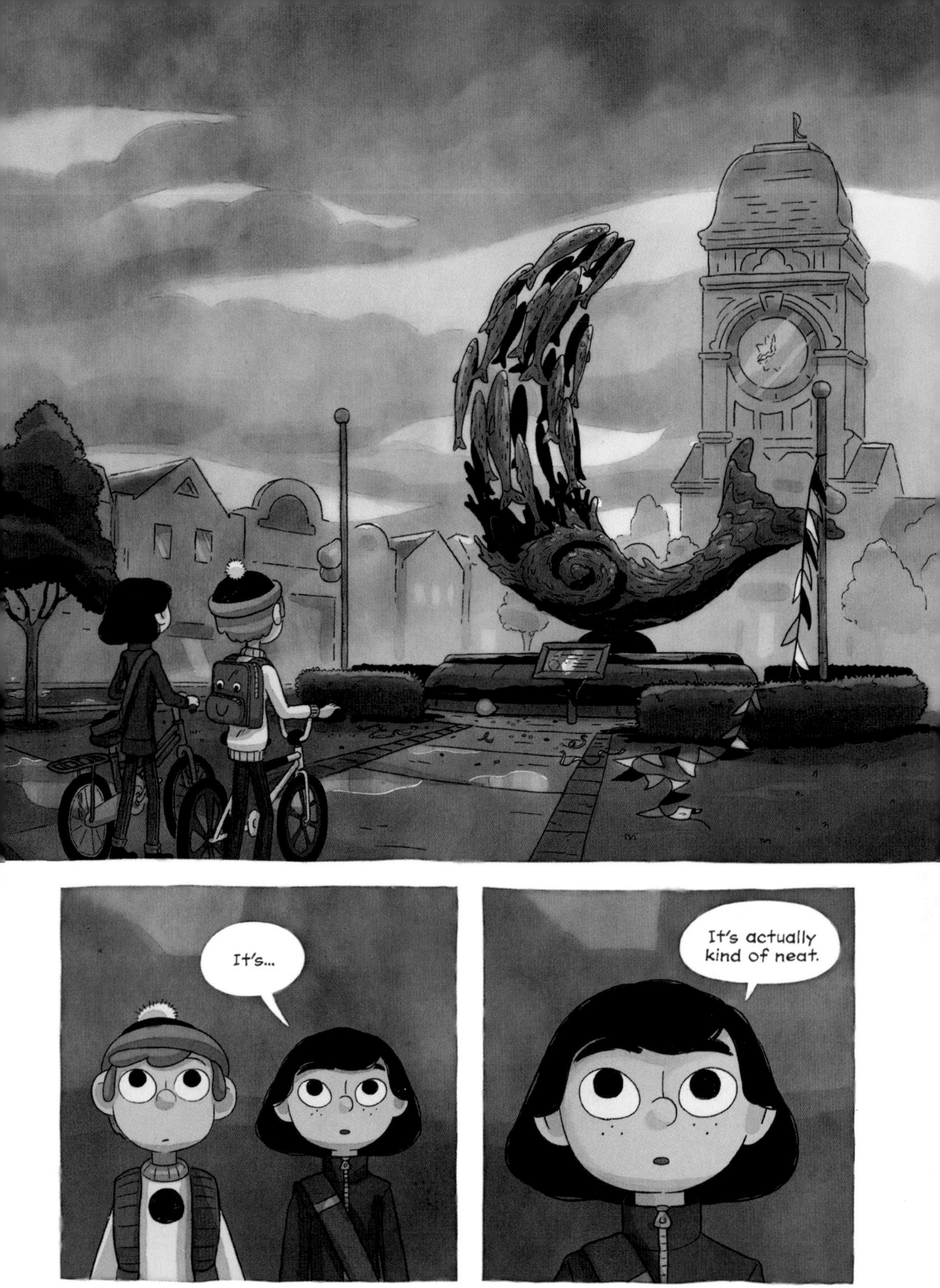
It's...
It's actually kind of neat.

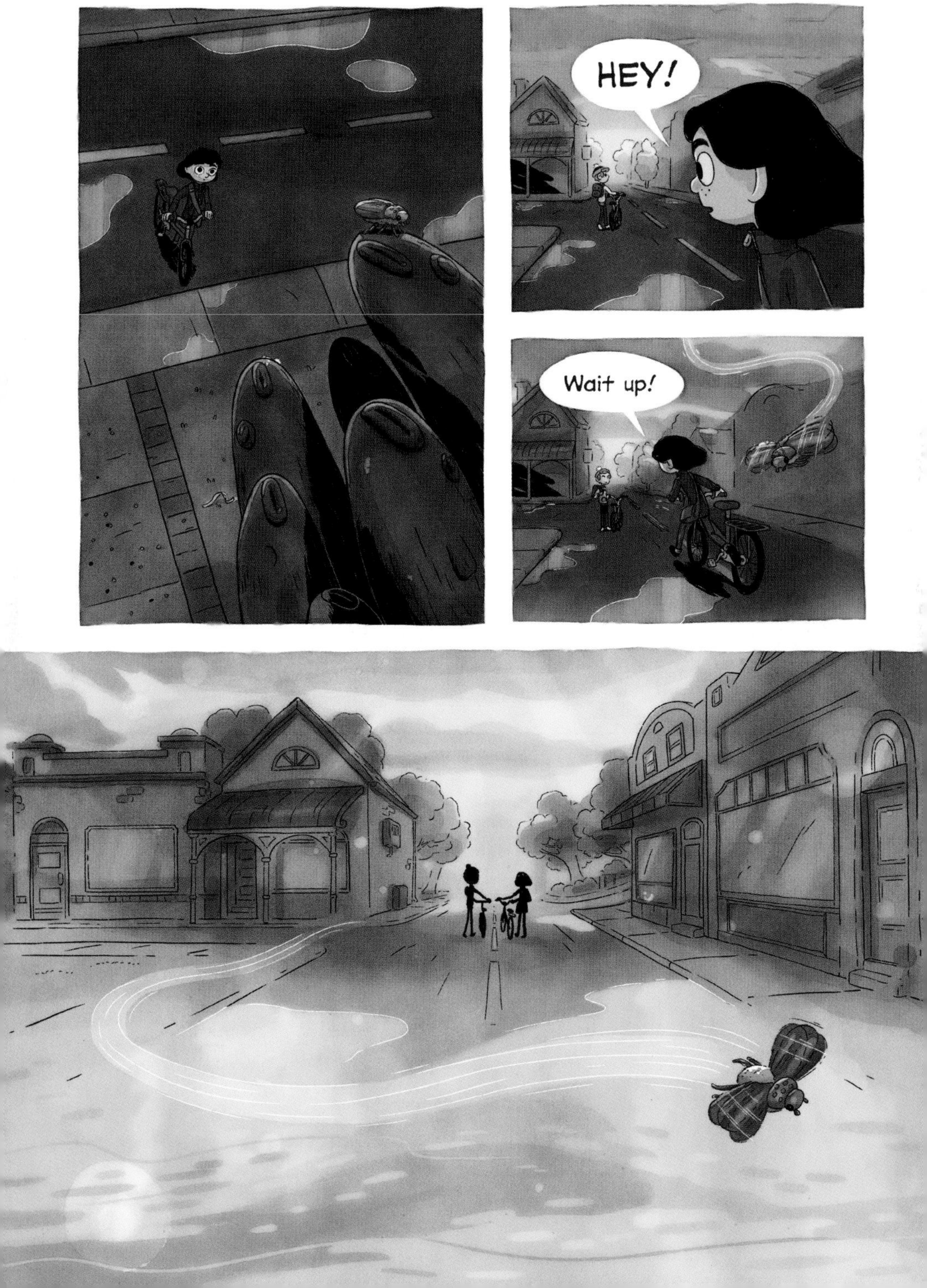
HEY!
Wait up!

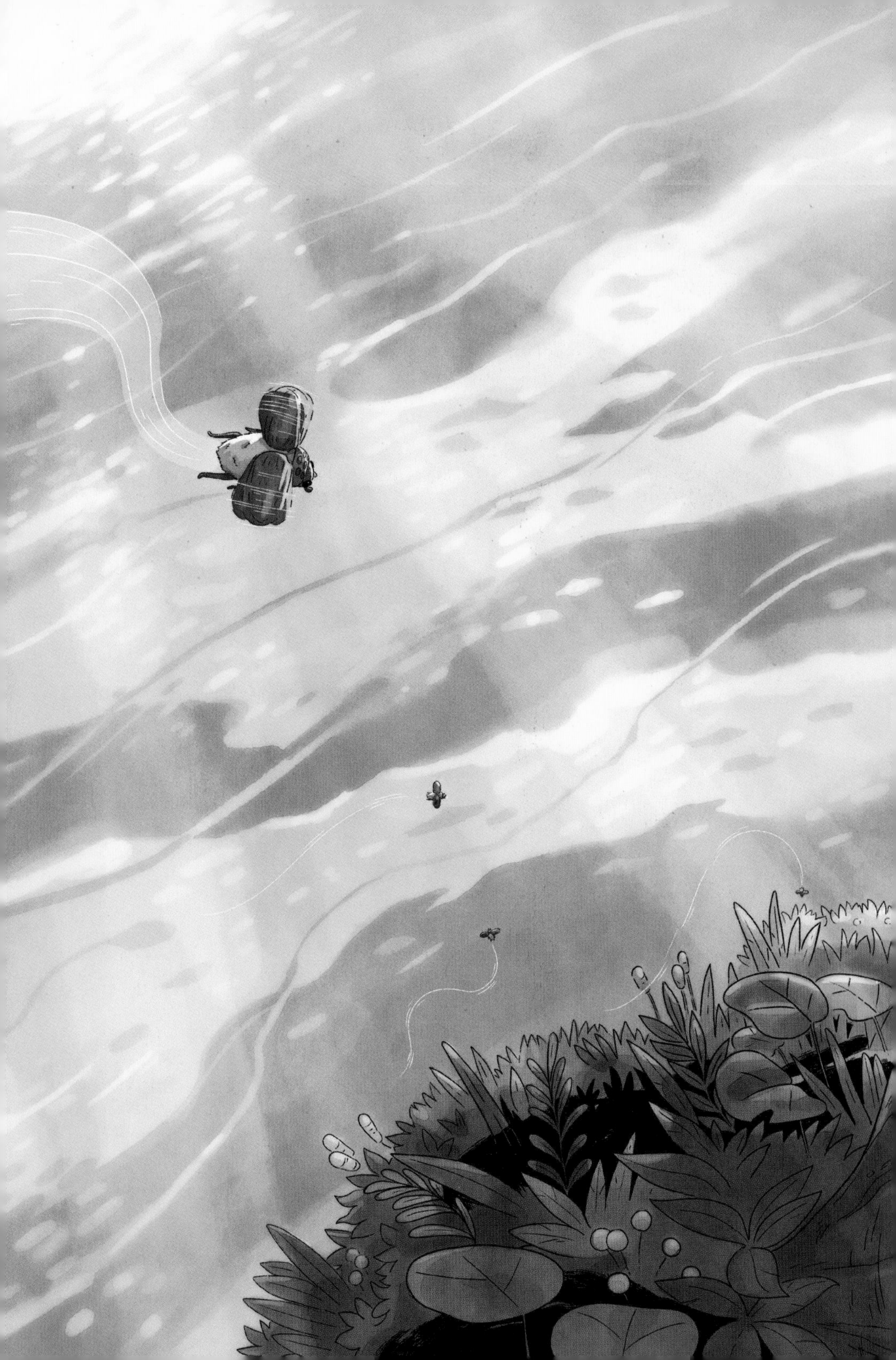

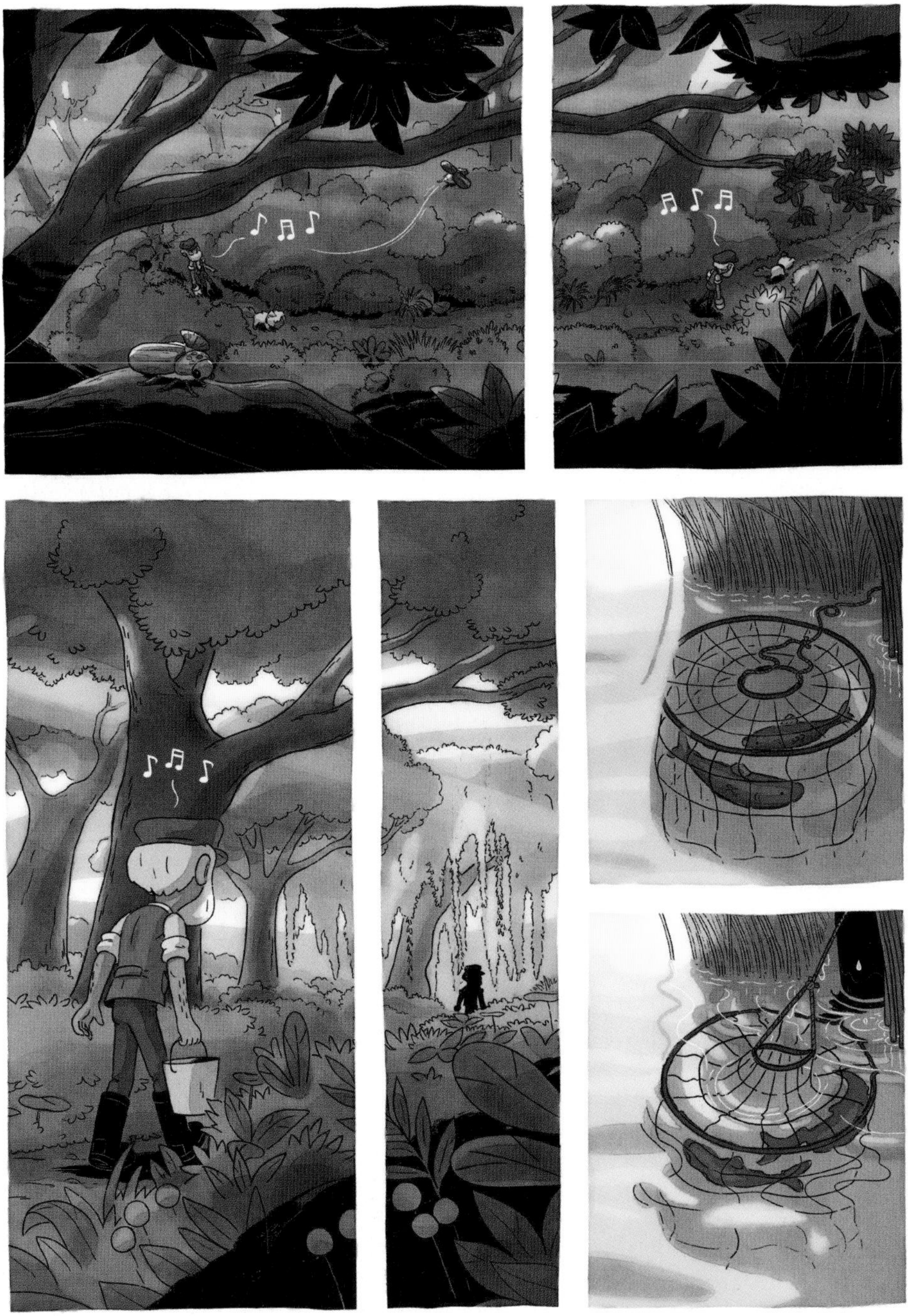

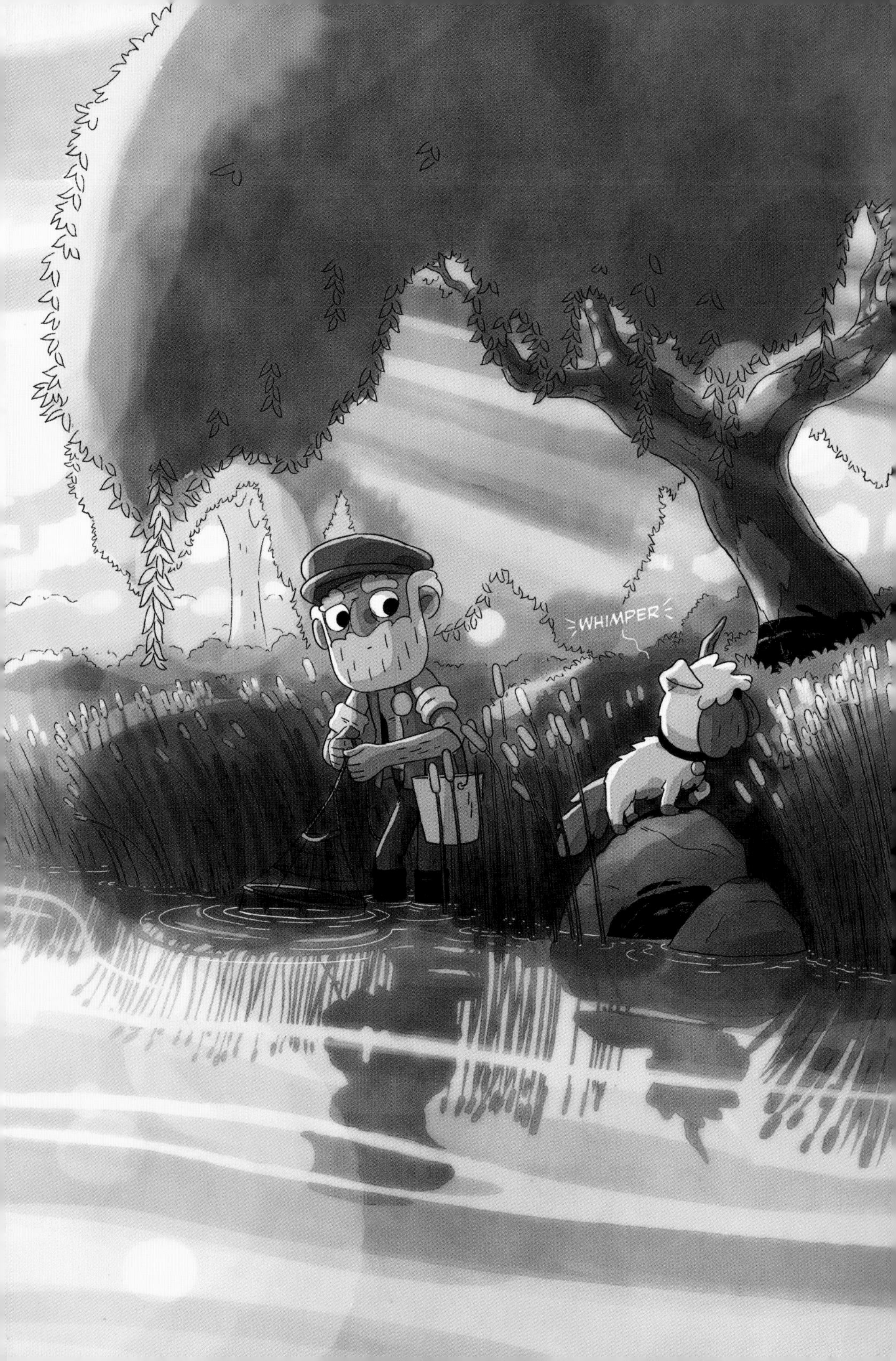
WHIMPER

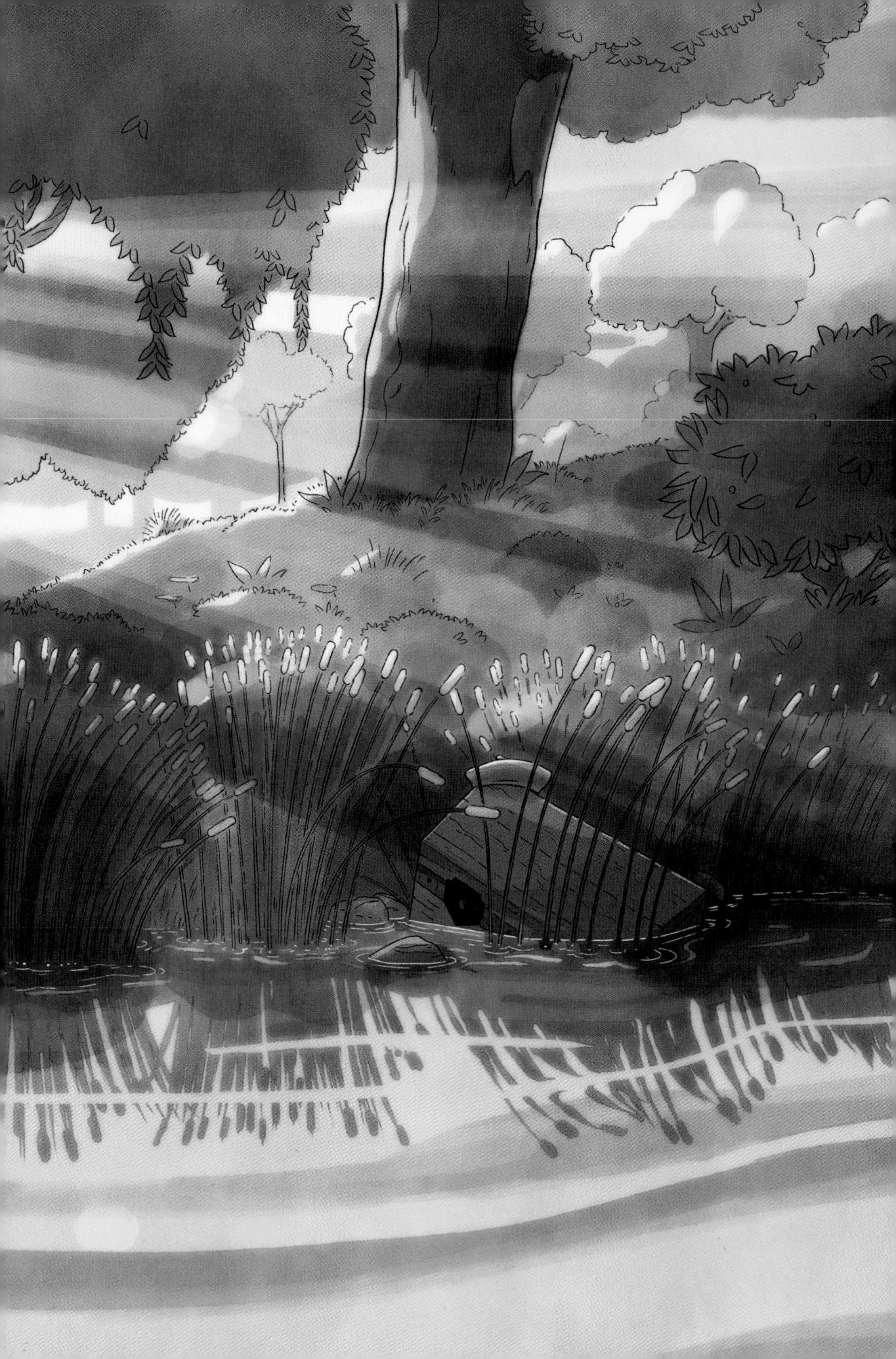

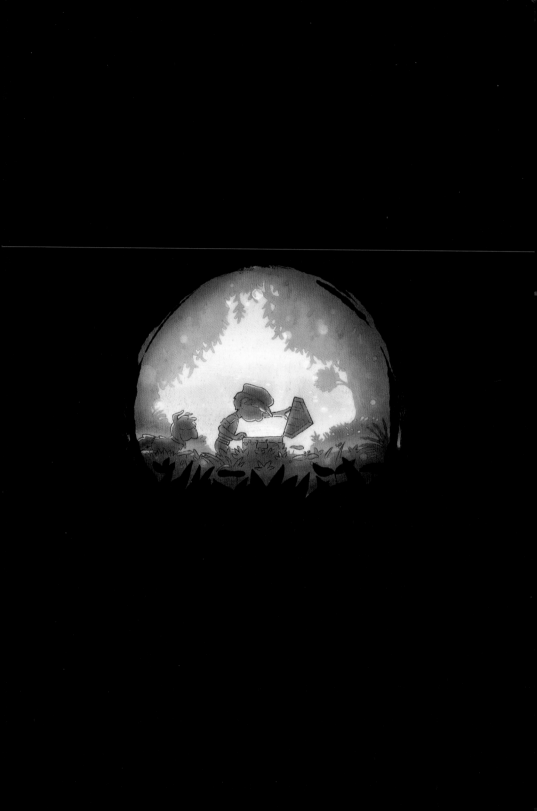

ACKNOWLEDGMENTS

Thank you to everyone who helped tell this story!

Thank you to Sara Crowe for your guidance and skill in finding the book a home. To my editors, Andrew Arnold and Rose Pleuler, for so thoughtfully and patiently helping me shape and refine the story. To Joe Merkel for your beautiful design, and everyone at HarperAlley for believing in this book. Thank you to Anna McFarlane for your valuable feedback and to the whole team at Allen & Unwin.

Thanks also to Chris Staros, Ari Gibson, Ryan Kirby, and Simon Westlake for your contributions over the journey.

Thank you to all my friends and family, especially my parents, for making me who I am.

Most of all, I'd like to acknowledge my incredible wife, Jessica, without whom this book would simply not exist. Thank you for supporting me and pushing me forward, the late night rewrites, the invaluable suggestions, and for your unwavering belief in me. ♡

DID YOU KNOW?

You may have heard of the lost city of Atlantis, but did you know there are submerged towns all over the world? It's true! Most were flooded on purpose to create reservoirs and waterways. Some were also the result of natural disasters and dams breaking—just like Ben and Lily's town.

Adaminaby

Between 1956-57, the Australian town of Adaminaby was moved to make way for a reservoir to power a hydroelectric system. Over one hundred buildings were lifted up and carried by truck. Two stone churches were even dismantled and reconstructed, brick by brick. Many buildings were sadly left behind, however. In 2007, severe drought caused the water level to drop so much that the old town reemerged! Surviving residents could walk the streets and reminisce about their childhood home.

Villa Epecuén

The Argentinian village of Epecuén flooded in 1985 after a nearby dam broke. Once home to fifteen hundred people, the town was slowly consumed by salt water, reaching a peak of ten meters (thirty-three feet). In 2009, the water began to recede, revealing the town once again. One man by the name of Pablo Novak even returned to live there all by himself.

Lake Reschen

Lake Reschen in Italy is home to a fourteenth-century church tower that sticks up out of the water's surface. It belonged to a town called Graun, which in 1950 was flooded on purpose in the creation of a dam. When the lake freezes over in winter, you can even walk out to the tower. People say that on some nights you can still hear the bells ringing, despite them being removed over seventy years ago!

PROCESS

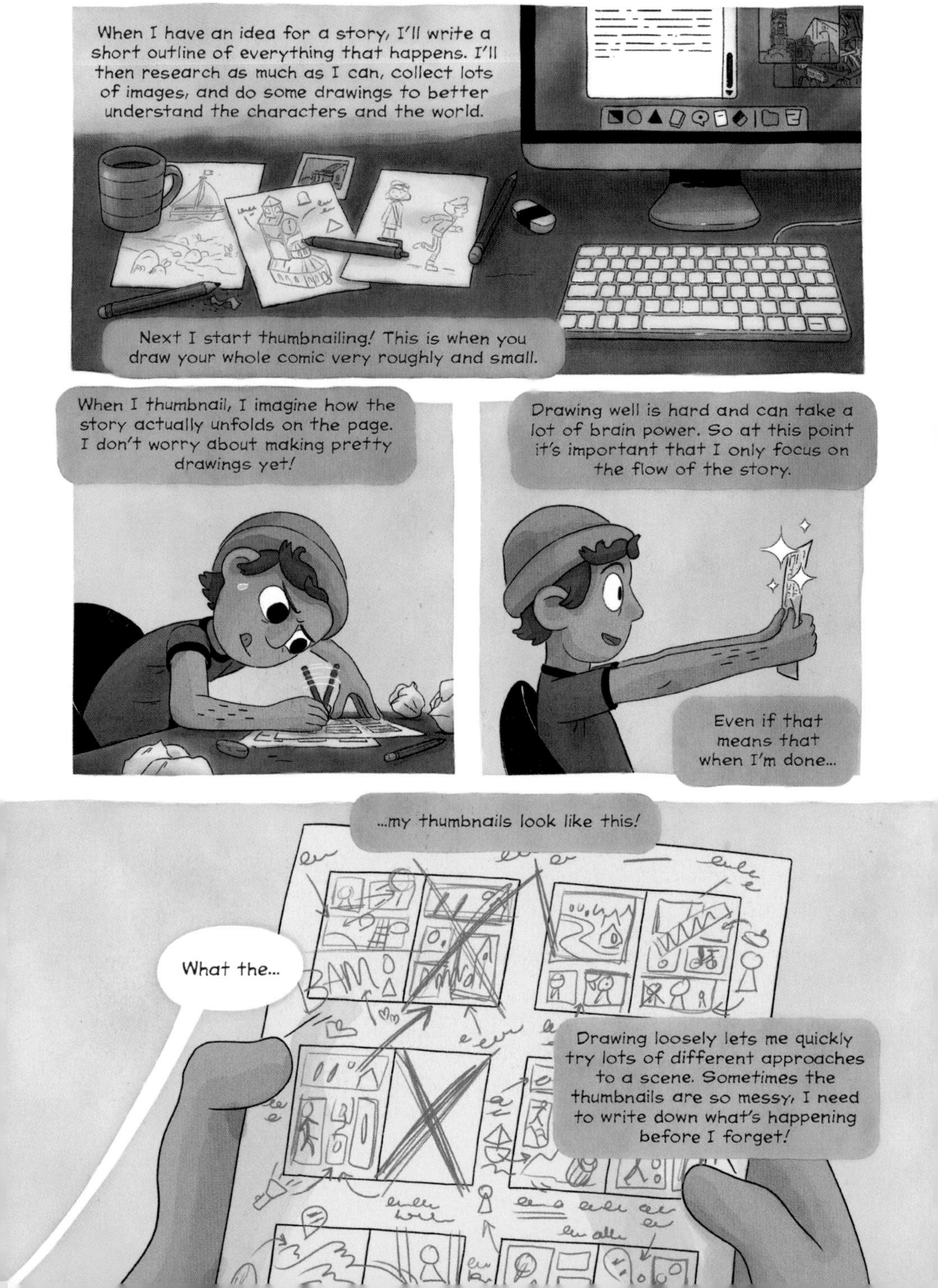
When I have an idea for a story, I'll write a short outline of everything that happens. I'll then research as much as I can, collect lots of images, and do some drawings to better understand the characters and the world.
Next I start thumbnailing! This is when you draw your whole comic very roughly and small.
When I thumbnail, I imagine how the story actually unfolds on the page. I don't worry about making pretty drawings yet!
Drawing well is hard and can take a lot of brain power. So at this point it's important that I only focus on the flow of the story.
Even if that means that when I'm done...
...my thumbnails look like this!
What the...
Drawing loosely lets me quickly try lots of different approaches to a scene. Sometimes the thumbnails are so messy, I need to write down what's happening before I forget!

EARLY SKETCHES

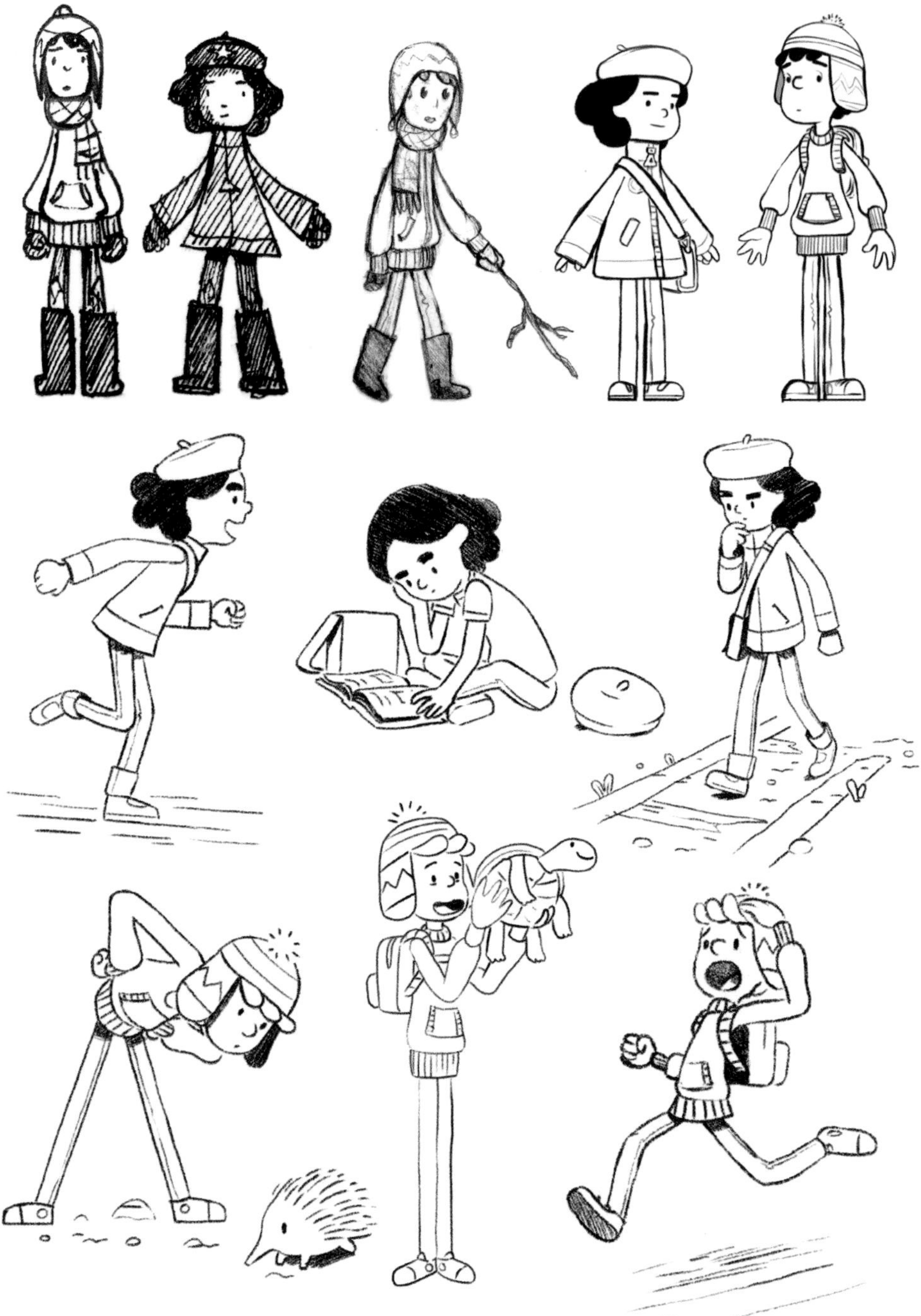

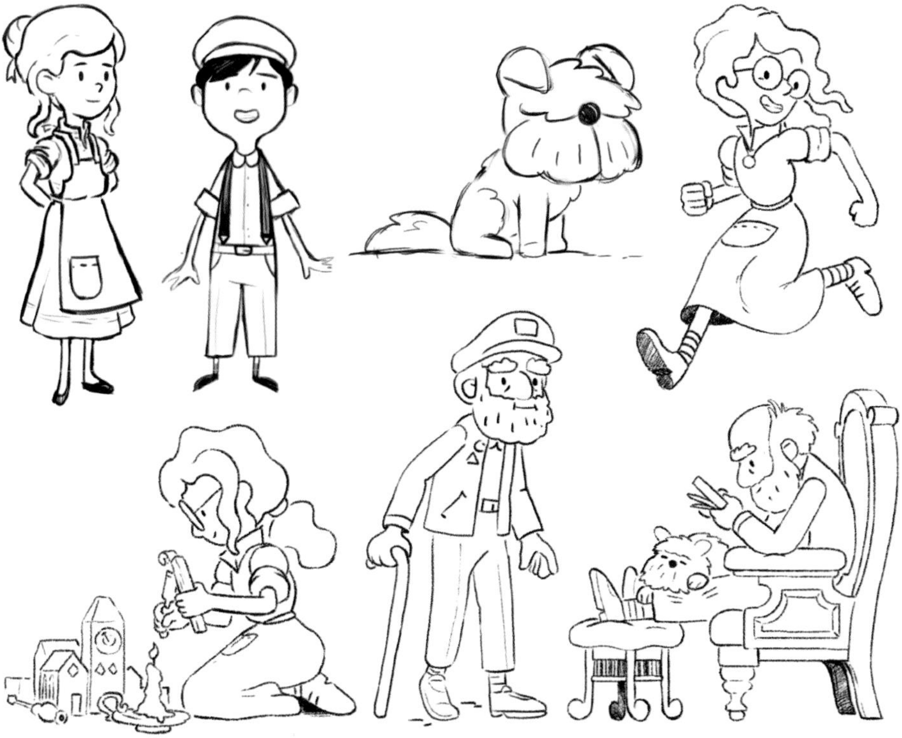

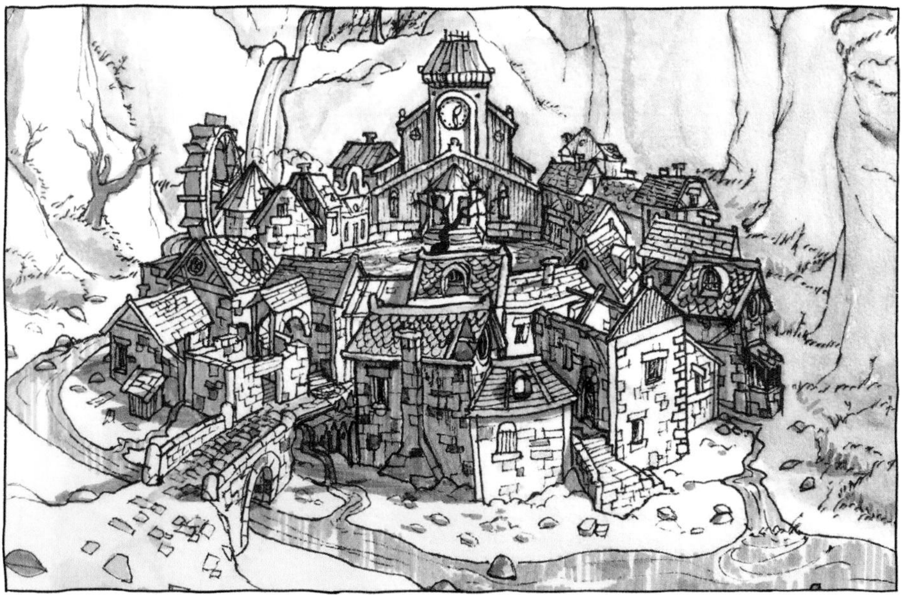

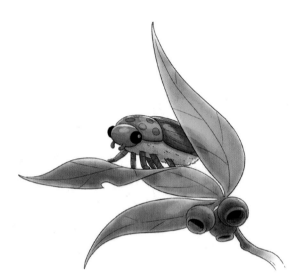

For Dad and Lilah.

HarperAlley is an imprint of HarperCollins Publishers.

Treasure in the Lake
Copyright © 2021 by Jason Pamment
All rights reserved. Printed in Spain.
No part of this book may be used or reproduced in any manner whatsoever without
written permission except in the case of brief quotations embodied in critical articles and reviews.
For information address HarperCollins Children's Books, a division of HarperCollins Publishers,
195 Broadway, New York, NY 10007.
www.harperalley.com

Library of Congress Control Number: 2021934291
ISBN 978-0-06-306518-5 — ISBN 978-0-06-306517-8 (pbk.)

Typography by Jason Pamment
21 22 23 24 25 EP 10 9 8 7 6 5 4 3 2 1
First Edition